Flicker of Defiance

C A Lewis

Copyright ©2022 by C A Lewis

All rights reserved. No part of this publication may be reproduced, stored or transmitted in any form or by any means, electronic, mechanical, photocopying, recording, scanning, or otherwise without written permission from the author. It is illegal to copy this book, post it to a website, or distribute it by any other means without permission.

This novel is entirely a work of fiction. The names, characters and incidents portrayed in it are the work of the author's imagination. Any resemblance to actual persons, living or dead, events or localities is entirely coincidental.

C A Lewis asserts the moral right to be identified as the author of this work.

ISBN: 979-8-9863413-0-9 (paperback)

ISBN: 979-8-9863413-1-6 (ebook)

Cover Design by Rachel Goering

Map created with Inkarnate

Typeset created with Atticus

To Joseph—
For always believing in me.

To Mom and Dad—
For giving me the wings to fly.

To Adam, Sophia, and Cody—
For never leaving me behind, even when I'm straggling.

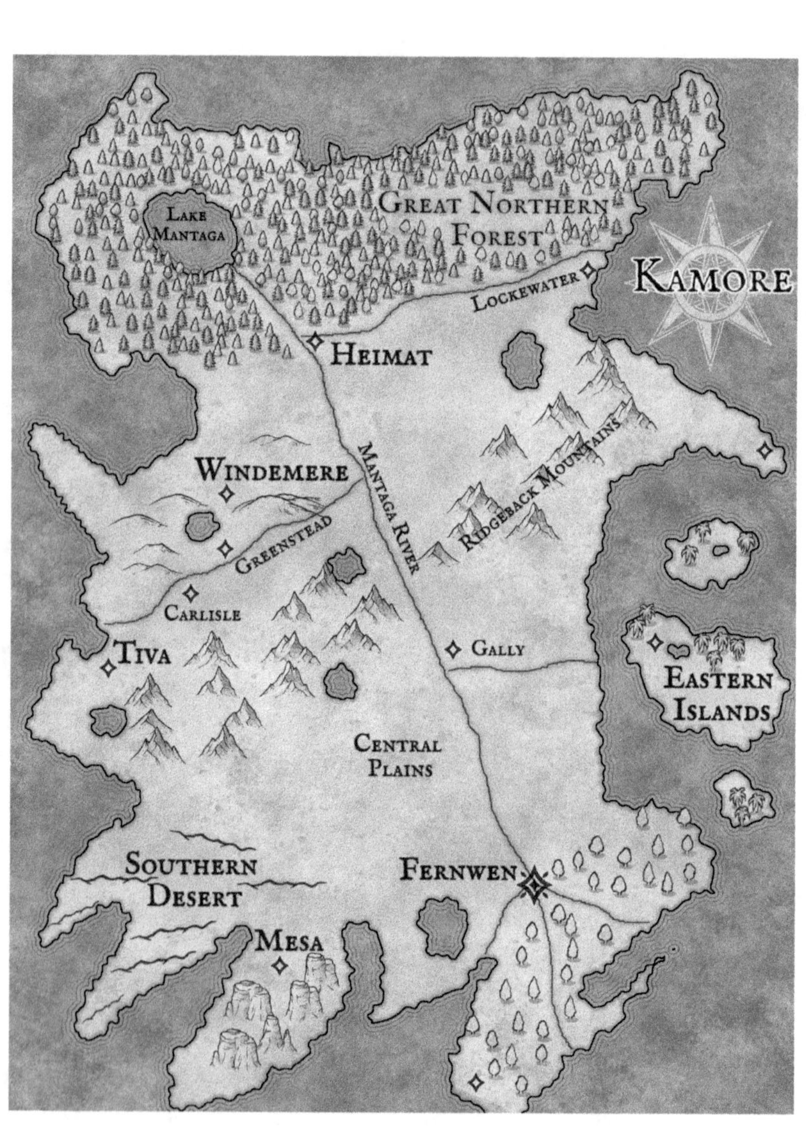

KAMORE
GREAT NORTHERN FOREST
LAKE MANTAGA
LOCKEWATER
HEIMAT
WINDEMERE
MANTAGA RIVER
RIDGEBACK MOUNTAINS
GREENSTEAD
CARLISLE
TIVA
GALLY
EASTERN ISLANDS
CENTRAL PLAINS
SOUTHERN DESERT
FERNWEN
MESA

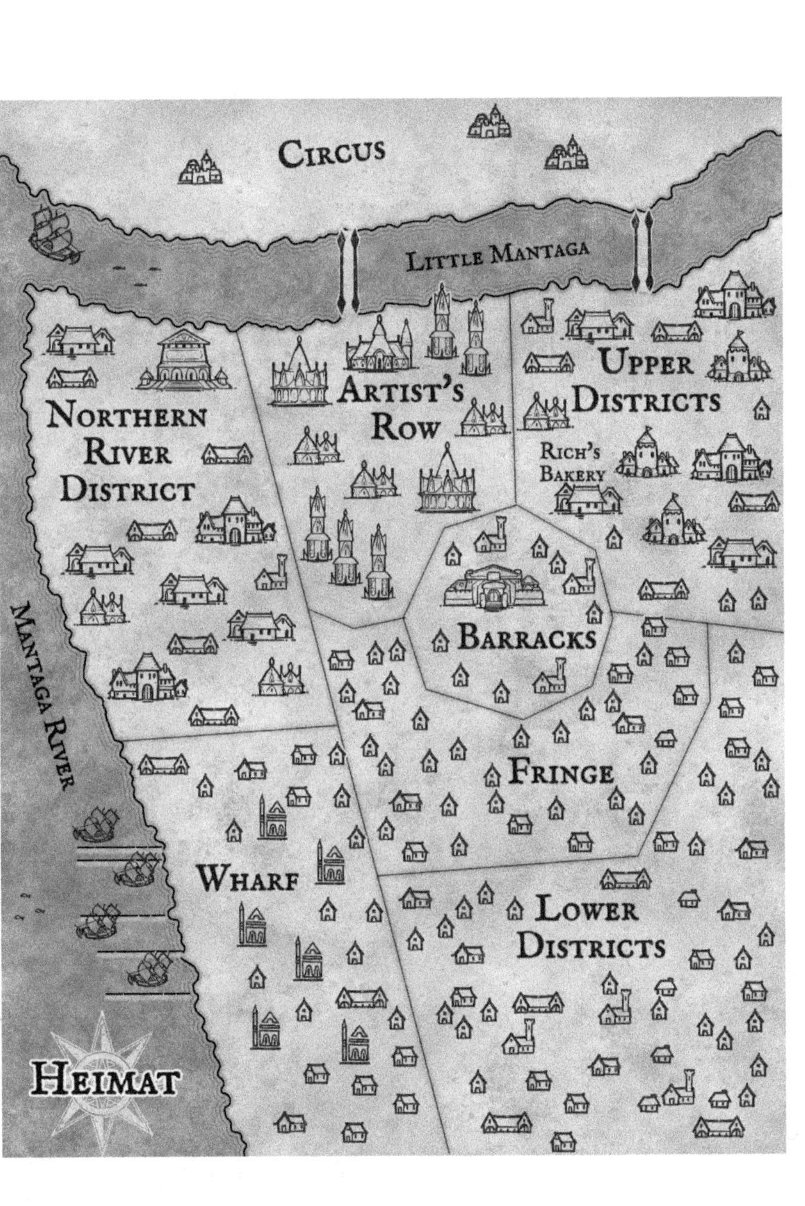

CIRCUS
LITTLE MANTAGA
UPPER DISTRICTS
ARTIST'S ROW
NORTHERN RIVER DISTRICT
RICH'S BAKERY
BARRACKS
MANTAGA RIVER
FRINGE
WHARF
LOWER DISTRICTS
HEIMAT

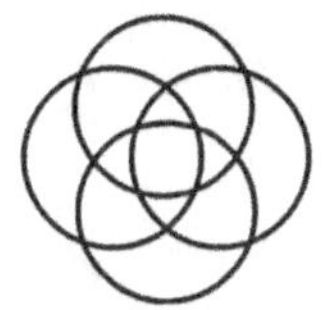

Chapter One

*S*moke filled her nostrils. Screams rattled inside her ears. And blood colored the walls she ran past.

A hand tightly gripped her small wrist, whisking her along the darkened corridors. It took all she had to keep up with the older woman. Suddenly, the hand tightened further and wrenched the girl to a stop.

"Shhh," the older woman hissed when the young girl let out a cry. "Quiet. We need to get to the stables." She watched with wide eyes as the woman cocked her head to listen for any pursuers.

In an instant, they were running again. Windows, hallways, rooms; they all blurred together in the rush of their departure.

The girl heard shouts coming from behind them and felt panic rising in her chest. She remembered her mother brushing a kiss on her brow and pushing her towards her aunt in everything but blood, telling her to go with Helene and be safe. Reaching up to her forehead with her free hand, the girl felt the ghostly touch of her mother's lips.

Shouts could be heard up ahead. Helene threw a glance behind them and pursed her lips, pulling them to a stop.

The little girl felt tears on her cheeks as her breath came in rasps. Her heart felt like it would beat right out of her chest, but she knew of another way to the stables. Staring at her protector, she said, "The servant's stairs. It will lead us to where we need to go." Her chin wobbled, but she kept her voice as steady as she could.

"Show me."

The hand on her wrist loosened, letting her lead the way. She tilted her head, listening for the people who were trying to find them. The shouts behind them were getting louder, so the little girl continued in the direction they were heading.

The wrinkled woman followed briskly, holding a hand out to grab the girl should they run into trouble. They weaved through the halls. One more turn and they'd be at the hidden door.

The little girl skidded to a stop.

Not soon enough.

Three men stood between them and the door they needed. The men smirked when they caught sight of their quarry. They laughed and pushed each other, talking about the riches they would earn for finding the President's daughter.

The little girl couldn't breathe. Helene stepped in front of her and pulled out a dagger. The men laughed louder, but the woman simply took a deep breath.

"Your job is to get through that door and down to the stables. A horse should be ready. Just take it and go little one. No matter what," Helene said through the side of her mouth, not taking her eyes off the men before them.

Before her charge could respond, Helene ran at the men, letting out a guttural cry.

The little girl froze.

Her limbs felt like lead and time passed in slow motion. She saw her protector slit one man's throat and knock out another.

She watched, eyes wide, until Helene turned back and knocked on the wall beside her. The hidden door swung inward, revealing the stairs leading to their escape. Helene yelled at her to move, but she could only watch the last man.

The little girl saw his hand move in slow motion, taking his dagger with it, until he thrust it into Helene's side in rapid succession. Helene cried out and faced her attacker, motioning once more for her charge to follow her directions.

Helene's cry broke through her paralysis. She rushed through the open door and thundered down the stairs, blood pounding in her ears. Fear, powerlessness, and anger raged inside her.

A loud thump signaled the end of the struggle up above.

Tears formed rivers across her cheeks.

She kept going.

She heard stumbling footsteps following her. Her heart jumped into her throat and she moved faster, flying down the stairs until she reached the door to the stables.

She listened, her hand on the doorknob. An enormous crash sounded above. She tensed but still waited. Her mind was racing, trying to determine whether the risk of seeing their pursuers was worth taking.

Another crash, louder than the first, rang in her ears.

She bit her lip and looked at the landing above.

Halting steps echoed in the hidden stairwell.

She held her breath.

Helene stumbled onto the first landing, one hand gripping hard to the handrail, the other clutching her side.

The tension left the little girl's shoulders as she ran to help the woman she'd known from birth.

"Silly girl. You should've gone." Helene glanced upwards. "Come on, Rae. Quickly now, they'll be here soon."

The little girl puffed out her chest before taking the woman's hand. She gripped her tightly and led her down to the door. They stepped through and made it to the horse that was waiting for them, saddled and bridled, ready to whisk them away.

The little girl climbed up and did her best to help her protector climb up behind her. They left the stables and were met with a blast of smoke and sound.

The city was burning.

Rae tossed and turned, drenched in sweat. She lay in bed, willing the traces of the memory to leave, but the echo of that night reverberated in her core and drove sleep from her eyes.

She forced them open, trying to escape the worst night of her life. Her limbs protested the lack of sleep, begging her to remain still. Rae knew she should've slept a few more hours, but her subconscious had other plans. Sighing, she left her cot and stretched her arms high above her head.

She needed to go for a midnight ride to clear her mind before the parade in the morning.

The Circus was coming.

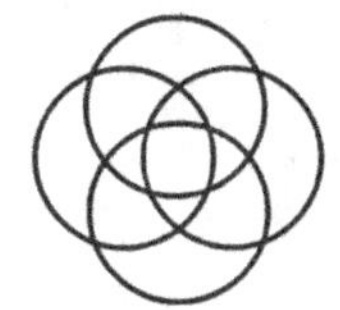

Chapter Two

Today was the day.

As soon as the sun rose, the parade would start, and the wheel resumed turning.

Dawn was when the Circus announced itself to the next town on the road they traveled.

Rae yawned, exhausted already, and they still hadn't started. Her night of restlessness was making it hard to concentrate on the task at hand. She stroked the palomino mare beneath her, reminiscing on the late-night run they'd taken, her long golden braid swishing behind her. Even the freedom on the wind couldn't drive away thoughts of the night her city burned.

She had been running ever since that hellish night and longed for the day when she could be still.

"Rae! You ready?" A cry came from her left.

As she turned to the voice, a smile graced her lips. "Always, Z, always." She forced the melancholy thoughts from her head, watching the owner of the voice come her way.

A young man with a slight build and silvery hair flashed her a grin as he brought his dappled gray gelding beside her palomino. "You look like you could go back to bed." He winked at the blonde next to him before waggling his eyebrows. "Did a certain equestrian find his way to your tent?"

Rae shook her head and urged her horse forward as Zeke laughed at her discomfort. She raised one finger in his direction before guiding Arwen, her mare, towards the front of the gathering of Circus performers. Zeke trailed behind her, sporting a wicked grin.

Dawn was coming, and it was time for her to play her part.

A sizable crowd gathered on the outskirts of the rural town of Windemere, despite the darkness of twilight. Parents murmured to sleepy children searching desperately in the dark. Everyone wanted to be the first to see the caravan of wagons, animals, and performers. Eyes darted between the scouting team, a few hundred feet away, checking the set-up field, and the top of the southern hill where the performers gathered out of sight.

The scouting team had arrived in Windemere a week ago. They prepared the town for the Circus's arrival by alerting local officials and ensuring the field they had used for the past decade was still available. They hung up posters, handed out flyers, and made announcements at public meetings. The scouts wanted every soul in town to know the very moment the Circus would arrive.

Windemere was the last stop on the road for this year's show season and the last time the scout team had to do their job. They needed this concluding parade to produce the biggest crowd yet.

A hush descended upon the people gathered in the minutes before the sun broke over the horizon. Older generations waited in anticipation, knowing what was coming. Younger generations quivered with impatience to lay their eyes on the spectacle they barely remembered from last year.

Gasps broke out as a single rider galloped to the top of the hill. They pulled their steed up into a rear, front hooves pawing the air as the sun rose with an explosion of color.

"It's the Golden Eagle!"

"No, that's the Silver Falcon."

"You're all wrong. It's the Night Rider for sure!"

Shouts and guesses were drowned out as more figures appeared on the horizon. Three riders joined the first and made their way down the hill. As the light of the sun illuminated more of the hillside, it revealed the costumes they wore as they raced towards the crowd. The crowd gasped as they realized no saddles separated them from their steeds.

Rae looked at Zeke and the other two riders next to them. All four of them were acrobats, traditionally performing on the trapeze during the Circus show. The parade into each town allowed them to display their acrobatic skills in a new way.

The flying trapeze was one of the headlining acts in the Circus, drawing a large crowd everywhere they visited. Rae was known as the Golden Eagle, Zeke was the Silver Falcon, Luciana the Black Swan, and Damien the White Raven. Their horses and costumes represented the colors and birds they emulated. By using them to start, the parade drummed up energy in the crowd as they did tricks on horseback. And this was only a prelude to the stunts they could and would do in the air on the trapeze.

With a nod, all four rose onto their knees and steered their horses apart. They zigzagged across the field, crossing paths and yelling. They worked as one, doing handstands and backbends on top of their horses as they passed by one another. The beauty and grace displayed in their movements were mesmerizing to the crowds in the valley.

They paired up, Rae with Zeke, and the other two riders, Damien and Luciana, or Luc as she was known, with each other. Rae gave Zeke a wicked grin before yelling.

At Rae's exclamation, the four hopped to their knees and then their feet, side by side with their partner. Each of them moved one foot to their partner's horse, so each pair straddled the gap between their horses. Rae and Luc placed a foot on their partner's leg and climbed to the men's shoulders. Zeke and Damien gave each of the women a hand, helping them settle into stable, seated positions. They rode like this, the men with one foot on each horse, their partner on their shoulders until they reached the field where the scouts waited. Rae and Luc blew kisses to the crowd before climbing down from where they perched.

Rae panted as she let Zeke help her back onto her mare. She squeezed his shoulder before looking at their friends. She shared a smile with Luc before all four turned their attention back to the top of the hill.

The townspeople went wild for the spectacle of the trapeze artists doing stunts on horseback. In the past, the four had done tricks and flips on the ground, but this year they were challenging themselves and the crowd loved it. Children shrieked with joy and adults broke out into applause. The riders had done their job, inciting the crowd and starting the parade with a bang.

More figures emerged on the horizon, framed by the sun rising behind them.

The menagerie was next. A multitude of animals descended from the top of the hill. First came a pack of dogs of all sizes, some walked on two legs, some on four, some with costumes and others without. A couple of trainers walked amidst them, using hand signals and dried meat to coax the dogs into doing flips, rolls, and jumps.

A pair of large wolfhounds did coordinated moves across the ground in front of their trainer. They zigzagged until meeting in the middle of the hill, one laying down as the other one jumped over him. They performed a synchronized roll before rising and giving a bow.

Next were the exotic animals. Pairs of lions, tigers, camels, elephants, and dozens more started making their way down.

Children screamed and cowered behind their parents when the big cats let out roars one by one. They slowly peeked in trepidation as the young man walking with them demonstrated their long, white canine teeth.

With a feral grin, he ran his hand along the sharp tearing instruments of one fearsome lioness. He moved to scratch her behind the ears, which earned him a nudge from the big-headed feline. The people stared in amazement as the big cats and other animals walked with no restraints, content to follow their handlers.

Rae lifted an eyebrow and shot Zeke a look at the man's display with the big cats. Zeke snorted and shook his head. "Don't do it, Sparks."

Rae smiled at the nickname, the same one Zeke had used since they met years and years ago as kids. That name held thousands of memories and inside jokes between them, including the one about the big cats' handler.

Rae held her pointer fingers out, about four inches apart, looking at Zeke with a questioning look. Her friend rolled his eyes and waved her off, not giving in to her antics.

She chuckled, her eyes drifting to Damien and Luc. Luc held her own fingers out, only two inches apart, mischief in her eyes. Rae laughed loudly before clamping her mouth shut. Her shoulders shook with mirth as the dark-haired woman giggled next to her.

Damien shook his head at their humor before turning back to the procession. The other three did the same, Rae and Luc occasionally sharing looks and giggling.

The stream of animals continued as the acrobats chatted, a pair of towering elephants moving apart to reveal a young girl walking beside a baby elephant.

Occasionally, one or the other would drape their long trunks over the girl's shoulder. Once they reached the middle of the hillside, both adult elephants let out a trumpet and raised one of their front legs to "wave" at the crowds.

The baby elephant moved closer to the young girl with pigtails in her hair as he took in the crowds below him. He used his trunk to grip the girl's hand as his ears fanned out and quivered. Once she gave a nod, the baby released her arm and gave a small trumpet of his own, running down the remaining hill to the flat field. The girl skipped after him with one last wave to the crowd, flanked by the enormous pachyderms. This display encouraged even the most timid of children to smile and clap in delight.

"Momma, could I have an elephant friend someday?" A young girl asked her mom with stars in her eyes.

"Oh sweetheart, maybe one day." The gaunt young mother pulled her toddler close, unable to completely lie to the innocent girl untouched by the troubles of life. "Maybe one day." She patted the top of her daughter's head and pulled the girl's thin coat tight around her.

A lone trumpet blasted across the grassy plain, its metallic vibrato instilling a sense of longing and loneliness in spectators and performers alike. Before they could identify the feeling, more and more instruments started up into a jaunty, silly tune.

The townspeople laughed in delight as a group of clowns in elaborate make-up bumbled down the hill. They performed a skit where they took turns trying to roll up the hill, only to end up back where they started. They earned a roar of applause for their antics.

Zeke gave Rae a playful shove and said, "Your favorite act is up next." He gave his friend a wink as Rae rolled her eyes.

"You're a prick, Z. Leave it alone." Her stomach clenched as a line of horsemen appeared on the horizon, her eyes focusing on the man in the middle.

Zeke chuckled as he followed her gaze.

The five riders thundered down the hill, crisscrossing and zigzagging as they did. The speeds at which they moved made it impossible to stay focused on one for long. Their display differed from that of the acrobats' as they highlighted the abilities and athleticism of the horses they rode, not the tricks they could do.

The crowds watched with bated breath, amazed the animals didn't fall or break a leg as the riders formed patterns on the hillside. Whispers of the Night Rider followed the dark-haired man astride the midnight-colored stallion.

He let out a cry as the five reached the bottom of the hill, causing all of them to rein in their steeds to an impressive stop. All five gave a salute before making their way to the field, where the performers congregated.

The Night Rider stayed the longest, flashing one last grin to the crowd before following his brethren to the ever-growing group of performers. As he turned, he caught Rae's eye and gave her a wink, smiling when he noticed the blush dusting her cheeks.

Rae broke eye contact and hid her face before Zeke or the other acrobats could notice, cursing the rogue under her breath.

After the horsemen came the side acts, a strong man and woman tossed giant logs and boulders between them; jugglers tried to outdo one another in the number and types of things they could juggle; an old fortune teller walked with a crystal ball and elaborate head covering; a weathered man flew different birds of prey while keeping a single falcon on his shoulder. The acts continued to stream down the hill until they reached their fellows. Wagons, crew, and livestock plodded behind the last of the acts.

The townspeople clapped and laughed in delight, waiting for the man of the hour to appear. They were met with silence as the top of the hill remained empty. Whispers ran rampant as people questioned whether they missed him in the chaos of all the performers. Above the noise, the band launched into a slow-building crescendo.

In an instant, the crowd was thrumming with thinly veiled excitement, whispers silenced. Everyone guessed this was for the Ringmaster himself.

Just before the music could make its big finish, a tall, slender man wearing a top hat appeared at the utmost point of the hill. As the last notes came to a close, he descended straight towards the crowds instead of moving toward his Circus of performers.

Rae lifted her head towards the other three acrobats to find them staring at her. She gave them a look. "What?" she demanded.

Zeke raised one eyebrow, inclining his head towards the crowd of townspeople.

Rae's eyebrows shot up. "Oh, shit. It's me, isn't it?" She frantically started guiding her palomino towards the edge of the performers. She called behind her, "Front handspring with a twist and then a double back one, right?"

"*Double* front handspring with a twist and then a double back handspring *with a salto.*" Luc corrected her, shaking her head in exasperation.

Rae drew a deep breath and went over the tricks she needed in her mind's eye. She kept Duncan, the Ringmaster, in her peripheral as he made his way down the hill, waiting for her cue.

He walked with purpose, purple coat tails catching in the wind and dark brown hair curling under his top hat. He had a lopsided grin plastered on his face as he addressed the townspeople of Windemere in his booming baritone.

"Greetings, my esteemed countrymen and women. We are honored to entertain you with our humble attempts at spreading awe and wonder. Thank you for the warm welcome. Did you enjoy the parade?" The crowd roared and shrieked their confirmation. "Ah, I see my family does not disappoint. Let me assure you, that is only the beginning."

The Ringmaster turned and gestured for someone to come forward. Rae slipped off her mare and made her way to where Duncan stood, keeping her chin up and smiling wide. She went through the tricks one more time in her mind, making sure she knew exactly which ones she had to do. One misstep could be disastrous for the people they came for.

"Let me introduce you to one of our stunning trapeze artists." The Ringmaster's voice projected as if the wind carried it. "Please welcome the extraordinary, Golden Eagle!" As most of the crowd clapped and whistled for the exquisite and poised acrobat, several people slipped towards the edge of the crowd. They noted which acrobat was called forward, but needed one more signal before they could prepare for the next couple of nights.

Once the acrobat made it to her Ringmaster, he reached for her hand and looked surprised when she snatched it away with a smirk. Without warning, she broke into a run and flipped forward twice, ending with a twist before she landed on her feet.

"Never underestimate the Golden Eagle," Rae said with a wink to the crowd. "You're all in for a treat the next couple of nights. The show is bigger and better than ever, from our family to yours." The golden silks of her costume trembled with the wind as she let the crowd soak in her presence. She sent a knowing look to the townspeople in front of her. "This year has been rough on everyone; let us transport you somewhere your troubles can't find you."

She ran off again only to return, flipping backward twice, ending with a somersault in the air, curling her body as it twirled in midair. Sticking her landing, Rae beamed. She knew she hadn't screwed up and there was no question what two tricks she performed for those watching.

"Let us delight your children and create memories that last a lifetime." She grabbed Duncan's hand and took a bow. "Welcome to the show," she said with a steely grin.

With the end of the acrobatic demonstration, those at the edge of the crowd left swiftly and quietly, trying to draw as little attention as possible. The second trick was what they needed to see. Their preparations needed to be made before the first show that night.

"Give it up for the ever-radiant Golden Eagle!" Duncan raised their entwined hands and spun the young woman, her silks twirling around her. "This display here has only been a fraction of what we have in store for you the next couple of nights," he continued as Rae took one last bow. She blew a kiss to the crowd before bounding back to her friends.

"Our first show will be tonight, once the sun has truly disappeared from the sky. And you, my friends, are all invited. Tonight's show will feature acrobatic displays of beauty and bravery, feats of strength, mind-blowing demonstrations of human and animal communication, along with so much more. Tonight is family-friendly, something for everyone. We will have a matinee tomorrow at noon, specifically for the children. They will have opportunities to meet and learn from our performers. Just beware, they may end up trying to run away with us!" The Ringmaster paused while the audience chuckled. A slow smirk spread across his features.

"Our third and final show tomorrow night will be adults only for a saucier burlesque show. Come after sunset tomorrow to indulge in the darker side of the Circus. It will be a show you will never forget. If you wish to see how we set up our nomadic city, please watch from a distance, maybe the hillside? And with that exciting news, I bid you adieu until tonight." The Ringmaster took his purple top hat off in a flourish and bowed deeply.

The crowd broke out into applause and whistles when Duncan finished his speech. Little work, school or otherwise, would be accomplished with the Circus setting up on the edge of town. When the Ringmaster straightened from his bow, he gave a last wave to the crowd, releasing them from the trance he inflicted upon them. Conversations resumed, children ran around to release pent-up energy, and the crowds started making their way back to their homes.

The message was obvious to the Circus's contacts within Windemere. The Circus was starting out with a bang and they needed to be ready. Tonight was when they saved those that needed a place of refuge; tonight would be the night the family of nomads grew. The other two performances would let them linger and look for anyone their contacts missed, to find those still hiding who they were from the world.

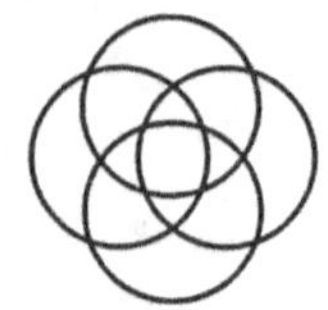

Chapter Three

The Circus performers and crew were not strangers to setting up their nomadic city. The process in each town they visited was the same, and each individual had a specific job to do. Everybody knew they needed to help if they wanted to welcome their patrons by dusk.

Before the actual work could begin, though, breakfast needed to be had. Duncan always insisted that sharing a meal after the parade was the first step to a successful set-up and subsequent performance. It strengthened the community and reminded everyone what they were working towards.

Besides, nobody wanted to work on an empty stomach.

The other performers began prepping for breakfast while Duncan and Rae, the Golden Eagle, addressed the crowd and their contacts within the agricultural community.

"For the last time Damien, keep your dirty paws off the bacon!" Luc complained, exasperation coloring her tone. She threw a look at Zeke as they laid the food out on the buffet table.

"Oh, mi amor! You wound me!" Damien clutched at his chest between bites of the greasy goodness.

The dark-haired acrobat rolled her eyes and pushed him out of the way, grabbing another tray from a runner before adding it to the spread of food.

Runners brought dishes from the cooks at the chuck wagons to the three acrobats before hurrying back to grab more. Everything was prepped the night before, making it easy for the cooks to heat everything once they reached the field. Luc, Damien, and Zeke made sure all the food was easy to access, plate ware was ready to be grabbed, and the food scrap and dirty dish stations were set up.

"Better watch out Dame. Don't want Luc to sock ya before opening night." Zeke shot his friend a wicked grin.

Damien held up his hands in defeat. "Huntress, like that time in Southton? I had a bruise for weeks!" Luc and Zeke chuckled at the memory, while Damien edged closer to Luc. She let out a shriek when he grabbed her wrist and spun her, ending with a dip. "That was the first time I laid eyes on such a beautiful woman."

Luc beamed as she struggled, blushing once Damien let her go. She gave the dark-skinned man a shove and shook her head. "Quit it! Before I give you another bruise. We have a job to do." She turned her attention to making sure food was accessible from both sides of the table.

Damien shot Zeke a wink as he snatched another piece of bacon behind Luc's back. Zeke snorted before grabbing more food from another runner.

The three acrobats did their jobs as others made coffee, some arranged wagons and livestock, and more roamed the grounds looking for anything else to assist in bringing their Circus to life. Everyone waited in anticipation for the food that was wafting delicious smells throughout the field.

"Tsk, tsk Damien, I thought you were better than lifting food behind your lover's back." Rae's eyes danced with mirth as she joined the other three acrobats at the buffet table.

Luc whirled around and glared at her partner. "How dare you," she seethed, stalking toward the man she had been with for years.

Rae shared a look with Zeke as Luc berated Damien for his duplicity. The four acrobats had joined the Circus in their youth, becoming inseparable as they grew in age and ability. They began their trapeze routine years ago and relished being able to perform beside their best friends.

Rae moved to grab the next tray of food from a runner but stumbled backwards as a gaggle of young kids almost ran her over while chasing a dog.

"Sorry, Rae! Max took Kim's doll again. We gotta get him before he chews the doll's head off!"

"No harm, no foul! Just make sure Kim knows she doesn't have to share with the dog," Rae said with a smile.

"That's what I said!" The leader yelled behind him as he continued chasing the mutt.

Rae moved back to the runner and grabbed the tray of food, still smiling. She looked up when she felt eyes watching her. Zeke laughed silently while he cradled a mug of coffee in his hands.

"Don't say it." Rae pointed a finger in his direction.

"Say what? That you almost let a group of six-year-olds take you out?" Her trapeze partner schooled his features into an innocent smile, Damien and Luc pausing their argument upon hearing what almost befell their friend.

"They didn't take me out! And what is this? No coffee for the only one working?" Rae lifted one eyebrow.

"Oh! So the Golden one expects to be waited on hand and foot." Damien shot her a wink. "Just because she did a couple of flips."

"We all knew this day would come. Pay up boys, you thought she'd last a couple more years." Luc held her hands out to the two men, a devilish grin on her face and mischief in her eyes.

"I'm going to fight all of you." Rae closed her eyes as if trying to find her patience.

The four broke out in laughter, enjoying the company of those that knew them best.

"Okay, but actually, did someone grab me coffee or do I need to go grab my own? I can feel the headache starting already," Rae asked, placing a hand on her temple.

"Here, Rae." Luc filled another mug from the jug they had grabbed from the coffee cart before starting at the buffet table.

Rae took the mug with gratitude, letting it warm her hands in the chilly morning air. She breathed in the nutty aroma and sighed as she took her first sip. The simplest of pleasures weren't taken for granted while they were on the road.

When the next runner came, Luc told him to let the cooks know the buffet was ready when they were.

The four chatted while enjoying their coffee, watching more and more of their troupe make their way to the long tables waiting to be filled.

The breakfast bell sounded in the distance, signaling the performers and crew to grab food. Lines formed on both sides as runners brought more trays from the chuck wagons to replace the rapidly declining dishes.

"I can refill this time, Luc. You go eat." Rae grabbed a refill of pancakes from the nearest runner.

"Are you sure?"

"Of course. You guys did all the work. I can do this. Besides, you know the boys won't wait."

Luc sighed. "They are the worst with food. Thanks, Hermana. Let me know if you need a break."

Rae secretly loved refilling the buffet because it gave her a chance to chat with everyone in the caravan. Ever the extrovert, she took pride in greeting every person by name. As people filed through, Rae's heart panged with the realization of rips in the makeup of the performers and crew.

It became harder to keep smiling while wrestling with her feelings of loss.

Finally, the cooks and Duncan made their way through the line. Duncan never ate before the people in his care. Rae smiled at the man that was like a father to her, but it didn't reach her eyes. Duncan gripped her shoulder and smiled kindly.

"You did well today, my dear."

"Duncan I—this was harder than I thought it would be." Rae hung her head.

"The grief only means you loved them. Never be ashamed of loving our people." Duncan gently lifted Rae's chin to look her in the eyes. Rae met his gaze and nodded, pulling out of his hold to hide the pain in her eyes. She grabbed a plate and went down the line, only taking a few things. The acrobat found her appetite lacking after recognizing the holes left in their community. She moved to sit with her three friends, hoping to drown out the thoughts of mourning.

Duncan turned to the tables filled with his people. They hushed each other as their Ringmaster opened his arms in preparation to speak. Hundreds made up the traveling city; meaning some finished eating by the time Duncan made it through the line. However, no one moved until he spoke.

"We all feel the loss of those that Tiva took from us. Our caravan will never be the same as it was. Grieving is inevitable and needed.

"Jason, Jose, Rochelle, and Naveen will always be remembered. They gave their lives to rescue as many as we could. Today marks the first set-up day since losing them. Be gentle with yourself and others. This day will remind you of what we lost. Lean into it and support one another."

Duncan let his words sink in.

A stillness fell over the caravan. Rae pulled her arms around herself, remembering everything that went wrong, including her part in all of it.

"We grieve for them while we prepare to save more of our people. Remember why we do this. Remember why we can't stop. The Magicae of this world need us more than ever. They are depending on all of us. Acknowledge your feelings, then choose to keep going despite the pain. We can do this together." With that, Duncan made his way to the nearest open spot, nodding to different groups as he went.

"As Rocky woulda said, 'No pain, no gain.'" One runner said loudly.

"No, no, no. She would have said, 'Just rub some dirt in it.'" Argued one of the tent crew, gaining a chuckle.

"Nah, yer all nuts if that's what ya think she'da said. Good ole Rocky woulda boxed yer ears and said, 'Suck it up, buttercup.'" Growled the oldest of the concession workers.

Soon enough, entire tables were arguing over what the rough and tumble, wiry, middle-aged carnival worker would have said. Eventually, the arguing moved to what the other three would have said to those that survived them.

Before long, it turned into a competition between who could do the best impersonation or tell the best story about those they lost. The entire caravan soon dissolved into a mix of laughter and sobs, remembering their friends lost in the last town they visited.

As the sun rose higher into the sky, performers and crew members started clearing tables and piling dishware to be washed. They needed to set up the big top for the main show, along with three smaller tents for side acts, concession booths for food, and carnival games for the children. There was a lot to do before dusk descended and the townspeople of Windemere filed in.

A warm wind rose despite the crisp morning air and traveled between the wagons, ruffling hair and sending caps flying.

The breeze spurred the Circus into action.

Oxen and draft horses were directed to pull the wagons to the outskirts of the field, making room for the Circus yard to be set up. Once the area was cleared, there was a fury of activity in the field. A large crew of burly men, women, and children pulled long metal stakes from the back of a wagon. They took turns pounding them into the ground in a large circle.

Once the stakes were set for the big top, the setup crew took out some poles from the wagon and laid them in the middle of the stakes. The crew then moved on to set up the smaller sideshow tents.

Other crews got to work setting up makeshift concession stands from a couple of specially-built wagons and setting more stakes for the long, rectangular carnival tent.

The cooks prepped the food for the concession stand and many of the performers, including Damien and Luc, helped set up tents in the players' yard. This would be where the individuals of the Circus rested their heads for the night while they stayed in Windemere.

Rae and Zeke were part of the canvas team. They helped pull the massive, rolled cloth pieces of the big top from a wagon and unfurled them within the perimeter of metal stakes.

Luckily, the wind seemed to blow in whatever direction the canvas needed to go.

Rae couldn't help but admire the red and white striped tent while unrolling it. She and Zeke worked side by side, laying the canvas of the tent out and tying panels together. They worked with little thought, performing the designated set-up job they had done for years.

The tasks needed to set up their nomadic city stayed the same, but the individuals found innovative ways to make their processes more efficient. Duncan gave free rein to the people he directed, as long as they were within reason. It was one thing to use their Gifts to make the job easier, but showing off for the sake of it was expressly forbidden. Rae had learned that the hard way when she first joined the Circus.

The two acrobats finished unrolling their section of canvas and tied it to the next one.

"Do you ever get sick of this?" Zeke wiped the sweat from his brow.

"What do you mean?" Rae asked.

"Well, the constant set up and tear down, never being able to stay in one place for long, not being able to lay down roots." Pain filled his eyes as he gave Rae a long look. "Losing the people we love. Does it ever get to you?"

Rae took a moment to process what Zeke was saying. "Zeke, I absolutely get sick of this. But I get sick of not being able to use my Craft more." Rae gave a quick look around before shifting to hide her hand from watchful eyes. She snapped her fingers, and they sparked, forming a single flame. She met Zeke's steady gaze before a breeze extinguished the flame.

"I get sick of having to hide who I am. If we weren't on the road so much, we wouldn't be able to use our Crafts without fear of being sent to the Capital. At least on the road, we can get away with practicing and harnessing our power without fear." Rae shook Zeke's shoulder. "Don't tell me you could give that up."

Zeke sighed. A wind rose around them. "No. My Craft is more important than laying down roots, I guess. I just wish there was a place where we didn't have to hide at all. Even here in Windemere, I feel like we should keep an eye out for danger."

"Hey, chin up. In a couple more weeks we'll be in Heimat. We won't have to hide there."

"Yea, but we won't have roots there either. I want somewhere that is truly our home. Somewhere we can practice our Crafts and use them to help the community. Don't you ever think about how much more you could do for our people if your hands weren't tied?" Zeke's voice shook with emotion. He clenched his fists as Rae gripped one of his forearms. "I want to do more for the orphans we find. Give them everything we never had." The wind turned into a fierce bluster around them.

Rae's nails dug into Zeke's arm. "Z, calm down. I agree with you. Staying on the road will never be enough. We need to find somewhere more permanent. Look at me." Rae looked into his eyes, willing him to calm down and gain control of his emotions. Zeke's wind Craft was responding to the acrobat's emotional distress and creating the storm forming around them.

Rae and Zeke were Crafters. They each had an element running through their veins. Zeke felt the wind, while Rae felt fire. The only clue to the power within was their metallic or jewel-toned eyes. A tonic was the only way to hide their abnormal iris colors when in close quarters with those that feared what thrummed in their veins.

Zeke's eyes were gray instead of their natural silver, while Rae's hazel ones hid the molten gold underneath. The tonic took away the metallic shine of Zeke's eyes, but not the power in his blood. His feelings of hopelessness were kicking up the wind around them.

Zeke breathed deeply while staring into Rae's falsely colored eyes. Anger flashed at the reminder of all they had to hide before he forced himself to take another deep breath. Once he regained control, the surrounding wind quieted. He patted Rae's hand in thanks. "I'm good. Set-up always brings out the worst in me."

"No, you're not, but no worries. I got you. Let's get out of the way while the crew and J get the poles set." Rae gave one more worried glance to her trapeze partner. "We can see if they need help with the other tents." The two friends stood to let the next crew take over; turning, they met the knowing stare of their Ringmaster.

Rae hugged Duncan, but Zeke turned sheepish at his rare display of un-needed power. "Splendid work, you two. The canvas has never been tied more tightly." The Ringmaster's eyes softened when he saw the young wind Crafter. Duncan moved to Zeke and placed a hand on his shoulder. "The wind can be a fickle thing, it's bound to get away from us now and then."

Zeke clenched his fists. "I'm sorry Dunc, I think I'm longing for what once was, instead of appreciating what I have." His gray eyes found Duncan's. "I could be on the streets or in the Capital or worse. I should be grateful for our family and the lives we get to lead."

Duncan adjusted his hand, causing a wind to ruffle Zeke's hair. "Never stop trying to change the world for the better. It's always a good idea to count your blessings, but never settle for less than what you can dream of." He looked to Rae. "That goes for both of you. Our people need young leaders that dream bigger and reach farther if we want our circumstances to change." He waited for the two Crafters to nod before dismissing them. "Good. Carry on, then. I won't stop you." He gave them a wink and made his way to where the entrance of the big top would be. Rae and Zeke gave him a wave before moving to the sideshow tents.

Duncan ran a hand through his slightly curly, dark brown hair, peppered with more gray than he would've liked. He glanced to the hillside where some of the townspeople gathered to watch them set up. Thankfully, nobody noticed Zeke's outburst and the Ringmaster could feel his heartbeat slowing, knowing his fear was unwarranted.

Being this close to those that wished his people harm always set Duncan on edge. The battle between staying safe and opening their doors to save more Magicae left a bitter taste in his mouth.

Most rural towns did not trust and even feared, the Magicae. The Magicae were any individuals with power from the Goddess in their veins. The Goddess's power could manifest in four different ways, creating four different affinities or Gifts. Crafters could control one of the elements, Shifters could transform into an animal form, Forgers could manipulate different materials such as cloth, wood, metal, and glass, and Herbalists were connected to plants, helping them grow and using them to create tonics for ailments.

Should the Circus be discovered for including fugitives of the law in their company, their people would be hunted for the price placed on the heads of Magicae and their sympathizers. It would become dangerous to stop in the communities they once entertained and delighted. The threat of discovery and the consequent hunt that would follow was a collective fear for those in the Circus. Magical Gifts needed to be used sparingly and away from eyes that could interpret what was happening.

Duncan sighed as he stood just outside a group of Forgers waiting to lift the red and white canvas. *If only things had gone differently.* He shook his head, scattering the thoughts of, *if only*, knowing they would only lead to unproductive spiraling. His faults and mistakes spurred him forward. Saving more lives was the only true atonement for the night known as the Uprising.

He let out a hiss when he noticed one Forger had a cut on her leg, a line of silver dripping down. Before Duncan could say anything, two others in the group quickly bandaged it, hiding the silver liquid from their spectators.

He gave the girl an encouraging smile when her wide eyes met his.

That was close. He thought to himself, looking at the crowd on the hill and giving them a wave.

Besides hiding their power, Magicae also needed to hide their tells. When the

Uprising occurred, Magicae that did not hide their tells were killed or taken to the Capital. Crafters had their unusual eyes in metallic or jewel tones, Herbalists had viny birthmarks somewhere on their bodies, Forgers had blood the color of silver, and Shifters kept their animal form's eyes even in human form.

Luckily, most things could be concealed with tonics or powders, or armor. Crafters took a tonic, Herbalists covered their marks with powders or cloth, and Forgers covered as much skin as possible to avoid cuts and scrapes. Shifters were the only ones unable to hide their tells effectively enough during performance stops. The Herbalists had been unsuccessful in creating a tonic that could alter the very shape of the eye. For this reason, they needed to stay in their animal forms upon arrival until departure from each town. It was safer to keep them hidden in plain sight with no way to distinguish a Shifter from an animal in their beastly form.

Shifters could communicate with and offer a calming presence to any animals they mimicked in form. For every animal in the Circus, there was at least one Shifter of the same nature. This made travel, training, and care a breeze, since the animals could communicate their needs and were soothed with a touch.

Each Shifter had a human counterpart trained in performance. They acted as the animal trainer during shows while the Shifter took part in the performance as one of the animals. This way, the animal performers stayed calm and comfortable while the Shifter went undetected.

Duncan inclined his head as a burly, redheaded woman made her way towards the group of young Forgers. This was Jess, his second in command and Head Forger on the governing Council that made the major decisions for the nomadic city.

She sent a smile towards Duncan before scowling at the group next to him. "Well? What are you lot waiting for? Those poles won't lift themselves."

The group of fifteen young, muscular men and women grumbled and gave the good-natured woman some snarky retorts, but started setting up the poles on the outer edges of the tent. They lifted the metal poles with ease, barely straining to set the perimeter poles into place. Most of them had an affinity for metal or cloth, meaning they could lift large poles and stakes with ease, manipulating the weight of the object to make it lighter.

Forgers could alter their Material into different shapes or different weights with just a thought. The Forgers were essential in moving and setting the heavy hardware all over the setup area. They had to be discreet, which is why they had crews comprising Forgers and Mortals setting stakes and lifting poles.

They also created most of the goods for purchase at the ticket booth and for the members of the Circus itself, providing things such as saddles, clothing, lanterns, and the wagons themselves.

As the group raised each pole, other members pulled the canvas over them and tied it to the stakes already pounded into the ground.

Duncan sent puffs of air underneath the cloth to make it easier to see what they were doing. He turned his head when he felt the ground shake underneath him.

One elephant made his way to the big top with the little girl in pigtails from the parade.

This was Juno, or J, as he was affectionately known. He was the Head Shifter and also on the Council with Jess and Duncan. He was a gentle and constant presence in the Circus.

Using him to place the long poles in the middle of the large tent was more efficient and was always a crowd-pleaser to the spectators they normally had. These long poles gave the big top three distinct points in its canvas and ensured it didn't collapse on their patrons.

Jess performed in one of the sideshow tents as a strong woman, using her Gift to lift the heaviest of items. Their patrons merely thought she was gifted with a large muscle mass when the power in her blood gave her the ability to alter the very weight of anything made of iron.

She always worked on the larger middle poles with J. The elephant wore a harness with a chain attached to its end. This dragged on the ground behind him and was used by Jess to wrap around one of the long metal poles. Once the chain was connected, J would walk forward using Jess's directions, pushing the canvas up as the pole was brought to the correct position. As they set each middle pole in place, a cheer sounded from everyone under the tent.

Jess could've lifted the poles herself but enjoyed working with the Shifter to accomplish the task. J could do it in half the time without needing help from anyone else, leaving more people free to perform other tasks around the yard.

Duncan watched the pair work together in tandem, occasionally sending torrents of air into the top of the tent to help Jess picture where the next pole should go. He admired the way the Forger and the Shifter worked together to bring the big top to life. They moved from the north side to the south side, methodically and swiftly raising the magnificent show stopper of a tent.

"Well, well, well. I think we set a record." Jess patted J's flank. "Big top is up!" J trumpeted his agreement.

Duncan smiled and waved at the pair before slipping out of the massive tent.

Jess sighed in frustration.

She knew the Ringmaster had other set-up duties to check on, but she worried he missed out on too many of the minor victories. Celebrating even the smallest wins filled everybody's spirits. Jess had noticed the gaunt look on Duncan's face as of late.

He needed his spirits lifted more than anyone.

Jess hid her concern as she waved the other members of the crew over to celebrate with the pair. The only one missing was Duncan. Smiles and cheers were had all around. Soon enough, a flask was produced and passed around. Jess offered J a swig before putting it in her inside jacket pocket.

"Alright, back to work, you rascals. This flask will be outside the coffee wagon after the show tonight. I don't wanna know whose it is, just pick it up from there once I'm out of eyesight." Jess shook her head at the antics of her team.

"Buzz kill!" One man gave a wolfish grin.

"You'll thank me later. I have more experience than all of you combined. It doesn't pay to be hungover for tomorrow's takedown. We have a job to do." The team sobered upon remembering their task for the duration of the two days spent in Windemere. Jess hated doing it, but she needed her team sharp for the next coming nights.

Living in violation of the law meant more and more people needed to be saved every day. The team broke apart and went to set up seats, the performance ring, and trapeze equipment.

J put his trunk on Jess's arm. She looked up at the kind, deep brown eyes filled with understanding. "Thanks, old friend." She patted his trunk. "You better take Eva back to the animal yard. I think we have a crowd." Jess had walked to the entrance of the big top while J followed, keeping his trunk on her shoulder.

Upon looking out, sure enough, townspeople dotted the hill to the southeast. Jess waved at the spectators and gave a bow. Moving to the side, she gestured to J, who lowered into a deep bow before giving a trumpet.

The crowd laughed in delight and broke into applause. The pair turned back into the tent and the safety from prying eyes.

Eva was the young girl from the parade that walked with the elephants. She was J's human partner and one of the youngest performers in the show. Their pairing elicited shock and awe from their audiences as they gazed in amazement at a young girl commanding such colossal beasts. She had joined the show several years back, as a Forger rescued from Windemere itself. Her immediate bond with J and the elephants brought about her role in the elephant act despite her affinity for manipulating wood.

Jess called Eva over, and she led J back to the animal yard to join the other elephants. Checking on them was J's number one priority. They needed to be ready for tonight's performance.

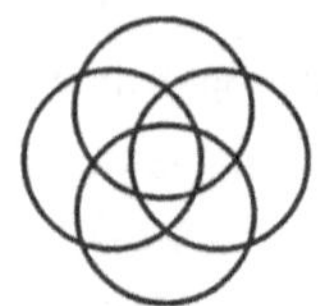

Chapter Four

Rae and Zeke finished laying out and tying the canvas for the three smaller side-act tents, two concession stands, and one carnival tent that would surround the big top. The sideshow tents shared their back wall with the big top but opened to the circus yard itself. They did not offer access to the main tent but provided a more intimate experience than that of the main spectacle on center stage.

The two acrobats walked around the circus yard, looking to see if anyone needed help before they reported for rehearsal.

The circus yard was set up to highlight the enormous tent that housed the center ring. Upon paying admission, patrons were funneled through an entrance that led straight to the big top's main entrance. On either side sat a side act tent. If patrons went to the left, they would reach the main concession stand after passing the entrance to the Raptor Show. Moving further, they would reach the Fortune Teller tent along the left, back corner of the big top. If they went to the right, they would reach the Feats of Strength tent and a smaller concession stand.

Rae and Zeke started at the main entrance, sending a wave to the ticket takers. The ticket booth sat right outside the main entrance, fashioned out of a wagon. A couple of people worked inside the wagon while others handed tickets out on the ground. Set-up was easy once they positioned the wagon correctly.

"Did you hear the news about little Izzy? Marv's daughter?" Rae asked Zeke, motioning toward the gruff ticket taker.

Zeke raised an eyebrow. "No, what about her? She's the one that made us flower crowns, right?"

"Yep! Cute as a button! Rumor is her eyes are showing flecks of copper." The fire Crafter beamed at her partner.

"A Crafter? Wow, I would've guessed Herbalist." He gave Rae a shrewd look. "What do you wanna bet?"

Rae feigned innocence. "Bet? Whatever do you mean?" She gave him a wink.

"How about a bottle of whiskey? I'll take wind."

"I'm gonna go earth." Rae waved at a group of children staring at the two acrobats. She smiled when they squealed and ran, knowing they'd been caught staring. She turned back to Zeke. "How mad will Luc and Damien be that they didn't get the first choice at Crafts?"

"Oh, you know Luc is going to make us pick lots. Gotta make sure it's 'fair.'" Zeke put the last word in air quotes as the two chuckled.

They made it to the first sideshow tent where Gar put on a Raptor Show with his son Bane in falcon form. He had several birds he worked with, including falcons, hawks, owls, and a magnificent golden eagle.

Curiously, Bane had found from a young age that he could communicate with and take the forms of raptors of all kinds, not just the falcon his animal form originally presented as. Thus, they added more birds to the show.

Rae poked her head in to check if Gar needed anything. He waved her on, already taking his birds out to run through rehearsals. A falcon whizzed past her, and circled Zeke, before returning to the small tent.

Rae lifted an eyebrow at Zeke as his neck flushed.

"Don't even, Sparks."

"I didn't say anything!" Rae threw her arms up in defense but waggled her eyebrows just the same.

Zeke shook his head but kept walking.

They stopped by the concession stand, grabbing their to-go lunches from the side of the booth. The main concession stand was set up to the left of the big top, positioned to serve patrons in the circus yard and troupe members in the player's yard behind.

The concession stands workers setting up the chuck wagon kitchens and concession stand waved at the two acrobats as they kept moving. The kitchen staff would serve everything from popcorn and honey candy to more substantial turkey legs and beef stew. There was no time to talk as they prepped everything for their patrons and the members themselves. Breakfast was eaten together as a group but lunch and dinner were grab-and-go, with performers and crew breaking for food when they could.

Betsy and Mac, head cooks for the nomadic city, ran a tight ship with Mac taking charge of the concession stand set-up and food prep while Betsy ran lunch and dinner services for the Circus members. They worked together seamlessly to provide hearty meals for their Circus family and patrons.

This was the one time a year for many in Windemere that they had access to sweets and actual beef. The concession crew knew when to slip in an extra candy or two for the children that would soon run wild. Food was another way to build trust and community in the towns they visited.

If only a good meal was all it took.

The two acrobats munched on dried meat and fruit while they continued looking to see if anybody needed anything. Moving clockwise around the big top, they came to Nan's sideshow tent where the old woman performed her fortune teller act. She read palms, tarot cards, and a crystal ball for a price. Luc was helping the old woman to set up, moving trunks and tables from a nearby wagon.

"Abuela, it's fine. Let me help you and Javie at least get the heavy stuff from the wagon." Luc argued with her arms crossed, not noticing her two friends at the entrance to the small tent.

"Nieta, stop fussing. The two of us are just fine. You should be helping set up the tents in the player's yard." The old woman sent a hard look at the young woman.

Rae and Zeke shared a grin. Nan was the oldest member of the Circus and was referred to fondly as "Abuela" by the members of the traveling city. She treated everyone like her grandchildren, despite Luc and her younger brother Javie being the old woman's only true grandchildren.

It was clear where Luc's insistence came from.

"Abuela! Need any more help?" Rae entered the small space, throwing an arm gently over the short old woman's shoulders, Zeke following behind her.

Nan tried to scowl at the two but quickly gave up. Wrapping one arm around Rae's waist, she smiled and shook her head. "You'd think I was old or something the way people keep asking if I need anything." She clucked. "No, no, no. You two move on and take this one with you." She pointed to her granddaughter.

Luc rolled her eyes and threw her hands up, exiting the tent.

Nan chuckled. "Just like her mother at that age. Go on then, run along. I have an act to set up."

Rae squeezed the Herbalist and followed Zeke, making her way to where Luc talked with her brother. Luc saw her friends and rolled her eyes again.

"That woman is infuriating. I'm going to stay and help Javie for a bit, maybe grab lunch for them. See you guys at rehearsal?"

"Sounds good!" The two Crafters chorused, continuing their walk around the yard.

To their left was the large carnival tent. It was in the back right corner, along the eastern wall of the circus yard, and housed the carnival games. Ring toss, darts, punk knock down, and milk bottle toss dotted the inside of the rectangular tent. The games were fun for all ages and were popular before the show started and during intermission.

The animal and players' yards were set up behind the main yard, separated by ropes and guards. This was where the performers and crew had their sleeping tents, ate meals, and prepped for their shows. The animal yards housed the creatures and Shifters used in performances, along with the oxen and horses used for transport and the livestock kept for food.

The two acrobats glanced at the crews of Forgers setting stakes and using poles to erect the carnival tent. There were plenty of people around to help with the tent, so Rae and Zeke kept moving, past the small concession stand by the carnival tent and making it to the last sideshow tent.

This was where Jess and Duke performed feats of strength.

Duke, a Mortal with considerable natural strength, performed alongside the powerful Forger, dazzling with all the things they could lift, bend, or break.

Zeke poked his head in and whistled. "You all alone here, Duke? Need any help?" Rae followed Zeke into the tent, helping Duke lug chairs to set up for the Feats of Strength side act. He was down a couple of crew members and gladly accepted the needed help.

In the big top, rehearsals were commencing. The family show had the most amount of acts, with the shortest lead time. There was only time for one full run-through and limited extra practice for each act. Duncan had already done an abbreviated intro, and the clowns were finishing their last bit when Rae and Zeke stumbled through the entrance to the enormous tent.

Everything had been set up in the big top without a hitch, the Forgers doing their jobs to perfection. A large ring sat in the center, with chairs and raised benches lining the perimeter. Two smaller rings sat to the right and left where performers could gather to watch and ready their acts. Where they joined the center ring, no seating was to be had. Instead, two large trapeze towers reached towards the top of the canvas.

Rae and Zeke shot into one of the side rings, trying to get to the closest tower to warm up. A voice caused them to halt.

"Good thing we switched the order of the acts, eh kiddies?" said a young man dressed in all black, sitting astride a midnight-colored stallion.

"Don't give me that, Tyee. We had to help Duke." Rae flipped her braided hair at the Night Rider, saying, "I didn't see you offering to help him." She turned on her heel and walked towards the trapeze area where Luc and Damien were already warming up.

Tyee whistled and patted his steed, Koko, as the horse pawed the ground. He looked at Zeke. "Someone's not in the mood today." He smirked. "Guess I'll have to try harder."

Zeke raised one eyebrow. "Good luck with that. You know how Rae can get."

"Aye, just let her know she doesn't get off that easy," Tyee said. "That's my cue." He nodded before guiding Koko to the middle of the ring and running through his act with his fellow horsemen.

With a last look at the horsemen whipping around the ring, Zeke followed his partner.

"Hey Z, think fast!" Zeke looked up just in time to see a baton headed straight for his face.

He quickly put a hand up and dropped to a crouch. Concentrating, he watched the baton slow its arc through the air until it floated to a stop inches from his outstretched hand. Grabbing the baton, he looked for where it originated from.

"Damien, what the hell? That was straight at my face."

"My friend, I knew you would catch it. Your competence in your Craft surpasses those that have studied twice as long." Damien draped an arm over his disgruntled friend. "Warm up the wind Crafter, check." He traced an imaginary check mark with his other hand.

Zeke brushed off Damien's arm with a huff. "There are better ways for me to warm up my Craft."

"Ah, but do they prepare you for the unexpected like my ways do?" Damien winked and gripped Zeke's shoulder. "Now you'll be ready if one of us misses a catch."

Zeke shook his head. "You are ridiculous. Let's get to work before the big cats get done." He made his way towards the southern trapeze tower, stretching and shaking out his muscles as he went. Luc and Rae were bouncing on the balls of their feet, deep in conversation, next to the southern tower. They were surrounded by several other performers that acted as spotters on the towers.

Damien followed at a light jog. He did a lap around the trapeze equipment before joining the other three.

"Okay, family fun show. We have three iterations to choose from. Which one did we agree on again?" asked Luc while grabbing some chalk from the bag attached to the trapeze tower.

"Well, Rae did the demo so Flying Eagle, right?" Zeke spoke up.

"Yep, that sounds good." Luc looked toward the center ring. "The horsemen are just finishing up. Big cats are next, then us. Let's get to work, everybody."

Zeke and Damien headed towards the northern tower while Luc started climbing to the top of the southern tower. Rae grabbed some chalk and looked towards the center ring. She looked straight into Tyee's expectant smirk. She felt heat creep into her cheeks as she quickly dropped her gaze.

Thoughts of the dark rogue had her stomach in knots. She tried to ignore the fluttering in her chest as he rode closer to the trapeze tower. *Please, just ride right on past. Huntress, please. Even if he stops, don't engage. We need to practice.* Rae thought vehemently to herself, invoking the face of the Goddess known to protect those on the road.

Tyee kept a wicked grin on his face as Koko brought him to where Rae stood, absentmindedly rubbing chalk on her hands and wrists. He dropped to the ground next to the fiery acrobat.

"And?" Rae lifted an eyebrow, keeping a cool demeanor despite the pounding in her chest.

"Your blood come in or something?" Tyee had the nerve to wink.

"None of your fucking business," Rae said, narrowing her eyes.

Tyee leaned in to whisper next to her ear. "Or are you dreaming of me again?"

Rae gave the tall rogue a shove. "Absolutely not."

Tyee gave a low chuckle. "I'll take that as a yes, then." He grabbed Koko's lead and headed towards the big top entrance, only turning back to wink one more time at the acrobat.

Rae growled. *I'm an idiot. Why does he always do this to me?* Rae shook her head. She needed to clear her mind to successfully run through their practice on the trapeze. If she didn't, Luc would make them redo it again and again until they got it right. She did not want to deal with her friend's perfectionist tendencies today.

Taking a deep breath, she climbed the trapeze tower to reach where Luc was already on the fly bar.

The two towers were directly across from each other, one on the north side and one on the south side. Rope ladders ran from the ground to the pinnacle of the big top and along the sides of the towers. Both metal structures were outfitted with two sets of bars, one higher, and one lower. This allowed the acrobats to swing in tandem across the center ring and interact with the two bars on the other side. Luc and Damien were starting on the lower bars, while Rae and Zeke were starting on the higher bars.

They ran through their performance with ease once the net was set up below. The Flying Eagle was a simple routine that started with all four artists doing tricks on their respective bars. They moved into taking turns flying across the center ring, performing twists and turns before catching the bar from the other tower.

Sometimes they did this in tandem, other times they took turns.

Eventually, the men caught Luc and Rae as they swung from their bars, performing flips and twists before grabbing onto their partner's wrists, and swinging precariously. They were then swung back around and thrown into the air to grab the bar waiting for them, courtesy of the spotters also on the towers. The spotters timed the bars correctly, so they were always ready for the female flyers to grab them. They also had hooks to grab the bars between tricks.

The four had been testing their limits on the bars since they were gangly kids, and it showed. Performers watched the four from below, awestruck. Zeke could've used his Craft at any point, but he never needed to; every leap and throw was pure precision. They had complete trust in one another.

There was little choice, being this far from the ground.

They performed together flawlessly, working in tandem at some points and staggered the next. The fluidity of each acrobat's movements seemed effortless. They demonstrated grace and power and complete control of their bodies as they flew around the big top.

Finally, Rae made her way up the rope ladder to the top of the tent, where a line of silk waited for her.

Unbeknown to the fire Crafter, dark eyes observed her. Tyee had left Koko in the animal yard before slipping back into the shadows to watch the performance, and one acrobat in particular. The rogue studied Rae's lithe form, admiring the strength of her muscles and the graceful way she moved in the air.

Rae took the silk, pulled herself up, and hooked one leg around the length of fabric. After wrapping it around one leg, she did the same with the other. Then she wrapped the end of the silk around her body and waited.

Tyee didn't register the other three acrobats and didn't see them perform the bit where Luc seemingly missed a trick and hurtled toward the net. No, his focus was on the golden girl that welcomed him with open arms that fateful night.

Haggard and running from a past he wouldn't face, he met her on the road and found a reprieve. She offered him food and water, and asked a few questions, but ultimately led him back to her people. He caught her using her Craft a couple of nights later and proved his mettle when he didn't run.

He was drawn to her from the first, floored by the way she cared for strangers, fought for her loved ones, and never backed down.

Not to mention those entrancing golden eyes.

Luc landed on her back in the net before jumping to her feet and out of the net to take a bow in the center ring.

Tyee was shaken from his reverie when suddenly, Rae dropped from the top of the tent, seeming to barrel roll down the length of silk, Zeke and Damien motionless on their bars.

Upon reaching the end of her piece of silk, Rae wrapped it around the length of her arm and spread her legs out into the splits. A couple of spotters used a pulley system to pull down on the silk and lift Rae high into the air, with only her arm suspending her. She flipped and twisted through the air.

The horseman frowned as he watched the acrobat grin, flying with freedom. He knew deep down the golden girl was hurting and had scars below the mask she wore for most. Duty and purpose kept her marching forward, but he noticed the times her mask slipped and sadness filled her eyes, tension taking hold of her frame.

His scars called to hers, begging for the relief she was sure to provide.

But Tyee wasn't that man. He locked those things away, deep inside. He wouldn't make that mistake again.

His eyes trailed back to the fire Crafter.

She had wrapped the silk around her middle, spread her arms wide, and swung her legs to get momentum.

Zeke jumped down to the lower bar across from Damien, both swinging, propelling their bodies through the air. They swung their legs up over their heads, turning to place one leg under the bar.

They hung upside down, doing the splits, and swinging back and forth. On the third swing, each of them hooked their front knee over their bar and hung from one leg. At the top of the arc, they both dropped face-first into the net below.

Tyee watched as Rae did her last trick, flying around the center ring, her arms mimicking bird wings. She continued until she lost her momentum and came to a standstill. Unhooking the knot, she wrapped the silk one last time around her legs. This time, she gathered the slack from the end of the silk and dropped, pinwheeling down the length of the silk.

She caught herself inches from the net.

Tyee let out a breath he didn't know he'd been holding. He slipped back into the shadows as the acrobat released the silk, bouncing to a stop in the net. The last thing he needed was for the woman to notice him.

Rae scrambled out of the net to the sound of her fellow performers clapping. Feeling her pulse race, she smiled and gave a bow in Duncan's direction. She joined the other three at the edge of the center ring, taking short, rapid breaths as she went.

"Nice job, Rae. Remember to point your toes. You tend to keep your feet flat. Zeke, don't forget to smile now and then. And Damien—"

"Hush, love. We all did a marvelous job." Damien put his finger to Luc's lips. "The kiddies will love it."

"But we should always try to be better." Luc protested.

"Ah, but of course, mi amor." Damien swung an arm over her shoulder and pulled her in close. "Just keep your notes until tonight's performance."

Luc squealed. "Ah, you are so sweaty! Let go, let me go!" She pulled away from the glistening acrobat and glared at him. "I'll stop giving notes if you get a towel or something."

Rae rolled her eyes. "It's not like you've never felt his sweat before."

Luc turned red, as Damien gave a wolfish grin. "We admit to nothing, my golden-eyed friend." He winked and followed a chagrined Luc.

"You're terrible. Let's go get some water." Zeke followed the couple, with Rae close behind, laughing at Luc's embarrassment.

All four acrobats watched from the side as the last performers did their run-throughs before making their way back to their tents to prepare for opening night.

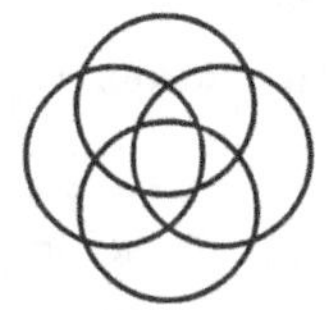

Chapter Five

The sun was sinking closer to the western horizon as the Circus bustled with activity. Most people were in the player's yard, putting on makeup and making last-minute tweaks to colorful and shimmering costumes. The sounds of children running, parents squabbling, and friends laughing filled the late afternoon air.

Once they were ready, performers and crew members made their way to the big top. A sea of sparkles, feathers, face paint, and animals streamed towards the center ring where their Ringmaster awaited, holding a lone torch. The lanterns used to illuminate their center ring were left unlit on opening night until after their Ringmaster spoke.

They gathered just before dusk on their first night of shows to share stories and confirm they knew the details of the rescue taking place during the show. Everyone needed to be ready to save the Magicae hiding in Windemere.

A cacophony of voices and sounds soon filled the big top. The only people not inside were the lookouts keeping their eyes peeled for the people of Windemere. Some townspeople could get a little eager to enjoy the delights of the Circus and try to sneak in to get a peek behind the scenes. The last thing they needed was for townspeople to catch them unaware in the red-and-white striped tent.

"Attention, my dear friends! Please, lend me your ears!" Duncan shouted. The crowd kept talking as if they couldn't hear him. He tried again, but this time he cupped one hand around his chin. "My dear friends! Please take your seats and quiet down." It was as if the Ringmaster had a megaphone to his lips. The performers and crew members immediately made their way to the wooden seats that would soon be filled with patrons. Conversations ended as everybody listened.

"Thank you. For everything you have accomplished today, I can only express my gratitude. Working together, we can do so much. Please, give yourselves a round of applause." Duncan looked around at his family and waited for the clapping to die down. "Tonight is the most important night in Windemere. Tonight, we save our people!"

The crowd broke out in cheers.

Duncan felt a lump in his throat, knowing the words he would say next would inflame his guilt and shame deep inside. But those new to the Circus deserved this story, no matter the cost to Duncan.

Green eyes found his from the crowd and gave him a small nod.

Duncan swallowed and continued, not letting himself find those green eyes again. "Tonight, I must tell the story of why this community was formed to begin with. A lot of you don't know this story. Those of you from Tiva, Carlisle, and Greenstead joined us recently and we are so happy to have you as part of the family.

"But that doesn't mean you haven't wondered how this traveling city came to be.

"Step back in time with me and learn why hiding in plain sight has served us so well for almost two decades. Eighteen years ago, our elected President and my dear friend lost his seat of power to his General, Myra Falkenrath. Myra used her soldiers to take power, ruling as a tyrant to this day, because President Andre had a little girl with golden eyes."

Duncan took a breath and clenched his fists, trying to keep his emotions in check, knowing this was painful for everyone in the audience. Myra's broad face and stocky structure came to mind. She was a cruel woman, more interested in gaining power than serving the ones she governed. She'd been in power for almost two decades and the country was more of a wreck than ever before.

The first time he'd met her she'd sneered and warned him to keep an eye over his shoulder. The woman was more at ease giving threats than thinking about someone other than herself. He kept telling himself they deserved to know how they ended up here and where they could expect to go.

"But I don't have to tell you that. We've all been through the hiding, the fear, and the hurt. That night made being Magicae unlawful. It put a price on your head and fear in your feet. I know, we all know. That night changed the course of our lives forever."

He paused and let his words sink in.

"Reeling from the loss of so many loved ones, I gathered as many of our people as I could, and we left Fernwen." Duncan looked to Nan, her kind eyes shining, remembering those first nights. She escaped with Duncan and her grandchildren from the capital city, never stopping to look back at what they lost.

His eyes returned to scanning the crowd, keeping his chin held high.

"We traveled for weeks, picking up people along the way. Stopping in towns became more and more dangerous as our caravan continued to grow. We spent less and less time in towns and more on the road. Hiding in plain sight was our aim, but more people meant more questions.

"As desperation set in, I thought back to my Mother and the advice she constantly preached. She would say 'Chin up, Dunc. No matter your circumstance, keep that chin up. Hopelessness is the beginning of anyone's demise.'

"Now my Mother was the smartest woman I've ever met. She raised me and my sister on her own, keeping us warm and fed, and being present anytime we needed her. I knew I needed to use her advice to see us out of this mess, to find some sort of safety for our people, and keep the hopelessness at bay."

Green eyes didn't miss the smile in Duncan's voice when he talked about his mother or the sadness that filled his eyes at the mention of his sister.

"We made it to Heimat months later. Heimat was the city I aimed for, desperately hoping it was far enough away from the capital to stay out of Myra's control. Its position on the Mantaga and near the Great Northern Forest made it an ideal place to settle for a community on the run.

"The people of Heimat welcomed us with open arms. They had Magicae friends and family they were determined to protect at any cost. Their generosity was and still is, unmatched.

"Many people joined seamlessly into the city, but all I could do was think about those we didn't save. The children born to Mortal parents with Magicae ancestors brought into a world that would hate them."

He rubbed the back of his neck with one hand. The familiar feelings of regret and shame at not saving more people the night of the Uprising threatening to overwhelm him.

"I couldn't let myself rest knowing there were more of our people in danger. When we had found a haven, it seemed selfish to keep it all to ourselves.

"I met with the first iteration of what became the Governing Council, the elders and representatives that guide our community, and we brainstormed for hours. We knew not everyone would want to give up their new haven to travel the road for the majority of the year, but some would, and they had families to bring with them. We needed a cover that explained the constant moving from town to town with children in tow."

A glint entered his eyes, remembering the cleverness that overtook them in those early stages. They were so proud when the ideas struck. It wasn't what they once had, but his community was thriving against all odds.

"Inspiration came as we observed our people interact with the residents of Heimat. Herbalists made and sold tinctures, and offered to diagnose patients and crops struggling to flourish. Shifters helped soothe tamed animals, performed tricks for children, and helped whenever needed. Crafters lit hearths, watered fields, and calmed the elements. Forgers created all sorts of goods for the town, working with local craftsmen and women to produce the most sought-after tools, but the shows for the children put on by the Shifters piqued our interest the most.

"The delight and joy in those children's eyes gave sparks to the imagination. If we could start a traveling show, nobody would question us or the children in our care. Our people could go undetected, using the Gifts we were born with discreetly, and save more Magicae in the process. We, the Governing Council, brought this idea to the leaders of Heimat. We wanted their blessing to recruit within the town and bring back the new recruits at the end of each season. With the enthusiastic backing of Heimat, we brought our ideas to our people, and thus, the Circus was born.

"We started small, relying heavily on the Shifters' animal performances, selling goods from the Forgers and tinctures from the Herbalists. We stayed in the North that first season, developing acts, deciphering what our audiences wanted, and adding in concessions and carnival games.

"We saved almost fifty Magicae that first season. By the end of the second, that number was up to a thousand."

Duncan paused, letting the numbers sink in, and letting the members of the Circus remind themselves why they risked everything on the road.

"The work we do matters. All of us have gone from being alone and fearing for our safety, to being part of something, creating a network of support for the people cast out by society. We welcome our new recruits with open arms, Magicae and Mortals alike. The relationships we've formed with one another, and the shared motivations we have, prove that power running through the veins of someone shouldn't be the cause for division. Vindictiveness, jealousy, and cruelty; those are what cause division in our country.

"You are part of a new legacy. We will keep our chins held high and weather the storm, preparing for a new day when hiding in plain sight is no longer necessary."

Duncan's eyes held fire as the members of the Circus cheered his words. He turned slowly, surveying his people and taking in their excitement, letting the guilt drop from his shoulders for a few precious moments, letting the weight of responsibility lift for an instant, and allowing himself a little time to recognize what he built for the Magicae of this broken world.

That relief was gone in an instant as his eyes recognized the holes where friends once sat.

"My friends, our pride and jubilation are warranted, as is the grief and hurt caused by the losses we have incurred." He bowed his head in reverence. "Jason, Jose, Rochelle, and Naveen will never return to us physically. But they live on in here." Duncan put a fist to his heart. "Jason lives in every Herbalist making a tonic, Jose is within every Forger lifting one of those heavy metal poles, Naveen is in the heart of every chef working a chuck wagon, and Rocky is in every crew member running a carnival game."

Green eyes welled with tears at the mention of her dear friend Jason. It would be a while until the raw ache of grief lessened. Her attention shifted back to the Ringmaster.

"These people are gone, but we can honor them every time we use our Gifts or talents to better the lives of those around us. This means our family, the people we save, and the people we visit. By the Huntress, let's put on the best damn show we ever have." The crowd erupted into applause.

"For Jason!" Duncan shouted.

"For Jason!" The crowd echoed, stomping their feet and thumping their chests.

"For Jose!"

"For Jose!" People clapped despite the tears that rolled down their cheeks.

"For Naveen!"

"For Naveen!" The crowd acted as if in a trance. All they knew was they had to keep going, had to keep their friends' memories alive.

"For Rocky, the hellcat we never thought we'd lose!"

"FOR ROCKY!" The crowd screamed and devolved into clapping and whistling.

Duncan had a sad smile that didn't reach his eyes. The guilt of losing their people weighed heavily on his shoulders. His gift for speeches could inspire those that followed him but seemed to leave him empty. Despite the pain and shame at his ability to manipulate using words, Duncan knew he needed to keep going.

"My friends, come, let us light the torches. It's time to welcome the masses.

Dusk is upon us." He gestured to the main entrance to the tent.

Everybody filed out into the Circus yard. They filled the space outside the big top, where four impressive torches stood, framing the entrance to the massive main event tent.

Once the torches were lit, townspeople would start arriving and opening night would begin. In the distance, children and adults alike waited in anticipation for when they would be welcome to enter the enchanting escape from their reality.

Rae filed out with the rest of the members of the nomadic city. She was dressed in her golden, shimmering, full-sleeved jumpsuit. The gold material was too loose to wear on the trapeze, with too much fabric to get caught up in, but Rae couldn't bear not to wear it. It reminded her of the dress her mother Naomi once wore to political events. As silly as it was, wearing it helped Rae feel closer to her late mother.

Underneath was her performance costume. She wore a pair of gold tights, one leg covered in a mix of golden, chestnut, and mocha-colored feathers, reminiscent of the magnificent bird she took inspiration from. Her golden, tight crop top had an asymmetrical feathered collar of the same colors. The half mask she wore had feathers on the brow and a nose that looked like the curved beak of a golden eagle. The jumpsuit hid most of her costume but provided needed protection against the chill in the autumn dusk.

She followed the crowd to the large torches outside of the big top. Wagons had been placed strategically to hide this spot from any early onlookers. Once the Lighting ceremony was over, they would move the wagons, revealing the beacons and inviting patrons to partake in the wonders of the Circus.

Rae moved to the front of the crowd. Her affinity for fire was rare to find, as the fire Craft was not known to announce itself gently or quietly. Most young fire Crafters were taken to the capital when their body parts started on fire or their emotions caused things to spontaneously combust. The fire Craft was routinely connected with destruction and was the most feared Craft by Mortals because of its potential for disaster.

Rae struggled deeply with that part of her Gift.

She devoted most of her time to learning how to restrain the magma running through her veins. Her control was hard fought but something she took pride in.

Fire was not something that wanted to be contained, yet Rae had done so. She could call forth a single flame or a raging inferno, and everything in between. She was one of five fire Crafters in the company. The two seasoned Crafters joined her at the front of the crowd. The other two still grappled with controlling the size of the flame they produced. They watched from the audience, wary of the danger they posed to their family and friends.

Rae looked to the gathering of the nomadic city, recognizing that everyone but those on lookout duty was present. She took a deep breath to hide her nerves. *Relax. You've done this a million times. Tiva was a fluke. You got this.* The acrobat gave herself a pep talk, driving thoughts of doubt from her mind.

Tiva was raided by the military before they could get there. They captured most of the children waiting to be rescued before the Circus could arrive. The Circus did what they could but only saved a fraction of the Magicae they'd been expecting. Jason, Jose, Naveen, and Rocky gave their lives trying to protect the remaining children from the soldiers still scouring the city.

Rae's emotions overwhelmed her, creating one of the biggest walls of fire most had ever seen. The flames ravaged the city while the Circus left with the children they could.

She needed to use the lighting ceremony to prove to her people and herself that she was as in control of her Craft as ever. She squared her shoulders and addressed her people.

"Tonight is special. Tonight, we light these four main flames for those we lost. They will be our guides in the night as we add more to our number."

Rae nodded and the other two fire Crafters stepped to the two outermost torches. Rae stood in the middle of the two inner torches. "Huntress, let these flames burn long and bright to guide anyone seeking refuge. Let the flames lead our people home." Rae bowed her head, invoking the protection of their deity. Lifting both arms palm-side up, she paused before snapping her fingers. Half a beat later, the other two Crafters did the same, leaving one arm by their sides, snapping the fingers of the hand they held high.

Rae's torches burned brightly, shortly followed by the other two. After a couple of seconds, they transitioned to a comforting, warm glow that crackled in the night.

The crowd watched the flames, but Rae looked to where the two young fire Crafters stood and motioned them to the front of the crowd. They shared a look, moving hesitantly through the throng. This was the first time they had been asked to join a lighting ceremony.

"Our memorial flames are lit. The last thing to do is bring light and warmth to our patrons." Rae addressed the crowd, shooting a warm smile to the two young Crafters making their way towards her.

"Rae, what are you doing?" hissed one of the veteran Crafters.

"Zalia, trust me." Rae turned to address the crowd. "Please welcome our young fire Crafters. I will draw on them to light the rest."

Zalia huffed, but stood stoically with her fellow veteran, avoiding Rae's eyes.

Rae knew Zalia was right to worry; it was risky to use the young, untested Crafters, but she felt a pull towards them she couldn't explain. She learned at a young age to trust her intuition and would not start ignoring the warm feeling in her bones now. They needed this reassurance as much as their people did.

Fire could be destructive, but it could also be warm and inviting. Reassuring those still learning and the surrounding people was of the utmost importance. She nodded to Zalia and the other fire Crafter as they stepped to the side, melting back into the crowd.

Rae looked at the two shocked initiates and whispered. "You can do this. On my signal, each of you will put a hand on my shoulder and focus on channeling your Craft to where skin meets skin. That's it. I will take what you give me and release the power slowly to light the lanterns and smaller torches." Rae adjusted her jumpsuit to leave both shoulders bare, waiting for a response from the young Crafters.

"What happens if we lose control?" One asked, eyes hard.

"You both have lots of power but haven't quite harnessed it yet. I want to give you a taste of what it feels like to rein in the flames. You can do this. Just follow my lead." The young Crafters nodded, determination in their gazes.

She looked back to the crowd, murmuring under her breath, "Let the games begin."

Rae gave a feral grin, flexing her fingers in preparation for the rush of power about to be had. She took a glance westward and noted the sun slowly sinking below the horizon. She closed her eyes as each of the initiates put a hand on one of her bare shoulders.

Rae chanted the words of the ceremony as she tilted her head back and spread her arms wide.

"Fire within, come to me,

"Fire within, become a flame,

"Fire within, burn brightly for all to see,

"Fire within, go forth gently to light the way." Rae kept chanting as she concentrated on the power found inside her core. The words were unnecessary to call her power, but they connected her to the rest of the Circus and those they came to save. By chanting the words, she invited others into the lighting of their world.

She felt the two Crafters touch her skin with clammy hands. Slowly, each of the initiates found their sparks and started pouring power into her. She gasped wordlessly as the twin rivers of liquid flame flowed into her, threatening to overwhelm her.

Sweat formed on Rae's brow. She frowned and battled to contain that raw power, channeling it to her outstretched hands. They soon blazed with fire so hot it burned a whitish blue. Rae's whole body tensed as she took in the unreined power from both initiates, regrets regarding her spontaneity beginning to form.

She needed to work quickly.

First, she concentrated on the lanterns. She saw them in her mind's eye and coaxed a flame to spring forth from each one individually. She heard cheers from the crowd as more and more lanterns alighted around the main yard, concession stand, and sideshow tents.

The last ones were inside the big top itself. Because of their size, she had to use more power to light these lanterns. She slowly allowed more and more power to eke out of her open palms to the larger lanterns. Recognizing when to stop was the crucial step.

She gritted her teeth and focused on the first lantern.

Just a little more heat.

She felt the glass of the lantern crack, forming spidery veins across the surface. A knot formed in Rae's stomach. It'd been years since she'd cracked a lantern. Thoughts of Tiva flooded in.

She rolled her shoulders back and tugged hard on the rope of energy connecting her to the lantern. The force of her pull lit the wick without exploding the surrounding glass.

She quickly closed both her fists, panting as she let the flames within burn her to the core.

Rae flashed a quick smile at the crowd, praying they didn't notice her distress. She continued to the other lanterns inside the big top. Sweat dripped down her brow as she struggled to control the power coursing through her veins.

Lanterns needed more precision to make sure the surrounding glass did not heat too quickly and explode. Once she finished lighting the last one, Rae breathed a sigh of relief.

Now came the fun part.

Each of the smaller perimeter torches was wrapped with fire cloth. Some Forgers had engineered this, making it easier for fire Crafters to light multiple things at once. A fire Crafter could focus on the fire cloth's signature and simultaneously light all the specially-designed cloth in an area at once.

She took one deep breath and as she exhaled, focused on lighting the dozen torches covered in fire cloth. Letting them flare brightly with full force, Rae finally felt relief.

She knew she had succeeded when the crowd started hollering and celebrating. She let the flames surrounding her hands die slowly, reversing the flow of power back into the initiates behind her. Unlike the inexperienced fire Crafters, she let the power trickle back to them slowly. This ensured a tidal wave of fire did not overwhelm them as she almost had been.

Once her hands were reduced to just being warm to the touch, she put a hand on each of her shoulders and gently peeled the initiates' fingers from her skin. She turned to look behind her and found both of them staring at their hands with wide eyes.

"Not what you expected?" Rae murmured, forcing her emotions out of sight.

"How did you do that? I've tried lighting lanterns before and it seems like one thought and they just explode."

"Find me on the road and we can practice. It's all about redirecting the flame. Let go of the fear and submit to the flame before it will accept your control. Prideful little bastard, that flame." Rae winked. "Says something about the rest of us, eh? Sometimes pride is our biggest downfall."

"Thanks, Rae, we will find you on the road. This was—words can't describe how much this meant. Thank you."

"Of course. We all have to start somewhere. Even the Elders were Novices once." Rae smiled as the two gingerly made their way through the crowd, performers and crew members offering smiles and back thumps in congratulations for a job well done.

Rae turned her head from the pair when she felt eyes on her. She found Tyee watching her closely, a small frown on his face. She squared her shoulders and stood straight, not letting her exhaustion show.

Tyee put an arm across his waist and gave her a half bow when he noticed her shift in attention. He cocked his head and raised an eyebrow after straightening.

Rae lifted a choice finger in his direction that earned her a chuckle.

Tyee turned away from the impressive Crafter to fetch Koko from the animal yard; it wouldn't be long before the show started. Rae watched his retreating figure become an outline. Before long, she was surrounded by her people, flabbergasted at her control over so much power. They showered her with praise and words of congratulations before rushing to their stations.

Opening night had begun.

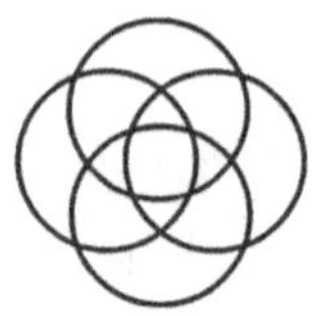

Chapter Six

The circus yard was a frenzy of activity.

Children dashed through the crowd, weaving haphazardly between groups of adults and performers. Concession stand workers shouted out their menus. Gar stood outside his tent, Bane on his shoulder, beckoning patrons to come and see the raptor show. Carnival tent workers challenged young people to their games of chance and skill. Jess and Duke took turns throwing boulders and tree trunks back and forth to each other. Duncan stood by the ticket takers, welcoming one and all to his city of nomads.

Inside the fortune teller tent, however, Nan already had a customer. She looked at the haggard young woman sitting across from her and felt sympathy. The woman wore a threadbare shawl she kept tugging at as if pulling it closer would make it warmer. She gave a grim smile when she noticed the old woman looking at her.

"Oh child, here, take this. You're gonna catch a cold with only that thin layer to keep you warm." The old woman got up, grabbed a blanket, and draped it over the woman's shoulders.

"You don't have to do that." The woman's features relaxed as the thick wool blanket chased away the chills.

"Hush. I was a young mother once, too." Nan sat down and placed a hand on top of the young woman's outstretched ones.

Distrust filled the woman's face as she dragged her hands away. "How did you know I was a mother?" She narrowed her eyes at the old woman.

Nan chuckled softly. "My dear, relax. I saw you and your dear one this morning. You were at the parade, no?"

"Oh, yes. Yes, we were. You noticed me?" She winced in embarrassment, then sighed. "I'm sorry. It's been a tough year." Tears glistened in the mother's eyes as she hung her head in defeat.

Nan gently lifted her chin to look her in the eye. "You are not alone, child. It's been a hard year for everyone." The old woman offered a handkerchief before continuing. "We lost four of our own just two weeks ago. Today was the first time setting up without them. You could feel it weighing on everyone."

"I'm sorry for your loss. Losing people is the hardest thing of all." The young woman gripped the fortune teller's wrinkled, leathery hands.

Nan gave her a squeeze. "Thank you for those kind words, my dear. We're working through it. Now, what can I do for a pretty thing like yourself?" Nan clasped her hand over her mouth in shock. "Oh my, I left the kettle on again. It'll be screaming at me in no time. Give me one moment here."

The small woman's smile didn't reach her eyes as Nan stood and moved to the back of the small tent. There was a twinkle in her eye as she set two steaming cups down on the table between them.

"A little herbal blend my own Abuela used to make. Warming, but doesn't make you sleepy. Perfect for a night like tonight." She sat down slowly and peered at the woman across from her. "Alright, my dear, let's try this again. What can I do for you? What did you come looking for?"

The young woman had steeled herself for this moment while Nan was getting the tea. Her eyes hardened, and she jutted her chin forward. "I'm here to learn my fortune, and what the Goddess has in store for me and my little girl. I have to make sure I'm prepared to do whatever's necessary to make sure she has the future she deserves." She swallowed a sob and continued. "Even if it means she is better off with someone else."

Nan's eyes widened. "What do you mean by that child? A little one is always better off with her mother." The hair on the back of her neck raised at the woman's admission. Nan ignored it, chalking it up to paranoia.

"No, you don't understand. I'm barely scraping by. Every day, I have to choose between feeding myself and my daughter. I—she deserves more than that." The desperate mother's voice cracked. "But if my luck is about to change, I'll make it work. We'll survive until then and she will get everything she deserves. But if my luck won't change, I need to make arrangements for my daughter." She looked at Nan as if she were a recovering alcoholic in the town's tavern.

Nan was the one that could change everything.

The old woman sipped her tea and studied the young mother across from her. She sympathized with the woman but knew she needed to be careful with how she responded. Her heart ached for the mother trying to do right by her daughter. However, lying to the woman would not help her or her little girl.

"Now, child, what arrangements are you talking about?"

"There's a merchant that comes to town twice a year. He takes children to the capital to be educated at the government buildings in exchange for cleaning and cooking services. He's coming next week and my little Wren is just old enough to be taken." She pulled the blanket closer and cupped her hands around the warm tea. Her eyes grew distant as she waited for the judgment bound to follow.

Nan blinked with surprise. This girl was naïve if she thought this merchant took his charges to the capital. He probably sold the children for a pretty penny to the flesh traders along the road. She sighed. "Let me see your hand. Our stories are told amidst the lines that traverse across our palms." She gently took the woman's outstretched hand. Looking into her eyes, she asked, "Now, is this the hand you use the most? The one you eat with and brush your hair with?"

"Yes, ma'am. Does it matter?" The young mother asked with a nod.

"Yes, child. The dominant hand shares the secrets of our past and the hope for the future. The non-dominant hand holds the keys to our character and what tendencies we carry with us." Nan spread the woman's fingers out and studied the lines on her palm. She brushed the woman's fingers gently and gave a small smile. "You have a water hand; an oval-shaped palm with long, narrow fingers. That means you are intuitive but can be sensitive to the opinion of others. Like water, you adapt to whatever life throws at you."

"You can tell all that simply by looking at my palm?" The young woman's eyes widened. Nan simply nodded. "What else can you see? Will my luck change?"

Nan turned her gaze to the woman's narrow hand. She traced a line that started just below her index finger and ended at the edge of her palm. "This top line here is your heart line. It is associated with feelings and emotions. Your line is deep. This indicates a strong heart. But this break, right here, you see? This tells me you have suffered great heartache."

The young mother's eyes filled with sadness. "That would be Wren's father. He took off once he found out I was pregnant."

Nan patted her arm. "Unrequited love is one of the cruelest things this world offers. You are stronger than you think, child." The old woman traced another line on her patron's hand. This one started between her index finger and thumb, continuing down to her wrist. "This, my dear, is your life line. It tells me about your health in this life. The bigger the space between your thumb and this line, the more vigor you'll have. Yours is a decent size, meaning you will have a healthy life indeed." She tapped a section where several short lines crossed the life line. "This right here, though. This indicates trouble. It could be an accident, an illness, or some other danger, yet unseen." The older woman frowned in concentration.

The young mother tensed with that bit of information. "Do you see anything else?" She whispered.

Nan traced a third line that started at the top of the life line and ran parallel, below the heart line. "This is your head line. This tells me about how you interpret the world. This large arc reveals your creativity, while the long, clear line shows abundant intelligence. Your creativity and intelligence allow you to adapt to life's hardships."

The woman sighed. "But they won't help me provide for my daughter."

"I have one more line to interpret for you. The fate line runs down from your middle finger. This is where we learn about your career and wealth." The young woman's hand tremored. Nan stroked her arm soothingly. "Oh child, I fear my services will not give you the answers you seek. This last line can give me information about your monetary wealth, but not the wealth that comes with a righteous life."

The young mother pulled her hand away and dropped her head into her hands. She rocked back and forth before whispering. "It's bad, isn't it?" She choked on a sob. "I'm going to have to give away my little Wren, aren't I?" Tears streamed down her face as she lifted her head from her hands to stare into the old woman's distraught eyes.

Nan sighed before gently grabbing the woman's hand. Again, she felt unease at the young mother's response. It was almost as if the woman's response was practiced. Nan pushed the thoughts away again. *Stop being ridiculous.* Trying to distract herself, she faintly traced the young mother's fate line. "This line is faint but wide. It means you will spend your life working hard but have little reward. This break here in the middle? It means you will have a setback in your career. But this new line that starts parallel to it means you will start a new one."

"But will I be successful once I start a new career path?" The woman asked with a tinge of hope in her voice.

"That, my child, is unclear. I can tell a lot about a person from the lines in their hands, but never the specifics. Life is too fickle for that." Nan shook her head sadly, unable to lie but wishing she could do something for the woman and her daughter. It was too risky to invite the suspicious young woman to join their family. Nan couldn't put her finger on it, but something felt off about the woman and she wouldn't put the entire Circus in danger.

"Thank you for your time. You have been very kind. I should get back to my little girl." The mother made to stand up.

Nan reeled inside. She could not let that sweet little girl end up in the hands of flesh traders. Her mind raced as she reached out and grabbed the woman's wrist.

"Wait. What if we found a place for your daughter here? The capital is so far away… this way you would be guaranteed a visit every year. You could still see her grow into a young woman."

The mother hesitated.

"I don't know. The merchant has been here many times and always brings updates of where others' children have ended up." She pulled her wrist from the forceful grip. "I need time to think."

Nan nodded. "I understand. Whatever you decide, stop by tomorrow. I would hate to leave without seeing you again." The woman shrugged off the blanket Nan had given her. "Oh, child, please, keep that old thing. I have plenty to spare."

"But I couldn't. You've already given so much." The woman insisted.

"Never you mind that. Take that home and use it to snuggle your little girl with. Take it for Wren, if nothing else."

The young mother shook her head and whispered. "Thank you. I will be back tomorrow." She rose from the table and left two coppers on the table as payment. Her eyes left no room for arguing when Nan tried to protest.

The old woman sighed and saw her out of the small tent, watching her dart through the crowds and back towards the village. Concern filled her eyes as she thought about the fate of the young mother and child.

Nan rubbed a hand down her face to compose herself before welcoming the next patron into her tent.

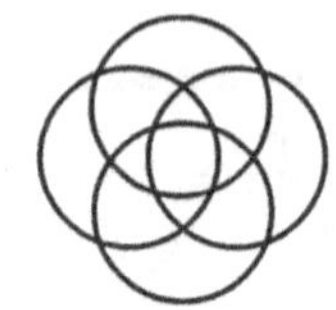

Chapter Seven

"Come one, come all! The main event is about to start! Take your seat in the big top to witness equestrian expertise, bumbling buffoons, and astonishing aerial acrobatics. Not a moment to lose! The show begins in ten minutes!" Duncan announced, using a giant horn to get people's attention.

He walked through the circus yard, repeating his message and gesturing to the large, colorful tent. He winked at performers and crew that knew the horn was all for show.

Their Ringmaster used the wind itself to carry his message.

A mad dash to the big top followed his proclamation.

Children and adults scrambled through the masses to get the best seats in the house. Lantern light twinkled as sound and color exploded in the once quiet performance area. Before long, every seat was taken and people were still crowding in. Children moved to the barrier acting as the perimeter of the center ring and adults lined the aisles.

The two staging areas on either side of the center ring could provide a larger performance area when necessary but did not have seats around them. Seating was only available around the center ring, explaining the mad rush.

Rae and Zeke hid in the shadows of the northern side ring, watching the people coming in.

"Where did Luc and Damien slip off to?" Zeke shoved some popcorn in his mouth before offering the bag to Rae.

Rae had her head tilted as she studied the lantern just above them. She could feel strings deep within her, each correlating to a different flame. A slight brush against each string and the flame gave a slight flicker. She was playing with the lighting in the tent, trying to see how much she could dim the lantern above.

Zeke looked at his partner and raised one eyebrow. He shoved the bag of popcorn into her face and, suddenly, the lantern above them roared with light.

Rae's eyes widened before focusing on dimming the light above them again.

"Zeke! What the hell?" Rae glared daggers at her friend.

"Sorry. I thought you were daydreaming. I didn't realize you were Crafting." Zeke said sheepishly.

The lantern above was flickering again. Rae frowned as she dug down deep and grabbed the inner string of her Craft firmly. She pulled it taut, slowly reeling it in until the lantern was reduced to a warm glow.

"There. Now what were you saying?" Rae looked at the other acrobat in expectation. "What do I have to daydream about?"

Zeke waggled his eyebrows, all traces of chagrin gone from the now-gray-eyed acrobat. "Oh, you know." He slid his eyes sideways to where the clowns and equestrians readied themselves in the opposite ring.

Rae huffed, but before she could retort, he continued. "I asked if you knew where Luc and Damien went."

Rae chuckled. "Like you don't know. They slipped off to the wagons for a little luck before the show tonight." It was her turn to waggle her eyebrows.

"Gross. I still can't believe they ended up together." Zeke grabbed more popcorn and held it out to Rae a second time.

"Thanks. And seriously? The two of them were panting over each other even as kids. They were each other's first kiss. Did you know that?" Rae said between bites of popcorn.

"Double gross. Almost like you and Tyee." Zeke winked.

"Yep, you got me. Took me that long to kiss someone."

"You said it, not me." Zeke held his arm up to ward off his vexed partner. "Oh, settle down. I'm just teasing. You're too easy to rile." Zeke offered more popcorn, but Rae shook her head. "You can't deny Tyee is nice to look at."

"Tyee is entitled. Have you noticed he always disappears before the work is done? He might have a pretty face, but there's no substance to him." Rae disagreed, ducking her chin as she thought about the rogue. *He is nice to look at, though. And those eyes... There's more to him than what he presents to the world.* Not wanting Zeke to question her thoughts, she looked sideways at her best friend. "Bane, on the other hand. Now that is one delicious example of a young man." Rae lifted an eyebrow as heat crept up Zeke's neck.

"Yea, I guess Bane is a nice guy." Zeke choked out.

Rae cackled. "I knew it! You were flustered when he showed off for you!"

"You're the worst." Zeke shoved his friend. Rae took it with a wild grin.

"You love me." Rae playfully punched his shoulder and changed the subject. "Are you ready for tonight? Not going to drop me?"

"I think I should," Zeke mumbled miserably.

The two looked up when Duncan entered the center ring after making his rounds outside. He waltzed to the middle of the ring with a spring in his step and a smile on his face. The crowd hushed as they waited for the mysterious man in the top hat to begin.

"Welcome, my friends, to the most amazing night of your life! Now is the time to let your worries and thoughts of tomorrow slip away. Now is the time to enjoy the magic of the show."

Duncan grinned wickedly before dropping a handful of powder, a special mix created by the Herbalists called Dust.

Chiara, the Head Herbalist on the Governing Council and Damien's mom, created it from a blend of herbs and dried grains. It was highly flammable and produced a large amount of smoke when burned. Chiara was the most accomplished Herbalist the Circus had ever seen. She was the mastermind behind the creams and tinctures that hid many of the Magicae's tells from their patrons and one of Duncan's closest friends.

Just as the Dust was about to hit the ground, Rae coaxed a spark and lit the powder. Fumes filled the center stage, and Duncan slipped away unseen.

In his place, five clowns sat, scratching their heads.

The crowd laughed while they yelled at each other, trying to figure out how they got in the middle of the ring. They continued to harass one another in a slapstick comedy fashion.

Rae and Zeke laughed along with the audience, enjoying the routine that never got old. The fire Crafter welcomed the reprieve from controlling the lanterns. She'd been on edge since the lighting ceremony, doing everything she could to keep her power in check.

After about ten minutes, four men dressed in black, astride beautiful, different-colored stallions rode into the ring.

They chased after the clowns, causing them to jump over the sides of the center ring and escape into the audience. Their patrons laughed while the riders paired up and rode the perimeter with their partners. They slowed to a trot before chanting in low, rumbling voices.

Rae admired the gorgeous horses, appreciating the way the equestrians guided them through their paces, moving from a trot to a canter.

The crowd sat silently, mesmerized by the beauty and grace of the four horses, straining to discern the language the men chanted in.

The chanting slowly gained momentum, in tandem with the speed of the four horses as they circled the ring.

Still working together, the inside riders pulled forward swiftly and fluidly. The four continued twice more around the ring in a staggered diamond formation. After the second lap, the two inside horses peeled away towards the middle of the ring. They arced into a smaller circle before falling in line behind the other two.

Their chanting continued throughout the transition, punctuated by the steady beat of their steeds' hooves. Watching the four race around the ring, most people didn't notice as they spaced themselves evenly around the circular area.

Rae furrowed her brows, readying herself for the next cue. As the riders finished another lap around the ring, she dimmed the lanterns as low as they could go, struggling to keep them from going out.

The chanting stopped in tandem with Rae's dimming of the lights.

The crowd held their breath and gripped their chairs tight. The only sound was the hoofbeats of the horses, pounding harder and faster as they broke into a gallop.

"AYE-AYE-AYE-AYE!"

The cry echoed throughout the tent long before anybody saw the torch streaking across the tent.

It was held by a fifth rider that could only be one person, the famed Night Rider.

The crowd whispered his name with reverence as he burst into the ring at a full gallop. The four other riders slowed to a trot and made their way to the middle of the ring, under the cover of the darkened lanterns. Upon reaching it, they fanned out into a line, leaving a gap between the two center horses.

"AYE-AYE-AYE!" they answered their brother.

He burst through the gap between them with an almost maniacal howl. They followed him in a staggered V formation until rearranging to avoid hitting the side of the ring. Soon enough, they were riding in tandem again, with the Night Rider leading their formation.

Sweat beaded on Rae's brow. She silenced a hiss between her teeth, trying not to divert Zeke's attention. She'd never had such trouble with the lanterns before. Rae concentrated on the power within, willing the flames into submission. She knew she'd need to devote more time to building her endurance if she couldn't keep the lanterns under control.

The crowd jostled one another to get a better look in the dark tent. They gasped when the torch carried by the Night Rider seemed to float back to the pair behind him, lighting the torches of those behind.

Three flames flew around the ring, flickering and dancing as the equestrians urged their steeds forward.

One flame reached behind and lit the last two riders' torches. It was a testament to the bond between each horse and its rider that none of them spooked at the flames above them.

All five riders carried a lit torch as they crisscrossed around the ring, with a series of whoops and yells.

The lanterns were still dimmed, leaving only the torches to light the way. The crowd watched the flames create a living, flickering pattern within the big top. They stared in awe as the riders maneuvered around each other, never colliding.

The darkness hid the sweat dripping down each of their faces as the men concentrated on making each pass. They had practiced this countless times, sometimes even with blindfolds on, but needed to stay vigilant. As they made their last passes, they ended in another V formation across the center of the ring.

As one, their torches went dark.

The crowd broke out into a roar as they clapped for the exciting performance. Rae furrowed her brows and clenched one fist as the lanterns around the center ring slowly brightened.

As soon as the ring was alight, the five riders took a bow, let out a cry, and took off for another lap around the ring. This time, they started doing acrobatic maneuvers on horseback.

Tyee started with a simple jump down, jump back up onto Koko. Once he finished, the next rider did the same maneuver. This continued down the line until all five riders performed the movement.

Tyee then began another move. This time, he scrambled backwards to give himself some room. He leaned down so one shoulder rested on Koko's withers and placed both arms on the horse's sides. With a deep breath, he kicked his legs up into a headstand. He held the position for a few seconds before dropping back down into a sitting position. The maneuver made its way down the line of riders as the crowd watched in awe.

"AYE-AYE-AYE!" Tyee called out with a wicked grin. He looked at the crowd with a twinkle in his eye. He looked back at his brothers by choice and whistled a couple of notes.

Rae knew the horsemen always improvised the last trick of their act and Tyee's whistle meant they needed to pay attention.

Without waiting to assess the reactions of his fellow performers, Tyee threw his leg over Koko's neck and spun so he was sitting backward on the tall, dark horse. Pausing for a beat, Tyee did the move again, resulting in a full three-sixty turn, and ending up back in a forward position. From there, he stood up and flipped backwards flawlessly. After landing on Koko's haunches, he jumped forward into a somersault, using his momentum to end in a forward sitting position. With that, he took a bow and rode to the center of the ring.

Rae smiled, noting how intensely the other four horsemen watched Tyee. The four men knew all the tricks Tyee could choose from but needed to know what order to perform them in. They were brothers in everything but blood, including how much they competed with each other. They wouldn't let Tyee outdo them.

They each performed in turn, ending with a bow before joining Tyee in the center.

Once all five finished, they took one last bow and filed out of the arena.

Rae let go of her control of the lanterns, sighing with relief, the tension in her shoulders easing slightly. She rolled her shoulders, preparing for a long night.

Adults and children, stunned by the performance, clapped and hollered as the men filed out. Women swooned as they passed and men stuck out their chests to mimic the lithe athletes.

Tyee rode past the crowds until he found Rae and Zeke sitting on the edge of the side ring. His eyes searched Rae's face until she met his gaze, noting her pale skin and the sweat on her brow. He nodded his head in acknowledgment of her part in the performance.

"Thanks for the lighting, Birdie," Tyee smirked, watching Rae tense at his nickname for her. He dismounted and continued. "You need some energy? You have quite the night ahead of you."

"Ha, not from you I don't," Rae replied.

"Why not? You too good for a little help?"

"I am too good for you. Thank you for noticing, so I didn't have to point it out."

"Rae, seriously. Don't jeopardize the kids." Tyee rolled up his sleeve and held out his bare arm. He looked her in the eye, one eyebrow raised in a challenge.

"Fine." Rae sighed and gripped his outstretched arm. Magic was written into Rae's DNA. It was as much a part of her as the color of her hair and the shape of her eyes.

But it also had limits.

Rae knew she was burning through the energy stores she had built up over the past couple of days. For whatever reason, her energy wasn't going as far as it normally would. She would be a fool not to take the help when it was offered. Her damn pride got her every time. But those kids deserved better. That's why she gave in, despite not wanting to appear weak in front of the tall rogue.

Just like a muscle, magic needed energy to perform and training to build endurance. She closed her eyes and focused on where their skin met, drinking in some of the dark-featured man's life energy. She had to concentrate and make sure not to take too much. The last thing she needed was to cause the rogue to faint.

Rae expected Tyee's energy to be as black as night. That was the way he presented himself to the world. Dark features, dark clothing, dark horse. Dark, dark, dark.

But when she closed her eyes and saw his life energy with her inner eye, he presented as warm maroon.

She was taken aback by the rich, almost inviting color. His hard edges seemed softer in this light and made him almost unrecognizable. She drew some of it towards her, taking care to only let a trickle flow between them. Taking too fast was just as bad as taking too much; she learned that the hard way at an early age, to her friends' detriment.

The rich, dark red had a chocolaty feel to it as it entered her veins.

It took all her carefully curated control to stop pulling after a few seconds; the maroon liquid was laced with more power than she expected. She shuddered as the liquid energy made its way to her center. Tyee's hopes, desires, and wounds were wrapped together tightly in that maroon liquid. The sense of them overwhelmed her for a beat before she came back to the present.

Rae quickly released Tyee's arm once she realized she still held it in an iron grip.

She looked up briefly, only to be met by a guarded expression on Tyee's face. His eyes were the only thing to betray the mix of emotions going on behind the stoic exterior. He'd known she would be able to sense everything in that small transfer of energy.

The first time a Magicae accepted energy from someone was always the most intense. He shook his head, trying to regain control of the emotions thundering in his eyes.

"Thanks," Rae whispered, unsure of herself after the exchange.

"No problem," Tyee said roughly. He turned and led Koko towards the exit of the side ring.

Rae watched him go. *Fuck.* Rae furrowed her brows as she sat deep in thought. *This changes everything.*

Zeke looked at his friend and cleared his throat. Rae jumped. She turned her head expectantly.

"You good there? I could've given you some energy if you needed some." Zeke said.

Rae stared with vacant eyes before processing Zeke's comments. "Are you kidding me? You need to make sure you're ready in case something goes wrong during the performance. I will not be the reason someone gets hurt."

"Yea, but you have a much bigger task ahead of you. I can spare a little and still be able to catch all four of us if something goes wrong. I highly doubt we have anything to worry about."

"It's not impossible for one of us to slip up. Remember, in Gally that one time?"

"Oh, come on! That was a long time ago. We were just kids." Zeke protested.

"I could've died that day. My point is we became cocky. We can't let that happen again." Rae insisted.

"Okay, okay. We won't sleep on safety." Zeke held up his hands with a wistful expression.

Rae nodded and turned her attention to the center ring.

Kaiser was running the lions and tigers through their paces. He was a reckless young man, delighting in stunning their audiences with his "brave" interactions with the big cats. His mother Nymeria indulged him, being the biggest lioness in the ring, but Conrad, the tiger Shifter, had little patience for his brazenness. He frequently let out a roar of protest when Kaiser tried to deviate from their routine.

The big cat show involved a lot of roaring, jumping, and wrestling.

No whips were needed since the two Shifters kept in communication with the other animals in the ring. Kaiser took care to interact mostly with Nymeria and Conrad. Occasionally, he would signal the other cats to do a trick, but they always looked to the Shifters before acquiescing.

Rae redirected her focus to the lanterns. She just needed to keep them steady for the big cats. Inside was pure turmoil as Tyee's energy melted into her own. Her skin itched as she tried to pinpoint what was off with the warm liquid.

The crowds oohed and awed while the big cats dominated the big top. They gasped when the big cats' claws and teeth got close to the gangly young man, making Kaiser give his signature feral grin. The energy of the crowd fueled him, making him bolder the more they responded.

By the end of the performance, the people of Windemere had adrenaline in their veins. Hearts racing and palms sweating, they didn't know whether to fight or flee. They reverted to screaming and clapping as the animals and their supposed handler took one last bow.

As the big cats followed Kaiser out of the ring, a spark flashed in the center, followed by smoke.

Duncan appeared again, thanks to some help from Rae.

"My esteemed countrymen and women, it is time for a brief intermission. I welcome you to indulge in some refreshments, explore our sideshow acts, and try your hand at the carnival tent. Our crew is waiting to host you and your family while our performers take a break and prepare for the big finish.

"Delight in the magic of the Circus while we set up for the act you have been waiting for. We will return with our trapeze artists, the Birds of Prey!" Duncan took his top hat off with a flourish and gave a deep bow.

The people roared with approval.

The trapeze artists' reputation preceded them. Their act was the most anticipated, as everyone loved watching them fly high in the air, throwing themselves across the tent without fear.

Excited chatter followed the adults and children as they made their way out to the circus yard.

Luc and Damien finally reappeared as their patrons exited. They needed to prep the trapeze equipment before intermission ended.

"Nice of you two to show up," Rae said with a knowing grin.

"Your jealousy is showing Rae-Rae." Damien winked with a sneer.

"Stop it, you two. We have a job to do." Luc pulled her hair out of her eyes and straightened her collar. She stared at the two acrobats in challenge, not hiding the purple mark on her neck.

"Of course, mi amor." Damien blew his partner a kiss before heading to the middle of the center ring. Rae waggled her eyebrows before running after the man dressed in white.

Luc shared a look with Zeke and rolled her eyes. They followed their friends to double-check their trapeze equipment.

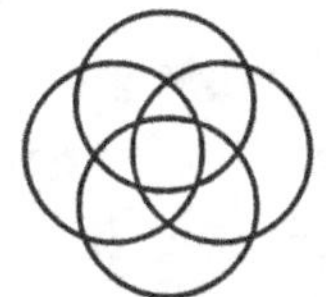

Chapter Eight

The big top became silent compared to the noise of the circus yard. Runners had prepped the crew for when the masses would return, in search of refreshments and entertainment.

The concession stand had bags of fresh popcorn and bowls of piping-hot stew ready to be served. The side acts were prepared for their ten-minute performances; just long enough to design a coherent act, but short enough to do several run-throughs within the intermission.

The carnival tent workers had the most complicated job. Not only were they trying to entice patrons to play their games, but they were also in charge of acquiring their new recruits.

Some were in charge of the games, a few disguised and guided the apprehensive new recruits to the player's yard, whereas others took charge of orientation for their new circus members.

Everyone in the Circus had a part to play in saving more of the Magicae and the Mortals that sympathized with them. The performers kept everyone distracted while the crew saved their people. The new recruits could slip away before or during intermission while the carnival tent was packed. Then it was up to family and friends to cover for their absences in the off chance someone noticed. The reality was many new recruits were abandoned by their family too scared to be associated with the Magicae, or orphans whose parents were stolen long ago.

The crew members worked with their contacts in the city to identify new members and stagger their intake. These contacts in Windemere consisted mostly of family and friends of those the Circus had saved. They roamed the smaller, surrounding towns and villages, gathering those that needed them and bringing them to Windemere when the time was right.

There used to be a time when the caravan of performers accepted Magicae and any family members that wanted to accompany them. Times were tough now, though. New recruits could only bring one family or friend with them these days. This made sure the caravan didn't get too big too fast, and that there was an opportunity to cover for those that left.

Hence why many of those loved ones became contacts in cities across Kamore, delivering the most vulnerable people to those that could save them.

This partnership reaffirmed the possibility for community building between Mortals and Magicae beyond the Circus. Magicae found hope in the way their contacts fought for them.

The stakes were higher tonight and tension ran rampant among the carnival tent crew. The Circus could not take any chances after arriving too late in Tiva. They wanted to get their people out tonight before something could go wrong.

Half of the new recruits were brought to the carnival tent before intermission. This staggered approach made it harder to notice that some of the crowd was thinning out.

Intermission was the tricky part since more people meant more distraction, but also meant a higher chance of detection. The carnival workers watched for the same signal from each contact without making it obvious what they were doing.

The contact wore a brown jacket while the new recruits wore some sort of red bow. Once that combination appeared, it was just a matter of time before they approached a predetermined game and asked for a special prize should they win.

"Step right up! Test your strength! Can you ring the bell with just one swing? Or are you weaker than a newborn babe?" One worker yelled.

"Come one, come all. Let's see how accurate your throws really are. Who thinks they can toss this ring on the milk jug?" Another one challenged.

"Need a release for all that anger? Come, throw a ball at the target and dunk the Jester!"

"Come on, big guy, your lady looks like she could use a prize. All you have to do is knock all three milk bottles down! Don't disappoint your beautiful woman!" Cajoled another.

The man approached the cajoling carnival worker and whispered something in his ear. The worker looked towards the booth and tapped three fingers discreetly on his leg. He held up a hand and gave the man a questioning look. The man grumbled but fished a couple of coins from his pocket for the carnival worker.

Turning to the crowd, the worker said, "Finally! Someone worthy of my task. You get three balls. That means three tries to knock down the bottles right there. Knock them all down in one go and you win the young lady a prize!" He took his cane and pointed at the jugs.

Several people stopped to watch the display and see if the man could win the game.

What the growing crowd didn't see was the assistant hidden behind the stand with a cane of her own. New recruits meant rigging the game so they could claim their prize.

Freedom.

And a new family that gave them a place to call home. The Circus might not be a permanent place for all the new recruits, but they did their best to make everyone feel welcome.

The man in the faded brown jacket wound up, the first ball in his hand. He took aim, let the ball fly, and missed all three jugs. The crowd laughed at the poor showing before encouraging him to have another go.

Secretly, many wanted to see the man fail once again.

He obliged the crowd and grabbed his second ball. He wound up again and let the ball sail through the air. It crashed into the top bottle with a loud clunk.

The crowd waited, but only the top bottle fell off.

They cheered and urged the man to use his last throw wisely. Many in the crowd had already tried and failed to win a prize at this booth.

The man looked at the carnival worker with a raised eyebrow after all three jugs were back in place. The worker nodded, confirming this last throw would win the prize as long as he hit at least one milk bottle. Contacts could choose the game they wanted, they just had to make their winning believable.

He gave another nod and took a deep breath. Picking up the last ball and widening his stance, he wound up, eyes focused on the three milk bottles ahead of him. The crowd disappeared as he thought about the little girl he sent to the Circus years ago.

He let the ball fly in a blur of movement.

The tinkling noise that followed was the sound of glass crashing on the floor. Members of the crowd whooped and clapped the man on the shoulder, not realizing their hero only knocked down two of the three milk bottles.

The assistant's stick came in handy after all.

"Congratulations, my good friend! You have won our grand prize! Please, take your lady and young ones to the side of the booth. My assistant will escort you to the back room. None of these prizes here are grand enough for the feat we just witnessed!" The carnival worker gestured towards where his female assistant waited to escort them to the changing tent.

He turned back to the crowd. "Alright, alright, who is next to see if they can win the grand prize?!" He picked one of the eager patrons from the crowd before leaning over the booth to grab the balls and set up the milk bottles. What his patrons didn't see was how he staggered the bottom bottles to better absorb the momentum of any ball being thrown.

The man followed the assistant to the back corner of the carnival tent with a young woman and two little girls in tow. Once they reached the tent, the assistant ushered them inside and pointed to a middle-aged woman that was folding and putting away clothes.

"Talk to Midge over there. She'll set you straight. Welcome to the show." She said, inclining her head to the young woman, before bounding back towards her booth.

The man went over to the short woman and cleared his throat. "I have three new members ready for transport, Madame."

Midge turned around with a hand over her heart. "My goodness, gracious! You scared me, cher." She bumped the man's shoulder in easy camaraderie. "Let me get a closer look at these pretty little things."

Midge finished folding the shirt in her hands and set it gently on the trunk in front of her. She turned her gaze to the three women in her tent. The two little girls cowered behind the woman when Midge took a step towards them.

She stopped and looked into the young woman's eyes. Her own softened when she saw the pain hidden in their depths. She put a hand in her pocket and pulled out two candies wrapped in foil. Midge knelt and looked expectantly at the young girls clutching the woman's worn skirt.

"Here little ones. Have some sugar while I pick out some new clothes for you." She extended the candies out for the girls to see.

They looked up at the young woman, who gave them a nod. The girls let go of her skirt and stepped towards the kind older woman. They took the candies and unwrapped them, promptly stuffing the sweets into their mouths.

"Here, let me take those wrappers from you." Midge chuckled and stood up. "Now, what are your favorite colors? I have blue, purple, or pink in your sizes. Any preferences?"

The two exchanged a look before chorusing, "Pink!" Midge opened the trunk to her left.

The young woman smiled at her two charges while they danced on the balls of their feet, waiting to see their new clothes. Simple things like this were what they needed. She looked up when Midge turned with two bright pink and ruffled dresses held in front of her. Gratitude shone in her eyes at the woman's thoughtfulness.

The girls squealed and rushed forward, all former shyness forgotten. They quickly put them on and admired them in the mirror. Midge turned to the young woman with a soft smile.

"And for you, cherie?"

"Oh." The young woman furrowed her brows in confusion. "Whatever you have available. I'm not fussy."

"Aye, but what's your favorite color?"

The woman bit her lip. "It's been so long since somebody's asked me that. Green." She choked out.

Midge thought for a second. "I think I have the perfect dress for you." She dug around in the trunk to her right before bringing out a beautiful, light green, woolen dress. "Here, try it on for me, cherie. Let me know if it fits." Midge gestured to a screen in the corner where she could change.

The young woman took the thick material into her trembling hands. She looked up with disbelief in her eyes before ducking behind the screen to change.

Midge sighed. *Poor thing is acting like she's never received a gift or kind word in her life.* She forced a smile onto her face despite the flash of disbelief. The girls and their protector deserved better, and Midge would make sure she did her part to make it so.

Once all three girls were dressed in their new clothes, Midge opened a back flap in the tent and let out a long whistle, followed by three short ones. Soon enough, a young boy sprinted up.

"How many ya got this time, Madame Midge?" He peered into the inviting tent. "Three plus a handler? I don't know if they'll be ready for them yet, but I can bring 'em to Betsy for a bite."

"That would be lovely, cher. And be sure to take one of these for your troubles." She held out a candy for the young rogue before turning to the four individuals in her tent. "Just follow this young lad and he will take ya to the kitchen cart. Grab a meal and wait for the orientation crew. It sounds like they are still finishing up with the last batch."

She beamed at the three newcomers to their family, her eyes lingering on the young woman. "And don't be shy. Stop by whenever you need a little sugar." She chucked one of the little girls under the chin, making her squeal in delight, and waved goodbye.

The four filed out of the tent behind the young boy. He grabbed the hands of each of the little girls and took off down the lowly lit path. He dragged them until they were running and laughing with him. The young woman turned towards the man that made all this possible.

"Thank you. Words won't do justice in expressing how much this means to me. If there is any way I can repay you, please, just say the word." She patted his arm. "If it is within my power, I will surely grant it."

The man patted her arm gently. "My daughter needed a safe place to call home a few years back. Some extraordinary people helped us get her here. I run new recruits to help repay the kindness shown to my family. Just tell Eva her Papa will be in the crowd tomorrow night. I'll meet her at the concession stand at the end of intermission." He squeezed her hand before letting it drop.

"I will certainly relay the message."

"You have my thanks."

They finally caught up with the three children as they reached the food wagon. Betsy handed a roll to the lad before he waved at the new recruits and took off towards Midge's tent.

The rolls were good, but candy was sweeter.

The man nodded at Betsy, took the outstretched bowl from her, and made his way out the back of the players' yard. It was easier for the contacts to slip out this way and not draw attention to themselves. He left, counting down the hours until he could come back and hold his little girl for a while. The time apart was excruciating, but knowing she was safe made it worth it.

"Alright, you three. Take a bowl of stew and wait right here. The orientation crew will be with you in a minute." Betsy beamed.

Three more had made their way to safety. This sequence of events would continue until they accounted for all the new recruits and their Circus family grew.

In the circus yard, the torches flared brightly, then dimmed, and back again. This was the signal intermission was about to end. People flooded back into the big top, racing to get the best seats. They needed to make sure they could view second-act favorites such as the trapeze act and elephant demonstration without obstruction.

The acrobats were already improvising high above their patrons' heads. They took turns swinging and jumping from the fly bars. Sometimes they caught each other, other times they fell into the net below. The audience watched in awe, stumbling over each other to get to their seats, necks craned to watch the impressive athletes.

After about ten minutes, the acrobats took their places on the towers. Once Duncan introduced them, they waved and smiled at the crowd before gripping their bars and taking flight.

They started with individual tricks; flipping different directions on the bars, curling their bodies up so they hung from their legs, moving to stand on the bar itself, and then dropping suddenly, using only their feet to suspend them high in the air.

Duncan's falsely gray eyes watched the acrobats whip through their routine, snagging on Rae in her golden and feathered costume. Something was going on with her. His eyebrows scrunched together as some lanterns flickered slightly, impossible to notice unless one was looking for it. He'd noticed her thinly veiled distress after the lighting ceremony but chalked it up to nerves after the fire in

Tiva.

He needed to talk to her. Worry caught in his chest for the woman he'd taken under his wing at a young age. She was his best friend's daughter, the friend he failed so long ago, and he loved her fiercely. She was compassionate, determined, and plunged head-first into anything and everything. He saw so much of Andre in her it hurt sometimes, but he was beyond glad he could watch over his friend's daughter despite his mistakes.

He watched some of the crew remove the net below while the acrobats still flipped and flew through the air.

The crowd gasped with the sudden rise in stakes.

The four acrobats looked at the crowd, shrugging their shoulders as if it didn't matter whether or not the net was there. With a cry from all four acrobats, the actual games began.

The friends worked together like a well-oiled machine. Everything went just as they planned. Every grip was tight, every flip was graceful, and every catch was steadfast. All four wore devilish grins by the end of their performance.

The audience was so enthralled by the acrobats, most didn't notice the helpers bringing the net back across the ring.

A wry grin slipped into place on Duncan's face, knowing what was to happen next.

They gasped when Damien pretended to lose his grip on Luc and dropped her onto the net below. A few people even screamed when they saw the Black Swan hurtling through the air towards the ground.

Sighs of relief were audible as she bounded up and out of the net before taking a bow.

Rae was already wrapped in her silks, just waiting for the boys to finish their last trick and dive headfirst into the net. Once they bounced backwards into a standing position, they too bowed and exited the net.

Rae's chest expanded as she took a deep breath before finishing her "flight" around the perimeter of the big top, wrapped in silk. Children clapped in awe as they reached their little hands up, trying to touch the amazing, flying Golden

Eagle.

Duncan's lips pursed as he studied the young woman. Her outward appearance hadn't changed, but he knew her better than most. The tension in her shoulders and the circles under her eyes revealed what she didn't herself. He would have to ask Nan or Chiara for their advice on a possible tonic.

Once Rae came to a standstill, she untied the knot and pinwheeled down the silk. Once again, she caught herself inches before the net. She jumped from the net and took a bow, not waiting for their patrons to recover from their surprise.

As soon as Rae exited the net, helpers and spotters aggressively pulled it out of the way so the four acrobats could take to the center of the ring. They took one last bow while the crowd clapped and screamed as loud as they could.

Duncan watched his surrogate daughter enter one of the side rings, whispering to Zalia as she went. The two shared the task of lighting the big top during performances. Duncan could only hope she would take a break and leave the rest of the performance for Zalia to handle.

After the net was taken away, another crew brought in agility items. They hauled out tunnels, bridges, and poles to be used in the next demonstration.

Once the items were in place, dogs raced into the ring, including the two big wolfhounds from the parade that morning. They were joined by a myriad of different canines, large and small, with long and short hair, mutts, and purebreds.

Several trainers walked into the ring as well, greeting and petting dogs as they ran wild. They took turns running the canines through the obstacle course and describing the personality of each to their patrons. Once each animal finished, the equipment was moved to the side. The wolfhounds took to the center ring while the other dogs took their places on top of the equipment around the perimeter. The wolfhounds started running patterns around the ring while the other dogs did tricks and struck poses at the trainers' commands.

Once they finished, the clowns appeared again. They acted as if they were lost yet again and eventually were chased out of the ring by a few of the smaller dogs. The audience loved it.

Duncan chuckled along with their patrons, enjoying the humor infused into the show.

Two of them ended up chasing the little dogs away and being the last two in the ring. They did a couple more bits before they stopped and stumbled all over the place.

They yelled and argued with each other about why the ground was shaking as the audience looked around with puzzled looks. They didn't feel the ground shaking, but the clowns were quite convincing.

Suddenly, one pointed out the door and started jumping up and down.

The crowd craned their necks and cheered when the elephants entered the big top. They chuckled as the two clowns shoved each other, trying to get out of the way of the large pachyderms.

The chuckles turned to gasps as one clown was cut off from the exit by one of the large animals. She beelined for the trapeze tower and started climbing.

J entered the center ring with the other adult elephant and her baby. They, of course, had Eva, and only Eva, by their side.

The baby elephant had developed a genuine connection with the girl and walked with his trunk on her shoulder. She spent as much time with them as she could, to the baby's delight, going for walks or taking baths in the stream.

The audience was so captivated by the little girl and her elephants; they forgot about the clown climbing for her life.

Eva and her elephant companion reached the center of the ring while J and the mother elephant took up positions on the outskirts. J strategically placed himself under where she climbed.

The clown on the ground made to help his companion, but let out a yell when she lost her footing.

J let out a trumpet, pushed himself onto his back legs, and reached towards the falling clown with his trunk. He deftly used it to grab the back of the clown's costume, redirecting her momentum into an arc. He swung her from side to side several times before setting her on her feet.

Her hair stood straight up as she leaned over, hands on her knees, trying to catch her breath.

The audience held their breath, adrenaline pumping as they watched the performer recover from what looked to be a terrifying mistake.

She took a couple of deep breaths before straightening. Relief was palpable in the stands as the clown righted herself.

The clowns made a couple more jokes regarding the elephants and falling off towers before waving to the crowd and making their exit.

Upon reaching the edge of the ring and making sure she was out of sight, the clown that fell turned towards J and lifted her right fist above her head. Holding her position, she nodded at the gentle Shifter. J lifted his trunk in a wave before returning his focus to his next act.

Nothing that happened in the ring went unplanned. Even improvisation was given a specific time and place. Duncan ran a tight show and learned from experience that any surprises usually ended in injury for his performers. He beamed with pride from the side ring, impressed yet again by the dedication of his troupe.

He watched the last act with a smile plastered on his face. His people had done it again. He'd witnessed the smiles, laughter, and pure joy on their patrons' faces when he walked the grounds during intermission. It gave him hope that with the right timing, Mortals and Magicae could find peace once more and the hiding could end.

They just needed to remember the humanity of both sides.

He could see the wonder and awe reflected in the audience while they watched Eva demonstrate the beauty and sheer power of her elephants. She was quiet outside of the ring, but you wouldn't know it with the way she educated the audience on elephant behavior. She was a force to be reckoned with.

All the new recruits had made it to the player's yard. A runner brought word by the end of the trapeze act, releasing some tension in Duncan's shoulders. It was always a challenge incorporating the new recruits during the season, with more mouths to feed, more idle hands, and more possibilities for exposure of their secrets.

But it was worth every risk.

Once they were on the road again, Duncan could relax. They had acquired the people their contacts identified, but more Magicae could still be in hiding. Shifters could identify Magicae with their Sight and stood near the entrance at every show, looking for anybody unidentified by the contacts in the city. Family and friends could make excuses should the absence of their loved ones be noticed, giving the Circus more time to find more of their people.

The Governing Council decided to stay for two more shows instead of the normal three extra. This meant leaving in the night, but the cover of darkness was for the best.

Duncan was the Head Crafter on the Council, voted for by the Crafters in the company. Each of the four types of Magicae was represented by a Head voted on by the corresponding Magicae, along with a Head Mortal voted on by the Mortals in the Circus. The remaining four spots on the Council were general positions voted on by everyone in the Circus. The Council was elected every few years, ensuring more voices could be heard.

They just needed to get to Heimat. Duncan would breathe easier once they reached the northern haven.

He sighed, adjusting his top hat, and looked back to the center ring. Eva was just about done. Once she—whoops, there was his cue. His eyes found Rae's across the way. With a nod, she sparked the ground for one last time that night. As the smoke grew thick, Duncan slipped into position while Eva led J and the elephants back towards the animal yard.

"My friends! The end draws near on a spectacular evening. It has been our pleasure to host such fine men and women. I hope you enjoyed everything you saw here today. Our very livelihood would not be possible without faithful patrons such as yourselves." Duncan took off his hat as he beseeched the crowd.

"Our purpose is to share the love we have for our crafts with all of you. We extend our hospitality to every city and town we pass through, only trying to bring a little magic to the people we meet. We truly couldn't continue our mission without every one of you. Please, give yourselves a round of applause." He took some time to let the people of Windemere clap for themselves, amused by the hidden meaning of his words.

A small smirk developed when he thought about the irony of this endeavor. By entertaining and serving the people that despised them, the Magicae could save their people and allies from ruin. When the clapping died down, Duncan continued.

"I would be remiss to say I could do all this on my own. Please put your hands together one more time for our wondrous performers!"

Some of the troupe were waiting in the side rings for this moment. Upon hearing their cue, they stepped into the center ring and took a bow. Each act was represented. Tyee, the acrobats, the clowns, Kaiser, Jess, Gar, and many others waved to the crowd after thanking their patrons. They moved to stand behind their Ringmaster while the crowd exclaimed their appreciation.

Duncan continued. "The performers have hard jobs to do. They are the face of our caravan and sometimes risk life and limb to perform their acts. Despite this, even they insist our crew has the harder task. Our magnificent crew includes the cooks, set-up teams, costumers, carnival workers, and many more. Please show them how grateful we are to have them in our caravan." If possible, the crowd seemed even louder than before.

Again, each mentioned position brought in more crew members. Betsy, Midge, a few runners, and many more strode to the center, took a bow, and waved at the crowd.

When the noise in the big top finally abated, Duncan reminded the people in the stands. "We are exhausted. But we are proud of what we have given you tonight. Remember there is a matinee tomorrow morning before lunch. It includes behind-the-scenes demonstrations of training techniques, opportunities to try your hand at some of our most beloved acts, and one-on-one interaction with some of our performers. This is a very special show, half-price, but for kids only. If they decide to run away and join us, remember, I tried to warn you it could happen."

Duncan paused while kids started pleading for permission to come to the show tomorrow. He cupped his hand around his mouth and made his voice louder.

"Not to worry. The adults are invited to a kid-free show tomorrow night as sultry as it is dark. It will follow two impossible lovers as they tempt the fates and explore their love for one another." Duncan's eyes glinted with mischief. "Leave your misplaced prudishness at home. All lovers dance in the dark, you see."

Duncan let the audience soak in his words. He hated the burlesque show, but the coffers never lied, sex sold, and they needed the money. "After our show tomorrow, we will pack up and leave by dawn. The show will be nothing but a memory. If we do not see you again, you have our gratitude and wishes for a better future. Good—"

"Before we say good night, this rag-tag group of orphans would be nothing without our Master of Ceremonies. Please, give it up for the Ringmaster himself!" Rae interrupted before nudging Duncan into the center of the ring. He obliged and took a bow. "Good night to all of you! See you in the morning!" The crowd clapped one last time before filing out of the big top.

Night one went exactly as planned.

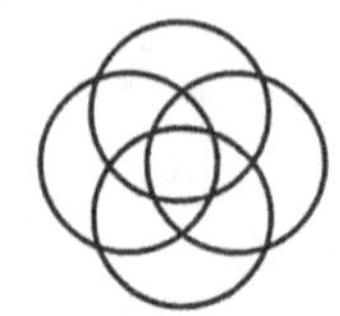

Chapter Nine

Performers and crew milled about inside the big top as patrons left. Everybody was anticipating the after-show bonfire. Much like breakfast, it was a way to connect and share in a job well done.

Plus, it was a great time to blow off a little steam.

They had to wait for the big top to clear out before they could clean, but some members got started before everyone left, impatient for the festivities to start. A bonfire meant food and libations; they had their priorities.

Others waited for their patrons to exit, discreetly hurrying them along and escorting them to the doors. They were the ones that wanted to work smarter, not harder. Once the people were gone, the flaps to the main tent could be closed, and the Crafting could begin.

As soon as the last person left the tent, Zeke led the wind Crafters in gathering most of the garbage left behind. He felt a thrill as the power in his veins rushed through him. This was what he loved, using his Craft to help the community. Even picking up garbage felt fulfilling when he could use his Gift. He looked around, watching earth Crafters call dust and dirt towards them, making a broom irrelevant for sweeping, and the water Crafter of the company called water to spray down the ring. The teamwork was inspiring to the young wind Crafter. He couldn't help but smile as he kept working beside them.

Zalia was the lone fire Crafter waiting for them to finish their duties before she snuffed out the lanterns and followed them to the circus yard. The other fire Crafters were down at the fires. They would reset the lanterns tomorrow morning after breakfast.

Once finished with one task, members of the caravan roamed the yard looking to see if others needed help, proving many hands made the work light. Everybody did a little to accomplish the colossal task of shutting down the Circus for the night.

Everyone moved from the circus yard to the players' yard behind it. They retired to their tents to change out of their costumes, wash off any makeup or sweat, and reflect on the night.

Children were put to bed, protesting they didn't want to miss the bonfire, but were unable to keep arguing once they curled up with blankets and pillows.

Once the children were settled, the adults made their way to the edge of the field where three piles of wood lay in the moonlight.

Rae stood next to the largest pile of kindling, waiting for Duncan to arrive. Her two charges from the torch lighting stood on either side of her. They had been almost giddy when she asked them to help her with the bonfires.

She looked at the piles of kindling and wood, deep in thought. Lighting the bonfires was straightforward, but the tricky part was keeping the burn going for just long enough. The fire Crafters needed to time the burn to allow the caravan time to celebrate, but not enough to cause too much trouble.

Idle hands were never good.

Soon enough, Duncan arrived and raised one fist over his head, palm facing out. Rae nodded at the signal and turned to her fellow Crafters. She told them to get ready to light. Duncan grinned and let out a whistle.

"I know many of you have called me long-winded." He let the crowd shake their heads at his cringeworthy comment. "Tonight I will keep it short and sweet. Raise your glasses for a toast." Duncan raised his mug of homebrew that tasted more like piss water. "Cheers to a successful operation and welcome to all our new recruits. Drink up, make some friends, and celebrate a job well done!"

Duncan waited for his friends to raise their glasses and shout their words of jubilation before raising the glass to his lips.

"That's it? No other speech to draw out?" Jess cajoled from the back.

"No story or anything?" Zeke added.

Duncan smiled. "Nope. Too much drinking to do." He took a long sip from the beer in his hand and grimaced before holding his empty glass in front of him. "Light the fires!"

Rae and the other two fire Crafters lit the kindling in blazes of white-hot flames. Each Crafter gently willed the fires to soften until each was a welcoming, crackling place to enjoy friends and discuss hopes for the future. They joined the throngs of merrymakers, keeping one eye on the fire that was theirs to watch over.

The caravan spent a couple of hours around the blazing warmth, telling stories about the patrons they saw and getting to know the people they saved. As the night marched on, groups and individuals ambled back to their tents to drift off into sleep.

The young woman from earlier asked around until someone led her to Eva's tent. She upheld her promise and let the young girl know her brave and kind Papa would be there for her tomorrow.

Eva lit up, replying he always had been and always would be. The elephant tamer went to sleep with a soft smile on her face, anticipating the morning sun.

The young woman made her way back to her tent and snuggled between the two little girls she came with, grateful to have found the place where they would be safe.

Slowly but surely, the time came to kill the lights. Rae had sent the other two fire Crafters to bed, letting their fires turn to embers. She kept the middle fire lit a little longer while stragglers said goodbye to friends and stumbled to their beds. The last few left as she doused the few remaining flames.

She whispered her thanks to the power running through her veins and lit the lantern in her hand. Lifting it, she stepped towards the path leading to where her friends slept. The three acrobats had stumbled off an hour ago after Rae assured them she would find her way back once the job was done.

Tyee left the bonfire hours ago. He preferred a pull of whiskey with Koko as his only companion to drinking with the entire caravan. He had indulged in one drink with his brother riders before feigning a headache and escaping into the shadows. From his vantage point, he could watch the fire Crafter unabashedly.

He hadn't been able to shake the thought of her since giving his life energy to her. Sharing the very energy from one's veins meant baring your soul to the other person. Tyee'd only given his life energy to one other person before and forgot how overwhelming it was. He'd felt all of Rae's emotions, fears, and desires in that single exchange. It rattled him more than he cared to admit, knowing Rae had felt the same such things from him. It left him feeling vulnerable and unsteady.

Not to mention, she'd been greedy. He didn't want to admit it, but when she pulled from him, he could feel the hunger. It made him shudder. She must have been dangerously low to have that reaction to a shot of energy. His gut had led him to her, but he never would have guessed she'd be so reckless.

He just couldn't understand why.

Rae had always been hot-tempered, but risking their mission was unlike her. He watched her closely while she interacted with people around the fire.

He noticed she smiled and laughed without letting the emotion get to her eyes. Something was going on with the acrobat.

Who cares? Tyee rubbed the back of his neck. His thoughts were going down a dangerous path. Better to turn back now. He straightened into a standing position and returned to Koko.

The sudden dousing of the flames caused him to look back. His gaze was drawn to the lone lantern in the darkness, clenching his jaw.

Tyee swore.

There was only one way to satiate his curiosity.

He strode towards his midnight-colored friend and swung his leg over the beast's back without slowing down. Tyee crouched low in Koko's saddle and urged him into a gallop. He would head her off at the oak tree. They could talk there out of earshot from the tents of other performers.

"Come on, Ko. Go get her." He whispered in the horse's ear.

Koko sprinted on, urged by his rider. Tyee gave him his head and stayed low to avoid falling off the powerful animal.

Koko had limited opportunities to sprint at full speed. He obliged with fervor, his muscles rippling with the effort. The stallion loved to race, and it showed. Even when his only opponent was the wind itself, Koko never held back.

Tyee knew they could intercept the vexing woman. It was just a matter of timing to ensure she didn't hear the horse crashing after her. He wanted to see if he could catch her unaware and elicit the truth from her.

He ignored the sinking feeling in his gut, telling him this was a bad idea. He knew he was headed for trouble, but couldn't resist the magnetic pull of the golden girl.

Tyee let Koko run for a few heartbeats more before reining him in as the trees thinned. The stallion threw his head in protest and snorted his displeasure.

Tyee patted his neck and murmured. "Oh, hush. Sometimes we need a little more finesse instead of just barreling in like some brute."

Koko trotted until the tree was in sight. Tyee quickly dismounted and sent Koko into the forest. "Go on, big guy. Have a snack and stay out of sight. I have some questions that need answering." He patted the horse's rump as he left the edge of the forest and headed to the tree.

Tyee climbed the old oak to get a better vantage point. Koko had gone as fast as he could, but the question was whether it had been enough. Once he reached the upper branches, he looked towards where the bonfires sat. His eyes caught on a floating ball of light bobbing across the clearing.

"There you are." Tyee rolled his shoulders and wiped the sweat from his brow. It wouldn't be long before the acrobat made it to his hiding spot.

He looked to the forest, making sure Koko followed his direction, but he needn't have worried; the stallion was nowhere to be seen, waiting patiently for the whistle to return to his rider. Tyee had known Koko since he was a colt; their bond was unbreakable.

Tyee's eyes shifted back to the bobbing light up the path, following the flame as it approached. He silently crept down until he crouched on a lower branch directly above the path Rae was on.

He held his breath as she approached.

He shifted his weight to the balls of his feet and clenched his hands into fists. The lantern drew closer and Tyee could make out Rae's features as she continued walking down the path. There was no sign that she sensed anything was amiss.

In the lantern light, he saw bags under her red eyes. *Has she been crying?* Tyee hesitated. Maybe an aerial attack wasn't the right move. He switched tactics and simply dropped in front of the upset young woman.

Tyee landed with bent knees and looked up with a smirk. Rae had instinctively dropped into a defensive position with feet staggered and fists up, no time to grab the daggers from her boots.

"How's it going, Birdie?" Tyee showed his teeth.

"Not tonight, Tyee." Rae eased out of her fighting stance and let her shoulders droop.

Tyee studied her. "What's going on?"

"Nothing. Just get out of my way." Rae tried to sidestep the horseman.

"Were you crying?" Tyee persisted, mirroring her movements, keeping her from moving past him.

Rae stopped and glared. "No. Not that it's any of your goddamn business."

"Birdie, you and I have a show to do tomorrow. Of course it's my goddamn business."

"Stop calling me Birdie." Rae tried to shoulder past the tall rogue. She was hot to the touch, catching Tyee off guard. "And don't remind me about tomorrow." She kept walking while he stood there, stunned by the heat he felt coming off the fire Crafter.

Tyee came to his senses and strode after the fiery acrobat. He gripped her wrist and turned her towards him. "Hey, seriously—"

"Seriously, what? Let go, Tyee. I don't want to hurt you. I can't control my emotions right now, so you need to back off." Rae said through clenched teeth. Flames danced at both her wrists, causing Tyee to let go.

He held up his hands. "Whoa. Take it easy, Rae. Why are you so keyed up? Talk to me." Tyee pleaded. "Keeping everything bottled up only puts everyone in danger. You don't want to start an inferno again, do you?" Tyee said, referencing her loss of control in Tiva.

He gently guided her to a large rock beneath the tree, gesturing for her to sit down.

She hugged her knees tight, letting her head fall until it rested against them. Tyee leaned against the oak next to her, giving her space to sort through her emotions.

"I would like to get some sleep tonight."

Rae lifted her head and narrowed her eyes. "Why do you even care?"

Tyee shrugged his shoulders. "I don't. But you look like you're struggling." *Lies.* Tyee thought to himself. Out loud, he continued, "Come on, lay the ugly on me. I can take it. Don't hold back."

Rae snorted and shook her head. "That obvious, huh?" She waited for Tyee's nod before continuing. She sighed. "I'm exhausted. But my power keeps growing. I just feel... out of control. I thought I was losing the endurance I'd accumulated, but that's not right either. It's as if nothing I do drains the fire inside, leaving a raging inferno that threatens to overwhelm me. It's as if I lose the ability to pull the fire from my core despite the flames claiming more and more of the space inside. Nothing makes sense anymore." She studied her hands before crossing them across her chest. She seemed to be barely holding herself together.

Tyee looked at Rae, really looked at the acrobat. She was thinner; he was sure of it. There was a gaunt look about her, with limp hair and hands trying to hide the way they trembled. The more he looked, the more worried he became. *Now what? This is beyond me. I don't know how to help.*

"Just because you can't feel those limits, they're still there. I felt that hunger. You needed my life energy." Tyee stared hard. "You need more right now." He moved to offer his forearm, but Rae pushed him away.

"Tyee, you don't get it. I can't take any more of that. You mistake this for something simple. Taking more energy doesn't stop this." She stared off across the field for a second. Suddenly, her head snapped back to the horseman. "Can I tell you something? A secret I've never told anyone?"

"Shoot, kid."

"I hate performing and putting on a fake smile for those bigots. Seeing their faces, I just want to—" Rae's voice quivered, and she clenched her fingers into fists. "I want to watch them burn. They took everything from us. And we have to parade around for their entertainment, all while hiding the power at our fingertips." Her fists erupted with flames as she struggled to check her emotions. "They murder our children and get away with it. It's despicable."

Tyee was speechless. He hadn't realized the true anger contained under that golden girl exterior. "Rae... I get it."

"No, you don't. How could you? You've never had to hide a piece of yourself that defines you. You've never been hunted or persecuted for something you can't change about yourself. My people have died simply because they had something others didn't understand." Rae sneered and stood up.

"You forget yourself," Tyee growled, straightening. "Just because I'm not Magicae doesn't mean I haven't had to hide pieces of myself. You think living out there is fun? You think being alone and hungry is the way to go? Let me tell you, Rae, you don't know how good you've had it. I grew up out there, where no one cares. You grew up here, surrounded by people that loved you. I was an actual orphan. Don't spout off bullshit to me about keeping something hidden."

He stepped closer to the acrobat, looking down his nose at her. "You think I get to show the side of me that kept me alive all those years? No. Nobody wants the selfish, resourceful thief I was as a kid. They say I need to 'be part of the community' and 'do my part.' But I can't Rae. I can't do all of those things." He pursed his lips. "I wasn't made to be part of a community. But I'm still here. Ask me why, Rae. Just ask me why."

"Why are you still here, Tyee?" Rae gulped, unable to look him in the eyes.

"I'm here for all those kids. They deserve more. I won't let them live the life I had to. And if you're going to jeopardize their safety, then I'm out. I will not let you do that to them. So get over your tantrum and pull it together. You're better than this."

"I didn't want this, Tyee. You're the one that asked what was wrong. You can't get me to open up and then berate me when you don't like the answer. This is ridiculous. You are so hypocritical." Rae pointed a finger into his chest. "I get you had a shitty childhood. Well, newsflash, we all did. Welcome to life in Kamore. Stop making me feel shittier than I already do." She hissed.

He stared down at her and pushed her finger away. "I don't know why I even bothered. I'm going to bed. You'll have to get your life energy from someone else next time." He whistled towards the woods, watching Koko race toward him. He swung up on the big stallion, gave a mock salute to Rae, and took off towards the tents.

Tyee missed the way Rae hung her head, her body sagging as the emotion left her limbs. She followed on foot behind him, with more on her mind than ever before.

Chapter Ten

Dawn rose over the city of tents.

Birds sang, animals brayed, and many people groaned in their beds. Some partook in too many libations, while others simply had a restless night.

The previous night's performance had gone well, but many were on edge, waiting for the other shoe to drop.

The kitchen crew had been up for a while, implementing another breakfast service for the entire troupe. Today, everyone would be invited to a sit-down breakfast, but the reality was people would trickle in as they got ready. Being hungover or exhausted made waking up and getting moving that much harder. Betsy and Mac created take-away items for those that slept in a little too late.

Rae lay awake staring at the inside of her tent. Her stomach was in knots as she relived the night before. It had been a disaster, causing her to toss and turn when she finally laid down to sleep, unable to shake her interaction with Tyee.

The rogue was an enigma she rarely thought about, or at least that's what she told herself. She was the one that found and welcomed him in, but spent little time getting to know him, wrapped up as she was in her own world. There had been those couple of drunken kisses, but never any real conversations. As much as she hated to admit it, he was right to call her out. She was insensitive and crass when she barely knew his story.

The worst part was Tyee had only been trying to help. She needed to apologize but couldn't bring herself to get up and just do it. Rae lifted her hands and started clenching and unclenching her fingers. Flames burst in her hands as she kept repeating the movements.

What's going on with me? I can't control these feelings. This anger inside is primal, threatening my handle on the flames. What do I do? She pondered, watching the flames dance across her skin.

The fire she felt was a comfort even as a little girl, providing warmth and relief, urging her to set more and more ablaze. The release of power was a balm to her soul, releasing her anger and hurt with it. Soothing her emotions with release wasn't working anymore, though; the anger and grief were too much. She needed to apologize to Tyee and start working through those emotions. It wouldn't be easy, but it needed to be done.

Rae quenched the flames in her hands and the pride in her heart.

She propped herself onto one arm and rubbed her face. Today's events would be interesting. The matinée would be easy; working with the kids was the highlight of the performances. It was simple to add a little extra magic without too much worry. Kids were always hungry for a little more magic.

The burlesque show would be another story.

Rae didn't mind showing off her curves or a little more skin. She knew she turned heads, but the problem was that Tyee would be her love interest. They'd done it before, but things changed last night. Their argument brought them to the precipice of something Rae wasn't ready to face. They had shared a few drunken nights in the past when Tyee joined the Circus several years ago, but they fizzled out as quickly as they started.

Her cheeks flushed with shame when she realized she didn't even know where he was from.

By the Huntress, I'm an idiot. Of course, I make something simple into a tangled mess. Every time. Rae shook her head and dragged herself out of bed. She slammed her foot into the trunk next to her cot and cursed.

"Bloody hell."

She threw the trunk open and grabbed the first pair of breeches she could find. She shrugged out of her sleeping clothes and jerked the soft, tight-fitting pants on. Finding a clean, loose top, she pulled it over her head and ran a brush through her tangled hair. She tied it in a braid before jamming her feet into the worn black boots she loved.

Her emotions jabbed into her like thorns, making her feel prickly all over. It would be hard to pretend nothing was wrong. She took a deep breath and pushed open the flap of her tent, promising herself she'd be back later to pack her things for move out.

Right now, she had a horseman to find.

Rae kept her head down and darted through the city of tents. She didn't dare stop by the breakfast spread, no matter how much her stomach grumbled. No, there was bound to be someone that demanded answers for her prickliness. The last thing she needed was to run into Luc or Zeke or Huntress forbid, Duncan. They worried enough as it was. She didn't need their concern turned her way. No, she just needed to make it to the animal yard.

Find Koko and you could always find Tyee.

Rae strode between the tents, taking care to look like she was on a mission. She ignored the smiles and friendly waves of passersby, only pausing to grab an apple from one of the snack barrels scattered around the player's yard. She finally made it to the animal yard and headed to the horse lines. A quick look at the horizon confirmed her dismay. She wouldn't have long before she'd be needed in the big top. *Better make this quick.*

She scanned the lines, looking for Koko's unmistakable, hulking form. She crossed her arms and tapped one foot when she didn't see him. If Tyee had already gone for a ride, she might be out of luck. She set her jaw and made her way to the golden palomino she called her own. There was no way she'd be able to perform in her current state.

"Hey, girl. We need to go for a ride. Wanna help me find someone?" Rae cooed at her mare as she offered her the apple. Arwen bobbed her head as she crunched on her favorite snack. She snorted her agreement, indicating the bribe was accepted.

Rae chuckled. "That's my girl. Let's go on a hunt." She started brushing the mare hurriedly, letting the rhythmic movements consume her thoughts. She checked Arwen's hooves, patted her back, and went to grab her saddle and bridle. Rae turned around and almost collided with the very rogue she was seeking.

"Watch out there Birdie. Wouldn't want you to hurt yourself." He grumbled, gripping her forearms to steady her.

"Tyee, I was coming to talk to you. We need—"

"Save it. I'm going for a ride. You coming?" He searched her eyes and noticed the uncertainty in their depths. He smirked and dropped her arms. "Granted, you probably won't be able to keep up, but you can try."

Rae bit her lip and furrowed her brows. She glanced at the horizon, noting the position of the sun. "I have to be back to help with the matinée."

Tyee raised an eyebrow. "You do? Aren't there three other acrobats to take care of the kiddies? What is the worst that could happen if you didn't show up?"

"Tyee..." Rae trailed off in protest, considering what he was offering. "I can't just leave my friends to do everything."

Tyee snorted. "The world does revolve around the golden girl. Catch you later, Birdie."

"Wait. Just wait." She rubbed her hands on her face, thinking frantically. She pursed her lips when she decided. "I need to send a runner to Luc. She'll cover for me."

She looked around for one of the animal hands tending the herds and flocks. Finding one, Rae strode over to him and asked if he could find Luc and tell her she was taking the morning off. She claimed the bonfire took more out of her than she realized and she needed time to clear her head before the night performance. He took off, excited to be given such a task by the Golden Eagle herself.

When she came back to her mare, she found Arwen already saddled with Tyee holding out her reins expectedly. He raised his eyebrows.

"Need help mounting?" A wicked grin graced his lips.

She glared as she snatched Arwen's reins from his hand. "I can get on just fine by myself."

Tyee gave a dark laugh and shook his head. He walked to where Koko stood grazing in the field and swung his leg over in one athletic movement. Looking down at the acrobat, he raised his brow before guiding Koko into the forest.

Rae flipped her hair, trying to rid the flush from her cheeks. Tyee knew what buttons to press to get a reaction from her. Maybe that was why they made such a convincing duo during the burlesque show.

She brushed at her breeches, chasing those thoughts far from her mind. She needed to keep her wits about her if she was going to best Tyee on horseback.

She swung into Arwen's saddle and murmured into her ear. "Let's show him just how hard we can ride." She gave the mare her head and chased after the dark rogue.

Nan was finishing breakfast with Javie and Luc when the runner came up. He whispered excitedly into Luc's ear, missing the fallen expression that slowly spread across the acrobat's features. She sighed when he bounded away.

"Sorry Abuela, Hermanito. I gotta go. Rae isn't coming to the matinée. I have to find Damien and Zeke so we can redo everything." Luc started collecting her breakfast dishes.

"What are you talking about, Hermana? Rae loves the matinées."

"I know Javie. I don't know what's wrong. She said the fire took too much out of her?"

Javie snorted. "Oh, come on. We all saw her light those lanterns. Lighting a fire is a drop in the bucket for her. She's lying to you."

Luc furrowed her brows. "Rae wouldn't do that unless she had good reasons. I'll talk to her later. Right now, I need to make sure the kids get taken care of. Excuse me." Luc stood up from the long table and brought her dishes to the scrap pile. She scraped her plate and set it with the others bound for the washing tent. She marched toward the big top where acts were already practicing, with only one thing on her mind.

Javie stared after his older sister with a frown. He shook his head before turning to his grandmother. "Why does she always let other people take advantage of her? She's Head Mortal on the Council! You'd think she'd be better about letting Rae walk all over her."

"Hush, Nieto. You do not speak about your family that way." Nan held up her hand when Javie protested. "What you mistake for weakness is your sister's biggest strength. She is loyal to a fault and always sees the good in others. She cares immensely for those around her. That's why she was voted to Head in the first place. Don't chide her for having a big heart." She fixed her grandson with an accusing stare until he looked away.

Javie crossed his arms but acquiesced. "Aye, Abuela. You're right. I just worry that heart of hers is going to get her into trouble one day."

Nan placed one of her hands over Javie's. "It most certainly will get her into trouble. That's why you and I are here to look after her. Now come help an old woman put her dishes away."

Javie obliged his grandmother and cleared both sets of dishes. He brought them to the washing pile and returned to the old woman.

"Do you need help, Abuela? I can walk you to your tent." Javie placed a hand under her arm to help her stand up and extricate herself from the bench.

Nan patted his hand. "No, I could do for a walk. You go start taking the tent down. I'll meet you there."

Javie nodded and headed towards the circus yard to take down the fortune teller tent. With the Circus leaving late in the night, its members were packing as much as they could before their last performance. Nan wouldn't need her tent, just the wagon to offer tarot and palm readings, and sell love tonics from.

The kids at the matinée were too young to need their fortune told. They had their whole lives ahead of them. It would be wrong for Nan to ruin the promise of the future for them as she had for that young mother.

She sighed.

Nan hadn't been able to tell whether the mother would take her up on her offer. The Circus accepted the relatives of the new Magicae because the stakes were high enough they could be trusted not to report its members to the authorities.

The young mother had been distrustful and desperate. Nan knew she would report them for the bounty it would bring her and her little girl. But she couldn't sit by and watch that child get taken to the flesh markets.

She had to try.

Nan needed to walk to the main gates and make sure the ticketers knew to alert her if a young mother in rags showed up with a little girl. The mother would spook easily and Nan wanted to make sure a friendly face encouraged the woman to make peace with her decision. Separating from her daughter would be hard, but at least her little girl would be safe. She made her way through the players' yard, chatting and checking in with friends along the way.

"Looking good today, Duke. Trying to impress someone?" She teased the strongman whom she knew had a crush on Jess, his performance partner.

"Only you, Abuela." He winked, unable to hide the flush creeping up his neck.

She laughed and waved at the predictable young man. If she were made matchmaker for this band of outcasts, Jess and Duke would be one of her first couples. The two fit together nicely. Jess just needed a push in the right direction.

She made a mental note to have a chat with the Head Forger. Lost in her thoughts, she walked right into the older man stopped in the middle of the path.

"Oof." She exclaimed, almost losing her balance.

"Nan! Careful there, lassie. You ran right into me." A gnarled older man quickly straightened and helped right the old woman before she could fall over. "Need to get yer eyes checked again? Or were you lost in thought?"

Nan blinked her eyes slowly, trying to regain her surroundings. When everything came back into focus, she shifted her gaze to look into weathered, kind eyes.

She looked up when her ears caught the distinct cry of a falcon. She looked to the older gentleman's shoulder and saw the bird staring at her with his head cocked. He made chattering noises at the older man as if he was chiding him.

"Bloody hell, Bane! I didn't try to knock her over. Give it a rest, ya tosser." The old man growled.

Nan placed her hand on his arm. "Thank you kindly, Gar. Are you headed to the circus yard by chance?" She carefully threaded her arm through Gar's and pulled him down the path in that direction.

"Yea, Bane and I are headed to the big top to make sure we're ready for the kiddies."

"Wonderful. Take me to the ticketers on the way?" She kept walking in the direction she needed to go, pulling the falconer away from where he had been standing.

Gar let out a deep laugh. "Aye, lassie. Yer not gonna give me much of a choice, now are ya?"

Nan chuckled. "No, not getting my way isn't my strong suit."

Bane let out another signature cry before flying ahead of the two of them. The two old friends continued after him, catching up on performer gossip and swapping old stories.

Conversations like these were the ones Nan lived for. She loved the feelings of connection and companionship they brought about. As she felt her age creeping into her bones, this was what the old woman longed for. She appreciated how Gar always indulged and made time for her. She soaked up the moment as they made their way to the front entrance.

"Why do you need to see the ticketers anyway, lassie? I thought I saw Javie running down the path earlier, assumed he was going to start packing up yer wagon." Gar asked.

"Aye, you're right. Javie is a good boy. Hot-tempered, but a good boy. I sent him to start tearing down while I deal with my bleeding heart. They need to send any young mother that turns up to me. I don't want them turning her away when I told her to bring her little girl here." She patted her friend's arm before letting go. They had stopped walking upon reaching the front entrance to the circus yard.

"Ah, lassie. You are too good for us. Want me to wait for you?"

"No, no. You've done enough, Gar. Besides, it looks like your son is getting a little impatient." She nodded towards where Bane was weaving in and out of the poles of the big top.

"He can wait. Just holler if you need me." Gar waited until Nan nodded before turning towards his unruly son in falcon form. Bane landed on the older man's outstretched arm and started chattering at him again.

Nan chuckled as she watched the pair. *Good people.*

She turned to the ticketing office and made her way over. Once she reached the closest window, she relayed her message to the young Herbalist sitting there. The Herbalist nodded and made a couple of notes while Nan talked. She assured the old woman any young mother claiming she needed to see the fortune teller would be sent to her right away.

Satisfied with completing her task, Nan made her way behind the big top to help Javie take down her tent. All she could do was hope the young mother brought her little Wren to the Circus and not the merchant.

Only time would tell.

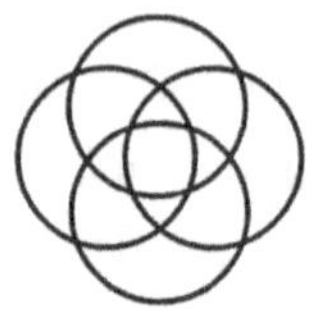

Chapter Eleven

T he sun was high in the sky by the time Rae and Tyee made it to the lake that sat outside of Windemere.

They'd ridden hard through plains and hills to get there. Both had been silent other than the occasional encouraging word to the horses. Tyee focused on leading them to where he wanted to go while Rae took in the beauty of the land they traveled.

Rae never relished what the road offered. Most of the time she was too fixated on the mission and practicing her Craft.

When their horses climbed the last hill and they could finally see the lake they aimed for, Rae couldn't contain herself anymore. She let out a cry and urged Arwen into a gallop.

They flew down the hill and barreled right into the lake itself. Rae laughed and stood on her saddle. Taking a bow, she performed a backward somersault, flipping in a tight spiral, right into the water.

What the hell? What a strange day. Who knew the illustrious Golden Eagle could let her hair down? Tyee thought while he watched the acrobat splash in the water.

He couldn't believe she was in the water with such a chill in the air. This late into fall was not the time he would consider pleasant to take a dip in the lake. Watching her, though, it seemed like the water brought pleasure to the fiery performer. *What happens if she catches a chill?* He guided Koko to the edge of the lake and called down to her.

"Well, well, Birdie. Never took you to be so daft."

Rae cocked her head, confused by what Tyee was accusing her of. "Daft? What the hell does that mean?" She furrowed her brows in thought.

Before Tyee could answer her, Rae's eyes lit up and a soft smile spread across her face. "Oh! You mean jumping into the water at this time of year, don't you?" She waited for him to confirm her train of thought with a nod.

Then she smirked. "I never took you to be so thick."

Tyee gave her an exasperated look. "Careful, Birdie. Wouldn't want anybody to think you're flirting with me."

Rae laughed and shook her head, droplets flying every which way. She took another moment to enjoy the refreshing feel of cold water, then walked out of the lake. Once she was only up to her ankles, she snapped her fingers and flames burst from them. She passed the flames over her skin and chased away the drops of water still clinging to her.

Tyee watched as her clothes began steaming from the heat of her skin. He felt stupid for forgetting the fire in her veins.

Of course, Rae wouldn't fear a little cold water.

It probably felt good on the skin that kept the liquid fire inside her contained. *I wonder if her skin is always hot.* Tyee mused as he watched the fire Crafter continue to drive the chill from her person. *I should pay more attention to the golden girl.*

He gulped as he felt heat pooling in his core. Thoughts like this could be dangerous. He needed to stop imagining fingers dancing over bare skin and eyes darkened with desire. To stop his thoughts in their tracks, he dismounted from Koko and walked the shoreline away from the woman consuming his mind.

Rae watched curiously as Tyee headed for an outcropping of rocks, stretching from the shore into the pure blue water. Rae's feelings for the stoic horseman were in knots ever since he'd given her his life energy. There was something raw between them that made heat pool in her core whenever he was near. He was more complicated than she bargained for and had challenged her when he asked her to join him on this ride, not expecting her to come.

Her acceptance rattled him.

She initially agreed to ride with him so she could apologize for her words the other night. Now, though, Rae wanted to learn more about the witty horseman. She followed Tyee once her clothes and hair dried from the heat emanating from her fingers and skin.

"Tyee! Wait! You're running like you've seen the Huntress herself. What's going on?"

"You don't have to shout, Birdie. We're not in the big top." Tyee stopped and watched her make her way down the shore. "Take a deep breath, this is what real air tastes like."

"You know little about me, don't you?" Rae asked sharply. "The woods have always welcomed me when I've needed a moment. Arwen is more than happy to race the wind and enjoy the trees."

Tyee snorted indignantly. "When was the last time Arwen had her head before today?"

"Last week. We went for a midnight ride when the caravan was asleep. Before the parade." Rae lifted a brow.

"What were you running from?" Tyee asked intently.

"I could ask you the same question. What were you running from to find this place?" Rae queried. "Why did you bring me here, Tyee? What do you get out of this?"

Tyee turned away and looked out over the water. After long moments, he scratched the back of his neck, looked at Rae, and bit his lip. "I didn't think you would come." He mumbled.

Tyee sat down on the rock he was standing on.

Rae walked over and sat down next to him. They stared at the lake in silence, watching an eagle swoop down and grab a fish in its talons. Rae followed it as it flew into a tree to eat its prey.

She started when Tyee continued, "Why did you come with me?"

Rae sighed. "I don't know. I think it was the way you dismissed me when I said I couldn't miss the matinée. It bugged me that you thought less of me for it. I couldn't let you be right."

She pushed the hair that had fallen out of her braid back. "Besides, Luc is always the responsible one. I had my reputation to protect. Being reckless is what I do best, after all." Her teasing tone had a slightly bitter edge, causing Tyee to look up when he caught her sharpness. "You said it yourself the other night. I do things that put those kids in danger. Is that the real reason you wanted me to skip the matinée? Don't trust my control after that outburst you witnessed?" Rae choked, struggling to keep the flames from her palms.

"Rae, do *not* think that low of me. I said a lot of things last night. I know you wouldn't hurt those kids during an actual performance. But you need to figure out what's going on before you hurt yourself or the wrong person sees you during an outburst." Tyee grabbed one of her hands and winced when the flames bit into his palm.

He only gripped tighter until Rae looked into his eyes. "Why did you come with me?" he repeated, looking into eyes that should be golden. He needed to know if this compassionate hellfire of a woman felt what he did. His eyes begged hers for answers.

"I woke up this morning knowing I needed to apologize for what I said to you last night. You were only trying to let me vent, and I directed my anger and grief at you. That wasn't fair, and I'm sorry." Rae licked her lips. "I thought riding with you would be the only opportunity I had to clear the air before our performance tonight. But then we kept riding, and I didn't want to ruin the moment and now I can't stop wondering why we came here." She hung her head as she finished in a hurry.

"This is where I always come before the night show in Windemere. It's a fair distance away from where we set up camp, but Koko can cover it and back quickly enough. I thought you could use a break from the act you have to put on." Tyee leaned so their shoulders were touching. "I thought this would be the best place to talk."

Rae slowly lifted her head. "Talk about what?"

"Rae. Clearly, you aren't doing well. Look at yourself. You're barely controlling your fire. You need to get ahold of your emotions before tonight's show." Tyee watched the corners of Rae's lips turn down into a frown. "Stop lying to yourself, Birdie. You and I both know the new act will push you to your limits."

Rae's eyes widened. "What are you talking about? We aren't doing the new version until next season."

"Birdie. Duncan changed all that after Tiva. He said we need to switch the act now to make as much money as possible since we're losing a day. I got the feeling Duncan knows something we don't."

"Shit." Rae stood up and started walking back to where Arwen and Koko grazed. "I gotta get back to the Circus."

Tyee sprang up and followed her. He grabbed her arm and spun her around. "No, you don't." He grated out of clenched teeth and stepped close to her. "Rae, slow down and let me help you."

"How are you going to do that?" Rae glared.

"Like this." Tyee's lips crashed against the fire Crafter's.

Rae responded to the kiss before she registered what was happening. One of Tyee's hands reached up and cupped the back of her head, the other drifted down until it rested on her hip.

Rae felt heat concentrating where Tyee's thumb drew lazy circles on the fabric of her breeches. The kiss was gentle but insistent, and Rae could feel the hunger behind Tyee's gentleness. She closed her eyes and focused on the feeling of soft lips against hers. Her hands rested on his chest, and she felt his muscles rippling under her fingers.

He was waiting for her to make a move before going any further. She parted her lips, inviting Tyee to deepen the kiss. He obliged, causing Rae to let out a soft moan. A wind picked up, whipping Rae's hair, but neither noticed, lost in each other as they were. She felt warm all over and pressed herself closer to the rogue.

Tyee started slowly running the hand on her hip up her side, stroking as he went. She felt the fire in her veins respond to the desire building in her core. She had to end this before she hurt the reckless man.

Rae pulled away from Tyee, panting. The pair stared at each other, breathing hard, the rise and fall of their chests the only movement between them.

Tyee broke the silence. "Did it work?"

Rae let out a manic laugh. "Fuck you, Tyee. A kiss doesn't change the fact I'm not prepared for the show that's happening in mere hours. Finally able to brag about kissing the golden girl again, eh?"

"Rae, stop. I'm not like that. Say the word and this never happened." Tyee growled. "I only did that to prove you wrong."

Rae searched his eyes while he continued.

"You're worried you can't handle this version, but you can. This first time around I'm following your lead. When you feel your Craft rising, tap two fingers and we're done. We can do this. For the kids." Tyee held out his hand.

Rae bit her lip and narrowed her eyes. *What a prick.* She hated that this man made more sense than she gave him credit for. She clasped his hand with hers and they shared a firm handshake.

"Thanks, Drifter. Good to know you have my back." She smirked, waiting for him to react to the nickname that sprang to mind. He raised an eyebrow but waited for her to finish. "We'll see how good your control is when I'm in costume. I'm sure Midge already has a new one all lined up." Rae winked before turning and sauntering over to where Arwen waited patiently.

This woman is gonna be the death of me. Tyee thought to himself as he followed the acrobat. He knew her flirting was bravado meant to hide her nerves, but damn, she was hard to resist.

His lips still tingled from their kiss, tasting like her vanilla and spice. Remembering the feel of her pressed against him made him shudder. He watched her walk away, eyes dark with need. Running a hand through his hair, he took a deep breath. He chased the lusty thoughts from his mind regrettably.

"Good one, Birdie. You nailed me on the head with that one." His sarcastic tone earned him a chuckle as Rae swung herself into Arwen's saddle.

Tyee knew Rae needed more than a few passionate kisses. He would give her space until she gained control of herself and her Craft. An inferno would be a disastrous way to end a roll in the sheets.

Rae had already taken off on her palomino as Tyee swung into Koko's saddle and urged the stallion after her. No way was she getting back to the Circus before him.

Javie and Nan made quick work of loading all her props back into her colorful wagon. They just had the tent itself yet, but were waiting for more crew members to come assist them. Nan was too short to be of much help and Javie couldn't do it by himself, no matter how many times he'd tried.

They were standing outside the tent when Javie had another idea of how to take the tent down by himself. He climbed to the top of Nan's wagon and leaned over to the tent, more than half his body hanging over the edge of the wagon.

"Quit it, Javie. You're going to hurt yourself. The others will be here soon." Nan hissed.

"I've almost got it, Abuela. Just give me one more second." Javie said through gritted teeth as he strained toward the tie holding the cloth part of the tent together. He groaned when he leaned too far and slipped over the edge of the wagon. Nan gasped, but Javie caught himself before he took a tumble headfirst into the ground.

"Get down here right now, Nieto." Nan stamped her foot. "You are going to give your poor Abuela a heart attack."

Javie grumbled but complied with his fretting grandmother's wishes. The tent crew would be here soon enough, so he could wait. Hurting himself would only make it more difficult for his Abuela, and making her life harder wasn't worth it.

"As you wish, Abuelita." Javie gave her a wide grin and scrambled down to stand next to her.

She cuffed his ear once he reached her, then pulled him into a fierce hug. "Don't you ever scare me like that again. I don't know what I'd do if something ever happened to you." She kissed the top of Javie's head before he pulled away.

"Alright, alright. I won't do it again, as long as you stop fussing over me." Javie protested. "I'm fine, Abuela. No harm, no foul. It looks like the tent crew finally made their way over here."

Javie raced to meet them before Nan could tell him otherwise. She shook her head as he started helping them take down the tent.

Nan leaned against the wagon that had been her home for over a decade. A lot of memories were made inside that rickety old thing.

A small smile formed on her face.

She remembered traveling for miles and seeing the beauty of the Huntress's creation, bonfires by the wagon, and painting it with her two grandkids. Laughing and screaming while they put more paint on each other than the wagon. Their lives on the road were far from perfect, but the hard times only made the good ones sweeter.

Nan never imagined she would raise her grandbabies like she raised their mother before them, but she cherished each moment she shared with them. She could feel the creak in her bones and the hitch in her breath when she overexerted herself. Yes, Nan knew that old age would take her sooner rather than later. She could only hope it was after she saw her people liberated.

Hope was a dangerous thing if it went too long unanswered.

Nan shifted her attention from the wagon to the bustle of people in the circus yard. The side act and carnival tents were being taken down to ensure the dismantling of their nomadic city went as quickly as possible. After intermission, even the concession stand would be packed away until it was needed again in Heimat.

The Circus did not trifle when it came time to leave their patrons. Duncan was a firm believer that leaving them wanting more was immensely preferred to overstaying their welcome. Plus, it made their presence more of a novelty.

And novelties could charge higher prices with bigger crowds.

Duncan was a businessman foremost, and it showed in the way he ran his show.

The bustle that caught Nan's attention wasn't the kind caused from tearing down, though. She started towards the commotion. Something pulled her there, an intuition she could not ignore after all the times it had saved her before.

As she approached, she realized it was the young mother and her daughter Wren. Performers and crew trailed the pair, whispering fervently and pointing at them. Nan knew they would be puzzled about seeing an adult so early before the night show, but this was a little much.

Some Circus members tried talking to the young mother, but she was getting frantic. She kept looking over the crowd with wild eyes. She hadn't been expecting quite the audience.

Nan knew she needed to intervene before the young woman changed her mind and bolted.

She reached the crowd and raised her voice. "Here you go, dearie. I'm over here. Bring your little one to my wagon and we can chat in peace."

The woman's face filled with relief when she found Nan waving at her outside the ring of people surrounding them. They parted as the young mother quickly marched her little girl to where Nan waited. As they approached, Nan studied the toddler. She was a precious little thing with light brown hair and a dress that showed the stains of too much time in the mud. The little girl felt eyes on her and lifted hers to meet them.

Nan gasped and put a hand to her mouth. *It can't be.*

She looked again, but Wren had already lost interest and was staring at the colorful big top, blowing in the wind.

"Thank you. I didn't realize there would be such a crowd at this time of day." The young mother held her daughter close and looked into Nan's kind eyes.

"Aye, the more we can get done now, the less we have to do later in the dark." She took the hand of the young woman not clutching her daughter. Nan tucked it under her arm and led both of them to where her wagon waited. "We're almost there now."

Nan walked slowly, letting the mother and daughter take in the sights and sounds of the Circus. She kept sneaking glances at the toddler while they walked. She wanted to catch another glimpse of the little girl's eyes.

Nan wasn't sure, but she thought she saw the dark blue jewel color in her eyes meaning this little girl was a Crafter. Time would tell what type she was, but Nan knew most people were thinking she'd be a water Crafter. Crafter eye colors were random, but certain colors always came with preconceived assumptions. Another water Crafter would be a boon for the Circus as they hadn't encountered one in years.

Nan needed to learn more about the little girl and decide whether her mother could stay with her. Nan tapped her fingers in frustration. This young woman could join their family if only she set her prejudices aside.

The world is cruel to those with little. Nan knew she had to be careful after the suspicion and fear the woman showed, but Huntress she wanted to keep these two together.

Nan looked behind them and hissed at the people still following the mother and daughter. She didn't want anybody doing anything stupid before she could convince the mother to leave her daughter with them.

Nan had a feeling the young woman would not take kindly to being asked if her daughter was one of the Magicae. She took her free hand and twisted it behind her back, crossing her two middle fingers. This was their signal for Mortals. She tilted her head to one side and prayed the onlookers would get the hint and get back to work.

Finally, they made it to Nan's wagon.

Javie and the tent crew were just finishing loading everything onto the top of the wagon.

"Ah, here we are dearies. Let me talk to my grandson quick and we'll have the privacy we need to get all this sorted out."

Nan released the woman's arm and motioned for the two to wait by the side of her brightly painted wagon. She stepped over to where Javie and the crew were laughing and chatting. She slipped a hand around Javie's waist and gave him a squeeze of thanks. Nan felt his arm settle on her shoulders as the group looked at her. "Thank you all for helping my Nieto. He almost hurt himself trying to take it down by himself."

"You did what?!" One gal interrupted. "You're thicker than I thought. We never attempt anything like that and we have Gifts to give us a leg up. You better quit those kinds of stunts before you give Abuela a heart attack." She punched his shoulder before inclining her head towards Nan to continue.

"I told him the same thing. But Javie has always been the stubborn one." Javie had the decency to look a little sheepish. Nan continued. "I'm sure you have lots more to do, but I wanted to make sure you knew you had my gratitude.

"Before you go, I have a favor to ask. If you hear anybody talking about my guests over there, please remind them the mother has not reacted kindly to the thought of our Gifts. They've had a rough go and I am going to do my best to convince her to leave the child with us. She has Crafter eyes."

The group gasped and turned towards where the little girl was tracing the colors on Nan's wagon, held up in the young woman's arms. "Aye, aye, aye. Don't all look at once!" Nan hissed.

"Abuela, should one of us go get Duncan? He might talk some sense into the mother." One of the tent crew asked.

"No, young one. This woman is desperate. She will do anything to give her child a better life, even if it means sending her away. I fear if we tell her everything, she will go to the authorities hoping for the reward promised to those that turn in Magicae. That way, *she* could provide her daughter with a better life. No, the only way we save the child is by keeping the mother in the dark." Nan hesitated. "She told me she was going to send the child to a merchant heading to the Capital."

Many in the group covered their mouths with a hand. Merchants going to the Capital with children only did one thing with them; sell them to the highest bidder at the flesh markets. Whoever the young woman had talked to was an accomplished liar and con. That was the only way any parent would give up a child to the likes of them.

Nan gave a grim smile. "Do not despair, dear ones. I just have to use my silver tongue to paint life in the Circus as glamorous." She got a couple of chuckles. "Please make sure nobody tries talking to the pair until after I'm done with them. Javie, I want you to wait on the other side of the wagon and intercept anybody that comes looking to talk. I just need a few minutes alone."

The tent crew gave salutes and Javie nodded before walking to the other side of the wagon. Nan made her way back to the mother and daughter. The pair were still looking at the colors when Nan cleared her throat. She held her hands up when the young woman pulled back and spun around. Seeing the old woman, she relaxed slightly but kept scanning the yard for threats.

"You're okay, dearie. Why don't you come and sit on the back of this wagon? Let's talk about what you've decided for your beautiful little girl." Nan moved to the back of the wagon to sit on the lower lip.

The woman looked at Wren and tucked a loose strand of hair behind the little girl's ear. She kissed her forehead and followed the old woman, carefully setting her daughter next to the fortune teller. Wren giggled when she was lifted in the air and immediately started moving towards the inside of the wagon. Her mother grabbed her ankle.

"Whoa, now. Let's not go in there. We shouldn't be messing with this gracious lady's things." She spoke softly, but firmly.

"Please, Mama?" Wren looked up at her mother through her lashes. She was quite the manipulator already.

"No, Wren. Come sit next to me." The little girl stopped squirming and sat next to her mother. She crossed her arms and flailed her legs to communicate her displeasure. "Hush, child. We'll only be a moment." She placed a hand on her daughter's head.

Nan watched this exchange and smiled. "Here, sweet girl. If your Mama says you can, have a sucker." She looked pointedly at the young mother.

She nodded her head. Nan held the treat out to the young girl, who accepted it with a shy grin. She hid at her mother's side while enjoying the sticky sweet.

The young mother kissed the top of her daughter's head and held her close. She looked over at Nan and a single tear ran down her face.

"Can you promise me she'll be safe?" She said.

Nan studied the steely-eyed woman, once again, trying to discern whether this woman could be trusted with their secrets. "You know I can't promise that." The mother hung her head. "I can promise she will be surrounded by people who will love her. I can promise she will never go hungry or spend a night in the cold. She will learn and grow into a strong, beautiful, independent woman. She will be challenged and will travel this rugged landscape." Nan paused.

"I can't promise she won't feel heartache. I can't promise she won't wake up missing you. And I can't promise she won't get hurt. But dearie, what is it you want?"

The woman sat stroking her daughter's hair. It was several minutes before she answered Nan's question.

"I don't know. I spoke with a couple of other parents, and they told me the merchant was a liar. They said the parents that sent their kids with him—, I don't know what to do." She squeezed her eyes tight and shook her head. "The letters stopped coming. They don't think... They don't believe... Their children are just gone." She sputtered. Nan put a hand on her shoulder. "This is the last place my Wren can go. I know it's the right thing to do. I just don't know how to say goodbye." The woman broke down into sobs.

Nan struggled. She desperately wanted to ask the woman to stay, but she couldn't risk her people.

"I know, dearie. I too have heard terrible stories about merchants selling children to the flesh traders. You are right to want more for your daughter, but you have the option to keep her with you too. Poverty does not mean she wouldn't be loved." She stroked the young mother's back.

The woman cried harder. Wren hugged her mother, sensing her distress.

Nan tried a different angle. "Dearie, your Wren has spectacular eyes. Did she get them from her father?"

The muscles in the mother's back tensed before relaxing again. "Yes, she got them from her father." She whispered.

"How does she feel about water? Or the dirt? Ever spent hours and hours playing in either of them?"

"Of course she does. She's a child." The woman sat up and shrugged off the comforting hand. She narrowed her eyes. "What are you trying to get at?"

Nan persevered. "Has anything strange ever happened when Wren has been around water or fire? Anything you can't explain when she plays in the breeze or mud?"

The young woman leaned away from the old woman, pulling Wren with her. "This was a mistake."

Nan gripped her arm. "Answer my question, please." She added, to soften her tone.

"I can't. Please. She is a normal little girl with a normal human soul. She does not have whatever it is you think she has. Magic has no place here. She's not any trouble." An edge tinged the woman's voice.

Nan felt a sinking feeling in the pit of her stomach. The woman had seemed sincere enough before, but she knew her daughter was a Crafter. Nan had a suspicion the mother wanted to rid herself of the little girl but didn't want to risk being denounced for having magic in her bloodline. She seemed to be searching for a place to dump the girl. Nan could only thank the Huntress her subconscious led her here. There was no way she could invite this woman to join their family.

"Hey, it's okay. I'm sorry I upset you. I just had to ask those questions. One cannot be too careful."

The woman's shoulders drooped in relief. It was clear she was more relieved that Nan believed her than anything else.

Nan knew this little girl would be their newest recruit. She just needed to make sure the little Crafter's mother left without seeing the truth about the members of the Circus.

"I promise you. My little Wren is just perfect." She gripped her daughter tight.

"Alright, then. I will have you say your goodbyes and then I'll take her to the supply tent." Nan slipped off her wagon and started toward Javie.

"Wait! I have to say goodbye now?"

"This is the time we have. I have to act swiftly before the next show and there won't be time afterwards, since we'll be rushing to pack up. You're out of time, dearie." Nan squeezed her arm and made her way to her grandson.

Nan reached Javie and looked back at the pair. The mother was whispering to her daughter, who was quietly crying. She couldn't understand what her mother was saying, but she knew change was coming. Wren did not want to stay with strangers and leave her mother.

The young woman did what she needed to and walked her over to Nan and Javie. She crouched down and gave her daughter one last hug, wiping the tears from her face.

She stood up and nodded at Nan.

"Javie, help this young woman find her way back to the entrance." She clasped hands with the mother. "You are welcome to come and see her anytime we are in town." She nodded and turned to follow Javie. She turned back once to wave at her daughter before following Nan's grandson.

Nan crouched down to talk to the Circus's newest recruit. "How about you and I take a walk to go see the elephants?" Nan waited for Wren to nod her head before offering her a hand. The little girl gripped it and the two walked toward the animal yard.

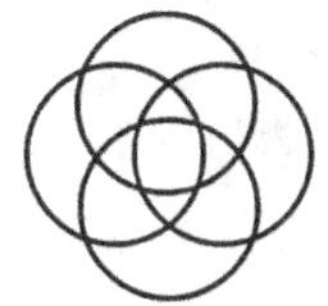

Chapter Twelve

Duncan stood inside the big top, watching the rehearsals for the night performance. His lips were set in a grim line as he watched his people go through their acts.

It didn't matter that the family show and children's matinée were spectacular. Now that they'd taken on all the new recruits, they needed to slip silently into the night and limit the chance of discovery. Duncan had half expected to find Windemere crawling with soldiers as Tiva had been, but, luckily, he was mistaken. However, that didn't mean they shouldn't be careful. Myra was getting desperate and sending her soldiers further than ever before.

Like that time Quinn Starski questioned her ability to lead an entire military operation. I thought Myra would draw her sword and decapitate the man then and there. Not one for subtlety, that's for sure. Duncan thought to himself before bringing his focus back to the young performers in the ring.

The night show was necessary to recoup the loss of their usual show schedule and make sure they had enough funds for the winter in Heimat.

But, Huntress, he hated how gimmicky this show was, focusing more on the flash of the acts and not the skill behind them. The whole Circus was a smokescreen, allowing his people to live in relative peace, but this show felt slimy. The costumes were always skimpy, the jokes were bawdy, and the story was overdone and cliché.

He sighed, watching Kaiser parade around the ring with Nymeria and Conrad flanking him in feline form.

Both the young men and women in the performances would be put on display for the entertainment of their patrons. *Huntress, I wish this was over.* Duncan closed his eyes and rubbed his temples.

His involvement in this show was minuscule. Luc took on the role of Ringmaster and storyteller, to the crowd's delight. She looked better in tights than the middle-aged wind Crafter and was a more dynamic tale weaver. *She gets that from her Abuela.* He thought with a small smile. *That and the way she carries herself. She is the youngest person to ever be voted to the Governing Council, and she's already making this community stronger. Nan should be proud her legacy will continue long after she's gone. The Circus will be in excellent hands with Luc at the helm.*

Duncan watched the young woman give Kaiser direction on when she wanted him to complete figure eights with his companions. She had a quiet confidence others gravitated towards. Luc could diffuse any situation and never shied away from hard work. She was the least selfish individual in their company, and he had no qualms about admitting that to himself and others.

Duncan was roused from his thoughts when he heard the pounding of hoofbeats headed straight for the big top. He motioned for Luc to continue when she gave him a look of alarm.

He made his way to the entrance flap and stepped outside. *The wayward return, it seems.* He shook his head in disappointment as Rae and Tyee barreled toward the main tent. He pinched his brows together and frowned when the pair approached.

"Duncan, we can explain," Rae said, sliding off Arwen to stand next to the Ringmaster.

Duncan held up his hand when she drew breath to continue. "Save it. Get in there and make it up to Luc. She's the one you need to explain yourselves to."

Rae's face fell while Tyee stayed mounted with a stoic expression.

Duncan wasn't close with the quiet horseman. Tyee had been standoffish towards the Ringmaster since Rae brought him to the Circus those years ago. Duncan never pried or pushed the young man to open up, knowing that wouldn't help the equestrian find comfort in his new community. Tyee cared about the kids they were rescuing; that was all Duncan needed to welcome the elusive man with open arms.

He waved the two inside, despite Rae's obvious dread.

Duncan slipped in behind the two performers and watched them make their way to the center ring. Tyee stopped just outside, still mounted on Koko. Rae handed him Arwen's reins and made her way to her friend. She looked apologetic and whispered words to Luc.

Luc's face went through a flurry of emotions as she listened to the fire Crafter. Anger, annoyance, and concern danced on the woman's face while she listened intently. Eventually, Luc clasped Rae's arm and made impatient gestures to get ready for a run-through.

Duncan watched Rae's shoulders droop and the lethargic way she moved back to report to Tyee. Concern and apprehension filled his eyes as he watched the two of them. *My, my do my eyes deceive me? No teasing? Who would've thought?* He watched the two interact, noticing something seemed different. *That look. Tyee is worried about her too.* He could see the emotion in Tyee's eyes as he handed Arwen's reins back to the acrobat.

Time would tell whether that concern hinted at a deeper emotion. *Ah, the promise of new love.* Duncan's face became wistful as he watched the rest of the rehearsal, lost in thought about a particular woman with green eyes.

Their future would be set on the shoulders of these young performers. *Huntress, help them.* Duncan pleaded as the show continued.

The energy inside the big top was thrumming. Everyone from Windemere old enough to be out of school made their way to the Circus for the last performance. A lot of them had seen the family show, but many more only came for the allure of something darker.

Luc stood in one of the side rings, cloaked in shadows. She closed her eyes, taking in the crowd and their energy, trying to steady her nerves. The acrobat always got nervous before the night show, not because she dreaded speaking in front of a crowd, but because she didn't want to let her community down.

One wrong move and they could all be in danger.

How does Duncan do this, performance after performance? Luc thought to herself as she opened her eyes, glancing to where the Ringmaster stood to welcome their patrons. *He deserves more appreciation than he gets.* She caught movement in the corner of her eye and turned toward it.

Rae appeared next to her, squeezing her shoulder. "An agate for your thoughts?" The Crafter held her hand out, a smooth rock visible in her palm. She wore a small smile, her eyes filled with an apology as she echoed the old joke they'd used as kids.

Luc studied her friend for a moment before covering Rae's outstretched hand with her own, accepting the rock and sentiment attached to it.

She spun the agate in her hand, staring at it, tuning out the noise of the crowd before meeting Rae's eyes.

"I'm thinking about the burden that must be on Duncan's shoulders every time he steps into the ring. Running the show comes with so many unknowns." Luc moved her eyes to take in the growing number of people in the stands, popcorn in hand, buzzing about what fantasies they would see.

"You're going to do great, Hermana. You've run through this a million times. There's no reason to doubt yourself now." Rae inferred where her friend's thoughts stemmed from.

Luc's deep brown eyes hardened as she held Rae's gaze. "Rae, that's not what I'm worried about. If it were up to me, the show would happen perfectly every time. But this performance depends on all of us. I can't control what happens with the performers or the crew. I can't control whether you self-combust or not."

Rae's look of shock gave Luc pause, but she barreled through, knowing she needed to get this off her chest to make things right between the two of them.

"You ditched us to go riding with Tyee when you've been struggling with your flames for weeks. How do I know you can handle this when you've acted like it's no big deal?"

Luc's eyes bore into Rae's as the acrobat stumbled for words. Rae turned to the center ring, tears welling in her eyes as she gripped the wall surrounding their performance area.

Luc immediately felt guilty for causing her friend distress and gripped her arm gently. Rae turned to her with watery eyes and Luc hugged her fiercely, stroking her hair and whispering, "What's going on, Hermana? Talk to me."

Rae swallowed her tears, refusing to have to redo her makeup. "Something's wrong, Luc. I'm losing control."

Luc pulled back to study the woman who was like a sister to her. She rubbed Rae's arms, asking, "Should we talk to Zalia? Get her to run the lighting, at least? Or switch places? You know the show as well as I do."

Rae shook her head, touched by the acrobat's concern. "No, I can do this. I just need to breathe." Luc searched her face, trying to find the words to convince her friend. "Please, Hermana, let me prove this to you." She hung her head. "Let me prove this to myself." Rae's voice shook with desperation.

Luc was skeptical, but looking at her friend, she couldn't deny her the opportunity to redeem herself. The Head Mortal of the caravan nodded, knowing it was a risk, but choosing to put her faith in the fire Crafter all the same. Luc firmly believed that people rose to the occasion when given the chance.

Rae's eyes were still filled with emotion as gratitude graced her lips. "I won't let you down." She whispered her thanks, gave Luc a last hug, and went to get ready for her performance.

Luc sighed and turned back to the patrons filling the tent, trying not to let her concern get the best of her. She just needed to have faith in her friend.

There were no games or sideshow acts in the circus yard tonight. Only a single concession stand selling a limited selection of snacks and drinks. Tonight was less about whimsy and more about the desires of the heart. And how much coin people would part with to have those desires realized.

Finally, darkness descended on the horizon. It was time for the show to start.

Whispers ran rampant when the Black Swan stepped into the center ring, her black feathered mask firmly in place moments before stepping into the ring. Whistles sounded as Luc made her rounds in the center ring.

A small smile danced on her face, knowing most people were expecting Duncan. Challenging other people's expectations always sent thrills up Luc's spine. She wore skintight leather pants and knee-high black boots with a black and maroon corset tightened to accentuate her figure. She wore long maroon gloves, one hand held a cane, and her long dark hair was pinned in an elegant updo, complete with a miniature top hat.

There was no mistaking who would be the master of ceremonies.

Luc smiled coyly as she moved to the center of the ring and took a bow. This earned more whistles and catcalls. She laughed and straightened to a standing position. Midge knew how tight to make the leather pants, so they hugged her curves without having to show any skin.

She sneaked a glance at Duncan and waited for him to give a salute. That was the cue her voice would amplify across the ring.

"Welcome to the show, ladies and gents." Luc paused, letting the crowd get some of their energy out, before continuing, "We have quite the show planned. Now I know some of you may miss our normal Ringmaster, but you're stuck with me tonight." Luc looked up from under her eyelashes at the crowd and strutted around the ring as the audience cheered.

"Now that the elephant is out of the room. Let's get started with our story. Our normal show includes single acts highlighting the talents within our caravan of misfits. Tonight is not that show." Her smile became a smirk. "As I'm sure you've noticed." She gestured to her outfit as the crowd cheered again.

"No, tonight will be a story that takes all night to tell. We will follow a tale told many times before, containing forbidden lovers and scorned spouses. It involves flames and dancers, sensual suitors, and feral felines. Come with me on a journey to fulfill a heart's desire."

An aerial hoop lowered behind Luc as she finished her intro. Once she was done talking, she stepped into the ring and took a seat, while some of the crew pulled the ring into the air using a pulley system.

As the hoop rose, performers streamed into the ring, carrying enormous snakes on their shoulders.

They were dressed in matching sparkly snakeskin leotards with huge white feather plumes on their heads. Their long white gloves and high heels drew the eye to their long limbs. They performed a choreographed dance, spinning, twirling, and leaping across the ring as a violin played a haunting melody.

Taking special care not to jostle the reptiles on their shoulders, they danced around the ring, drawing all eyes to their sensual movements. So enraptured was the audience that most people didn't notice when Tyee and his horsemen rode into the ring.

The five horsemen wore slim black masks hiding their eyes and tight, dark breeches, their chests bare and oiled. They raced around the ring, chanting and pounding their fists on their legs. Soon enough, the melody of the violin trailed off and drums picked up the rhythm of the hoofbeats flying around the ring.

"Long ago, before you or I, a soldier was going off to war." Luc began, pausing as the dancers spread out to either side of the ring, taking care to stay out of the path of the galloping horsemen.

She let Tyee guide Koko into the middle of the ring, watching the black stallion rear up on his back legs, front legs pawing the air, announcing his part in the evening show.

Luc continued, a lantern hanging from the hoop she perched on and lighting her face. "Before leaving, he took it upon himself to visit a gentleman's club for a little company in the night."

Tyee dismounted and gave Koko a pat on his rear, moving the horse from the ring. The other four horsemen followed suit and dismounted, joining Tyee in the middle of the ring. The girls in snakeskin moved to the men and began dancing on them, snakes still in hand. "But alas, these cheap thrills were not what his heart yearned for."

Tyee kissed the woman dancing on him hard on the mouth and twirled her into the open arms of another. More women came out and surrounded the five men.

They began another choreographed dance where the women took turns trying to dance with Tyee but were rejected despite each new girl's increasing lack of clothing. Finally, a dancer in a nude bodysuit forced herself upon him, shoving her tongue down his throat.

Tyee threw her off of him, and the center ring darkened. Lanterns flashed and drums mimicked the sound of thunder while the musicians created the sound of rain using their instruments.

"No, our soldier wouldn't be satisfied by the girls in his homely village. He knew the capital was the only place with a woman that could satisfy his needs. He traveled with his brothers in arms to the largest city on the peninsula and where the government had its seat." While Luc narrated, the dancers in snakeskin slipped out of the center ring.

Once they were gone, Tyee and his horsemen swung back into their saddles and took off again. The ring darkened, with only the sound of hoofbeats indicating the horsemen raced around the ring. Luc's lantern was the only illumination in the big top, highlighting her words.

"When they reached their destination, they took in the sights and the sounds of the city with awe. Being from rural farmland, the men were shocked by the people and places they witnessed." Performers streamed into the ring wearing colorful costumes and yelling in different languages as lanterns flashed, putting different groups on display for the audience.

"Before long, they arrived at the bathhouse in the center of the city." The lanterns went bright to highlight a structure in the middle of the ring, the colorful townsfolk forgotten. It had low sides and a shallow pool concealed within.

Tyee and his men dismounted, making their way to where Jess sat on Duke's lap, both of their leotards showing off skin and the rippling muscles hidden beneath. Duke stood up abruptly, dumping Jess to the ground in his haste to perform his duty and defend the structure behind him. Jess dusted herself off and took the seat previously occupied by the strong man.

In the sky, Luc continued. "The soldier spoke with authority as he addressed the guard of the bathhouse. He asked about Maria, the famed golden virgin, untamable and wild, that many a man had tried to bridle, all to no avail. The muscular guard welcomed the soldier with enthusiasm. He knew this army man had no chance with the woman inside, but encouraged him all the same, if only for some entertainment."

Tyee gave a wry smile as he made his way to Duke. He was the one that convinced Luc to add in the flowery language, adding some humor at Rae's expense. He kept his composure as he clasped forearms with Duke before making his way to enter the structure.

"Inside the bathhouse, the soldier finally met the woman he had been dreaming of. Maria, the golden virgin, rose from the water inside her place of refuge, and the courting began."

Rae straightened from inside the structure, her sheer gossamer gown sticking to her body as water ran down her skin. Her hair was loose but slicked back by the water she rose from.

Tyee felt his heart stop and his mouth go dry as he gazed at the beautiful woman in front of him. The memory of her lips on his from that morning sent heat through his core.

His eyes moved over every inch of her before meeting her gaze through the golden mask covering the top half of her face. Rae's stare was filled with mirth as a coy smile danced on her lips.

She knew where those ridiculous phrases originated from.

After a heartbeat, Tyee grabbed the dripping acrobat and whipped her into a waltz. Music started, propelling Duke and Jess and the other horsemen accompanied by dancers in silver into their own waltzes.

Tyee leaned down with a smirk and whispered into Rae's ear. "Be sure to look like you're swooning now."

"Tyee, you're going to make me break character!" Rae hissed, concentrating on her steps.

"Just follow my lead." He used his arm to send her out into a spin before bringing her back to him. "You good?"

"Yea, it's just a lot. The lanterns..." Rae said through gritted teeth.

Tyee gave her a concerned look but continued their dance. Before long, the cue in the music sounded, and he dipped her as the music stopped.

Breathing hard, they stared into each other's eyes.

Tyee was prepared to perform but needed Rae to confirm she had enough control to pull it off. He knew this show rested on her shoulders. No matter how hard he pushed, Rae refused to switch places with Luc. He needed to tread lightly and make sure the firebrand didn't hurt herself or the rest of the big top. Rae nodded slightly after a moment.

That was all Tyee needed.

He bent his head to hers and kissed her slowly, keeping his lips gentle and his desires in control. A single violin played softly as Tyee dipped the acrobat lower, not breaking the kiss and using a hand on her neck to support her. Tyee's other hand hooked her knee around his waist and slid up her thigh, following a slit in her dress, exposing more skin as it traveled.

Tyee was oblivious to the crowd, lost in the woman he held.

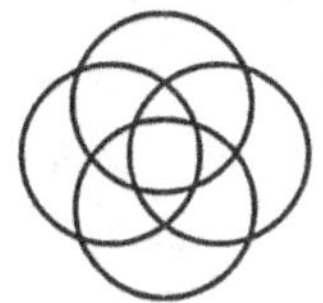

Chapter Thirteen

Luc studied the crowd and the scene below her.

Rae and Tyee performed a little too convincingly. She would have to drill Rae about that later. The paired dancers continued waltzing and dipping their partners with the melody of the music. The lanterns in the structure burned brightly, while the ones on the perimeter of the center ring were a muted glow.

A small smile tugged at Luc's lips as she appreciated the way the lighting highlighted the scene inside the bathhouse. Luc had given Rae the chance to redeem herself and prove she could control her flames, but the Head Mortal would be lying if she claimed she hadn't had her doubts. It seemed like those doubts had been unwarranted; Rae was doing everything flawlessly, even with the recent additions to the show. Her brown eyes glanced at where the two kept kissing. They could do this.

She felt the crowd's energy shift as she noticed more people growing restless. Time to move the plot along.

"The courting didn't last long. The soldier knew what he wanted and pulled out every trick he had to convince her she wanted the same thing. Soon enough, she gave in and invited the soldier to her bed."

Tyee straightened, so the pair were standing, but still close enough to be touching. Rae put her arms around Tyee's neck, jumped up, and wrapped both legs around his waist, kissing him as he carefully lowered her to the ground.

The lights in the bathhouse went dim as catcalls and whistles came from the audience, the other dancers slipping silently out of the ring.

"That night, the pair spent hours memorizing each other's bodies, but when the sun came up, drums made the call for war." The lanterns in the bathhouse slowly brightened as the drummers played a loud, pounding beat.

Tyee and Rae were a tangle of limbs on the floor of the structure. Tyee, clad in only a pair of underwear, disentangled himself and stood up. He put a hand to his ear, listening to the drums before pulling up his breeches. Rae scrambled up, the gossamer gown slipping over her lithe form, and grabbed his arm, trying to prevent him from leaving her.

"Maria was alarmed by the way her soldier so readily made to leave her. She'd finally taken a man to bed, and he was treating her like a common whore. She raged and begged him to stay."

Tyee pulled Rae towards him, kissed her roughly, and pretended to throw her to the ground. She hit her fists on the floor of her bathhouse before clutching at the horseman's pants. Tyee pulled her hands off him, kissed them, and pushed her away once more before making his way to the exit of the structure.

"The soldier did not heed his lover's pleading and left the bathhouse. He stopped by the guard and told him of his conquest, entreating him to keep the woman safe and isolated until he returned. Our soldier had no intention of letting this woman go now that he'd found her. He wanted to make sure no other man tried to take her while he went to war."

Tyee stepped to where Duke leaned against the bathhouse. They mimed a conversation before Duke clasped Tyee's arm in brotherly congratulations. Tyee put some coins in Duke's outstretched hand and thumped him on the back. Duke made a show of pocketing the coins and nodding his head, accepting the responsibilities he was tasked with.

Tyee blew a kiss to the bathhouse before running and leaping onto Koko. The other horsemen reappeared, already mounted and ready to ride.

The five men on horseback did a lap, yipping and hollering, as the drums of war continued to sound. Then they rode out of the ring and the lanterns dimmed once again.

When they brightened, the bathhouse structure was gone, with only several platforms remaining in the center ring.

A woman dressed in the same gossamer gown as Rae took the Crafter's place as Maria on one of the new structures. She started contorting her body into shapes that didn't seem possible. The drums of war were joined by the violin and other instruments to create a melody of power and anger.

Luc explained the situation unfolding below. "Maria grew angry as she spent days, months, and even years trapped in the bathhouse. Her reputation became a cautionary tale for many young maidens, warning them to never lay with a soldier until after the wedding. Maria's name meant beloved and rebellious, but her bitterness only grew as the soldier spent years at war."

The contortionist lit a baton on fire and placed it in her mouth. She continued to twist and bend as the flames of her baton danced to the cacophony of sounds that accompanied her movements.

The crowd became entranced as the woman lit two more batons. She kept one in her mouth and grabbed one with her toes. She kept the third in her hand and rolled to another platform. The fake Maria took the baton from her mouth and positioned herself so she could bite down on the mouthpiece in the center of the platform. She did so and lifted her legs behind her, a baton in each hand and the third held in her toes. She marveled the crowd by supporting her weight with just her mouth.

The crowd clapped and hollered, sending praise to the daring contortionist. She brought her legs back down and released the mouthpiece. She performed a couple more tricks before the music came to a crescendo and the woman put out all three batons.

The music changed to a slow, keening of the violin as she hugged her knees to her chest and sobs racked her body. The lanterns in the ring dimmed once more as the violin continued its somber song.

"A couple of years passed before Maria heard a commotion outside the bathhouse. She left her place to peer down at what was happening outside her window. As she watched, a falcon flew to perch on her shoulder."

The lanterns brightened, and the bathhouse was back in place, the platforms removed, and Rae back in her role as Maria. Duke stood outside the structure, miming a conversation with Kaiser and Damien, clad in government dress.

Bane, in falcon form, flew from Kaiser's shoulder to where Rae waited in one corner of the bathhouse, peering over the low walls of the structure.

"The commotion was a government official coming to warn the guard that the bathhouse would be taken down in two days. Maria jumped with joy at that proclamation. She would soon be free..." Luc paused, adding some drama, "or so she thought."

The crowd gasped as Zeke dropped into the bathhouse from a rope above. He grabbed Rae and held her by the waist as the rope raised them to the trapeze tower high in the sky. Bane let out a cry and left Rae's shoulder to fly back to Kaiser.

Kaiser cocked his head as if he was listening to the bird now on his shoulder. Suddenly, he ran past Damien and Duke to the entrance of the bathhouse. He motioned to the other two, convincing them to come and see.

"Now the three men were dumbfounded as to where Maria could have gone. There was only one entrance and exit to the bathhouse, and they stood in front of it. They scratched their heads, trying to figure out where she had disappeared to."

The three men stood in the bathhouse as Rae's gossamer gown floated to the floor of what was once her prison. Duke, Kaiser, and Damien shrugged their shoulders and left, not acknowledging the gown at their feet.

"A prince of thieves came and claimed Maria for himself. He whisked her away to his palace below the city. He gave her the finest silks and jewels to clothe herself in. All he asked in return was her hand in marriage."

The lanterns in the ring went dark. Only the ones on the northern trapeze tower blazed for this next act.

Rae wore a golden bikini, studded with gems, and gold silky shorts. A strip of golden cloth covered her eyes in place of her golden mask. Her hair was still slicked back, but contained in a bun, prepared for the trapeze routine that was to come. Zeke wore silver shorts with a silver strip of cloth across his eyes, matching Rae's golden one.

They stood on the lower bar of the trapeze tower, the upper bar tied, and Luc's hoop pulled to the southern tower to keep from interfering with the duo's act.

Their performance began when the music started, upbeat but insistent, led by the beating of the drums and the sound of a horn.

Zeke dropped, so he hung by his knees, hooking his ankles around the sides of the bar. Rae stayed standing, doing a couple of turns and shimmies to the beat of the music.

As the large bass drum sounded, she stepped off the bar and plummeted to the ground in free fall.

Zeke caught her arms and spun her around several times as the audience gasped in relief.

Zeke continued to throw Rae around, catching her by her arms, swinging her, and letting her go, only to catch her by her knees.

Rae reached up and let Zeke grab one arm and spin her in a full circle. Then he readjusted and grabbed both her wrists, swinging her so she could flip all the way around before he caught her by her ankles. Swinging her again, he performed the same move, catching her by the wrists again. With no net below, the audience watched in awe at their daring and sheer strength.

They started another sequence where Zeke held Rae's wrists and she used her legs to grip his waist. She then lifted her upper body until she reached the bar and pulled herself into a standing position onto it.

Rae's heart pounded with effort as she welcomed the slight reprieve built into the routine. She struggled to control her breathing and the flames on the trapeze tower. Luckily, she only had to keep track of a few torches and lanterns for the duration of their routine.

She returned her focus to the bar as Zeke unhooked his knees from it, hanging one-handed while the drum pounded. Rae moved to one side of the bar and allowed Zeke to swing into a sitting position next to her. They held their poses while Luc continued her narration.

"Maria was hesitant at first to accept the prince of thieves' proposal. She enjoyed the perks that came with being tied to a man as wealthy as he, but she couldn't stop thinking about her soldier. Even though he'd left her, Maria still yearned for the rough touch of his calloused hands and hungry lips.

"Maria let the prince of thieves court her for months before giving up on her soldier and acquiescing to the prince's wishes."

Zeke made to stroke Rae's leg, and she kicked him off the bar until he hung only from his ankles. She still stood on the bar looking forlorn and lost.

The music turned melancholy as the drums quieted and the violin played louder. She twisted and lifted her body, using the ropes on either side of the bar they performed on.

Eventually, the drums sounded louder and Rae seemed to relent. She let Zeke pull his upper body to the bar and grip it using his hands. He took the time to readjust, hooking his knees around the bar's sides and letting his upper body hang. Rae lowered herself so one leg dangled precariously while the other stayed rigid, holding her body suspended away from her partner. She leaned her head back and closed her eyes while Zeke stroked her leg intimately. The lanterns dimmed so only Luc was visible high above.

"Maria wed the prince of thieves and became a princess herself. She learned the underbelly of the streets and watched her husband control its people with ease. Their new life together was filled with glamor and untold riches, while the soldier was long forgotten."

The lanterns lit once more to show Zeke still hanging by his knees, but now Rae hung suspended from Zeke's ankles on the other side of the bar.

The crowd gasped at the recklessness of the two acrobats.

Rae swung her legs up and over the bar, and plunged down on the other side, Zeke catching her by the waist. He dropped her to get a hold of her wrists and ran through a set of throws and catches, using her arms, legs, and feet. He ended the sequence, holding her around the middle.

Rae threw her arms out as if she was flying, and they held the position. She rolled over in his arms and he held on to one wrist again. He twirled her before gaining ahold of both wrists and swinging her up so her legs could wrap around his waist.

Once again, Rae pulled herself into a standing position on the bar. Zeke gripped it with both hands, unhooked his knees, and drew himself up into a sitting position on the bar. This time Rae straddled him and Zeke leaned back, his hands on the sides. They held the position again, allowing Luc to speak.

"Lost in their new world, they missed the trouble brewing below. And that is where our story will resume after a brief break."

All the lanterns brightened inside the big top. Rae and Zeke stayed on the trapeze bar and waved as some of their patrons left to get snacks. This would be their last chance to get food from the concession stand before it was taken down.

Other patrons stretched or stole glances at the attractive trapeze duo, not willing to leave their seats for fear of losing them. Rae and Zeke were deep in conversation, not noticing the curious glances from below.

"Rae, you sure you're good? You look exhausted. I could feel you shaking during that last sequence. Can one of the other fire Crafters control the lanterns for this next act?" Zeke grabbed the pole one of their spotters offered and held on while he pulled them to the tower.

Rae had her eyes closed and rubbed her temples. "I can do this, Zeke. Just a couple more scenes and I can sleep. Zalia might be able to do it, but she won't know the cues. Honestly, this was the hardest thing I had to do. The next few scenes will be less intense." She opened her eyes when she felt their bar pulled towards the tower. She accepted Zeke's hand, letting him help her onto the sturdy structure. Her legs trembled with effort, but she gritted her teeth and started climbing down.

"We can tweak stuff to make it easier too. Just say the word, Sparks."

Rae patted Zeke's cheek when he finally reached the ground next to her. "Thanks, friend, that means a lot. I'll be good." She turned to get some water and swayed a little. Before she could lose her balance, she felt an arm around her waist. She leaned into the warm presence. "Hmm, thanks, Zeke. I didn't realize how tired I was. Just need a little rest and some water and I'll be right as rain."

"I highly doubt that." Came the rough response.

Rae straightened quickly once she realized Zeke wasn't the one supporting her. She looked up into her rescuer's face and relaxed a little when she recognized Tyee.

"Hey, Drifter. Thanks for the lift." She murmured, her eyelids drooping, missing the small upturn of his lips at the nickname.

"Come on, Birdie. Don't pass out yet. We need you. I'm bringing you to the fire Crafters now. They told me it would be too dangerous to use my life energy, but luckily they offered theirs. We just need to get you to them."

The two made slow progress to where the other four fire Crafters waited in the shadows of one of the side rings. Zalia, the second most powerful fire Crafter, rushed to Rae's other side.

"You stubborn fool." She whispered rawly. "Set her on this bench, Tyee. It's a good thing you came to us. Keep her awake now."

Tyee did as he was told and squeezed Rae's hand when he set her on the bench. He continued to talk to her, making her laugh weakly and roll her eyes.

Zalia knelt beside Rae and cut a shallow line on her own forearm. She did the same to Rae's hand and pressed them together. She murmured under her breath and motioned for the other three to come over. They each put a hand on Zalia's bare shoulder and poured some of their Craft into the short, older woman. She directed the heat to enter Rae's veins, which it did willingly.

Rae's eyes flew open as she felt the fire burn within her. She writhed in pain, unable to break Zalia's grip. When the Crafter finally released her arm, Rae snatched it towards herself, cradling it against her chest. She lay on the bench, rocking back and forth in pain, waiting for the heat to run its course.

Zalia put a hand on Tyee's shoulder and motioned for him to follow her. They stepped to the side, but Rae could still make out the older fire Crafter's words despite the pain. "She'll be okay, son. Just give her a minute. Let us know if she needs anything else." She dropped her hand and turned to go.

Tyee gripped her wrist before she could leave. "Thanks, Zalia. I didn't know what else to do. Thank you." He whispered, dipping his chin.

"You're welcome. Make sure she knows her actions have consequences." Zalia and the other fire Crafters went back to the player's yard to continue helping with dismantling tents.

Rae heard their soft footsteps as she held in a scream, beseeching the Huntress to have mercy and make the pain go away. Anything was better than the heat flaring through her veins.

Zeke had followed the two and watched the proceedings with a frown. *What is Rae doing? Why won't she ask for help?*

He shook his head and went to Rae's side when he noticed she stopped rocking in pain. Her body relaxed as the fire fizzled out. He held her hand as she sat up.

"Oof. I feel like that time we got into Mac's top-shelf whiskey." Rae put a hand to her head to steady herself.

"Rae, you scared me." He squeezed her hand, eyes wide with concern.

She patted his hand. "Sorry, Z. I think I overdid it again. I don't know what's going on. I should be able to do these lanterns in my sleep. Something is sapping my fire and I don't know how to stop it. Was Zalia as pissed as I thought she'd be?" She looked at Tyee as he walked back from his interaction with the fire Crafter.

The horseman rubbed the back of his neck. "Yea, I'd say, pissed and exasperated. She called you a fool."

"She's called me worse." Rae chuckled. Zeke cracked a smile, thinking of all the times Rae caused the brusque Crafter to snap. She wasn't wrong in her sentiment and Zeke felt some of the tension in his shoulders dissipate at her dry humor.

Rae swung her legs over the bench and started to stand. Her legs wobbled but then held steady. Zeke stood next to her, hands hovering to catch her if need be.

"I'm good, guys. That shot of pure fire is just what the doctor ordered. I'll talk to Abuela while we're on the road. She'll know what's going on, or at least be able to point me in the right direction." Rae waved off the two concerned men. "The show must go on." She said with a weary smile.

The three slipped behind the flap that led to the water cooler for the performers. They joined the throng and listened to Luc's words of praise and encouragement. They soaked in the compliments and steeled themselves for the next and last act of the show.

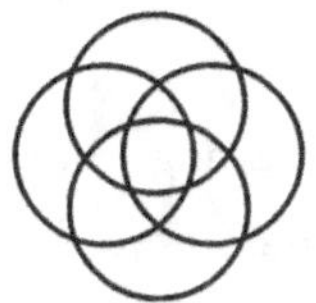

Chapter Fourteen

The lanterns inside the big top and the circus yard flashed several times. Intermission was over and the second act was about to begin. The remaining patrons in the yard made their way to the big top and found their seats. The unlucky ones found theirs taken and scrambled to find new ones.

Music started playing, and the lanterns in the big top dimmed. A single lantern beamed high above the audience. Their eyes were drawn upward to where Luc perched in her hoop once again.

"Welcome back, my friends. We have quite a second act in store for you! Filled with betrayal, broken hearts, and dirty dancing." Luc laughed as the crowd cheered. "Now where were we? Oh yes, trouble was brewing despite the happy couple's bliss. The soldier returned from war to find the bathhouse demolished and his woman disappeared without a trace. He searched long and hard for the guard that betrayed him."

Hoofbeats sounded as Tyee rode in with his fellow horsemen. The lanterns brightened to show the ruined bathhouse, the gossamer gown still on the floor.

Tyee leaped off Koko before he came to a stop and gripped the gown in his fist. He whipped his head around, looking for the woman that once wore it. His head turned when he heard noises outside the ruins. He walked over as one horseman dragged Duke towards the ruined bathhouse.

"The soldier finally found the guard, thanks to one of his brothers in arms. He beat the man until he got the answers he needed. The guard gave him the names of the government officer and his assistant that were there the day Maria disappeared.

"The soldier released the guard and started a search for the two men who'd seen his beloved last."

Tyee mimed giving Duke a beating while his brother horsemen held the strongman. Duke held up his hands before making exaggerated gestures towards one side of the ring. Tyee pretended to throw Duke to the ground and strode over to Koko, whistling to the other horsemen. They swung into their saddles and rode hard around the ring, following the rogue.

The drums beat as the lanterns dimmed and Luc continued. "They searched far and wide before happening on the two men. They approached and asked for clarity about the day's events. The soldier had to quell his temper and appear subservient to the official, as much as he hated it. If he wanted Maria back, it all depended on how he handled the situation."

When the lanterns brightened again, the ruined bathhouse was gone and Kaiser and Damien sat sprawled on two chairs next to a table. Bane perched on Kaiser's shoulder and Nymeria and Conrad lounged at their feet in feline form.

The five horsemen gathered in a line and dismounted. Tyee marched towards the two men and waved his hands angrily. Kaiser and Damien jumped from their chairs, knocking the table over as Tyee thrust the gossamer gown into their faces, still gesturing wildly. Nymeria and Conrad scrambled up and put themselves between the two men and Tyee. They bared their teeth and let out low growls.

"Needless to say, controlling his temper was not one of the soldier's strong suits." Luc paused, listening to the laughter of her audience. "The two men stopped when they saw the gown once worn by the golden virgin. They'd both tried to tame the wild woman, to no avail. Shocked to meet the man that finally bridled her, they recounted the day she disappeared.

"The official's henchman relayed that his falcon was the one to alert them that the woman had vanished. They concocted a plan to use the raptor to lead them to where the woman could be found." Down in the ring, Tyee and Damien continued their conversation while Kaiser moved to the side and cocked his head in Bane's direction.

He nodded as the falcon chittered in his ear. Finally, he interrupted the other two men and held out the falcon on his arm. They listened intently as Kaiser made gestures towards the falcon and the gown.

The music of the drums and the horns started once again. This time, the five horsemen mounted their horses and trotted around the ring. Kaiser and Damien walked behind them while Bane began an aerial routine to display his prowess in the skies.

The falcon flew to the top of the tent and started a nose dive, spiraling down in a circular pattern. This allowed him to gain more momentum. Yells and screams sounded throughout the audience as Bane continued his descent, looking like he was going to crash into the dirt floor of the center ring.

At the last possible moment, Bane pulled out of his dive and soared over the audience.

He let out a screech of joy as he continued around the tent. The Shifter perched on Luc's hoop briefly before diving into the crowd and snatching a flower from a bouquet held by one of their patrons. He flapped his wings and presented the flower to Luc. She took it with a grin while Bane flashed his wings and flew back to Kaiser's shoulder.

Bane chittered once more in Kaiser's ear and the man offered him a piece of meat. He pointed across the ring and stroked the falcon's wings. He motioned to the big cats in the ring and they joined him as he marched across the performance area. Damien followed behind, keeping a lookout for the woman they were seeking. The flames dimmed once again, so the audience shifted their attention to Luc once more.

"They traveled far and wide looking for Maria. They came across dead end after dead end, even though their quarry resided just under their noses. Maria played her part as the princess of thieves with ease, but her heart still yearned for the soldier that left her. When she got word that he was looking for her, she couldn't resist sending him a clue as to where to find her."

The lanterns illuminated the scene in the ring. A platform had been wheeled to its center with two thrones sitting atop it. Rae lounged in one with a golden tiara gracing her brow.

The horsemen continued trotting around the ring while Damien and Kaiser stood with their feline and falcon escorts to one side. They studied a map while a dancer pranced up the platform to whisper in Rae's ear.

Rae sat up straighter as the dancer continued to inform her of the happenings in the city. She put a hand to her mouth and then moved it to her chest. She steeled her features and pulled out a golden handkerchief; giving it to the dancer, she pointed across the stage. The dancer left it on a pedestal and bounded out of the ring.

"Maria told her informant to leave the handkerchief outside the hidden entrance to their underground palace. She did not know the government official traveled with the man she was still besotted with. This official had been hunting for her husband's lair for years. He would arrest her husband on sight if they found the entrance."

As Luc stopped talking, Bane took to the wing and soared around the big top. He flew over the heads of the crowd, creating a breeze that ruffled hair and clothes. Gasps were sounded by those unprepared for the closeness of the raptor.

He veered to the center of the ring and grabbed the golden handkerchief from its place on the pedestal. He landed on Kaiser's shoulder and offered him the prize he had snatched, eliciting a cry of jubilation from the young man. Kaiser motioned Damien and Tyee over, proffering them the piece of cloth in triumph. Tyee grabbed the handkerchief from Kaiser's fingers and did a victory lap around the ring.

"The three men celebrated their luck and sent the falcon to lead them to their prey. He did so, and they entered the domain of the prince of thieves.

"Meanwhile, Maria confessed her transgressions to her husband. They were deep in conversation when the men attacked their underground kingdom."

Zeke slid down a rope from the pinnacle of the big top and landed on his throne. He pulled Rae into his lap and started nuzzling her neck. She put a hand up to stop him and began talking rapidly, telling him what she had done.

While the pair conversed, the three men strode to the pedestal. Tyee dismounted from Koko as his brothers followed his lead. The five joined Kaiser and Damien and their animal escorts next to the pedestal. The music became a cacophony of drums and horns and strings as the men rushed to the foot of the platform.

Zeke scrambled, dropping Rae into a pile at his feet. He quickly took in the scene and climbed atop his throne. He gripped the rope with one hand and was pulled into the air.

"The prince of thieves was a master escapist. His kingdom was compromised and his princess was about to be captured. He made a getaway, knowing he would live to fight another day.

"The official and his assistant were frustrated that the prince outmaneuvered them yet again. The soldier licked his lips with satisfaction when he saw Maria on the ground. He'd gotten what he came for, and let the official and his assistant lick their wounds. He was ready to remind this woman of his claim by worshiping every part of her."

Zeke was pulled out of sight into the darkness of the top of the tent. Bane fluttered around the space the acrobat once occupied but eventually returned to Kaiser's shoulder. Rae struggled to her elbows, looking up to where Zeke disappeared. Losing sight of him, her gaze shifted to where the men stood at the bottom of the platform. She scrambled up and leaned her back against the throne she once sat on.

Her tiara askew, she gulped when she saw Tyee lick his lips. He strode up the platform while Kaiser and Damien argued at the bottom of it. He sat on the throne that was still warm and gripped Rae's wrist forcefully. Tyee lifted her by one arm into his lap and started stroking her bare thigh. He gave her a feral grin before calling down to his men. The four horsemen escorted Damien and Kaiser out of the ring, taking Nymeria and Conrad with them.

The lanterns dimmed so only a couple on the platform were left, illuminating where Rae still sat in Tyee's lap.

Tyee continued to trace her skin but whispered gently so the crowd couldn't see. "You good, Birdie? Remember our signal. You tap two fingers when it gets to be too much."

"How presumptuous of you, Drifter." She patted his cheek, leaning into her role of a woman reunited with the man she never stopped thinking about. "Thanks again. I don't know if I would've made it without your intervention. Burnout was a lot closer than I realized."

"That's been happening a lot lately." Tyee shifted Rae, so she straddled his lap. He lifted an eyebrow as he stared into her eyes.

"Your guess is as good as mine. My fire is like a well. Every time I use my Craft, I draw from the well, having to dig deeper and deeper as I use more and more. Right now, it's like I'm drawing from an endless well, and every time I reach, the power is right there. I can't tell when it won't let me stop pulling from it." She bent her head towards his as he ran his hands up the bare skin on her back.

He furrowed his brows. "What did it feel like if the well was getting dry before?" He placed a hand on the back of her head and brought her in for a quick peck.

"I could feel how much power was left as I pulled the flames toward me. The more I had to dig, the less power I had left. Once I reached a certain point, I knew it would be dangerous to keep going and would stop.

"It just doesn't make sense because I've trained for this. My well should be deep enough to handle two days of shows." She placed her forehead on his, breath ragged.

"This is the part where we make out." She searched his eyes.

"I know this is supposed to be that part." Tyee closed his eyes, putting the decision on Rae. "But we don't have to. No use in burning the tent down."

"Luc is waiting for us."

"She can improvise if need be."

Tyee leaned back until his head rested on the back of the throne. He still had his eyes closed when he felt lips press against his own. Tyee lifted one hand and gently cradled Rae's head while the other ran circles on her thigh.

He knew it was only an act, but Huntress he wished it were real.

He made sure his hunger for her was held in check and kissed her slowly. Rae had her own ideas, though. He let her deepen the kiss, surprised by the woman's boldness. The heat intensified as she drank him in.

Her hands knotted in his hair and she pressed herself into him. He grunted as he tried to think of anything else. It was no use. He waited for the two-finger tap, but it never came.

All too soon, Luc started talking again, and the lanterns dimmed. Rae gave him one last kiss before pulling apart. They disentangled themselves while Luc narrated from her perch, but kept eye contact.

Rae held a hand to her lips, fingers tingling with the sparks that lingered there. Luc narrated above, but Rae didn't hear a word. Her body shuddered as she thought of the kiss. *Fuck.* She bit her lip and dropped her hands, emotions racing. *That was one hell of a kiss.* Her eyes burned as she saw the same hunger mirrored in Tyee's.

Sorry, Luc. Rae thought as she moved closer to the rogue, still oblivious to the tale her friend wove high above. She was tired of performing and wanted something that felt real. Even if it wasn't.

Tyee held Rae's eyes as she straddled him, confused by her actions. He searched her eyes and found exhaustion tinged with pain in their depths. He started to question her, but she put a finger to his lips.

His breath hitched as she leaned in close, whispering in his ear. "I need this."

She studied his face, running fingertips along his jaw, slowly tilting his chin up. He gave her a slight nod, letting her know he understood how the weight of keeping her Craft in check was eating her from the inside out. Rae dove head first into another kiss as Tyee pulled her close. She clung to him as she let herself fall apart at his touch, losing herself in the fire between them.

While Rae and Tyee indulged in each other, the lanterns in the big top flickered. Luc was forced to improvise but paused as the hair on her arms stood up. She had a feeling something terrible was about to happen.

"My esteemed guests. Our story is just about over, but it seems something is happening with the lanterns. In case of an emergency, please make sure you know where your closest exit is."

The crowd grew restless after Luc made her announcement. People jostled each other as the lanterns kept flickering.

Suddenly, they all flashed too bright and burst from their glass holdings.

Broken glass rained down and fire flared from the ruined lanterns. Soon, the magnificent fabric of the big top itself started smoking.

People screamed and rushed towards the exits. Crew members sounded the alarm and helped guide the panicked crowds to safety. Spotters pulled Luc's hoop to the tower and helped her dismount. Luc climbed down the tower quickly, beelining for her friend.

On the platform, Tyee heard the sounds of glass shattering and felt the heat of untamed flames on his face. Glass fell all around while the woman on top of him suddenly went limp in his arms. He started shaking her and calling her name.

"Rae. Rae, wake up. We have to get outta here, Birdie. Wake up." Tyee rolled the unconscious woman off of him, setting her gently on the ground next to him. He tried shaking her shoulder again. "Shit! Rae, don't do this to me."

Damien and Zeke appeared at Tyee's shoulder.

"Looks like she's out cold. We need to get her out of this tinderbox." Damien tried to shoulder past the horseman.

"I got her." Tyee pushed back and gently scooped the fire Crafter into his arms. "She feels ice cold. Where do I bring her?" Tyee's voice was raspy as he felt himself spinning out of control.

Damien and Zeke shared a look. While the men debated what to do with her, Luc came rushing up. She looked at Rae and her face fell. She placed the back of one hand on her friend's forehead.

"Damn it, I knew something was going to happen. She only wanted to prove herself." Luc stroked Rae's cheek.

"Not helpful. We need to get her out of here. But where do I take her?" Tyee repeated his question to the usually intuitive acrobat.

Luc's eyebrows knitted together before she snapped her fingers. "Take her to Abuela's wagon. Javie will be there to help you get her in safely. Abuela should have a fire tincture to melt the ice in her veins. Hopefully, that works again."

Tyee took off, trying not to jostle her limp form too much. He didn't wait for the other two men to offer their help, just left as quickly as possible.

The three acrobats shared a look. Zeke voiced what they were all thinking. "I didn't see that one coming." Damien let out a booming laugh while Luc just shook her head.

"Come on, you two. We can gossip about Rae and Tyee later. There's a fire to put out."

"Literally." Damien winked at Zeke, making his friend snort.

Luc rolled her eyes and strode towards the stands to help escort those lost in the press of flesh.

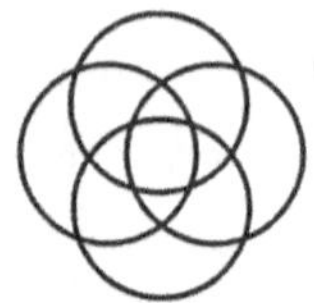

Chapter Fifteen

The Circus worked efficiently to save the red and white striped tent.

The other fire Crafters had returned to the side rings to make sure they were close by in the event of an emergency. Zalia wrangled the lanterns to emit a soft glow that illuminated the tent. The other three worked to contain the burning fabric of the big top.

They couldn't put it out just yet, but they could stop it from spreading. They needed water to make putting the fire out seem plausible.

Eva had to leave her father to get J, their best asset in this situation. She hugged him fiercely before running to the animal yard.

Her father helped direct traffic but had no choice in leaving when several townsfolk recognized him. He blew a kiss in Eva's direction and prayed to the Goddess she would understand why he had to leave.

Eva returned on J's back, his trunk already full of water.

He sprayed it on the largest flames, allowing the Crafters to discreetly purge whatever flares survived the spray.

He moved to the next largest fire and did the same, using the buckets of water brought by the crew and performers. Some troupe members threw their buckets of water on the smaller flames, but all continued until the flames were put out.

Once the crisis was averted, J grabbed Eva by the back of her shirt and lifted her off his back. He placed her on the ground so she could run to where she had last left her father.

He watched, sadness in his warm, brown eyes, as Eva searched in vain. They both knew he had to leave with the crowd. Eva trudged back to him, tears running down her cheeks. He wrapped his trunk around the young girl.

J connected with her the first day she joined the Circus. He had been surprised when so many other performers failed to gain her confidence. She was one of those kids that kept to herself.

He hoped the new little Crafter would be good for her, help her open up a bit more. He worried about Eva, but when Nan brought the little girl to see the elephants, she gripped Eva tight and wouldn't let her go. Eva did her part and took the new recruit's hand to show her around the animal yard. He had a feeling he was about to gain another charge, whether he liked it or not.

The two made their way back inside the patronless big top.

Their last performance was one the town would never forget.

Crew members had already started dismantling the trapeze towers and hauling pieces of it out to the storage wagons. Others packed up the seats and props inside the ring. Jess and Duke were leading the crews in, taking down the smaller poles on the perimeter of the big top.

Seeing J, Jess made her way over to her old friend and placed a hand on his flank.

"Well J, what do you say we get started on the big poles?" Jess patted his side as he let out a trumpet of affirmation. The two got to work taking down the long, thick poles holding up the enormous tent.

Luc finally made it to her Abuela's wagon. She had been trying to slip out of the big top for hours but kept getting wrangled into helping with more tasks.

Finally, it was just the tent left.

The tent crew was well-manned and no one protested when she stepped into the darkness. Zeke would be cross that she got to go check on their friend while he was stuck untying knots in the canvas, but Damien would stay and help.

She knocked on the back doors of the wagon with three beats followed by two. That had always been their signal. It let her Abuela and Javie know who was at the door.

Luc frowned when no one answered.

She went around the front and found the oxen hooked up, but nobody held their reins. She circled back to where she started and tried the doors. They swung open easily and were accompanied by a small cry.

"Good heavens, child. Give an old woman some warning." Nan exclaimed from where she sat next to the still unconscious fire Crafter.

"I knocked." Luc protested. "How's she doing?"

Nan touched a finger to her lips and raised it above her. "Not well, mi Nieta. The fire tincture brought the heat back to her skin, but she still hasn't woken up. Come and sit with her while I look in my cabinets."

Luc climbed into the wagon that felt like home. She sat on the other side of her friend and gripped Rae's hand. She watched her Abuela search cabinet after cabinet. Finally, she opened a book and turned to a page with a woman lying on a bed with her eyes closed.

The old woman stared hard at Rae before grabbing the ingredients listed. She added them to a bowl, whispered some words, and started grinding the ingredients together. She called for Javie and told him to grab some of the liquid boiling on the fire outside her wagon.

Once he brought it to her, she added it to the bowl and poured it into a glass. Nan brought the awful-smelling concoction to where Rae lay prostrate.

"Lean her up, dearie. We have to make her drink this. If this doesn't work...we may have to just wait and see what her body can do." Nan said.

Luc mulled over her Abuela's words as she lifted the limp fire Crafter, supporting her head. Rae would be okay; she had to be. Otherwise, the Circus would never be the same.

She watched Nan tip the cup back and pour the red mixture down her friend's throat, clutching her hands anxiously, her eyes never leaving her friend's face.

Nothing happened.

Luc looked at her Abuela with tears in her eyes and watched as the old woman's eyes drooped and her lips pursed. She rubbed her granddaughter's shoulders.

"Hush, child. Give her a minute."

"Should I get Zalia? Maybe another transfusion is what she needs." Luc pulled out of Nan's grasp, restless and wanting to be of use to her friend.

"Nieta, sit." Nan gave Luc a look and continued only after the young woman sat back down next to her friend. "You know Zalia has her limits too. The tincture brought her back from the edge, we must let her body heal at its own pace."

Luc sighed, picking at her skintight pants. She turned to the woman next to her, tears welling in her eyes once more. She didn't know what she'd do if the Crafter didn't wake up.

Nan, Luc, and Javie were some of the first in the band of nomads. Duncan helped them get out of the Capital after they lost Luc and Javie's parents. Luc had been a runner between Midge and the orientation crew back in those days following the Uprising. She was one of the first people to encounter the fire Crafter after several years on the road, and the two became fast friends.

For a long time, it was just the two of them. Running between the tents, splashing in the creeks, and laughing until their sides hurt. She would always remember those times fondly. She reached out to tuck a strand of hair behind her friend's ear.

Rae stirred.

Luc's head whipped towards Nan and they shared a smile of relief, while Rae coughed and murmured something, her eyes still closed.

Luc quickly grabbed Rae's hand once more and squeezed. It was faint, but Luc felt a responding squeeze from the acrobat. Rae's eyes fluttered open and a moan escaped her mouth.

"Ugh, my head hurts." Rae squirmed on the makeshift cot. "Everything hurts." Her voice sounded like sandpaper, and it seemed to take all of her effort to keep talking.

"Don't overdo it now." Luc fussed and fluffed her pillow. "Just get some rest."

"Arwen-" Rae croaked out.

"Your friend said he would take care of her." Nan offered.

Rae searched Luc's eyes desperately.

"Tyee was the one that brought you here. He must have said he would look after Arwen for you." Luc answered.

"Yes! The Night Rider. I blanked on his name. He ran off soon after getting Javie to help him place you on this cot." Nan pulled a blanket over Rae and moved towards the front of the wagon.

She opened the front doors but turned back and said, "Luc, stay and watch her. I'm going to check on Javie and see where we're at in terms of transport." Luc just nodded as she watched Rae doze back into a restless sleep.

Duncan found himself wandering to Rae's tent after receiving word she had regained consciousness. The runner reported the fire Crafter was sleeping soundly in Nan's wagon.

Good. She needs it. He thought to himself as he made it to the lone tent left in the player's yard.

Before he could enter, someone exited the tent.

Tyee stopped with wide eyes as he noticed Duncan standing there.

"Sir." He acknowledged with a nod.

Duncan watched Tyee place the things he'd grabbed from within the tent into an open trunk just outside.

"I packed all her things in there; even her cot folded up enough to fit. The only thing left is to take the tent down." Tyee ventured.

"Let me help," Duncan said, moving to the opposite side.

The two men worked together to take down the simple structure, fold the canvas, and tie the poles together. They placed everything inside the trunk.

"Where does this need to go?" Tyee asked.

"She always puts it in one of the supply wagons. Move it to that pile over there and it'll get loaded with the rest." Duncan frowned. "Don't you put your trunk on one of the wagons?"

"Oh. No, everything I need is in my bag or Koko's pack. We travel light."

Duncan studied the horseman. "You've readied Arwen, I take it?"

"Aye. I figured I would be more than qualified to take care of the golden girl's horse." Tyee bristled.

Duncan raised an eyebrow. "Of course, I would be a fool to suggest otherwise. Just be careful with her." Duncan walked away, leaving Tyee to figure out if he meant the horse or the girl.

Rae woke up in flashes. Sometimes it was dark, other times sunlight danced across her face. Sometimes Luc sang her a song, sometimes Damien told fantastical stories, and sometimes Zeke droned on about all the gossip she was missing.

She floated in between sleep and wakefulness, most of the time unable to differentiate between the two. She finally woke with a start, fearing her golden palomino had been left behind.

Luc snored in the chair next to her while Abuela and Javie slept soundly on the floor. Guilt panged her heart when she realized they had given her their bed while on the road. Riders traveled with bed rolls on the back of their saddles, but wagons had the advantage of holding cots to sleep on.

I owe Abuela and Javie something sweet. She thought as she took stock of her limbs. Her body felt heavy and achy, but there were no sharp pains or burning sensations. She steeled herself and sat up slowly, being as quiet as possible. Rae paused, letting her head stop spinning, and climbed out the front of the wagon.

She almost fell off the side of the front seat when a muscular arm kept her from hitting the ground.

She looked into the dark eyes of the man she'd been secretly yearning for. Tyee helped her climb into the saddle behind him. She wrapped her arms around him and rested her head on his back, trying to keep the world from spinning. He guided Koko to where the other horses stood, hitched to a line strung between the trees.

Rae slipped off Koko's back when she caught sight of a familiar golden coat. She ran up to Arwen and buried her face in the mare's mane. Tears slipped down the fire Crafter's face.

"What's wrong with me, Arwe? Why can't I keep it together?" She whispered under her breath. Arwen's ears flicking back to her was the only response she got. She took a deep breath of Arwen's rich aroma and turned back to where Tyee stood next to his steed.

"Thank you. Again." She smiled, but it didn't reach her eyes. "Never pegged you for the rescuing kind."

"Never pegged you for being the damsel in distress," Tyee smirked and held an arm out to steady her. "Let's get you back to bed."

Rae could only manage a nod as Tyee lifted her into Koko's saddle. He mounted behind her and guided the ebony stallion back to Nan's wagon. He helped her inside before returning to his nightly sentinel outside the wagon.

It was three more days on the road before Rae could leave the wagon for Arwen indefinitely. Her friends made her take it slow, but she refused to stay in the wagon a moment longer than was necessary.

Heimat was getting closer and closer.

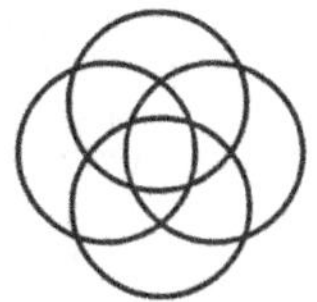

Chapter Sixteen

The air was brisk with the promise of winter. The smell of leaves, crisped with death, mingled with the rich scents of the earth. An icy wind blew through the hills, chilling the bones of those traveling in the nomadic city.

Rae rode ahead of the caravan, trying to put space between the shame and guilt she felt. She patted her golden mare, wincing as she failed to outrun the consequences of her transgressions. She leaned low on Arwen's neck and whispered in her ear. "Faster."

The horse snorted and threw her head before lengthening her stride and obliging. Running was something the palomino cherished but never got enough of. Soon, the caravan was just a speck in the distance.

Her heart twinged as distinct memories drifted towards the forefront of her mind, her heart willing anything but thoughts of Windemere and her latest disaster to come forward.

She closed her eyes and saw a younger version of herself stealing warm bread from the kitchens, but laughing too much to get away with it. Her mother kissing her cheek goodnight, dressed in golden silk for an event she needed to attend. Her unruly hair bouncing as she pounded down the steps and leaped into her father's arms, only for him to spin her around.

Rae brushed roughly at her face as her eyes flew open. *That wasn't any better,* she thought, cursing her treacherous mind. She reined Arwen in, slowing the horse from a gallop to a steady lope, rocking with her horse's gait. She forced her eyes shut again, letting herself get lost in the rhythm of her horse.

She was met with an image of dark features, blazing eyes, and a wry smirk. Calloused hands reached for her.

Rae's eyes flew open as she groaned. *Not going there either.* A flush crept up her neck and into her cheeks while she struggled to chase thoughts of a certain horseman away.

She lifted her chin, embracing the bite of the wind hitting her face.

Rae knew many of her fellow performers were cross with her, especially Zalia. It didn't take long for the fire Crafter to lay into her once Rae had recovered.

Reckless. Arrogant. Selfish.

Zalia's words rattled inside her brain, eating away at her and fueling her guilt more than ever. She pushed Arwen a little faster, knowing nobody from the Circus would follow her after what happened in Windemere. Even the two young fire Crafters avoided her; the trust and admiration they once felt washed away with a single incident.

Her friends were giving her space. Rae had told them she needed some alone time, seeing as Luc was determined not to leave her side. Luc only obliged when Damien and Zeke convinced the Head Mortal Rae needed some breathing room.

And Tyee. Tyee had barely spoken to her since the first night she was conscious. She knew it was because she'd been actively avoiding him, running away whenever he got near.

Coward.

Her inner voice was right, but she couldn't seem to find it in her to care much.

She was shocked from her reverie as the shadows of trees started to cross their path. They made it to the outskirts of Heimat faster than she thought they would. She'd have to turn around and return to the Circus. She halted Arwen and reached into her saddlebag for an apple.

"Better turn around here, girl," Rae said, wistfulness in her voice as she set her worries aside and offered the horse a treat. "This is the last one I have. I'll try to get more when we stop tonight."

Arwen bobbed her head while munching on the treat, her sides slick with sweat as the horse took the much-needed rest. Rae scratched her steed's neck until the mare's ears pricked and she gazed up the road towards town.

Voices sounded up the path, heading in their direction. Rae quickly dismounted and guided Arwen into the brush, not wanting to deal with the people coming towards her.

"I swear I saw someone on a golden palomino coming this way," a slender young man in a dark overcoat panted as he slowed down and looked behind him.

Rae heard someone wheezing and slowly another, older man, this one plump, came to stand next to the first.

The two men were complete opposites. The first man was tall, dressed in a dark gray coat, breaches, and boots, quiet as his eyes flicked up and down the gravel road. The second man was short, dressed in as many colors as possible, and made a racket as he tried to catch his breath.

"Huh—I still don't think... You saw anything," gasped the second man.

"Good Goddess, Rich, get ahold of yourself. All of Heimat knows where we are by now." Whispered the tall man furiously. "I saw a girl with golden hair on a horse shimmering like the sun. She was–"

"Young woman, actually," said Rae, stepping out of the shadows, having recognized them as townspeople by the invocation of the Goddess herself, protector of all the towns and cities in Kamore.

Arwen nickered nervously and nudged her rider, seeming to signal flight was better than fighting. Rae patted the mare and continued, "Why are you looking for me?"

Rich finally caught his breath and glanced at the tall man. "Look at that, George, there she is! You were right after all!" Looking at Rae, beaming, he extended his hand and said, "Miss Goldie, it is my pleasure to meet you. Your act in the Circus precedes you."

"Good to meet you..."

"Call me Rich! I own the bakery in town."

"Good to meet you, Rich," Rae said, clasping his hand. Looking at the other man, Rae asked "George, right?" He nodded, and she continued, "Why were you looking for me, George?"

As he hesitated, Rae had an opportunity to study him for the first time. The gray outfit made it seem like he wanted to blend into the background. His body language was relaxed, but Rae's trained eye caught the taut muscles underneath that false front. She caught the way his eyes never stopped studying his surroundings.

George was more than he seemed.

"Everyone in town knows the Circus is coming. Merchants from Windemere brought word yesterday. Rumors were the Golden Eagle sometimes rides ahead." George paused and glanced at Rich. The two shared a meaningful look, and Rich's face fell. George continued, "The snow in the forest falls fast, and an avalanche is building."

Rae blanched at those words. She was not part of the Council, but all performers knew what those words meant.

Heimat was compromised.

They wouldn't find safety here anymore and she needed to prepare the others.

George looked her right in the eye and understanding passed between the two of them. Time was of the essence. Their carefully laid, backup plans would be put to the test.

"Time to batten up the hatches and prepare as best we can. I will alert the Ringmaster at once."

George and Rich nodded somberly as Rae mounted her horse. Rich grabbed her hand, saying, "Bless you. Once your troupe has settled, send a runner to the bakery. I'll have fresh bread for you."

"I will," Rae promised. Rich squeezed her hand, smiled softly, and turned away. George nodded as Rae turned Arwen back the way they came.

Rae's heart pounded as she rode hard, only easing up once she reached the outskirts of the slow-moving caravan. She searched for Duncan, turning her head this way and that while her thoughts ran wild and her frustration mounted.

"Has anybody seen Duncan?!" Rae exclaimed, trying to keep the desperation from her voice.

"Rae, he's over there. Everything alright?" Nymeria, the lioness Shifter, called out, pointing towards the back of the caravan.

"Thanks, Mer. I need to talk to him first." Rae barely looked at the concerned performer as she made her way swiftly to Duncan.

Her stomach was in knots as she replayed the exchange in her mind repeatedly. She clenched her jaw to hold back the tears and rage she felt. The fire roared in her veins and it took everything she had to stay in control. Her skin felt too tight as she fought down the anger in her throat.

They couldn't let Heimat go without a fight.

Rae found Duncan towards the back of the caravan, deep in conversation with Chiara the Head Herbalist. Both looked up when they heard hoofbeats pounding their way.

"Chiara, will you excuse me? Someone needs to speak to me it seems." He said, noticing the fire Crafter's disheveled hair and frantic expression.

"No problem." Chiara moved her horse away from the Ringmaster, concern glittering in her gaze. "Everything okay, Rae?" She directed the question at the fire Crafter once she was in earshot.

"I just need to talk to Duncan, Ms. Rutter. Thanks though." Rae met the woman's kind green eyes and inclined her head to the older woman.

"Of course, but please, call me Chiara. We are well past the need for formalities." The Herbalist insisted as she made her way from the pair.

Rae nodded, still preoccupied with her thoughts.

Duncan studied the usually composed acrobat. Once Chiara was out of earshot he guessed what happened. "So I take it Heimat needs our help."

Rae's bewildered expression was all he needed for confirmation. "How did you know? Did the scouts send word?"

"My dear, we never send the scouts to Heimat." Duncan winced. "No, I've had a feeling ever since Tiva that something like this would happen. Myra is getting more desperate as her lack of leadership shows. Finding the Magicae is the only thing left to earn her people's approval."

"We can't let them take Heimat. We need to fight for our last city of refuge. Duncan, I can't let them do this. Not Heimat." Rae's voice cracked with emotion.

"Rae, we need to be smart. We lost people in Tiva, almost lost our cover in Windemere." He gave her a look, but Rae's eyes still blazed. "Our caravan is filled with children and elderly. They won't be able to fight." Duncan hesitated like he was holding something back and Rae shot him an expectant look, frustration building at the situation and knowing her mentor was keeping something from her. "I know you're hurting, but we need to *think*. Those are your father's words, not mine."

Rae felt her world spin; Duncan rarely mentioned her father. She gave him a searching look.

"I need to tell you about that day. The day everything went wrong." Duncan sighed. "You know that your father and I grew up together. Fernwen was a dirty, crowded city even when I was a boy. It reeked of sweat, sewer, and dead fish, yet no other place was as beautiful.

"Your father and I spent entire days on the pier, pestering sailors with questions, chasing seagulls, and sneaking glances at the ladies walking by. Our nights were spent standing outside the pubs, waiting for some drunk to drop a bottle, still half full of whiskey or rum. On successful nights, we would take the bottle to the city limits and stare up at the stars while passing it back and forth." Duncan had a far-off look as he remembered those days.

"We talked about everything and anything. Our dreams, our families, politics, sex, and so much more. Don't give me that look. I'm sure you talk about much worse with Luc." Rae had the decency to look sheepish when chided. "We grew up but never apart. Eventually, your father became President of Kamore with myself and others as his official advisors. He was an outstanding leader. He was fair and just, but fear has a way of corrupting even the best people."

Duncan's face scrunched with pain and he continued, "I think about that night often. Your father and I were running in the streets again, but not for the feeling of freedom we once chased. This time, a mob followed. Your father made me continue while he turned to face his once loyal citizens. I tried to get him to come with me but he wouldn't listen. Protecting others runs in the family, I fear." Duncan smiled sadly and roughly ran a sleeve across his face. He reached into his bag and pulled out a weathered envelope, discolored from age.

"He asked me to give this to you when you needed his words the most. Your father was an idealist. He always believed in the best of people, even Myra. But he was also wicked smart. He knew a wave of fear and turmoil was coming fast. He was prepared to protect the Magicae with his dying breath."

"You mean to protect me, right? I was the reason Myra could manipulate the people into forming a mob, to begin with. Me and my stupid golden eyes." Rae hissed and looked at her hands.

Duncan gripped Rae's arm hard. "Never say those words again. Being Magicae is not something to be ashamed of." He squeezed her arm gently to get her to look at him. "Your father loved you deeply and wouldn't even consider giving you up, despite multiple advisors trying to persuade him otherwise. He knew there would be consequences, but the message of giving you up was one he refused to send. Your eyes may have been the spark to the Uprising, but the tinder had been laid generations before."

Rae narrowed her eyes. "Some days I wish he had. Maybe our people wouldn't be in such a mess then." She pulled her arm out of his grasp.

Duncan shook his head. "Just like your father. Rae, our people would be in this mess no matter what happened. Somewhere down the road, it turned into us versus them. I don't know when and I don't know how, but the mistrust between Magicae and Mortals slowly grew into outright fear. This fear led to our current conflict. Stop blaming yourself for something that was out of your control."

"Do you believe that?"

"Wholeheartedly, my dear. If you don't believe me, read this. Maybe your father left some more convincing words." Duncan handed the old letter over to the writer's intended recipient. "I've made a lot of mistakes since that night, but keeping this safe wasn't one of them. I was only waiting until you needed them most."

"Thanks, Duncan." Rae took the letter gingerly as if she was afraid it would turn to ash at any moment. Holding her father's words in her hands was beyond her wildest dreams. She was in shock. Suddenly, her eyes went wide. "And what about Heimat? We can't ignore this loss."

"Absolutely not. I will talk to the Council and figure out a plan of action. Our priority will be getting those kids out. We will spread the word quickly so everyone is prepared." Duncan's eyes grew weary. "We will get through this like we always do, together."

He patted Rae's shoulder and urged his mare toward the other Council members.

Rae looked down at the letter in her hands and let a single tear fall. She turned Arwen away from the caravan to read her father's words in solitude.

Rae needed time to process this. Duncan had these words in his possession for years and never told her about them. That stung more than she'd like to admit. *Why wouldn't he give them to me when I joined the Circus?*

Unfortunately, the luxury of time was never on her side. Knowing her friends would find her sooner rather than later, Rae took a deep breath and sighed heavily. It was now or never.

She slid her finger between the envelope and its flap to undo the seal. The crisp release indicated no tampering or resealing had befallen the envelope. Her father's words would be for her alone.

Rae closed her eyes and tried to bring the memories of her father to the surface. Time dulled them from when she was a toddler, but she remembered brawny arms holding her tight and swinging her up into the air. She remembered gentle hands tucking her into bed and kind eyes glinting with mischief.

Andre had been Rae's idol. After the Uprising, she spent many nights imagining he escaped the mob and was on the run just like her, looking up at the same stars she was. In her young mind, both her mother and father were out there, she need only to find them.

Foolish child. Rae admonished. She learned years later her father was publicly executed and her mother presumed dead as well. The grief racked her frame once again, searing pain running through her veins.

Her palms burst into flame.

"Fuck!" she exclaimed, beating the flames on her pants before they could consume the letter she needed.

She reached within and yanked the fire into submission. Returning to herself, she took a deep breath, trying to steady her pounding heart. Rae inspected the letter and relaxed her shoulders, realizing only the edges were singed.

Finally, Rae took the leap.

She opened the flap and took out the letter, hands shaking. She wiped one sweaty palm on her breeches and looked at the neat, concise lettering. Her eyes darted rapidly across the page, brimming with tears as she took in her father's last words to her.

Little one,

I love you. Those three little words will never be enough to encompass how I feel about you. They are just the closest I can come to putting my feelings into words.

Watching you grow, I know you will be more like me than not. That fills me with pride and terrifies me at the same time. Your vibrant curiosity and big heart will take you far.

Love, you must have so many questions. I don't know how to answer most of them, but I can try. Above all, this is <u>not</u> your fault. Many, many people advised your mother and me to give you up upon realizing the power in your blood. We both agreed it couldn't be done. We were selfish, little one. We feared a broken *heart more than the potential political consequences.*

Our actions doomed the Magicae.

They doomed Duncan, Helene, and so many more. Yet, I would do it all over again in a heartbeat. The past four years with you made everything worth it.

Again, I am a selfish man who loves his daughter.

I did what I could to ease the tension between Magicae and Mortals, but my efforts weren't enough. There is too much fear of the unknown.

But your magic is not something to be ashamed of. Your mother and I knew if we let you go, we were sending the message to you that your magic is shameful. It is not. It is part of who you are and what makes you unique. Please, do not stop developing your abilities. Be the strong, independent, and compassionate woman I know you will become.

We may not have had a lot of time, but some things cannot be changed.

All my love,

Daddy

Rae was a mess. She reread the letter several times, her fury mounting each time she read that last line.

Fire burst from her hands and this time, she let it consume the letter she already knew by heart. She watched it burn, turning to ash and leaving with the wind.

Shuddering sobs took over as the fire in her hands died and her mouth tasted like ash.

Some things cannot be changed.

She was raging at the words from her father, at the way he didn't fight for her, and the magic in her veins. By the way he didn't fight for Duncan or Helene.

The betrayal cut like a knife, deeper than anything else.

Rae screamed as loud as she could, releasing her outrage, and urged Arwen into a gallop. The horse flicked her ears back and gave a soft nicker, but did as her rider bid. Tears streamed steadily down Rae's face, landing like rain on her loyal mare's coarse coat. Rae couldn't care less where the horse took her. As long as she kept moving, she wouldn't have to face her grief.

They ran for what felt like hours until the mare was drenched in sweat and breathing hard. The Crafter reined her in, giving Arwen the rest she deserved. Rae was patting her steed when she noticed one of Arwen's ears shift backward, hearing something in the distance.

She aggressively wiped at her face while listening closely. Sure enough, hoof-beats sounded somewhere behind her. Without turning, Rae knew Zeke had found her. With a sigh, she leaned forward to scratch Arwen between the ears. She kept her mare walking, making sure Arwen didn't stiffen up too much.

"Good girl. Let's see what happens next." Rae murmured to the mare, feeling raw and hollow after the release of emotion. She didn't want to face her friend but was grateful Zeke came alone. He wouldn't judge her as harshly for losing control.

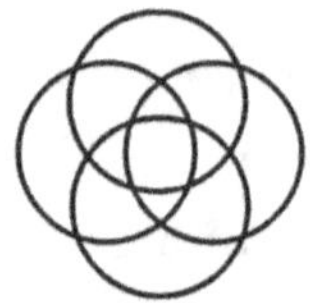

Chapter Seventeen

The Circus performers felt dread and anguish as they neared the city that had once been their unofficial home. The northernmost city in Kamore always meant safety and a respite from the act they put on. Every year, they spent the winter on the outskirts of town, some of the new recruits choosing to find permanent residences while others threw themselves into prepping for life on the road come springtime.

The caravan sludged forward, dragging their feet, trying to avoid their new reality. Even the young kids, unaware of the magnitude of this change, were somber and kept out from underfoot.

Duncan made good on his word, alerting the Council and creating a plan to disseminate the news to the masses. Once the word was out, it spread like wildfire. Set-up would be done without magic, the number of shows would be reduced, acts would perform as if they were in Windemere or any other town, and they would be moving more kids than ever before.

Tensions had never run so high in the nomadic city. Heimat was the tipping point and everyone knew it. A choice to fight or flee was coming, and the question was how they did either without losing more of the ones they loved.

As the oldest member of the Circus, Nan had a long memory. She remembered the time before all the fear, all the hiding, and all the pain. She remembered a time of peace, prosperity, and cooperation.

She knew the only way for those three to come again was to keep hope alive for her people. And there was no better way to do that than by telling a story.

"Javie, be a dear and pull the wagon ahead. And keep your ears open. I expect you to be listening too." Nan moved from her seat next to her grandson and made her way to the back of the wagon.

"Yes, Abuela. I *always* listen when you speak." Javie snapped the reins to speed up the oxen, a smirk in his tone.

Nan chuckled to herself as she moved past shelves of vials and glasses that lined the inside of her wagon and onto the back platform. Javie's wit would get him in trouble one day, but she had already told him that time and time again. She opened the back door quietly, securing it to a hook inside the wagon.

She sobered as she spied a familiar young couple talking in hushed tones astride their horses. Her heart ached, knowing they were discussing the loss of their safe place. This was why she needed to take action before the despair became impenetrable.

"Luc, Damien, gather everybody you can. It's time for a story." Luc looked at the old woman with tired eyes. She urged her mostly black paint to a trot to get closer to the old Herbalist.

"Abuela," she hesitated before continuing, "Is now really the right time for that? Our people are reeling. They need time to grieve and heal. Losing Heimat is devastating."

"Child, a story is exactly what people need right now. Look around you! If we don't do something now, we won't make it through the next three nights."

"I agree, Abuela, but a story? Those are for children."

"Stories have more power than you know, dearie. They can teach, strengthen community, honor loved ones, and most importantly, inspire hope." Nan swung her legs over the back of the wagon and grabbed her granddaughter's hand. "Our people need that more than anything. Hope will keep this fight alive."

Luc searched her grandmother's kind eyes and slowly nodded. "Yes, Abuela, we're on it." She turned to Damien. "You go find Rae and Zeke. They can help gather the riders and the walkers; I'll focus on getting the wagons to stop."

"Aye, aye, my love. Your wish is my command." Damien gave a salute and turned his horse in the direction they had last seen their fellow acrobats. Turning his head to look behind him, he called, "We'll have everybody here before you know it, Wise One." He urged his mare into a trot without waiting for Nan to reply.

Nan chuckled and shook her head. "You have your hands full with that one, Nieta."

"Tell me about it." Luc looked after her partner with a wistful expression. "Sweeter than molasses and more charming than a prince. Huntress have mercy! Don't worry, we'll get the job done Abuela." Luc directed her horse to the nearest wagon, yelling to hail its driver.

The wind whipped across the field, ruffling the hair of both riders as their horses walked aimlessly. Neither noticed as they argued.

"Zeke, I've told you a million times. I'm fine." Rae huffed at her fair-colored performance partner.

"No. You are not *fine*, Rae." Zeke spat her name as if disgusted he was using it. "By the Huntress, we've been performing together for almost a decade. Give me a little credit. I know you better than you know yourself." Zeke shifted slightly to look Rae dead in the eyes. His features softened as he said, "You can trust me Sparks, just talk to me."

Rae couldn't bear the searching look and gentle concern in his mercurial gaze. Dropping her eyes, she stroked Arwen's neck, trying to keep her hands busy while her mind raced.

"Z, I hate knowing this place will never be the same. It's been a tough year. We've lost so many places and people. I never thought we'd lose Heimat, too." Flames danced in her palms as her emotions raged. She clenched her fists to quiet her fire and shook her head. "Our people deserve better. I can't stand by and let her take this place, too."

Zeke angled his mare close enough so he could nudge her boot. "This isn't your fault. Duncan has—"

"Duncan has lost touch with what our people need. He doesn't understand that striking back needs to happen now. We should've come back here sooner. Maybe we could have prevented this." Rae wiped away a tear of frustration. She knew her anger was misplaced. Rae was still aching from the letter, the words it contained, and the failure in Windemere. She kept them close to her heart, not ready to probe the bruises they left there.

"Rae, all is not lost. There are still people here that need us. People that are depending on us to get their loved ones out." Zeke grabbed Rae's hand and squeezed. "Our job has to be getting the kids and vulnerable adults out. Once they're safe, we can strike back. You're being too hard on Duncan. His focus is and always will be the people we set out to help."

Rae pulled her hand away gently. She took a moment to decide her next words carefully. "I can't stop thinking about that night." She hung her head and willed her eyes to stop the tears that were welling. "This feels just like when they took the Capital; when they took my father and my mother, and when Helene gave her life to save me. My heart feels like it's being ripped apart again."

The sound of approaching hoofbeats caused the two to look up. Seeing it was Damien, Rae quickly wiped her eyes and tried to compose herself.

Zeke sighed as the rare moment of vulnerability was lost. Rae had always been too strong for her own good. Bottling her emotions to please the people around her was what she did to protect herself; very few ever saw this side of her. Damien rode up to his fellow performers with a flourish.

"Sorry to interrupt, but our most gracious Wise One requests your presence at once." Damien attempted an impersonation of their Ringmaster with an exaggerated bow. As he straightened, he noticed Rae's puffy eyes and the tension palpable between the two friends. His smirk turned downward into a slight frown. "Hey, what's going on friends? Is everything okay?"

"Just peachy, Dame!" Rae said with a tense smile.

Looking between the two, Damien got quiet. "Rae-Rae, don't. You insult me by trying to put on this mask. What's going on?"

Zeke interjected, "Heimat is hitting some of us a little harder than others. Classic Rae, pushing her people away so she doesn't have to deal with her feelings."

Rae slumped away from her closest friends, trying to retreat inside herself. She knew better than to hide from the acrobat, but some habits were hard to break.

"Ease up, Z. I'm trying to be better. I just wasn't expecting to lose this place too. Losing all those kids and our people in Tiva wrecked me." Rae closed her eyes before continuing, "We got there too late, fanned out, and went looking for anyone the soldiers missed." A single tear rolled down her cheek. "They attacked Rocky, Jason, Jose, and Naveen... I wasn't fast enough to stop the violence." Her eyes were bright when she opened them, swimming with grief and guilt. "My fire tore out of me, matching my rage. I couldn't stop it." She hung her head. "And then I almost fucked up Windemere, too. Thank the Huntress, we had already gotten the kids out. Who knows how many we missed because we had to cut the last show short." Rae's voice cracked as she spoke. "Now we have to evacuate Heimat, too. What if it goes wrong again?"

"Tiva was a tragedy. Those people needed our help, and we were too late. Windemere was a fluke. Something is going on with your Craft and we weren't prepared, but this is different, Rae. We have a plan, and we aren't too late. Falling apart will not help *these* children." Zeke insisted.

Rae and Zeke were at a standstill. Rae knew she couldn't afford to fall apart. *Some things cannot be changed.*

Rae bit her lip, swallowing the grief bubbling up. *Stop. Pull it together.* With that thought, she clenched her fists and raised her chin.

Zeke made an important point. To make it through the next three days, she had to stay strong and not dwell on the past. Remembering that feeling of helplessness would not save the lives of the Magicae in Heimat.

"You're right." Rae sat up straight, squared her shoulders, and stared hard at the two young men. "We need to focus on getting our people to safety.

What happened in Tiva won't happen again and I won't let what happened in Windemere take place again. We evacuate Heimat and then we strike where it hurts. We'll go straight for her at the Capital."

"Rae-Rae, let's slow down. Myra is only the head of all the people trying to find and enslave us. Maybe we start with something a little more manageable?" Damien ran his fingers through his hair. "Shall we say, doing what the Wise One says?"

"Oh, yea that's why you came and found us. What does Abuela want anyway?" Zeke welcomed the distraction with a concerned glance towards Rae.

"Glad you asked, my silver-haired, clever friend. The Wisest One that has ever lived wants to entertain the entire company with a story. And we are to gather everybody not in wagons."

Rae rolled her eyes. "Of course, Abuela wants to tell a story at a time like this. Well, you're right. Better get to it then." A glint came into her eyes. "Bet I gather more people than the two of you combined." She turned Arwen and took off at a gallop towards the main part of the caravan.

"You're on," said Zeke as he took off after her. Damien let out a cackle and followed.

Chapter Eighteen

A crowd gathered around the colorful wagon where Nan delighted children with bedtime stories and stored the tonics she created as an Herbalist. It held the memories of her grandchildren and reminded her of traveling with her own Abuela.

Tonight, she would make that fierce woman proud.

More and more people joined the throng outside her wagon as the acrobats did their duty. Wagons were arranged in a half circle at the edge of the gathering of people. Several bonfires blazed to ward off the chill of the night.

Nan searched the crowd. She saw a myriad of people, of her people. The sounds of community warmed her heart. Children laughed as they jostled for a spot to sit up front. Adults stood in small groups chatting and greeting one another as more people joined. The crackle of the bonfires and the clank of mugs and dishes filled the air.

A nervous energy weaved its way among her people. They were on the edge of a precipice as they gathered just outside Heimat, terrified for the moment that decided whether they fell off or stayed on the edge.

Her gaze was drawn to another sizable group settling their horses as the light of dusk faded away in earnest. She watched three figures peel away from the group to sit with Luc where she was talking to Bane, taking advantage of the Shifter's limited time in his human form.

Despite knowing Heimat was lost, the Magicae in the troupe were holding onto one more night without having to hide.

Nan watched fondly as the trio joined in the conversation with her animated, raven-haired granddaughter. The acrobats' arrival meant her story could begin; they wouldn't have come until the entire Circus was in attendance.

She sighed, a weight settling on her shoulders. The spirit could only take so much heartbreak before it began to dim. Her most important job tonight was setting spirits aflame with purpose again. She nodded to Javie, and he lit the lanterns hanging on both sides of the back of her wagon.

"Come closer my dears. We have not gathered like this in a long time." The caravan quieted as Nan locked eyes with Duncan. He gave her a salute, and she continued, her voice now projected. "We live in dark, dark times. Heimat has been a symbol for all of us. A symbol of peace, of sanctuary, of hope for a return to what we've lost." She paused, letting her words sink in. The performers and crew moved closer to their loved ones as they listened to this affirmation of their grief.

"It is necessary to acknowledge the loss of this place. Most of us have feelings of despair, fear, and anger that need to be expressed. Once expressed, we can work through them and take action. Our very souls are crying out for vengeance and justice. How we go about answering those cries will depend on how we work through the pain." Nan watched Rae lean her head on Luc's shoulder.

She continued, "A long, long time ago, when I was a little girl—,"

Quiet giggles could be heard in the front row amongst the children. "Yes, as hard as it is to believe, I was once as young as Miss Izzy here."

Izzy squealed with delight to be called out by the old storyteller, her copper-flecked eyes flashing in the darkness. She was one of Nan's frequent attendees at story time and loved the old woman. Nan's eyes crinkled with mirth.

She went on, "When I was a child, I would spend my days running through the forest and my nights sitting at my own Abuela's fire. I learned how to listen, how to heal, and how to enjoy the company of others. I learned the art of conversation and the power held within the tales we weave for others.

"My Abuela ended every night with a story.

"One night stands out in particular, and it's the one I want to share with you on this harrowing eve. That night was a rare one, as just Abuela and I shared her fire.

"Boy, do I miss that circle of warmth and light.

"My Abuela spent hours laughing and loving by that fire, making it a safe place to rest." Nan's eyes became unfocused as the memories swelled up unbidden. Calloused hands, a booming laugh, and the smell of stew on the fire swirled inside her head. She brushed her long skirt, forcing herself back to the present.

"I was staying with my Abuela for several days. My parents were on a hunting trip and I had her all to myself.

"I couldn't be happier."

The members of the circus laughed at the image of a young Abuela bouncing with energy, ready to have endless attention from her own grandmother.

Nan smiled, "Little did I know, I was in for something special. While I sat by her fire, anticipating having her all to myself, she was preparing to share her story for the night. She sat next to me and gently, but firmly, grasped my hands between hers. She looked me straight in the eyes and brushed a piece of hair out of my face.

"She seemed to struggle to find her words as she sat staring into my eyes. Finally, she said, 'Bonita Nieta, this story I'm about to tell you is special. I have seen what is to come of this world. When everything seems dark, when the flame of hope is flickering, this is the story our people will need. Listen carefully and remember it often, mi amor.'"

Nan paused and gestured for water. Javie brought her a glass while her audience waited patiently. Rae leaned over and whispered to Luc, "Has Abuela talked about her grandmother before?"

"Only in snippets. She always looked pained if we asked about her, so Javie and I stopped asking. She's never told this story before."

"Ladies, ladies, the Wise One speaks again." Damien chided. Luc shrugged her shoulders as both young women turned back to the colored wagon.

Nan gathered her thoughts. "I am going to share this origin story with you. Many of us don't know where we came from or how we got here. This story inspired me as a young girl and I hope it inspires you as well. We will get through these dark times. Just like our ancestors before us." The old woman shifted forward in her seat and began.

"A long, long time ago before people spread across the land, wilderness reigned. The world was a wild, wild place where only the strong survived. Deer grazed in the fields, salmon swam in the streams, and eagles soared in the sky. Bears and wolf packs roamed while vegetation grew without bounds.

"In this world, people were the visitors. They had no roots or influence on the environment they inhabited.

"One tribe was traveling through a valley when they encountered a pair of wolves. The two parties studied each other carefully before going their separate ways. As the tribe moved through the valley, they hunted the deer, fished for the salmon, and gathered berries, but never stopped moving.

"Slowly but surely, small groups broke off as they were seduced by the idea of a home, at the idea of not living on the road, and just being. What they didn't know was how dangerous stopping in the wild could be. Just as slowly as they had left, their fires sputtered out."

Nan paused for effect as her Abuela had done. She let the story weave its magic and entrance her audience. Javie offered her a glass of water, but she shook her head and continued.

"I know what you're thinking, dear ones, the wolves had to be the ones that did it. Oh, but that would be too easy.

"Wolves have been the villains for so long that we've forgotten how misunderstood they are. That they have families to feed and a community to nurture. They hunt to survive, not because they enjoy killing. We are more like them when we pause to think. Our story is more compelling than blaming it on them.

"When these small groups left the main tribe, they were smart. They took supplies to sustain them for a few days, along with the equipment needed to build a new life. Things like tents, blankets, knives, baskets, and much more. No, they weren't lacking in anything material. They were devoid of knowledge, of skills, and, most importantly, *magic*."

Nan spread her hands wide, sending drops of the tonic concealed in her hand to the ground below. Flowers sprang up in the grass surrounding the children in the front row.

The crowd gasped as the children squealed in delight and clapped their hands. Soon enough, the ever-fidgeting young ones started picking the beautiful blooms for crowns and chains. The rest of the crowd recovered from the shocking display of magic, miles from a city besieged with soldiers.

"She always had a flair for the dramatic." Luc stretched her legs out in front of her. "When we were kids, Javie and I would beg her to use her tonics. No matter how many times she did the same display, we were stunned and delighted. Every time she would laugh with sparkling eyes and just do it again." Luc picked at her sleeve before continuing. "I can't believe she would do that so nonchalantly. It's not safe."

"She's doing it for us. This is her way of revolting against the militia. Only Abuela could be this positive when our last haven has been taken." Rae said.

"Absolutely. That woman has a reason for everything." Zeke crouched down to where the girls were sitting. "She's just as devastated as we are. Most likely more so since she's watched city after city become unsafe." Damien nodded his head in agreement but kept his gaze on the old storyteller.

"I think the Wise One is about to continue." Damien's eyes never left the colorful wagon, deep in thought about what the old woman was doing. The other three quieted and brought their gaze to the front of the crowd. Javie could be seen trying to quiet and herd the children back to their spots.

On the back of the wagon, Nan continued. "Now where was I?" Nan looked down at the barely settled children. "Oh yes, that's right, magic." Her eyes danced as the kiddos squealed with glee. "Now, now, my dear ones, listen closely to the rest of this tale. We can all find something to hold on to if we listen."

And just like that, even the babies and young children quieted themselves. Everybody wanted to hear the rest of Abuela's story.

"You see these small groups that broke off were part of the fringes of the tribe. They didn't understand how their leaders kept them safe. There were four entrusted to lead the tribe, their names lost to the sounds of time. Our ancestors gave them false ones long ago to honor and remember the four brave, young people that led our ancestors through this strange new land. These are the names I will use tonight.

"We begin with Malachi. He'd learned from an early age he could coax plants and herbs to grow taller and ripen faster. Green things were drawn to him; when he walked in the forest, vines reached for him and flowers bloomed in his wake. He could read the healing properties of each plant with a single touch. You've probably guessed already, but from his bloodline came the Herbalists.

"The second leader liked to work with her hands. Salma could take one look at something and realize its potential. From cloth to rocks to animal hides, anything physical could be manipulated by the wiry young woman. A touch here, a pull there, and sure enough, she had created something magnificent again. These clothes, those wagons, our tents, and so many other things can be attributed to the first Forger.

"The third leader was hard to find most of the time. One minute Ezra was there and the next he was gone again. Most of his time was spent pulling a wagon. His affinity was for animals and he could take the form of anything he'd seen before."

Gasps and grumbling could be heard among the people gathered. These ancestors were more powerful than any of those gathered. Herbalists were divided into Growers and Healers, the prior coaxing plants to flourish while the latter could create tonics for certain ailments using the innate properties of different plants. Forgers and Shifters specialized in only one material or form. The idea of infinite options was foreign to the members of the Circus.

The people were filled with dread at the suggestion that the magic running through their veins wasn't as potent as it once was. Why had their power dwindled?

"Yes, yes, surprising I know. Let me finish." Nan waited for her people to quiet and nod their acquiescence. "Like the other three, he believed in serving his people first and foremost. That was why he offered to pull a wagon and give the oxen and draft horses a break. It was also a convenient way to listen to the frank conversations of other tribe members. His example is what still inspires our Shifters today."

Nan nodded respectfully towards where many of the Shifters had gathered. It was always hard to find the elusive Magicae that could so easily slip into the wild and never return. So many were killed as babes because of their "demon eyes" that gave a hint of the wild contained within. Having so many in the troupe was a blessing, especially for what was waiting in Heimat.

"The fourth leader and final ancestor was beauty and power in the flesh. Even her skin glowed with the elemental power running through her veins. She could control not one element, but all four. This was Yana. She was the one the other three leaders deferred to and the one you've probably heard of before. Yana is the one we still tell stories about, Yana is the one that brought magic across the land, and it was Yana that sacrificed so much for our people.

"My dear ones, you've never heard this part of her story. This was before the

Great Drought, before the Prophecy, before everything. In this part of her story, Yana was young, barely past womanhood, but she was a leader.

"She was brave and bold, and headstrong, but more than anything, she had heart.

"She was one of those individuals that genuinely listened when others talked. Yana always thought about what she wanted to say and how she wanted to say it. She was taught from an early age that actions spoke louder than words. She grew up watching her father conserve his words to make them more powerful.

"Her parents begged her not to leave on this expedition, but she was tired of living in the shadow of their accomplishments. She was young but ready to become the leader she knew she could be. When she volunteered to lead the expedition to the new land, her parents had no choice but to support their determined daughter."

Nan stopped to take a breath. She felt a little lightheaded but brushed it off as hunger. She skipped the midday meal while they had been on the road. She took one more deep breath, in through the nose, and exhaled, letting the exhausted air seep through her mouth. The story would flood from this point forward, she wouldn't have time to stop once she started.

Pursing her lips, she continued, "Let's get back to those that kept leaving the group. Nobody was privy to their leaders' abilities and what they provided for the tribe. The four leaders and their types of magic worked seamlessly together. Malachi, the Herbalist, kept everybody fed and healthy while always finding a safe place to rest in the forest. Salma, the Forger, fashioned supplies and weapons from their raw materials and the ones they found along the way. She was also the best mechanic on this side of the Mantaga River. Her motto was anything broken could be mended." Nan surveyed the crowd to let them absorb the words that clenched her heart.

Anything broken can be mended. Huntress, let that be true. Nan thought to herself before she continued.

"Ezra, the Shifter, reminded the others what servant leadership looked like. He emphasized they base their success on the most vulnerable of their tribe. His presence made sure the young and the old were considered in every decision. Their pace, their rations, their supplies, and where they stopped each night. He made sure everyone was taken care of.

"Yana, the Crafter, was the spokesperson for the group. She relayed their decisions and information to their people. She used all four of the elements under her control to help her tribe. She found water to drink, created fire to heat, blew a breeze to cool, and eventually, broke the earth for planting. Her extensive power was the biggest reason why she was tasked with exploring this new land.

"My dear ones, these wanderers enjoyed this wonderful new world. Even with the strange plants and sometimes treacherous terrain, this tribe had *life*.

"They traveled across this wild, wild country and the four young leaders stressed community over individuals. A chain is only as strong as its weakest link after all.

"However, not all shared this mentality. It was why small bands started leaving. They didn't want to continue at the reduced pace or share their rations. They were sick of listening to the same stories told by the elders and the whining of the young ones.

"They grew restless and left the group, planting seeds of doubt within their inexperienced leaders. The four knew they were stronger together but needed to find a way to prove that to their people. They met by moonlight to discuss tribe morale.

"'We need a new plan. Three more left last night. Our people are dying out there.' Salma blew her hair out of her face as she sat on a stump. She looked towards Ezra and asked, 'Have you heard anything, my friend?'

"The other two looked towards the tall wisp of a man with cat eyes. 'I've only heard the usual grumblings. We're going too slow, why can't we stop and settle down, why are we following a bunch of kids?'

"Yana winced. She knew they were young but her hands were tied. How could they make their people believe in them when they had to stay hidden? Before she could voice her thoughts, there was a rustling in the thick underbrush behind them.

"The four exchanged glances and Yana nodded towards Malachi. He stretched out his arm and took a step closer to where the rustling had come from. The Herbalist widened his stance as he furrowed his brows and gazed into the leafy array. As he concentrated, branches and foliage began to disperse. While Malachi cleared a path the other three spoke in hushed tones.

"'Does anybody see anything?' Salma bit her lip and bounced on her heels.

"'Calm down. I'm sure it was just a deer.' Yana squeezed the Forger's shoulder and looked at the Shifter. 'Can you sense anything?'

"Ezra closed his eyes and gritted his teeth. He could sense something, but it was unlike anything he'd encountered before. Ask any Shifter and they can tell you animals always evoke certain emotions that could be identified. Birds evoked freedom as they left the ground, wolves evoked a sense of family, and squirrels caused panic as they scoured the ground for food before winter.

"People on the other hand were much harder to read. They were a patchwork of dreams, emotions, fears, and desires. They constantly changed, making their auras hard to distinguish, even for one as powerful as the first Shifter. He pressed his hand to his temple and shushed the murmurs of the others.

"'I can sense something…but it's strange.' He opened his eyes and stared into the now silent forest. 'It's like an onslaught of intense emotion that changes faster than I can comprehend. I am left with the aftertaste of an emotion before I realize it switched in the first place.' He groaned as he put his head in his hands.

"Malachi turned back towards the others and gazed at his distressed friend.

"'I feel something too. These trees, it's almost like they're resisting me, as if they listen to the call of someone else.' He trailed off as he leaned down and touched a protruding tree root. The Herbalist felt not only the tall, mighty oak but the song it sang.

"Animals evoked emotions but plants could sing." Nan's eyes met Javie's. When he was younger, that's how he always described the plants he came in contact with. Javie was a Grower that mostly ignored the power in his veins. But that was a story for another time. Nan looked back to the crowd and continued.

"Just being in the wilderness, Malachi heard symphonies. Each vine and flower and blade of grass comprised a unique melody. Each shrub and herb and young tree had a different tune.

"The Herbalist heard it all.

"Touching the root helped him hone in on the oak's rich, buttery tone. It felt like a mighty drumbeat, pounding strong and true. Mixed with a deep bass, its song reverberated with power.

"As Malachi listened, the song changed. It moved from a heartbeat to one of longing. He listened to the haunting, beautiful tune and slowly expanded his consciousness to the other plants. Curiously, he noticed that sense of longing in every song he heard.

"Plants? Longing for something? No. He knew they were longing for some-*one*. Someone with greater power than his."

Nan noticed the tightness in many of her people's faces. The elder Herbalists in the group knew what was coming, they knew what people this story referenced.

Nan continued, "'I think we should move out. Someone is coming.' The Herbalist murmured.

"Ezra's head shot up as the rustling in the trees resumed. 'It's too late for that.'

"The four sprang into action as the rustling got louder. Malachi drew his bow, and Salma dropped into a fighting stance, drawing two throwing knives. Yana pulled her sword from its sheath and lit its edge on fire. Ezra dropped to all fours and took the shape of a black panther. They made a formidable force as the lithe figure finally appeared from the trees.

"'Young ones, relax.' A middle-aged woman walked towards them with her arms raised. 'You are welcome here. Lower your weapons so we can talk. Your people are in danger.' She was dressed in mottled colors that matched the forest behind her. Her leather shoes moved silently across the grassy terrain of the forest and her face had the lines that came with easy smiles, and much laughter. Her eyes were kind as she regarded the four Magicae.

"Yana and the others exchanged glances. They had never seen a woman quite like her. Something was off. But she spoke a truth none of them could deny. With a shared nod, they lowered their weapons.

"Ezra stayed in his panther form and slinked closer to this strange being. This indeed was what he'd sensed in the woods. He drank in her scent as he moved closer, forgetting where he was. She smelled of the forest and fresh rain, smoke from a fire, and the sweat after a hard day's work. His heart pounded as he closed his bright green eyes and tried to read all the emotions being thrown at him.

"'You're the one the plants sing for, the one they long for.' Malachi cocked his head to the sound of the greenery.

"The woman lowered her hands and clasped them behind her back. She turned her gaze from the panther and rested it on the dark-skinned healer. With a gleam in her eye, she smirked. 'Aye, and they'll keep longing if they know what's good for them.'

"The Herbalist widened his eyes. 'But why? What do they want?'

"She gave a small smile and knelt beside the oak's root. She motioned for him to join her, and pressed his hand with hers to the root.

"Yana exchanged a glance with Salma. The Forger shrugged her shoulders; answers would take time it seemed.

"'What do you hear? What do you see?' The woman's eyes searched his face for signs of understanding. Keeping one of his hands on the root, she grabbed his other one and placed it over his heart. 'Use this to see, to hear. Reach down deep. What does the tree seek?'

"Malachi stared at where their hands met the tree root. This strange woman made no sense. How could his heart see what his eyes and ears failed to show him? A glance at the woman had her giving an encouraging nod.

"He closed his eyes and pictured the mighty oak in his head. As he concentrated, the rhythm of his heartbeat matched the pounding of the tree's drumbeat. Malachi's eyelids flew open in shock seeking the comforting, experienced gaze of the older woman.

"'Ah, there, you felt it.' The woman's lips lifted into a coy smile.

"'But what does it mean? The drumbeat quieted once my heartbeat matched it.' He wrenched his gaze from the woman and turned towards Yana and Salma. 'The plants never stop singing. The music never fades.' He shook his head and pulled his hand from the tree.

"The woman quickly grabbed his wrist and shoved it back towards the root. 'Think. You told me their song yearned for me. Why?' She said with a voice like iron. She held her other hand out towards the quietly growling Shifter. 'Down Kitty. He can find the answer. You all can. You just need a push in the right direction.'

"'I got it.'

"Everybody looked towards their friend as he slowly disentangled his wrist and helped the woman stand. They waited expectantly for him to continue.

"'They yearn for connection.' He rolled his shoulders and continued, 'I never thought about the loneliness associated with standing still. This tree has been waiting for someone or something to recognize its worth.' His face lit up with excitement. 'This part of the forest has been recognized before, hasn't it?'

"The woman clapped her hands in delight. 'Aye, it has. Part of my duty is to check in with my quadrant of the forest. To connect with the trees and grasses and search for any sickness.' She swiped at the strands of hair that came loose from their tie. 'When they sense my presence, they tend to forget themselves.'

"'I've never connected like that before. Plants have always heeded my presence and responded to my touch but that was...extraordinary.' His eyes drifted to the tree in awe. 'I can still feel it.'"

Chiara's green eyes filled with sadness as she listened to Nan's tale. As Head Herbalist, it was her duty to keep track of the Herbalists, Growers and Healers, and their education in using their Gifts. Only a few Herbalists could hear the singing of the plants these days. The power within was indeed weaker.

The question was whether they would survive long enough to get the answers they sought. She gave her attention back to the old storyteller.

"Ezra finally decided to shed his panther form. He rose to a standing position and clutched at his head. 'What are you? You're giving me a headache.'

"Yana and Salma exchanged worried glances.

"'Maybe you should sit down?'

"Ezra shook off Salma's hand. He winced before turning towards the woman expectantly.

"'Ah, may I?' She spread her hands, palm up, and waited for the Shifter's nod before moving closer. Mumbling, she drew gentle symbols on each of his eyelids with her thumb. 'You have the Sight then, don't you?'

"Ezra slowly opened his eyes to search the woman for meaning. 'The Sight?'

"'You can sense the feelings and movements of living things. My kind is difficult to comprehend, no?'

"'Your kind? What do you mean by that?' Yana's voice wavered.

"'Well, there's no use in denying it. All four of you have been studying me since I made myself known. My people live among the trees. We believe in being connected, with each other, with the plants, and with the animals whom we share this earth with. We call ourselves Skovnisser; you may know us by another name though.'

"Something clicked in Yana's mind.

"'My parents led an expedition here long ago. They mentioned your people. I think they referred to you as the Elven.' Yana studied the short, fine-boned, older woman. She had high, angled cheekbones and toned muscles that rippled as she moved. She leaned lightly on a wooden staff covered in strange symbols she had grabbed from the forest floor. Her copper-colored skin shone in the lamplight, providing a stark contrast to her raven-colored hair. This woman had the confidence of an adventurer that had faced many dangers head-on. Her head cocked to the side as she met Yana's probing stare.

"'Aye, those visitors were here years ago. The more I think about it, I think I remember your Ma. She was strung taut, just like my bow. Just like her daughter.' Her lips curled up into a knowing smirk. 'All four of you seem that way.' Her almond-shaped eyes narrowed and her brows pinched together. She sighed as understanding flashed in her gaze. 'You're all so young. Yet so powerful. Your people are leaving. Why? What do they know of your sjel evner?'

"Yana's brows shot up. 'You mean our magic? No one knows what we can do.' She rubbed a hand through her hair.

"Salma's demeanor visibly changed. Her muscles tensed as she curled her hands slowly into fists. Her lips pursed together and she muttered under her breath. The Elven woman noted this reaction and shared a pointed look with Yana.

"'Your friend does not approve.' She mused.

"'Of course not! These people are supposed to be trusting us and we are lying to them.' The Forger's jaw clenched hard as she gritted her teeth.

"'I've told you so many times. We are not lying to them. We're just—'

"'Yana. Stop. Omitting the truth is worse than lying.' Salma's cheeks flushed with passion as she paced the forest floor. 'They will never trust us if they find out about our magic. Our lies are already pushing our people apart. We need to come clean before we lose more.'

"Yana took a figurative step back in her head. She knew her friend always spoke her mind and truly loved their tribe. Her anger was laced with an edge of fear, the same fear weighing on Yana's mind.

"Her gaze slid towards the men. They looked on as Salma paced, their expressions conflicted. Yana knew this weighed on them too. It was a burden they all carried. Yana had to decide whether telling their people was worth risking the uproar it could cause."

Nan needed some water.

She looked towards the side of her wagon and saw Javie gesturing to the table beside her. Looking at it, she realized her grandson already had one waiting for her. She reached towards the glass and paused. There was a peculiar tingling sensation beginning in her fingers. She pulled her hand back and gave it a quick shake.

The joys of getting older, she thought to herself and reached for the water again.

A sharp pain flared through her arm.

Nan cried out and fell forward as the world spun.

She heard a loud *crack* and everything went dark.

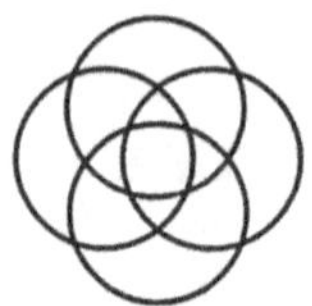

Chapter Nineteen

"For the last time, Simone, we're positive that woman was the Golden Eagle from the Circus. We followed protocol and so did she. The reports came back, and they've bedded down just hours from town. They should be all set up by tomorrow night. That means we only have one day to prep for three nights of shows," Rich said through gritted teeth.

Simone looked like she was about to argue again, but George stood up and spoke.

"We're all nervous. We've never had to evacuate our people like this before. This is unfamiliar territory for us and for the Circus. This is their home too, and I bet they're reeling just as much as we are.

"You know we had to warn them; our esteemed mayor would have arrested them on the spot. We have to trust each other and the Circus performers. Our friends, our family, and our children are counting on us." George asserted, looking into the faces of those standing in the basement of Rich's bakery.

The community leaders had gathered to discuss the evacuation of their people, despite it being past curfew. Rich had called the meeting after he and George encountered Rae, known as the Golden Eagle by the townspeople. They risked a lot in meeting after curfew but had to make sure everything went according to plan to get as many people out of Heimat as possible.

It was tough enough concealing the Magicae of Heimat for the few months since the new mayor came to town. The country of Kamore had been under militant rule for almost two decades, but the city of Heimat avoided infiltration until three months prior when Myra finally sent Darren Vincenzio to "civilize the north."

For years, community leaders were preparing for this, however, now that the time was upon them, many were still in denial. They refused to believe their haven was no longer secure. Simone was by far the most vocal, but nods could be seen among the others as she made her points.

"George, I hear you, but we need to make sure everything goes exactly right. We have a lot of people to move with a lot that could go wrong." Simone concluded.

"Absolutely, let's go over the plan one more time," Rich said quickly before George could make a sarcastic reply. "The Circus will get in tomorrow morning, set up, and put on their first show tomorrow night. Usually, they put on five nights of performances, but this time, there will only be three.

"Our first priority must be the children. All of them will join the Circus, along with one adult for every five children. Crafters and Shifters get first dibs on account of their marks. The same goes for Herbalists with face or hand marks. Forgers, just be careful not to get a scratch."

Rich took a drink of water and continued, "George will be stationed at the Circus itself, overseeing the accumulation of our people and subsequent transport to safety. He will only return once Heimat is safe again."

His eyes turned to the tall lanky man, leaning against a beam in the basement. Rich's features softened as he replayed their conversation before this meeting.

"Rich, you can't go. You're a figurehead in this town. Vincenzio will notice your disappearance in a heartbeat and it's much safer for me to go. The girls need you here. Just promise to check in on my Ma now and again."

Rich had argued with the younger man, to no avail. George wouldn't budge on taking the position at the Circus. The two of them held official positions as liaisons to the Circus, and part of their contracts was that one of them would go with their people should Heimat become compromised. The Magicae and Mortals in Heimat wanted the reassurance their children would be safe and trusted the two men unequivocally.

George was giving up everything he'd ever known for the good of their community.

Mikel, one of the older leaders, clapped George on the back, while the others shot him appreciative glances. Only Tommy and Reg seemed unenthusiastic about the man leaving.

Rich inclined his head to the brave man, his eyes filled with gratitude. "The city has been divided into seven sectors; each of you is in charge of one of them. Simone has the Lower District, Eddy has the Wharf, Tamara has Artist's Row, Reginald has the Barracks–"

"Make sure you're careful, Reg. I can help if need be; the mayor is in your sector, so be smart," George interrupted to address his childhood friend.

"Yep. I will take yer help a course, Georgie. I know the Barracks like the back-a-me hand, but that mayor is a wily one. Better safe than sorry, I say." Agreed Reg, one of the younger community leaders of the group, and George's closest friend.

"Right. Continuing on, Johanna has the Fringe, Mikel has Upper District, and Tommy has the Northern River District." Rich redirected the group. "As leaders, you have volunteered to stay behind and help shepherd any remaining or future Magicae. We appreciate and honor your sacrifice and service."

Rich stopped and met the gaze of each individual. They were an eclectic group of all ages and backgrounds, yet they were united in their purpose: defy the mayor and protect their people. Their demeanors belayed their nerves, but their eyes showed only determination.

This was a cause worth fighting for.

Each acknowledged the recognition, some with a nod, others a smile, a wink from Tamara, and a fist pump from Reg. Rich continued, "Make sure everyone knows they need to be there on the correct night. We are trying to be as subtle as possible by staggering the intake of our people. George will run through details with the Ringmaster and grab numbers from each of you before your assigned night. The Fringe and Lower District sectors are up first. Johanna and Simone, make sure your people are ready by tomorrow night." Rich finished, looking the two women in the eyes.

"We'll be ready. Come on Jo, let's get started," Simone said. She grabbed Johanna's arm and almost dragged her up the stairs.

"Yeah, I guess we'll be going then!" Johanna half yelled down the stairs as everybody chuckled. "Good luck everyone, we got this. Once they're all out, the mayor is going to wish he never took this position." She stated forcefully, making her way up the rest of the stairs.

The two headed out of the bakery, being careful to keep to the shadows. The last thing they needed was to be caught after dark.

"We're trying to space the sectors out to rouse the least amount of suspicion. We don't want anybody noticing the kids are gone until it's too late and they've been saved. Our people will do what they can to shield us from suspicion, but it's always better to be safe, rather than sorry." Rich shuffled his papers as he composed himself, thinking about all those kids being sent away from their families.

Waves of emotion crashed over the older man as he thought of his young granddaughters. He would do anything for those two little firecrackers.

George put a hand on Rich's shoulder, recognizing the older man's far-off look. "The second night of performances, Tommy and Eddy, you're up. Have those kids ready to go."

"We'll make a game of it, won't we, lad? Give those kiddies something to keep 'em occupied." Eddy looked at George and Rich. "Do you know if them Circus rebels need a getaway boat?" He straightened his shoulders with a wicked gleam in his eyes. "I know some solid guys and gals that could wait on the Mantaga. They're discreet. And more importantly, raging about the new dock taxes that went into effect last week."

"Rich and I will get back to you on that. We have a general idea of their rescue protocol but don't know how open they are to modifications. Excellent suggestion, though, Eddy." George nodded at the Wharfman before looking at his older, more colorful counterpart.

Rich scratched the back of his neck, straightened his patchwork coat, and clasped Eddy's shoulder.

"We'll keep you in the loop, old friend. Tell your guys and gals to be ready. We'll get word to you by tomorrow night."

"Thanks, Rich, George. We couldn't do this without you. Our people will be ready." Eddy gave a nod and headed to the stairs.

Tommy stepped towards George and embraced his brother before shaking Rich's hand. "We won't let you down. See you on the flip side, brother." He turned to follow Eddy up the stairs to exit the bakery basement.

"Oi, and Tommy? Say hi to Sara and the kids for me."

"Say hi to them yourself, you lazy bastard."

"I don't think I'll have time. I'm stopping by to see Ma tomorrow, and then I'll be at the Circus. This will be the last time I see you."

"I'll bring Sara and the kids to Ma's tomorrow. This won't be goodbye yet." Tommy crossed his arms, jaw set, daring his older brother to argue.

George recognized the denial and defiance in Tommy's eyes for what it was. He grabbed his brother by the shoulder and squeezed. "I'll see you at Ma's tomorrow."

Tommy nodded and made his way up the stairs after the Wharfman.

George wrenched his eyes from his brother's retreating figure. Leaving the only place he had ever known left a bitter taste in his mouth.

His gaze traveled to the bare, chilling walls of the basement. His mind wandered as he took a moment to compose himself. Growing up between the Fringe and the Barracks hadn't been easy, but having Tommy and his Ma to look after gave him a sense of purpose. It filled him with dread to not be around for weeks, months, or even years. Knowing they'd be taken care of was the only reason he'd agreed to go. Thinking about them too much made him question everything he was doing.

"We'll take care a'them, mate." Reg put his arm over his best friend's shoulder. Reg had grown up an orphan until meeting George. George's mom practically took the scruffy, hungry seven-year-old in as a third son when she found George sneaking him food.

"Thanks, Reg. I'd never forgive myself if something were to happen to them while I'm gone." George gripped Reg's forearm, shifting his stance to look him in the eyes. "I know you and Tommy are fully capable, and I trust you to take care of them. You'll stop by Ma's tomorrow?"

"T'wouldn't miss it. Let's finish this so we can grab a pint and I can best your arse in cards one more time."

The two turned back to the group to finish planning for the next few days, and to keep planning for the changes to come.

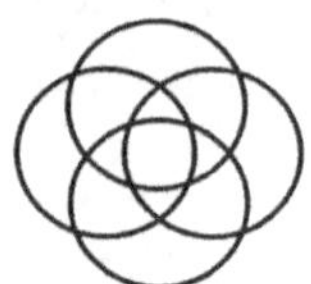

Chapter Twenty

"*D*uncan, just go. It's me they want. Myra whipped these people into a frenzy about my daughter, not yours."

Andre tried to push his friend towards the town hall.

"I'm not leaving you. Until the end, remember?"

Andre just shook his head. "Until the end..." He reached into his pocket and took out a letter. "You are my oldest and dearest friend. My true brother. I need you now more than ever."

"Dre—"

"Stop. We both know this won't end until my daughter is dead. Help me make sure that doesn't happen. Give this to her when she needs it most."

Andre handed him the letter and pulled him into a one-armed hug.

"Now go. Get them out. Please, Dunc. This is my fault. Let me pay the consequences."

"Andre, no. I am not leaving you here with this mob. We can get out of here together." Duncan gripped his friend's forearm.

Andre extricated himself from his friend's grip. "Duncan. I know we can get out of this, but my children can't. Naomi can't. The staff can't. Not without you. Let me distract the mob and you go save our people. They need you."

Duncan stared long and hard into his friend's eyes before nodding, accepting the weight on his shoulders.

Duncan woke with a start. Dreaming of the last time he saw his best friend was the nightmare that never ended. He lay on his cot, rubbing his face to try to wipe the memories and shame away. Duncan knew his efforts were in vain. The only way to chase that night from his head was to get up and face the day.

Sighing, he sat up and swung his legs over the side of the low-hanging bed. He groggily dressed into his Ringmaster garb. After putting on his breeches and long-tailed tunic, he sat down to put his weathered boots on. Once that was done, he shifted forward to lean his elbows on his knees and hang his head in his hands. He took a moment to reflect on that fateful night.

Duncan had made many mistakes in his life. However, that night was the biggest. He left his friend for dead and never made it to save Andre's family. He got all the staff out of the town hall but was too late to save Naomi and the children.

Helene ended up giving her life to get Rae out of the city before the mob found her. Naomi, Rae's mother, and the baby she carried never made it out. Andre was publicly executed, but nothing was ever concluded about Naomi's fate. Duncan could only assume she and the babe never made it. Luck brought a young Rae to the Circus, but it was weeks before Duncan recognized her for who she was. Many people in the Circus, especially its newer members, were unaware of Rae's origins.

Duncan knew dwelling on the past was not productive. The only way to make up for his mistakes was to keep pressing on and saving all the Magicae he could. It was the only way to atone for failing his friend.

With that thought, he stood up and made his way out of the tent.

Duncan took a deep breath of crisp fall air and headed towards the coffee wagon. In the darkness before dawn, Duncan started when he found he was not the only one driven to wakefulness.

"Couldn't sleep again?" The Head Herbalist with green eyes said while she started a fire to get the coffee going for the day.

"Aye, ya got me there, Chiara. And yourself?"

Chiara's eyes filled with emotion as she studied the tall, serious-looking man.

She hesitated, taking in Duncan's open expression before shaking her head. "Just the shadows of the past making themselves known. Yourself?"

Duncan's purple eyes found hers, rippling with understanding and pain. Chiara wasn't the kind to burden others with her problems. "Same. Why do they always come knocking before the sun?"

Chiara laughed. "So inconsiderate. At least wait until dawn to remind me of all my failings." She leaned forward and squeezed his forearm. "Do you want to talk about it?"

Duncan studied the dark-skinned woman. He sighed and gently pulled his arm away from the Head Herbalist. "I can't Chiara. You know that."

"Why not? It might help to talk about it. You would be surprised by who understands the pain you are dealing with," Chiara challenged.

"Not now, though. We need to get through the next couple of nights before I can even think straight again. Heimat means so much to our people; they need me to lead them through this."

"Duncan, your guilt is written all over your face. You need to work through it instead of burying it. I'm worried about you." Chiara stepped closer to Duncan, touching his cheek to get him to meet her gaze.

His eyes found hers and he knew he couldn't avoid this anymore. Chiara was the one person in the Circus he couldn't hide from.

"You need to fill your cup before you can fill the cups of others. Let me help."

"Chiara, I can't. Not right now. Dawn is almost upon us. Please. I'll come to your tent after tonight's performance. We can talk then." Duncan grabbed Chiara's hands and cradled them. "I promise."

"Dunc—"

The pair turned towards the configuration of tents that housed most of the people of the Circus. They could hear a pair talking and making their way to the coffee wagon. With a glance, Duncan dropped Chiara's hands as she turned to hide the flush creeping up her neck and into her cheeks.

"Aw hell yea! Come on Luc, I think the coffee is on already. Let's grab some before the other two can guilt us into bringing some for them." A good night's rest added brightness to the fire Crafter's tone. The past few weeks had been taxing, but choosing to focus on the positives was a testament to her spirit. She almost ran into Duncan while looking back at her friend. "Whoa! Didn't see you there Dunc. Oh, and Ms. Rutter, my apologies to you both." Rae furrowed her brows. "Are we interrupting something?"

Duncan and Chiara shared a look. "Of course not, dear. We couldn't sleep, so we thought we'd get an early start on the coffee." Chiara patted the young woman's arm and shook her head. "And I thought I told you to call me Chiara. I'll let Damien know you two will bring him a coffee." She winked and filled her mug before making her way back to the tent she shared with her grown son.

"Are you kidding me? Why didn't she grab him a mug? This is uncalled for." Rae grumbled.

"Settle down, Rae. She was only joking. Ms. Rutter would never. She's always complaining about how spoiled Damien is. She's going to make him get his own, you watch." Luc said with a yawn. "Morning, Duncan. Ready for tonight?"

"Once I finish this coffee, I will be. Can I trust you two to keep brewing while I go check on Abuela? She was sleeping when I checked last night, but I thought I would stop in again. Then I need to figure out where the big top will be going."

"Absolutely!" The women chorused as he turned towards the big top.

Luc added, "Abuela hit her head pretty hard, but Javie and I were able to scrape together some tonics with Chiara's help. They brought the swelling down, but we still don't know what happened. She gained consciousness a little after midnight. We got her to drink some tea and chew on some ginger root. She descended into sleep soon after."

The young woman had bags under her eyes but flashed a genuine smile. Everybody was concerned about the caravan's eldest member, but her relative stability meant they could continue with preparations for that night's show.

Duncan gripped her shoulder as he made his way towards the fortune teller's wagon.

The Circus woke slowly on the outskirts of Heimat. The buzz that usually accompanied their arrival in the northern city was all but gone. Its members dragged themselves out of bed, not ready to face the reality that they needed to prep for new recruits yet again.

Unvoiced questions hung in the air like smoke.

The biggest one being, where would they go after Heimat? They usually spent the winter months here before traveling the coast come springtime. There was nowhere further north they could travel.

Duncan felt the stares and heard the whispers as he walked towards Nan's wagon. Sweat dripped down his sides despite the chill in the air.

His family had questions he didn't have the answers to. They would expect him to speak at breakfast, but he had little solace to offer them. Duncan hated not having a plan but needed to make it through the next three nights before figuring out where they would go. The Council Meeting was postponed because of Nan's accident, but their people would demand reassurance, regardless.

Nan would be their greatest asset in figuring that out. She grew up traveling the country with her Abuela and knew Kamore better than anyone he'd ever met. The caravan depended on her for more than just stories.

She was the living history book of their land and its people.

Duncan made it to the wagon without talking to anyone. He had nodded and waved at people, but resisted his usual inclination to exchange small talk. He greeted Luc's brother as he approached.

"Hey, Javie. Anything new to report?"

"Nothing new, Dunc. Abuela is still sleeping." Javie said from the front seat of the wagon. He yawned. "She's a tough old bird, though. Not her time to go, as she'd say. Did you need anything else?"

Duncan chuckled softly. "She's as tough as they come, that's for sure. Tell her she must have deserved a break." Duncan clasped the young man by the forearm. "You let me know if you need anything. Have you had enough people to cover shifts?"

"Yea. Luc and her crew have it taken care of. All the kids made get-well cards and Betsy even said she'd bring us breakfast. Never thought I'd see the day when I'd get breakfast in bed." Javie rubbed his chin.

"She'll be okay, kid." Duncan studied Javie closely. He noticed dark circles under the young man's eyes and a tense set to his shoulders. At heart, Javie was just a grandson worried about his grandmother. Duncan was proud of their people for supporting Nan and those closest to her.

"You don't know that, Dunc. Nothing makes her different from Rocky or Jason or the other ones we lost." Javie looked to the horizon. His voice wavered, and he clenched his fists. "I don't know what I'd do without her."

"We'd all be lost, me included. But she's stable right now, correct?" Duncan waited for Javie to nod. "That's all that matters. Let's just take it day by day." He shook Javie's shoulder.

"That's all we can do." Javie sighed. "I'll let you know if anything changes. I should go in and see if she needs anything."

"Thanks, Javie. I'll be back later to check in on her and you."

Javie nodded and ducked into his grandmother's wagon. Duncan took a last look at the colorful home on wheels, then walked towards the horse line. He mounted his dark bay mare and headed towards the place where they'd set up their big top in the past.

He let his horse run, noting the terrain they traversed. In years prior, the first snow had already fallen, making arrival harder with the wagons.

At least we won't have to deal with snow. Duncan thought with a mocking smile.

He finally made it to the part of the field where they set up last year. He dismounted and scanned the ground before nodding to himself. Bending down, he felt the ground and ran some of the dirt through his hand. This spot would do again; few rocks, pretty flat, and solid ground. Perfect for the many visitors they would welcome once the sun went down.

Tonight would be pivotal in getting many of the children out of what was once a haven for the Magicae. Duncan needed to make sure his Circus was ready. Tonight would set the tone for the next three nights. They needed to get it right.

Duncan gazed back the way he came, to where his people camped. He sighed and hung his head. *Damn it. I knew this would happen.* He shook his head, trying to clear his mind.

He needed to figure out what he was going to say to his people. He needed to find the words that would reassure and inspire. Duncan didn't know where they would go after this, but he knew the time had come for them to strategize their next move.

He lifted his chin and went to his mare. It was time to pack up and mobilize for their people.

The sun was high in the sky by the time the big top was set up again. Duncan had done his job and gotten the city of nomads to pack quickly and make it to the field on the northern side of Heimat. Set-up happened swiftly and run-throughs were beginning.

Rae wiped her brow and focused on her hands within the shadows of the large tent. They were soon bathed in flames. She glanced around and turned her back to the entrance.

She stared once more into the flames and willed herself to dig deep. *Come on.* She furrowed her brows and flexed her fingers. After a couple of minutes, she let out a frustrated cry. *This is ridiculous. Even a child can recognize their limits.* Rae extinguished her flames and left the big top in a whirl.

She needed to speak to Zalia. There was no way it would be safe for her to perform and control the lanterns. Rae needed to swallow her pride and ask for help from her former teacher.

Luckily, there were a lot fewer light changes in their regular shows compared to the burlesque show. Zalia could handle it, but she'd use it to needle Rae later.

Tyee watched the fire Crafter leave the center ring. He heard her frustrated cry and saw her risking the flames in her hands before marching off.

The two had spoken little since the night after their disastrous performance.

Tyee was grateful Duncan had no intention of performing the burlesque show in Heimat. When Rae brought word back that they needed to evacuate the city, Duncan and the Council decided to model their shows after the family ones they had been performing across the country.

This made it easy for the caravan to fall into a familiar rhythm, setting up, prepping, and rehearsing for the show that night. Tyee had wanted to comfort Rae several times since arriving in Heimat, but he couldn't find the words or courage since she seemed to avoid him.

Coward. Tyee thought to himself.

That word filled him with shame, but he knew it was true. Tyee placed a hand on his temple.

Thoughts of Rae and the old fortune teller's story ran circles in his mind. It was enough to give a man a headache. He traded his feelings of shame for ones of intrigue. He focused on what the old woman was saying before her accident.

Something about Abuela's story didn't sit right with the horseman. He chewed on his bottom lip, trying to determine why the story seemed so familiar. He felt like he was trying to remember a dream. The details were foggy, but his emotions ran high.

"Tyee!" A voice called from across the big top.

Koko pranced underneath him, shaking Tyee out of his reverie. He reeled wildly, looking for the origin of the call.

"Tyee!" Someone called again.

Tyee located the caller and realized it was one of his fellow horsemen. He flashed a couple of hand signs, asking Tyee if he was ready.

Tyee raised a hand and signed back his affirmation. His brothers began their dance and Tyee took a deep breath. *The work never ends.* He thought and let himself get lost in the motions of the performance.

The town of Heimat went about its daily routine as normally as possible. Kids went to school, washerwomen did laundry, bakers tended their ovens, and so on. The coming of the Circus was like the seasons, always returning despite what transpired in town.

The Circus's arrival was no surprise, but now the stakes were higher.

Much of the town comprised new recruits that didn't want to travel with the caravan, and performers and crew that grew tired of the road. The Circus brought much-needed supplies and animals the town could barter for. This symbiotic relationship between the two had been cultivated and growing for years.

But change was here.

The leaders for each section of the city spent the night spreading the word to their constituents and planning the best routes for the children to take. The Magicae of Heimat were part of the fabric of the city and their absence would be felt. That was why it was important to get everyone out within the next few days. Surprise was the only thing left on their side.

George started the trek from his loft in the city to his mother's farmstead on the outskirts of town. He and Tommy had built it for her a couple of years ago and surprised her with it for her birthday. They had saved, schemed, and built for years before it was complete.

George knew it would always be his greatest accomplishment.

He took his time walking through his city. He knew every road, every alley, and every corner. It would be hard to leave, despite knowing it was what he signed up for. The extra coin he earned being a second liaison to the Circus was why he took the job, to begin with.

George made it to his Ma's all too quickly. He stood with one hand on the gate. Taking a moment, he gripped the fencepost to steady himself.

The unknown was unnerving, but leaving his family to fend for themselves was terrifying.

A dog barking alerted the robust woman to his presence.

"Georgie," she beamed and walked towards her eldest son, "Come give your old woman a squeeze!"

A smile broke out on George's face despite the pit in his stomach. "Hey, Ma." He opened the gate and walked into the barnyard. A border collie danced around his legs, yipping in delight. George knew better than to indulge the dog before hugging his mother. He continued walking until he reached the stout woman with salt-and-pepper hair.

She grabbed him by the shoulders. "Let me take a look at you." After rubbing his cheek, she pulled him into a bear hug. "A little dirt on your face and the weight of the world on your shoulders. Some things never change." Her smile faltered slightly, only her eyes betraying the sorrow behind her cheery demeanor. "Come, help me finish the stew before your brothers get here."

George knelt and scratched the dog behind his ears. The dog's tongue lolled in pleasure and his back foot thumped the ground as George scratched his itch. He gave the dog one more strong pat on the back before straightening up and following his mother into the kitchen.

They worked in tandem, gossiping about other townspeople and discussing happenings on the farm. His Ma's kitchen was the place George felt the happiest. He cherished this rare time between just the two of them. Soon enough, the sound of crashing children and excited dog yips could be heard through the window. The pair shared a look and a smile before George opened the door and stood in the doorway.

"Who's making all that racket in my yard?" George boomed from the back stoop of the modest house.

Wild squeals and giggles sounded as three children ran straight for their uncle. George stepped out of the doorway and onto the ground before the flock of kids could topple him off the stoop. He grunted when they collided with him and made a show of falling to the ground under the weight of his nieces and nephew. The group wrestled for a couple of minutes before George gained the upper hand and started tickling all three of the small children.

"Do it again Uncle Georgie! Do it again!" They chorused between screams of laughter.

George smirked. "You couldn't handle that!" The kids tried to prove him wrong but were left breathless when he started picking them up and swinging them around.

"Now you've done it. They won't leave you alone for the rest of the afternoon after all that." An amused voice sounded from the gate.

George looked up long enough to wink at his sister-in-law. "Perfect." He shouted as he continued to throw the little ones around.

Sara shook her head and carefully maneuvered her protruding stomach into the yard. Tommy gripped one of her hands and kept his other on her back as he guided her to the picnic table already laid out with silverware. She sat down gratefully and smiled when her husband kissed her on the cheek.

Being seven months pregnant made everything more difficult.

After making sure Sara was settled, Tommy went into the kitchen to see if his mother needed more help.

She greeted him with a kiss and handed him a basket of bread. "That's a good lad. Take this to the table and make sure your wife eats something."

"Aye, Ma. I told her we could take the cart, but she insisted we walk. Wear the kids out she said. I think the fresh air made them wilder than ever."

She patted his cheek and smiled. "No, that was your brother that got them all wound up. They'll settle in once the food is out. Are we just waiting on Reginald?"

"Aye. He should be here soon, I reckon." Tommy took the bread to the table, rubbed his wife's shoulder, and returned to grab more from the kitchen.

Wild screams announced the adopted member of their family as the children stormed the gate. Reg laughed but held a hand up, trying to balance a box in the other.

"Back, ya beasties! Or do ya ruffians wanna spill the cake?" He asked the children with a glint in his eye. They backed off and attacked George again, keeping a close eye on their other uncle.

Once he set the cake down, all bets were off.

Reg took a seat next to Sara but kept the box in his hands.

"Good call." Sara smiled, nodding towards the cake.

"Aye. Tis' the only thing keeping those beasties off me." Reg said fondly.

Before they could continue their conversation, George and Tommy's mother rang the dinner bell hanging from a hook next to the back door.

"Time to wash up, kiddos. Granny has a feast prepared, so hurry up now!" She looked pointedly at the grandchildren she loved dearly. "Ah, ah, ah. You too Georgie. Go wash up."

George followed the kids to the wash bin and helped them get cleaned up. The four then made their way to the table to join the others. They said grace and tucked into the wonderful spread put out by their mother and grandmother.

Time passed as stomachs filled and laughter rang. The cake was cut and frosting covered the mouths of the three little ones.

After a while, George cleared his throat.

"It's time everybody. I have to go speak with the Ringmaster about a couple more details." He struggled for words. "Then it will be time for me to finally join the Circus." He cracked a soft smile as he recited the old threat he would make when he didn't get sweets for breakfast. His voice broke. "I'm going to miss all of you. I don't know when I'll be back." He rubbed his face roughly. "Promise me you'll take care of each other." He looked everyone in the eyes.

His mother had silent tears running down her cheeks. She pulled him into a hard hug. "This isn't goodbye, my boy, just until I see you next. We'll look out for each other." She whispered in his ear. She pulled back to look him in the eyes. "Look to the stars and know I'm looking at the same ones. Be safe." She enveloped him in a tight hug, small sobs racking her body.

The rest of the table watched the exchange quietly. Tommy stood up and hugged both his brother and his mother. The three broke apart just for George to pull Tommy into another embrace.

"I'll look after them, Georgie. Count on me. Just get those kids to safety and come home to us." His brother whispered in his ear.

George couldn't do anything other than nod, afraid his voice would fail him.

He put an arm on Sara's shoulder and kissed her cheek. "Don't let those little ones wear you out too much." She laughed and patted his hand. George turned to Reg, who jumped from his seat.

"I'll walk with ya, Georgie."

George nodded and bent down to hug his nieces and nephew.

"Now you kids listen to your Ma and Da. I'll be back soon with more stories for you, but you gotta be good while I'm away. Got it?" The three kids nodded seriously before clinging to their uncle.

George disentangled himself from the kids, gave his mother one last hug, and went to the gate.

Reg said his goodbyes and joined his dearest friend. George waved one last time, opened the gate, and headed towards the big top.

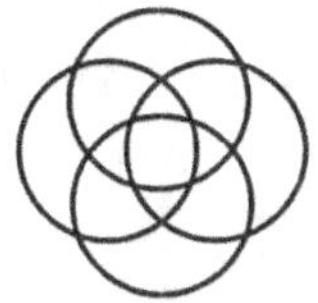

Chapter Twenty-One

Rae stood outside Abuela's wagon, waiting for Luc. The old woman had finally woken up, cutting the trapeze rehearsal short.

Javie sent the runner to find Luc as soon as Abuela had stirred. Luc left the acrobats to go see her Abuela without a second thought. The other three continued for a couple of tricks, but still ended early, needing Luc to finish practicing their routine.

Damien and Zeke were roped into helping set up the carnival tent. The late start in the morning meant all hands on deck, but Rae had slipped off to go check on their friend before getting sucked into another task.

Rae leaned against the wagon and rubbed her arms. She picked at her jacket while she waited to hear how Abuela was. Luc and Javie were in with her, making sure she was comfortable.

Rae knew Luc would appreciate her checking in, despite knowing Abuela wouldn't go down without a fight. Rae refused to believe the old woman could be leveled by anything, but she knew Luc worried, nonetheless. Her friend could use the support.

Besides, the fiery acrobat needed a minute of peace before the lighting ceremony tonight. It would be the first time she wasn't the lead fire Crafter in years. Heads would turn and all eyes would be searching for her. She knew she needed to face her people and what she'd done, but struggled to quench the pride in her heart. Focusing on helping Luc kept her thoughts and feelings at bay.

Rae clutched her arms tighter and attempted once again to feel where her fire ended.

Rae was lost in her attempts to master her Craft. She started when she heard someone clear their throat. Looking up, she met the deep brown irises of her fellow acrobat. Luc had unshed tears in her eyes that she tried to swallow as she looked at her friend.

Rae immediately threw her arms around the other woman and pulled her in tight.

Silent sobs racked Luc's frame as she wrapped her arms around Rae. The fire Crafter held her close without saying anything, offering silent support to the woman she considered a sister. Eventually, Luc pulled away and wiped her eyes.

"She's weak, but she's okay." Luc wiped at her face again. "I was so scared. I don't know what I'd do without her." Luc grabbed Rae's arm. "Thanks for being here, Hermana."

"I wouldn't be anywhere else." Rae gripped her friend's arm in turn. "What's going on with her?"

"She's awake. We told her to stay in bed, even though she could sit up. She ate a little something and chewed on more ginger. Abuela said she didn't have any other pain and told us to get some of the other Herbalists to come and see her. They can make her some tonics that should chase the illness from her body." Luc took a deep breath and leaned against the wagon. She tilted her head back until it hit the weathered wood of the wagon's side.

Rae moved to lean next to her.

"That's great news. I knew we shouldn't underestimate that woman of steel." She nudged her friend and earned a chuckle. "She'll be able to instruct the other Herbalists in creating something to help her."

"I know she will. They'll take care of her." Luc shifted to look at Rae. "She wants to see you."

Rae furrowed her brows. "Me? Why?"

"I don't know. She said she didn't get to finish what she had to say. She seems to think that's why the Huntress struck her down. Abuela's convinced she didn't get to the point quick enough and you're the one that needs to hear the end of the story." Luc sighed and toyed with the pendant hanging around her neck. "Rae... I think it has to do with your Crafting problems."

"Really? She never said anything to me that night we left Windemere." Rae wiped her palms on her breeches as she felt her heartbeat race.

Luc shook her head. "Yeah and she feels bad about that, but she said you weren't ready then? Abuela has always been shrewd, but this is different. She wanted to get out of bed to come and talk to you. Javie and I convinced her to let us bring you to her. Javie is in there, making sure she doesn't leave while I went to find you." Luc looked down at her fingers that still rubbed the pendant around her neck. "You need to go in there, but I have this feeling that it's going to be something bad. Abuela refused to let me bring anyone else, not even Duncan. She insisted only you should be brought to the wagon."

Rae shrugged her shoulders and straightened her tunic. "I guess I better get in there." Rae disentangled Luc's fingers from her shirt when she lunged for the fire Crafter. She continued gently. "Hermana, let me go. I need answers whether they're good or bad. I'd rather meet them head-on. We don't have much time before the torch lighting. It's now or never."

"I'll be right here if you need me."

"No. Go find Damien and Zeke. They were heading to help with the carnival tent the last time I saw them. They should get an update on Abuela and know how you're doing. Let them love on you." Rae squeezed Luc's forearms before pulling her into one last hug. She released the woman and made her way into the wagon. She waved one more time before Luc gripped her pendant tight and headed to the carnival tent.

Rae opened the door to what promised to give her the answers she desperately wanted.

George gazed at the horizon, judging how much light he had left before he needed to be in place at the Circus. He crossed the river at one bridge and walked along one of the alleys in the Upper Districts. George needed to check in with Johanna and Eddy before the sun sank too low in the sky. He rubbed sweaty palms on his pants as he stuck to the shadows.

He had spent the latter part of the afternoon going over plans with Duncan. This was only the second time he'd interacted with the Ringmaster, but he remembered being unnerved by the man's lavender eyes.

George needed to do a double-take when he saw the man again.

Duncan's eyes were now a steel gray color.

George didn't know whether the purple or the gray was more alarming. Regardless, he appreciated the older man's no-nonsense personality that allowed them to run through scenarios quickly and thoroughly. As soon as they finished, he left to run back into the city.

He was on his way to check in with Johanna and Eddy to ask about a head count and confirm the drop-off point. He shifted the bag on his shoulder, heavy with supplies to keep their people hidden.

George took a shortcut through one of the alleys and made it to the street Johanna's tannery shop was on. He looked both ways before leaving the comforting darkness of the deserted walkway.

There were several soldiers down the main road to the left. He waited until they were deep in conversation before crossing without attracting their attention.

George rapped on the side door of the tannery three times in succession. The door cracked and upon recognizing the lanky man; it opened fully to reveal the dusty-skinned woman inside.

"Jeezez, Boss! You frightened me. Get in here before someone sees you." Johanna motioned him to step inside from the doorway. "Aren't you supposed to be at the Circus already?"

"I was already there and firmed up all the details with the Ringmaster. I wanted to swing by and check that everything is ready for tonight. See if you had any questions I could answer." George brushed off his coat and took in the delicious smell of newly made leather.

"Ha, you came to me because you knew Simone would have a million," Johanna smirked with a wink. George rolled his eyes, giving his intentions away. "Nope, I think we're all good. I have seven kiddos and two adults and Simone has twelve kiddos and four adults." Johanna held up a hand when George started to speak. "Hear me out first. There are two Crafters with jeweled eyes and two Herbalists with face markings. We needed to get them out of here. They've been stuck inside their houses for months, fearing for their lives. We already turned away so many. One extra won't make a difference.

George nodded, tight-lipped.

"Oh. The couple of questions we needed clarity on were, where is the drop-off point and when do we send them there?" asked Johanna.

"Split them up into groups, like an adult and so many of the kids, and send them to the carnival tent before the show starts and during intermission. Just stagger them, so they go at different times. Anything else?" George asked gruffly, reaching into his bag to pull out some bottles, creams, and strips of cloth.

"Got it. Simone and I are meeting in an hour to walk our route and pick up our people. What are those for?"

"These are tonics for the Crafters and creams for the Herbalists. Have the Crafters take two drops of the tonic and the Herbalists plaster this cream over their markings. It should conceal their eyes and marks, respectively. These bandannas are similar to the ones they'll be handing out. Each night, different colors will be given out, but only we get the purple ones. Have each individual wear one so the carnival workers can identify them. Are any of the kids Shifters or Forgers?" George handed over three bottles of tonic and five jars of concealing cream.

"One dog Shifter whose eyes can pass as Mortal and I believe two Forgers." Johanna placed the bottles and jars in a leather bag.

"Okay, that's fine then. Tomorrow, I need you to pass any extra bandannas, bottles, and jars onto Tommy and Eddy. I have to stop by the Wharf and talk to Eddy about his getaway boat idea. I'm going to give him some too, but just to be sure, we will pass them around. He'll pick up more tomorrow for Mikel, Tamara, and Reg."

"That's easy to do, Boss." Johanna nodded.

"And let everybody know about the drop-off point. Just tell them to form groups and stagger them. Any Shifters that can't pass as Mortal are welcome to join the animal yard after the show during the night. They will have people posted just in case. I think that's all unless you have any more questions." George tapped his chin, trying to think of anything he'd forgotten to tell the formidable Forger.

"Got it. Nope, we are all good. I will make sure the others know. Do you need numbers from everyone?" Johanna ran her fingers over the leather she had been working on before George knocked on her door.

"I'll get them from Eddy and tell him to grab numbers from the last three. Duncan just likes to know how many to expect in case something goes wrong." George started towards the door. "Anything else?"

"I don't think so." Johanna could see the tension in George's shoulders. "Take care of yourself, George. Don't get too attached to the Circus life."

George laughed without humor. "Don't worry about that, Jo. I have every intention of getting back here as soon as I can." He slipped out the door after checking for soldiers. Johanna locked the door after he left and got back to work on her leather.

Javie looked up from his seat next to his grandmother when Rae entered at the back of the wagon. He nodded at the fire Crafter before leaning down and kissing Nan's cheek. She gripped his wrist and whispered something in his ear, too soft for Rae to hear. He murmured back softly before squeezing her hand and exiting out the front of the wagon.

Rae took hesitant steps toward the old woman once Javie left.

Nan coughed but motioned for Rae to get closer.

"I hear you have something you want to talk to me about." Rae sat down in the chair Javie had occupied, her heart thundering in her chest.

Nan cleared her throat and reached towards the glass on the table beside her cot. Rae took the pitcher and poured some water into the cup before handing it to the old woman. Nan drank deeply before setting the glass down on the table.

"Ah, much better. Thank you, dearie." Nan paused and observed the young woman before her. "Help me sit up a bit?"

Rae moved quickly to help Nan readjust herself and her pillows, so she sat up higher. Rae could feel bones beneath her sagging skin and felt the alarm Luc had displayed when she left the wagon. Seeing the grizzly of a woman reduced to such frailty was unnerving. Rae silently prayed to the Huntress for a full recovery of the old woman. She waited for Nan to speak again.

"Now, you have questions about your Craft. I'm an Herbalist but I have seen many Crafters in all my years of wandering. None of them had the power that you do, my dear." Rae snorted in disbelief, but Nan continued. "You may not feel powerful now, but something is changing inside you. Crafts are wicked things. They rule their Crafters viciously, no matter how good of a person you are. Your fire seems like a friend but it wants freedom as much as you do and will stop at nothing to get it." Nan sighed, seeing Rae's confused expression. "You don't want to believe me, but it's true."

"Abuela, I mean no disrespect, but my Craft has been the only thing keeping me sane most of the time. After the Uprising... after Helene..." Rae gulped down those memories, squeezing her eyes shut. "When I was alone, my Craft was the only thing that kept me alive. It was how the Circus found me. Abuela, the fire in my veins means more to me than anything. How could it be wicked?" Her voice cracked as she opened her eyes to gaze at the Herbalist.

Nan looked at the young woman with sympathy. "Dearie, just look in the mirror. You've lost weight, you look hollow. Those circles under your eyes tell me you haven't been sleeping. Your fire is destroying you from the inside out." Rae's blood roared in her ears as she tried to focus on what Nan was saying.

The old woman's words cut her to the core as her mind reeled. A squeeze of the weathered woman's hand brought her back to the present. "Your Craft has become too powerful. This phenomenon is rare, but I have seen it before. I prayed to the Huntress herself it wasn't true, but the signs are unmistakable. You have the Crafters' Curse; your fire will consume you if you don't bind it." Nan squeezed Rae's hand as emotions warred on the woman's face.

"Bind my fire? What the fuck, Abuela?" Rae put her hands in her lap to hide the tremors coursing through them, struggling to keep her voice in check.

"Aye, child. Your fire would be quenched forever. Your golden eyes would be the only thing that separates you from a Mortal." Nan's eyes turned hard. Rae's reaction wasn't out of the ordinary, but the old woman wouldn't be cowed. "This is a lot to take in, but Rae, your life is on the line. This is not a joke."

Rae gave the woman an incredulous look and rose from her seat next to the old woman. "I need to leave." Rae thrust her hands into her jacket, holding on desperately to the flames, pushing for release.

Nan reached for the Crafter but recoiled with a cry, her eyes widened in alarm. "Rae! You're burning up! Hear me out, child. As much as you don't want to."

Rae hesitated, looking back at the woman she revered. She bit her lip, hand on the door of the suddenly too-small wagon. "Abuela, I need a night." Fire blazed in Rae's eyes as thoughts swirled through her head.

Not my fire. Anything but that.

There must be another way, something else I can do to alter my fate.

Tears brimmed in her eyes as her father's words threatened to overtake her.

Some things cannot be changed.

Rae's sharp eyes caught Nan's nod, and she fled the wagon, not saying another word.

The bedridden Nan coughed and called for Javie, but Rae didn't stop to hear what she wanted from the young man.

The main road that connected the Fringe, where Johanna's tannery stood, and Eddy's home, the Wharf, was littered with soldiers.

George bypassed most of the length of it, using alleys and side streets, but he was out of options. He pulled his hood up and waited for the soldiers' attention to shift.

George grew up hiding from everyone whenever he left his house. He made it his goal to go from home to school and back again without anyone noticing him just to prove he could.

Silly games long ago suddenly had new relevance.

George silently thanked the Goddess for his childhood zeal; he still knew every crevice and back alley of the city. The past few months had been exhausting, but at least George had some practice at going undetected.

A farmer traveled down the road, pushing a cart full of vegetables, causing a throng to form behind his slow, bulky form. George took his chance, blending seamlessly into the crowd. With a little luck, the soldiers wouldn't notice one more person among the masses.

He weaved down the path until reaching the alley that would take him to the back door of Eddy's place. He made a sharp right and flattened himself next to the wall of the alley. George waited until he was sure no one followed him. He needed to be careful not to expose the Wharfman, no matter how tough or gruff the man was.

He moved down the alley soundlessly until he came to the back of one of the many fish shacks in the area. Each district in Heimat had a unique character and architecture. The three in the south composed of the Lower Districts, the Fringe, and the Wharf were the rougher parts of town. George grew up at the edge of the Fringe with Tommy and Reg and a bunch of other dirty, poor, and sometimes orphans. George and Tommy made it a point to prioritize getting their mother out of the one-bedroom, dirt-floor, house once they reached adulthood.

George didn't know if he would've left had his mother still been in the Fringe. There were a lot of decent people there that looked out for one another;

nonetheless, poverty made even decent people desperate. No, the farm was the best thing they could've done for her.

The Wharf was a little rougher, where docked sailors congregated and made trouble with coins in their pockets. Brothels and bars dotted almost every corner. George hated coming here but needed to update Eddy.

He rapped three times on the back door of the shack, waiting to be let in.

The door opened outward in a whoosh of air.

George quickly stepped behind the door as a fishing knife whirled through the open doorway, thrumming as it bit into a pile of old wooden crates behind the humble structure.

"Damn it, Eddy! It's just George. Hold your knives! If you cut me, I swear to the Goddess. You will meet Her sooner than you'd like." George yelled into the darkened doorway.

"Georgie?" The callous dock worker stuck his head out cautiously, one knife in each hand. Seeing the tall, hooded man, he sheathed both knives. "Why didn't you just say it was you? Only them ruffians have the courtesy to knock. They try to lure you into an ambush." He looked the man up and down. "You're a long way from home."

"I had to stop by to update you on your getaway boat. Plus, I have a couple of things to give you," said George.

"Ah! The boat! Yes, shall I get a crew manned for our friends in the Circus?"

"The Ringmaster said that sounds like a fine idea. Have it waiting near the northern bridge by sunset on the third night. He claims you can never have enough backup plans." George started pulling supplies out of his backpack.

Eddy laughed. "He seems like my kind of guy. Sounds like a Wharfman." He thumped his chest and looked at George's pack curiously. "Whatcha got there, lad?"

"I have some supplies for you and Tommy. I stopped by and gave some to Johanna as well. She'll hand off any of her extras in the morning. How many people are you expecting to bring tomorrow?"

"I have nine kiddos and two adults. They're a mix of Herbalists, Crafters, and

Forgers. No Shifters in the bunch. Bandannas?" Eddy picked up several of the pieces of cloth set out by George.

"Aye. They'll be handing them out at the show. Only we have the purple color so the crew can pick out who needs shelter. Make sure everyone puts one on after getting to the show." He explained the tonics and creams he brought, asking the Wharfman to pass off any unused supplies to Tamara. George handed the supplies over to the older man and asked, "Do you know Tommy's numbers? I forgot to ask him earlier."

"I believe the lad had seven kiddos and three adults. Don't gimme that look, lad. I know what the orders were, but she has a babe with Shifter eyes. We couldn't separate a mother and her babe. You go for it, though. I'd love to see Luna take a bite outta ya." Eddy protested when George's expression hardened. The younger man sighed.

"No, you two did right. It just complicates things." He rubbed the back of his neck. "I also need you to get in touch with Tamara and Mikel to get their numbers. Reg didn't know them when I asked him earlier today. I'll be waiting at the entrance of the Circus tomorrow night. I need you to come with those numbers."

"I can do that. Tam and I will be in the same gambling outfit tonight. I'll ask her then. You gotta get back to your band of misfits, I take it?" Eddy nodded in the direction of the Circus as he put the supplies into a crate on the shelf above him. He noted George's nod and added, "Good luck to ya, Georgie. Performing for a living? No, thank you. I'll stick to the docks. Have they put you into an act yet?"

Eddy howled while George protested. "I am not performing in any kind of act. I'm just making sure our people are okay." Eddy tried to compose himself and failed. "Laugh all you want, Wharfman. You are more than welcome to take my place." Eddy finally sobered enough to reply.

"No, no, no, lad. That's all you. I'm too selfish for that job." Eddy held up his hands in surrender. "You're a better man than me by far. Anything else I need to do before tomorrow night?"

George slung his pack over his shoulder and pulled his hood up before stepping to the door. "Nope. Just keep everybody safe until the drop-off. I'll see you tomorrow night."

Eddy nodded as George opened the door and disappeared into the back alley. He had to get back to the Circus quickly and discreetly.

The rescue began tonight.

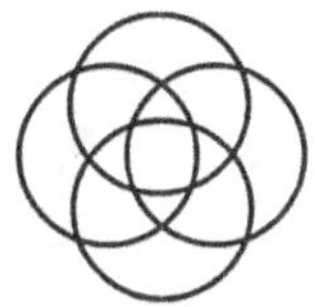

Chapter Twenty-Two

R ae sped from the fortune teller's wagon. She didn't have a direction, just knew she had to get away before she hurt someone. She left the player's yard and made her way to the river, craving the promise of cool relief should something go wrong.

Rae didn't trust herself with the emotions broiling inside.

She found a bare spot along the river bank and sat down, hugging her knees to her chest, as she rocked back and forth. She stopped to lift her head high enough to see her hands as she released her flames for a couple of moments. The flames danced in her vision as she emptied her thoughts, solely focusing on the flickering fire.

The tears came as Rae's fire died down. She cried silently, pressing her face into her knees.

A hand on her back roused her from the empty darkness inside.

Rae lifted her head and watched Duncan take a seat next to her, slinging an arm around her shoulder and pulling her in close.

The pair sat side by side as the sun started its descent in the sky.

Rae brushed roughly at her face and steadied her breathing. There was steel in her voice as she spoke. "I'm not binding anything, Duncan. I won't lose my Craft."

Duncan kept his arm over her shoulder but fixed her face in his gaze. A slight crease formed on his forehead as sadness filled his eyes. "Rae, I don't think you have a choice."

Rae's eyes narrowed. "Yea, I know, some things cannot be changed. But that's shit, Duncan, and you know it. I'm going to do whatever the hell I want, consequences be damned. I won't lose this. I can't." Her voice cracked on the last sentence, revealing the vulnerability beneath the fire Crafter's bravado.

Duncan stared at the river, recognizing the words Rae uttered and inferring where they came from. "Your father took comfort in the idea that fate made his choices inconsequential. But it's a terrible thing to say to a young person with the rest of their life in front of them. He shouldn't have written that." He looked back at the acrobat, feeling her tremble. "Rae, you can make that choice. You can run off and let the fire in your veins consume you from the inside out. Don't give me that look. I've seen it happen before. But you would have to leave the Circus."

Rae's eyes widened as Duncan continued. "I can't have you putting others in danger. Leaving would be the only way to keep our people safe. You would be alone, Rae. You need to understand that before you make a rash decision."

Rae bit her lip, soaking in Duncan's words.

"This Curse is devastating, taking too many Crafters before their time, and no antidote to be had. Many have tried to outrun it only to be caught unaware, leaving their loved ones grieving. I don't want you to end up like them, but it's your decision."

Rae picked at her coat, speechless at the misfortune she found herself in. "I feel it taking more and more."

Duncan studied her carefully, staying silent and encouraging her to continue.

"But who am I without my flames, Duncan? How can I just accept this and move on?"

"Losing them won't make you less, it will challenge you to be better. Acceptance will come with time, my dear. Your fire isn't the only thing that defines you."

Rae let out a sigh. "I need a night, Duncan. I need a night to sort through my thoughts and decide what I want. Give me one more night with my friends."

Duncan pursed his lips, but nodded, moving to stand. He squeezed her shoulder before heading back towards the Circus. "Take the time you need, but don't wait too long." His voice belayed the anguish he felt at losing her even as he stood and left her on the riverbank.

This decision rested with Rae alone.

Rae made her way back to the player's yard shortly after Duncan left her. She missed the Lighting ceremony but barely registered the time as she wrestled with her emotions.

Her feet took her to her tent unbidden.

Rae pushed through the flaps separating her space from the rest of the caravan and shuffled to her trunk, placed there by the tent crew. The Crafter felt numb as she opened it and pulled out her golden, feathered performance costume. She set it on the cot to her right and stared at it blankly, Duncan's words rattling in her brain.

I can't have you putting others in danger.

Slowly, the acrobat sank to the ground and let out a scream, clutching at her face.

The tears started, and she flailed about, looking for something to break. She took her water pitcher and hurled it at the side of the tent.

Water and shards of clay littered the ground around her.

Rae paused, her breathing turned ragged as she let the relief of violence wash over her. She scanned her small tent, looking for something else to throw.

Her eyes caught on the trunk, still open from when she had pulled out her costume.

She lunged for it and toppled it so the trunk listed on its side, clothes, and belongings scattering across the floor. The tears streamed down her face and a strangled cry left her throat as she wheeled for more.

This time, she flipped the cot over, relieving it of its bedding. Rae stood over the ruins of her tent and slammed her hands into the side of her trunk. She repeated the motion again and again, screaming as she did so until her hands were bloody and throbbing.

Finally, Rae stood still, her chest heaved with shuddering breaths as silent tears continued falling. She was a mess and the release of her anger left her hollow.

She sank to her knees and sobbed, feeling unmoored.

Without her Craft she was nothing.

She heard footsteps headed for her tent and braced herself for one of the other acrobats. They would be looking for her before the show.

"Birdie? You decent?" Rae started when she heard Tyee's rough baritone. She couldn't bring herself to answer him, sobs still racking her body. "I know you're in there, Rae. I'll give you another minute and then I'm coming in." Tyee tried again.

Rae brought her knees to her chest and hugged them tight, burying her face in them, and trying to calm down.

Tyee opened the flap of her tent gently and whistled at the sight of the destruction within. Things were shattered on the ground and her few pieces of furniture were strewn haphazardly across the room.

He stopped when he caught sight of Rae on the ground.

He hesitated, not knowing what to do.

After a couple of breaths, he sat next to her and placed an arm around her shoulder.

Rae's sobbing slowed as she leaned into the horseman. They sat without talking, listening to Rae's frantic breathing become more even. Eventually, she lifted her head to look at the man beside her.

Tyee reached to wipe her tears but hesitated just before touching her cheek. He stared into the acrobat's wide eyes with a questioning look. Rae wrenched her gaze away and leaned her cheek on her knee.

"My Craft is trying to consume me. It's a sickness that happens when the Craft becomes too powerful. The only way to stop it is to bind my fire, quench all my flames." She choked out. She wiped her nose on her sleeve and sniffled. "It's either that or risk myself and others."

Tyee couldn't stifle his gasp as he pulled her closer, at a loss for words. Rae losing her Craft was akin to him losing his ability to ride. She gave a heavy sigh and stretched her legs out in front of her. Tyee looked into her watery eyes.

"Who told you this?" He asked.

"Abuela did. She said she's seen it before. She didn't want to believe it was happening to me, but she said the signs were all there. Abuela told me the only options were binding or dying." She called forth the flames begging to be released from her palms. A gentle glow emanated inside Rae's tent as her hands burned gently. "I don't understand how this can be the end. I could feel the power rising within me, and I felt my limits expanding, then nothing. It was like my fire had become endless. I felt it using me, desiring more."

She met the horseman's stare and winced. "When you gave me some of your life energy, I could feel my Craft pulling too much from you. It took everything I had to shut it down. That's why I couldn't take from you again." She dropped his searching gaze and traced circles on her knees.

Tyee struggled to process everything she was telling him. "So what happens during the binding?" He drew his words out, broaching the subject delicately.

"I didn't ask." Rae gave him a hard look but noticed Tyee was clad in his blacks, ready for the show. She cursed and started searching through the rubble for her costume. "Damn it. I set my feathered garb somewhere over here."

Tyee watched while she searched, not knowing whether to offer his help or stay out of the way. Rae grunted as she hoisted her cot out of the way. She still couldn't find the damn thing but noticed Tyee out of the corner of her eye.

"You better get going, Drifter. The first night of shows is about to start. I'll find my costume or something close to it and get to the big top." She turned her head and nodded at the concerned horseman. "Go on, Tyee. I just need some time to compose myself."

"When will the binding take place?" Tyee asked, refusing to leave before hearing her answer.

"I didn't say there'd be one." Her eyes were steel as she stared at the horseman.

"Don't be daft, Birdie. I'll be there when it happens." Tyee left before Rae could respond.

Bastard. Rae thought as she continued to look for her costume. She nudged the trunk a bit and spotted the leggings with the feathers. She lifted slightly and tugged them out from under the heavy trunk. Rae quickly slipped them on and kept looking for the rest of her costume. She found her mask and felt relief.

She knew she could just grab the next fitted top she found. It had to be tight, so there was no chance of catching on the trapeze.

She threw on a dark shirt and rushed to the big top.

Zalia would man the lanterns, leaving Rae to focus on the second most important part of her identity. Performing for those that discriminated against her people always made Rae's skin crawl, but Heimat was different. Here, performing in the center ring, flying on the trapeze, feeling her muscles twist and stretch as she asked them to flip, was pure freedom.

She looked forward to a racing heart and straining muscles. The physical activity would give her a respite from the thoughts swirling around her mind.

Rae made it to the big top and entered one of the side rings. She joined the other three acrobats and prayed they didn't sense her dread of what was to come.

Zeke motioned for her to come closer and threw an arm around her shoulders when she did. He tucked her into his side as they watched the first night of performances, waiting for their turn in the ring.

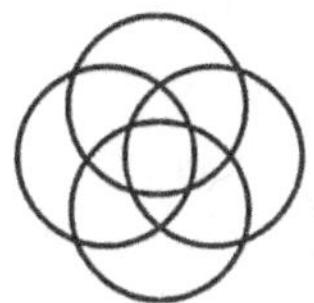

Chapter Twenty-Three

Intermission ended in a hurry as the acrobats warmed up on the trapeze towers, the familiar setup putting them at ease as they flew in the air.

Heimat was traditionally the place everyone experimented with their acts. Tyee and his horsemen sometimes created grand spectacles, jumping from horse to horse, tandem riding, and jumping through flaming hoops. The acrobats became more daring, relying on Zeke's Craft to keep them from ending up on the ground. Shifters walked freely in human forms and Herbalists cured ailments and crops without hiding anything. Everyone tested their limits with the rare opportunity to add their Gifts into their acts without fear.

It was freeing to perform for people that accepted every part of you.

This was why having lost Heimat was devastating. Losing that freedom dampened everyone's spirits, but it also fueled their desire to get their people out quickly. The children were depending on them to escape the unsafe conditions they now found themselves in.

The performers and crew were ready for the next few nights, no matter what happened.

Rae flew on the fly bar, performed a flip, and gripped Zeke's waiting arms. She let out a cry, letting Zeke know his timing was perfect as he grunted and swung her arms, spinning her sideways before catching her by the ankles. He spun her again until he gripped her wrists.

This time, Rae faced the fly bar she had come from. She swung from Zeke's hands and launched herself into the air, somersaulting high in the sky before grabbing the fly bar.

She swung on the bar for several oscillations before dismounting onto the trapeze tower. She bowed in tandem with Zeke, and the lanterns switched their focus to Damien and Luc on the lower bars.

A slight breeze blew the loose hairs from Rae's braid.

Rae breathed hard while she took a break on the trapeze tower. Zeke was resting across from her on the other tower while Damien and Luc went through their sequences, flying and spinning on the lower bars.

She looked at her partner and gave him a thumbs up, but watched in horror as he slipped, mid-wave, and hit his head on the side of the tower.

The audience didn't notice, entranced by Luc and Damien below.

One of the spotters pulled Zeke up before he lost his footing completely and helped the acrobat regain his balance. Rae watched as they exchanged words, the spotter frowning with concern at the performer. Zeke shook his head slightly and grabbed the fly bar anyway, getting ready for the next sequence. Rae watched with apprehension, noting the way his arms shook.

Something was wrong.

Zeke leaned over the trapeze tower but didn't jump to start the next sequence. *He's leaning too far forward.* Rae's knuckles went white as she gripped the sides of her trapeze tower.

Zeke was going to fall and didn't seem to be in any condition to use his Craft to save himself.

Panicking, Rae let go of the tower and waved her arms, trying to get the attention of Zeke's spotters without alerting the audience to her distress.

If only one of them would look.

Rae jumped up and down until one spotter shifted and saw her.

She frantically pointed at his trapeze tower, feeling a burst of wind run through her hair. The spotter gave her a quizzical look before pointing at Zeke. Rae nodded, relief washing over her, and gave him a thumbs up.

Rae felt like the world slowed down as the spotter took a step towards Zeke too late. The acrobat tipped forward as the spotter grasped at empty air.

Rae screamed.

Zeke plummeted to the ground.

The lanterns in the center ring went out.

Rae's heart dropped into her stomach. Her body froze as her mind struggled to process what was happening.

She felt her Craft welling up in her center and instinctively clamped down on the sensation. But her blood felt cool, not the warm magma she normally felt from her Craft.

Surprised, Rae let her Craft take control and move her body in unfamiliar movements. She crouched down and moved her hands in circular motions, ending with a gentle downward movement of her arms.

Once her hands reached her sides, Rae snapped out of the trance she was in. She focused on controlling the unruly Craft, terrified Abuela and Duncan were right and the sickness was already unstoppable. She reached for her fire—

It wasn't there.

Instead of warmth, she felt coolness, instead of a molten core, a storm cloud raged, and instead of flames, she called forth the wind. She looked at her palms in awe as she felt the wind traveling between them.

Rae furrowed her brows and stared at her hands while screams and panic filled the big top. She closed her eyes but expanded her focus, amazed to find she could feel the air currents in and out of the tent. A sense of euphoria filled her as she plucked the currents with her Craft and saw them switch.

The raw power of the wind took her breath away.

She released her focus and opened her eyes. A breeze wrapped around her and cooled her sweaty skin. The unfamiliar feeling caused frantic searching for the heat that was her constant companion since childhood. Not finding it made her shaky, bringing her back to reality within the center ring.

The crowd was being directed out of the tent. Lanterns flickered on and off, trying to provide visibility and privacy at the same time.

The Ringmaster announced for people to enjoy a free drink at the concession stand and game at the carnival tent while the big top transitioned for the next act.

Rae barely registered hearing Duncan and seeing their patrons leaving. She fought to keep the panic attack at bay, sitting down and putting her head between her knees. She forced herself to take deep breaths and tune out what was going on down below.

When the tightness in her chest eased, she looked down and saw some Herbalists hovering over a heap beneath the southern trapeze tower. Her heart squeezed when she realized it was Zeke.

She scrambled up and pushed past the spotters to the ladder that would take her down the tower to her friend. She made it to Luc's platform and kept going, deaf to the shouts around her.

Reaching the ground, she sprinted to the opposite side, only skidding to a halt when she came to the group of people.

"Is he going to be okay?" Rae asked, trying to peer around the ring of Herbalists surrounding her friend.

"He has a pretty severe concussion, but no other major injuries." The tall Herbalist scrunched his face like he smelled something rancid.

"Can I see him?" Rae pressed, knowing full well Zeke had to be more injured than that.

The Herbalist grunted and Rae immediately pushed herself forward, kneeling beside Zeke's limp form.

"Z? Z, can you hear me?" The Crafter groaned and pulled his brows together. "It's Sparks. Come on Z." She reached for his hand and gave a gentle squeeze. Her heart fluttered in relief when she felt her friend squeeze back.

Zeke groaned again and shifted. Indiscernible noises came from his mouth and Rae looked at the Herbalists.

"Does anybody have any water?" She asked, impatience creeping into her tone. *Honestly. You'd think a bunch of Healers would know to have water ready.* She bit her tongue to avoid voicing the thoughts in her head. Snark wouldn't help Zeke get the care he needed.

"Working on it. Simmer down lioness." The youngest Herbalist smirked at

Rae.

Rae looked up, ready to snap but laughed instead, seeing it was Freya challenging her. The young Healer was only a few years older than them but had always been the one they wanted to emulate as kids.

Freya put her hands on Rae's shoulders, gazing into the Crafter's eyes.

"We have to move him, Rae. Once the stretcher gets here, they're taking him to the med tent. Be quick. Carlos doesn't like having non-Herbalists around during a stretcher carry out." She squeezed her shoulders before releasing the acrobat. Freya turned to join a discussion between the other Herbalists, not waiting for Rae to respond.

She turned her attention back to Zeke and wiped his brow. "Come on Z, talk to me," Rae whispered.

Zeke's eyelids fluttered before opening briefly and closing again. He tried to clear his throat and let out several coughs. "Duncan?" Zeke's voice rasped, barely audible with the sounds of patrons moving and the Circus crew setting up agility ramps in the background.

Rae felt ice fill her veins. She tried again. "Nope. Z, it's Rae."

Zeke's brows scrunched together. "Sparks? Where's fire?" It still labored Zeke to speak much. He settled for croaking out a few words to get his point across.

Rae's hand tightened on Zeke's. "I don't know. It's gone." Her chest tightened when she reached for the warmth in her core, only to be met with the chaos of a raging storm. She tried to crack a sad smile, but it came out as a grimace. "I think I'm a wind Crafter now."

Zeke groaned and made more incomprehensible noises. Rae leaned down closer to her trapeze partner, but still couldn't make out what he was trying to say. All too soon, Rae felt a hand on her shoulder.

"Time to go, champ. Come visit him after the show. He might be lucid then." Freya said firmly, leaving no room to argue.

"Is he going to be okay?" Rae asked, standing up.

"Don't tell them I told you, but he should make a full recovery. Just might have a gnarly headache for a few days." Freya frowned. "It's a good thing his

Craft caught him before impact. He wouldn't have survived that fall otherwise."

Rae started to respond but stopped herself. Freya raised an eyebrow and looked at her expectantly. "It's nothing. I... do you think his Craft would've been able to save him even if he was out cold?" Rae asked carefully.

"All I know is Duncan was talking to the townie over there and missed the whole thing. If Duncan didn't save him, who did? None of the other wind Crafters were around; it had to be him." Freya said matter-of-factly, inclining her head to where George watched from the side of the ring. She became distracted, helping the other Herbalists move Zeke onto the stretcher. She waved to Rae as she took a side and walked Zeke out of the big top.

Rae stood for several moments, ruminating on what the Herbalist told her. *It had to be me. But how?* She ran a hand over her braid.

"RAE! YO! RAE-RAE!"

Rae started, looking around for the voice calling her name. She saw Damien and Luc on the opposite side of the ring, standing behind the low wall separating patrons from performers. They hadn't made it past the Herbalists, herded to the side before reaching their friend. They waved their arms frantically to get her to come over.

Once Rae reached them, Damien asked, "What happened? One minute we were finishing our set and the next we heard your usually whimsical voice twisted into a scream."

Rae ignored him and grabbed both of their wrists. "Do I feel warm to you guys?" She asked intently.

"No," Luc answered automatically. She jumped after processing what she just said. "No, you feel like ice. What happened to you?" Luc clutched at Rae, feeling different parts of bare skin. "Nowhere is warm. Rae, we should take you to the med tent." She frowned, looking closer at what Rae wore. "And where is your feathered top?"

Rae's expression turned sheepish as she rubbed the back of her neck. "Well, my tent is kind of in shambles right now. I had to throw on the first thing I found to make it here before intermission. I don't know where it went."

Damien moved a hand to grip the bridge of his nose and furrowed his brows. "All this information is overwhelming me. Start from the beginning, keeper of secrets." Luc looked exasperated at her partner's inability to keep up with the conversation.

Rae started at the beginning. She told them about Abuela's insight, the binding, Duncan's ultimatum, the incident in the tent with Tyee, and finally, Zeke's accident on the trapeze. Luc and Damien were quiet, absorbing everything their friend confided.

"I think I was the one that saved Zeke. Freya said Duncan was distracted and no other wind Crafters were around. Zeke was shaking on the bar and looked so weak. I don't think he would've been able to save himself." Rae said quickly. "When I reach for my fire, all I find is a raging storm. Instead of flames bursting in my palms, I feel winds blowing across them." She held her hands out to the pair, palms up. Both of them widened their eyes when they felt the breeze on Rae's palms.

Luc bit her lip. "So you're a wind Crafter now?" She drew out each word.

"I think so? Oh! Zeke thought I was Duncan too. Even after I told him several times that it was me. I think he sensed my Craft and assumed it was Duncan." Rae mused out loud.

Damien held up his hand, willing his brain to catch up with the onslaught of information. "Slow down. Do we know if that's even possible? To switch Crafts? Is this just a side effect of the Crafter sickness Abuela was insisting you had?"

Rae stopped and closed her eyes. She reached inward once again, trying to grab hold of the raging storm. She finally gained a grip on it and prodded the winds she held. Satisfied, she opened her eyes and shook her head at her friend.

"This feels different from my fire. The whole makeup of it is strange. My fire was a mass of sparks and flame, while this is made of individual winds. I don't know how they'd be the same."

"You should go talk to Abuela. She's seen this sickness before. Maybe she'll know if this is another symptom." Luc hesitated. "Hermana, you still need to consider doing the binding. This might just be a hiccup."

Rae's face fell before her eyes turned to steel and she lifted her chin. "Or it's the answer I've been waiting for." She felt the power within, recognizing its differences from her fire but feeling whole all the same. She refused to believe the binding was necessary with this change in events.

Luc and Damien shared a concerned look as they followed the Crafter to the side ring, watching the lanterns flash, and signaling to their patrons it was time to return to the big top.

Rae watched the rest of the show, preoccupied with the events of the night. The clarity that came with the trapeze was gone. She rubbed her hands over her arms and let Luc put an arm over her shoulders. She leaned into the warmth she was unaccustomed to feeling from someone else and prayed to the Huntress she was right about this.

And just like that, night one of the performances was done.

Rae, Luc, and Damien hurried to make it out of the big top before the crowds could. The ending hadn't come soon enough for the friends who were anxious about one of their own. They stood and waved as people left, greeting some by name. As the throng thinned, they slipped away before someone could guilt them into helping with clean up.

The three acrobats kept to the shadows and made their way to the med tent. They knew it was wise to listen to the Herbalists, but couldn't help feeling they should have checked in sooner.

Herbalists were split into two categories, akin to the four different Crafts for Crafters, each with their particular gifts. Healers identified and used plants to create tonics, creams, and tinctures that were then used to treat maladies in the med tent. Growers foraged for plants that could be used for cooking and consumption and could use their Gifts to help plants grow faster.

The three acrobats arrived at the med tent just as Freya was leaving. She saw the three and said something to the friends she was with. She walked over to the acrobats.

"You guys here to see Zeke?" When they nodded, Freya continued. "He was awake a bit ago but might have dozed off. He's got quite a lump on his head, but he'll recover." She shrugged her shoulders.

"Thanks, Freya. We appreciate you looking after him." Rae said. "Your shift done?" She nodded towards the other young Healers still waiting for her.

"Yep! Time to let off a little steam. Do a little dancing in the dark, if you know what I mean." She winked and waggled her eyebrows. She turned towards her friends and called back. "See you at the bonfire!" The Healers left towards the player's yard.

Luc and Damien followed Rae into the med tent. They greeted the chief Healer who pointed them towards Zeke's cot where he lay sleeping. The three exchanged looks before spreading out around him. Rae crouched near his head while Luc and Damien stood at the foot of his cot.

Rae shook Zeke's arm gently. The wind Crafter stirred in his sleep but didn't wake up. She looked at Luc, who nodded for her to try again. They just needed to hear Zeke's voice to know he would be okay. Rae took his hand and squeezed.

"Z, can you hear me? Damien and Luc are here too. We just want to see how you're doing." Rae felt Zeke squeeze her hand and roll over. He murmured. Rae shot a glance at the other two, but they shook their heads.

"Didn't hear that, Z. Can you speak up?"

"I said a guy can't get any sleep around here, can he?!" Zeke rasped louder, turning to look at his trapeze partner. His hand strayed towards his head and he groaned. "Augh. Moved too fast. Makes my head hurt."

"Z, we were worried about you. I'm so glad you're okay!" Luc moved closer and hugged him.

Damien gripped his friend's foot over the blanket. "You've missed a lot, my fine fellow. Glad to see you up and kicking." Luc hit Damien with a hiss as she moved back. "What?" He asked her, eyes wide.

"Z doesn't need to worry about all that." She shook her head. "He just needs to focus on healing."

"Worry about what?" Zeke asked weakly.

Rae placed a hand on his arm. "I'll come by tomorrow and fill you in. A lot is going on, but you need rest. Go to sleep. We're just relieved we could talk to you." She leaned down and hugged him.

"You better. I'll send Kim after you if you don't." Zeke turned over once more and started dozing again.

Rae smiled at the thought of the little girl trying to find her. She shook her head and left the med tent. Damien and Luc said their goodbyes before following Rae out.

The three walked together until they got to the player's yard.

"You going to the bonfire, Rae?" Luc asked, Damien's arm draped over her shoulders.

"I don't know. I need to sort out the mess in my tent, but then I might wander down. Are you guys?" Rae responded.

Luc shared a look with Damien. "We might make it down there for a bit." Damien nuzzled her neck. "Or we might turn in for an early night." The two shared a smile.

"I have to check on Abuela, though. She should be out of the weeds, but best to be sure. Some of the Herbalists were meeting with her during tonight's show. I'll check in and see what they could do for her."

"We will." Damien corrected with a kiss to her forehead, a knowing look passing between them.

"Yes, *we'll* go check on Abuela." Luc beamed, intent on filling the old woman in on what happened with Rae.

"Augh. Just get a tent already. You make me sick." Rae chided.

Damien threw his other arm around the Crafter and pulled her close. "Don't worry gorgeous, you'll find your heartmate one day. No need to be so jealous of us." He smirked. "Maybe explore a little something with a certain horseman."

"I hear he's quite the rider." Luc giggled.

Rae threw Damien's arm off while he cackled at Luc's comment. "You two are worse than Z. I'm leaving." She stalked towards her tent.

"Have sweet dreams, heartbreaker! I hope they're filled with the sound of hoofbeats." Damien called before joining Luc in a fit of laughter. The two walked in the opposite direction towards Nan's wagon.

A flush crept up Rae's neck as she marched to her tent.

Her feelings for the horseman were complicated, and the lust she couldn't deny would only lead to trouble. Those feelings only heightened when he found her sobbing in her tent and offered consolation and comfort without hesitating.

Tyee was not who she expected him to be.

Her thoughts mirrored the storm raging in her core. Her friends' teasing tempted her to consider pursuing something with the tall rogue; consequences be damned.

Rae blushed when she thought of Tyee's hands running up her sides, her lips consumed by the taste of his kiss, and finally giving in to that heat pooling in her core. She rubbed her face while sorting through her conflicted feelings.

Reaching her tent, she stopped to listen.

Sounds were coming from inside.

She crouched and shuffled to one side of the structure. Rae pulled a dagger from inside each boot and reached for her Craft.

Might as well use the wind while I got it. Rae thought as she stepped to the front of the tent and held her daggers aloft. She pulled the wind to wind around each of them before jerking both hands forward, punching the wind into the tent flap. The flap flew inward, and she heard a thump as the person inside dropped to the ground from the force of the wind.

Rae moved quickly to take the intruder by surprise. She positioned her knees on either arm and pinned the person to the ground. Rae held a dagger to their throat while the other stayed menacingly above their head. She panted as she held her position and the tent flaps swayed back into place.

"If you wanted to straddle me, all you had to do was ask Birdie." The intruder grunted.

"Tyee?" Rae questioned, lowering the dagger held above him but keeping the other one at his throat. "Why are you in here?"

"Easy, golden girl. I was trying to clean up a little for you." He moved his eyes to the side, trying to get her to notice the trunk that was now righted. "See?"

"But why?" Rae stuttered, unable to comprehend the man's motives. "What's your game Tyee?"

The man cleared his throat. "How about you remove the dagger from my neck and you can find out?" He threw her a wicked grin.

Rae let out a frustrated cry and leaped off the horseman. She placed both daggers back into her boots, straightened, and turned towards Tyee. "Talk."

Tyee sat up into a sitting position, knees bent slightly and rubbed his neck. He studied the woman before him, taking in her disheveled clothes and windswept hair. "You can control the wind now?"

Rae gritted her teeth. "I said talk, not ask questions."

Tyee sighed. "Fine, I thought it would be helpful if you came back to a tent that didn't look like a battle zone. I saw Zeke fall and heard you scream. I just wanted to help, but you've been avoiding me, so I didn't know if I was welcome."

Rae snorted. "You invited yourself in here just fine earlier."

"But you needed someone. You would've let Kaiser in here if he was the first to find you. You were in no state to turn anyone away." He ran a hand through his hair, still on the ground. "I'm sorry I barged in, but I couldn't leave you like that." He looked up to meet Rae's searching eyes.

Rae bit her lip, not sure if she wanted to utter the words at the tip of her tongue.

Fuck it.

"I'm glad it was you," Rae said softly, staring down into Tyee's dark eyes. She didn't break eye contact as he slowly stood up and walked towards her.

"Say that again." Tyee's breath caressed her skin. He was so close to her. His hands stayed firmly by his sides as he waited for her to respond.

Rae's eyes darted between his as her pulse quickened. She tried to speak but had to swallow before she could. Tyee's gaze followed the movement in her throat before finding her eyes again. "I'm glad you were here this afternoon."

Tyee's eyes turned molten as he drew closer to the acrobat, careful not to touch her. "Why?"

Rae licked her lips before pursing them together. *Make a decision, it's now or never.* Her internal monologue didn't make the decision easier. Tyee's closeness made Rae's body thrum with the promise of heat and pleasure. Her breathing was ragged while she teetered on the edge of letting go. She searched his eyes again, finding only desire in their dark depths.

She closed the space between them and tangled her fingers in his dark hair. His hands went to her hips and pulled her close. She lifted her head and their lips met in a jolt of heat and passion. Tyee deepened the kiss and Rae moaned with need. She gently nipped his lower lip and took charge of the kiss. Her hands pulled him closer, while his clutched at her back, trying to do the same.

Their bodies were fire everywhere they touched.

Rae's hands moved to the hem of his shirt and tugged it out of his breeches. She kept kissing him forcefully when he tried to pull away. He grabbed her hands gently and pulled away again.

"Rae, stop." Tyee rasped. He pushed a strand of loose hair behind her ear and studied her before both hands lifted to cradle her face. "Slow down, Birdie. We need to talk first."

Rae leaned into Tyee's touch and breathed deeply. "I'm sick of talking, Drifter." Her hands slipped under his shirt and traveled up his back. Her lips teased his with their closeness.

Tyee's hands moved to the back of her neck before becoming tangled in her hair. Their lips danced together again, both getting lost in each other. Rae tugged Tyee's shirt up again, and he didn't stop her this time. They separated long enough for Rae to pull it off his and study the horseman's scars. Her fingers were feather-light as they traced each one. Her eyes caught his and asked the question she couldn't formulate in words.

"Troubled past, remember?" Tyee growled before capturing her lips and drinking her in again. His hands were at her waist again, sending goosebumps along her exposed midriff. He held her close and whispered in her ear. "This is dangerous, Birdie. You could hurt me." She could feel his smirk as he trailed kisses up her neck. He ended at her jawline and placed his forehead on hers. Both panted, trying to catch their breath, pulses racing. Rae closed her eyes, breathing in the scent of leather and horseflesh.

Suddenly, she felt empty air where Tyee had been. He sat on her trunk, gazing steadily at her with a tormented expression.

She moved to stand between his legs and brushed a hand through his hair. It moved to rest on his cheek while she searched his eyes. "I could. You need to decide if it's worth the risk."

"What do you mean?" Tyee closed his eyes.

"I can't promise you anything, Tyee. There's too much going on in our lives right now. But we can take comfort in each other for the night. We can indulge ourselves this one time." Her hand moved to his chin, lifting it to look at her.

He opened eyes that blazed. "No strings?" His voice had an edge to it that took Rae aback. She bit her lip and nodded.

Tyee stood again, pulling the acrobat into a fierce kiss. One hand held her neck while the other toyed with the bottom of her cropped shirt. Heat pooled in her center when he teased her, moving his fingers just below her waistline.

Tyee backed her to the cot, still askew in the tent. He let go of her to right it and heard Rae shed her performance costume. He swallowed when he felt nimble fingers undoing his breeches. Once they were off, he pulled the acrobat on top of him into the humble bed.

They descended into a tangle of limbs, letting their desires consume them.

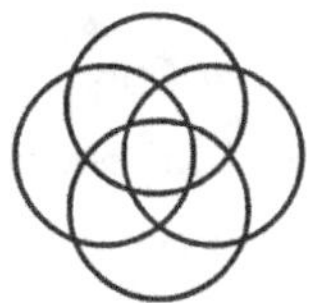

Chapter Twenty-Four

Sunrise dawned on the city of Heimat and the nomadic city settled on its outskirts. The air was crisp and a light frost dotted the grass, giving it a white sheen. Townsfolk and players alike woke from their beds and cots, yawning and rubbing their eyes. Many attended the show the previous night and witnessed Zeke's fall from the trapeze. They talked in hushed tones, exaggerating the story and their part in it.

Most people in Heimat knew Magicae lived among them.

The city had worked hard to build a community around Magicae and Mortals alike. They knew which merchant ships and caravans could be trusted and which ones needed to be kept in the dark about their community. Their northern latitude meant long, cold winters that kept most migrants at bay. Those braving the cold were met with strict new land ownership laws and regulations, making settling a chore. The only way to get around the restrictions was a closely guarded secret. Sponsorship allowed newcomers to buy land but was rarely extended to new Mortals without strong ties to incoming or established Magicae.

The people of Heimat knew they were possibly the last community welcoming Magicae to their ranks. They wanted to keep it that way for as long as possible.

When Darren Vincenzio made his debut, all that hard work was undone. The government of Heimat was overturned by Myra's decree and given to Vincenzio alone. He declared himself mayor and systematically replaced city officials with high-ranking officers and friends or family that dared to brave the cold. He took up residence with his soldiers in the city center, taking the largest city structures to provide housing for his troops. The whole lot were brutes, spending their free time at the brothels and bars down by the docks of the Wharf.

Laws and regulations were overturned with the new government in place and newcomers were welcomed into the city with open arms.

The end of the prosperous community was swift and rang with finality.

Most of the Magicae left the city or hid in fear. Some were reported by the newcomers and shipped to the capital when they were captured by Vincenzio's men. The Circus was the last hope for many, Magicae and Mortal, that wanted to save their family and friends. They depended on their former city leaders and the Circus to get as many out as they could.

Despite the chaos of the previous night's accident, all the children and adults from the Fringe and Lower Districts arrived to the Circus safely. All were accounted for before Zeke took his fall. Johanna had made sure their people followed directions and Simone found efficient ways to coordinate the staggering of groups heading to the carnival tent. Both woke up and made rounds in their respective districts to listen for whispers of children disappearing. Satisfied there weren't any rumors flying around, they met at Rich's bakery to give him a report.

Once that was finished, Johanna made her way to Eddy's to give him their extra supplies. Simone knocked on Tommy's door to give him tips on how to coordinate staggering their groups in the carnival tent.

Both men greeted the women warmly and welcomed their help in finding the best ways to save their people.

Their tasks done, Johanna and Simone went about their daily tasks, keeping one ear to the ground in case trouble began to brew.

The Circus was abuzz with energy, even in the early dawn. Orientation guides brought the newest recruits to different tents and wagons, introducing them to as many people as they could.

The adults nodded and made small talk while the children rubbed their eyes and yawned. They hugged stuffed animals close and clung to their caregivers. They made it through the tour and introductions, ending at the breakfast tables. A large group of children ran to their newest playmates, eager to make new friends despite the early hour. They gripped the newcomers by the hand and hurried them to their table for games involving sticks, rocks, and their imagination. Soon squeals and giggles were heard from the whole mob of them.

The adults watched with soft smiles before forcing their attention back to the overly informative orientation leaders. A couple suppressed yawns while noting the need to identify possible ways they could contribute.

One woman disregarded the bubbly Circus members and kept her eyes glued on the children. She watched a small group of girls whispering, their heads together, until they noticed one newcomer sitting by herself. They moved their circle to include her and slowly, the loner warmed up, talking in excited whispers with the others.

The woman breathed a sigh of relief.

Her little cousin was so shy, she worried she'd have trouble finding friends. With her fears alleviated for the moment, she returned her attention to the young man instructing them on breakfast protocol. She hoped this would become easier after she went through the motions herself instead of trying to commit everything to memory.

"Is this our newest batch of recruits?" A tall man with dark, slightly curly hair said with a smile. The orientation leader stuttered in response. "I will take that as a yes. Let me take over, for now, Bart. Splendid, splendid job, go take a break and enjoy your breakfast." He squeezed the man's shoulder and looked at the six adults huddled together. "Welcome, friends. This place is as much yours as anybody else's. Please feel free to—"

"Are you the Ringmaster?" A middle-aged man asked.

"Please, call me Duncan." He stretched his hand out to shake the man's hand.

The man narrowed his eyes but accepted the handshake. "Where's George?" Whispers started among the group, realizing their point man was absent.

"Seems like he slept in." Duncan winked. "He should be joining shortly. Once the meal bell sounds, it will be a mad dash for the food. I would wait as close to the start of the line as possible. There will be plenty, so please help yourself once the chefs are happy with their offerings."

"Sir?" The young woman with the little cousin asked before the Ringmaster could turn around.

"Madam, please, call me Duncan." The wind Crafter gave a slight bow.

"Duncan, then. How is this place governed? Who's in charge?" Her face was stoic as she stared at the Ringmaster.

"We have a Governing Council with five heads, one for each type of Gift plus a Mortal Head, all voted on by the individuals with those particular Gifts. There are also four general seats voted on by every member of the Circus. The Council is in charge of making the major decisions for our nomadic city and always encourages input from its members. Everyone is welcome to meetings of the Council and encouraged to bring forth new ideas or concerns to any of its members." Duncan noticed the small frown the woman was trying to hide. "You are welcome to attend as long as you partake in our travels." Her frown became more prominent. "Did I say something wrong?"

The woman ducked her head and balled her fists in the plain tunic dress she wore. "When are we going to save the rest?"

Duncan scratched his head. "What do you mean? Speak plainly, I'm a simple man. The more you can spell it out, the better." The new recruits stood next to the beginning of the line for the buffet. More and more members of the Circus were making their way to the breakfast tables. Some joined the group, intrigued by the conversation, while others hung back, torn between being polite and wanting to hear the young woman's response.

"The Magicae in Heimat. When are we going to rescue the rest of them? The ones that can blend in and pass for Mortal?" She clenched her jaw. "When do I get to see my parents again?"

Duncan looked stunned. He noticed the crowd growing and felt the pressure of their stares weighing on him. He closed his eyes, trying to calm his mind. The only thing he could do was be honest. He whispered, holding the woman's gaze. "I don't know. Our priority is getting the children and those in danger out."

"But all Magicae are in danger. Heimat is the last place we could live without fear. We can't just leave them here." The woman snapped.

Duncan's face turned grim. "That is exactly what we must do." He sighed. "We must trust in them just as they trust in us. We need to gather our people and prepare for the battles to come. The next time we return to Heimat, it will be to the drumbeats of war."

"Pretty words, but that doesn't explain why we can't fight now." She hissed as her eyes became watery. She wiped at them with her sleeve, trying to hide the emotions bubbling inside her.

Duncan and the woman were at a standstill. The woman had her arms crossed as if to protect herself from the realization she could do little to change the Ringmaster's mind. Duncan studied the woman closely, trying to find the words to make her understand.

The crowd around them grew larger. Many people wanted to listen to the argument and even more joined, curious to find out what the commotion was about. Furious whispers sounded as the crowd parted to let someone through.

"Can someone explain what's going on here?" Nan asked as she made her way slowly through the crowd, holding on to Luc and Javie's shoulders, going easy on the old legs, stiff with disuse.

Duncan broke out of his reverie to answer his old friend. "This woman is frustrated with me."

Nan cackled and then doubled over in pain. "Don't do that to me, dearie.

You're going to hurt these old, worn-out bones." She shook her head with a smile. "I can see you've upset the poor thing." She turned her attention to the woman. "What has Duncan said now?"

"We can't leave them." The woman's voice cracked.

Nan furrowed her brows and shot Duncan a look. "Child, we aren't leaving anybody. We're saving those we can and going to find a place for our young and old." She paused to look at the surrounding crowd. "Heimat is a special place to all of us. We would never abandon it, but I'm a hindrance in a fight. The children are a hindrance. We can't ask them to bear arms against our enemies."

She searched the young woman's face before she shrugged off Luc and Javie. Cutting off their protests, she took a couple of shaky steps toward the woman. Nan rubbed the woman's upper arms and smiled sadly when she instinctively used her forearms to support the old woman. "Understand me when I say we leave now to fight another day."

The woman nodded as the tension left her body. Nan patted her cheek and looked at the crowd. "The day is coming when all of you will be asked to make a choice. The Resistance will need all of you to succeed. Be honest with yourself and decide if you wish to join the front lines or man the home front. Each will be challenging in its own way. Be vigilant and don't do anything stupid."

Nan took a deep breath and Duncan frowned. The old woman still wasn't herself just yet. He feared she was overdoing it and made to step towards her when Luc and Javie took both her arms and led her to a table. He noted the way her body sagged with relief at the support from her grandchildren and his frown deepened. He'd need to talk to Chiara to see if there was anything else they could do for the old woman. The meal bell sounded and the crowd dispersed.

Rae and Tyee were the last ones to make it through the breakfast line.

They overslept after spending most of the night indulging in each other.

Rae's cheeks flushed when she saw heads turn and whispers following the two of them. She straightened her shirt and tried to flatten her disheveled hair.

Tyee leaned into her from behind and whispered in her ear. "It's useless, Birdie. You're better off letting people talk. They'll do it regardless of what you say to them."

She stepped forward quickly, shaking her head and clenching her teeth. The last thing she wanted was rumors to start as people came to their own conclusions about the two of them. It was their own damn business and everyone should leave them alone.

Tyee ducked his head to hide a smirk. The fiery blond couldn't be reasoned with when she was like this. He became engrossed in watching her while she walked through the line in front of him. His only thought was how badly he wanted to take her back to her tent and ravish her again. He licked his lips as he envisioned kissing her until she was dizzy and worshiping every inch of her skin.

Best to stop that train of thought before I get too carried away.

No strings, remember?

The horseman shook his head and took a plate. Rae grabbed food quickly in front of him and shot him a look. He nodded at her, encouraging her to sit with her friends. Her eyes were grateful as she smiled at him. She nodded before turning towards the tables.

And ran right into George.

"Oof." She tried to save her plate, but it went flying out of her hands, following the momentum she had when she turned. She was able to stop herself from falling, but only just. When she straightened, she noticed George hadn't moved an inch.

"Can I help you?" She asked loudly, not realizing who she had run into. "Or are you just going to stand in my way?"

"Excuse me?" George asked, clearly distracted.

"I said move your ass!" Rae dusted herself off and looked him in the eyes, taking out her frustrations on the tall Mortal.

"You don't have to yell." George turned around and looked down his nose at her. Recognition flashed in his eyes as he continued. "Maybe you should watch where you're going next time."

Rae missed the glance Tyee threw at her. He knew this wouldn't end well for the newcomer. Before he could intervene, Rae seethed.

"Don't talk to me like I'm an idiot. If you weren't in my way, I wouldn't have wasted so much food." She fumed as she recognized the man before her. "I know you're new to the Circus, but we don't have the resources to waste here." A wind picked up, blew through the breakfast area, and buffeted the lithe man. He stumbled a bit but remained standing.

Everybody, even the children, paused their eating and conversing when they felt the wind. Most people were unaware of Rae's afflictions and sat dumbstruck as the wind obeyed her beck and call. She missed the look Nan shot her and the way the Herbalist's lips pursed and her fingers steepled while watching the exchange.

George leveled a gaze at the angry woman. "Resorting to threats now? How high and mighty of you." George straightened. "If you want to hurt me, be my guest. It says more about your character than mine."

Rae glared at him. "If I wanted to hurt you, it would already be done. Just stay out of my way."

George nodded in acknowledgment before Rae brushed past him to the scrap bucket. Any leftovers or uneaten food were collected, sorted, and brought to the animal yard to be recycled. George looked at the tables and shook his head when he saw eyes on him. He left towards his tent in a huff.

Rae finished collecting her fallen food and turned to start over. Heat crept up her neck as people resumed eating and talking, shooting glances toward her every so often. She held her head high as she started towards the front of the line.

Tyee stepped in front of her and thrust a tray filled with food on top of her empty tray. She looked into his face, confused.

"Take it, and go eat with your friends." He turned to grab another filled tray and moved past her to sit with his horsemen. He had an idea for the evening's show he wanted to run by them.

Rae murmured her thanks to empty air before going to sit with Luc and her family. Luc touched her arm when she sat down, offering unspoken support. Rae smiled at her friend before tucking into the food Tyee grabbed for her.

As she ate, she felt eyes on her. Looking up, she caught Nan staring warmly at her.

"So the wind, eh?" The old woman asked.

Rae ducked her head. "I'm sorry, Abuela. I was going to find you before breakfast, but I overslept."

Nan raised one eyebrow with a knowing smile. "I can only speculate why." She winked before taking a deliberate look toward Tyee's table. She laughed when the acrobat's face took on a rosy glow. "Good for you, child. I would have done the same."

"I'm out." Javie stood up and grabbed the empty plates from the table. He sorted the scraps and stacked the empty plates before joining a table of young men his own age.

Nan chuckled before bringing her attention back to the Crafter across from her. "Just know I approve. Now, when are we doing that binding?"

Rae glanced at Luc before jutting her chin out. "My fire is gone. There's no need for binding anymore."

Nan frowned. "What do you mean, gone?"

"I can't feel it. My core is a storm, not the inferno it once was," Rae replied. Her hand tightened around her fork as she gazed inward. Once again, where she once felt heat, she now felt ice. "Look." Rae held her hands out and called her

Craft. Gentle breezes toyed around them instead of the sparks she once had.

Nan mulled over Rae's words, concern knitting her eyebrows. She gripped both of Rae's hands in hers and turned them over and over, trying to find answers that weren't there. She looked up at Rae, finally accepting her words.

"Have you ever seen or heard of this before, Abuela?" Luc asked. "I don't think you quite believed me last night."

Nan's gaze shifted to her granddaughter, and she rolled her shoulders back, releasing Rae's hands. "Never. In all my years, this has never happened." She pursed her lips. "My Abuela told me years ago there were some Crafters born with two Crafts. Sometimes, they didn't learn they had the affinity for more than one until later in life, but never has one Craft simply overtaken the other." Her eyebrows furrowed together. "Did you feel a shift in your Craft or did it happen without warning?"

Rae thought back to the night before.

Huntress, did all that happen just yesterday?

Rae's mind fluttered past learning her condition, trashing her tent, and settled on just before intermission. "I used my fire in my tent, right before intermission, but not again once I got to the big top. There wasn't a shift, just the normal feeling of it wanting to be released. I reached for it as I saw Zeke falling—Huntress, I forgot about Zeke." The color drained from Rae's face thinking about her trapeze partner. She turned to Luc and asked, "Have you seen him today? I should go check on him."

Luc placed her hand on Rae's arm when she tried to stand. "He's resting. Let him be Rae." Luc searched her friend's wild eyes. "He'd want you to stay and figure this out."

Rae looked between the two women. She gulped down the dread she felt and continued, "When I reached to control my Craft, it felt different. It was so cold... I was paralyzed. And then something happened, and my body went through these motions as if I was trying to slow Zeke's fall. It happened so quickly... if there's a switch, I have no idea how to flip it."

Nan stared intently, drumming her knobby fingers against the table. "Hmm.

Your color is better. As is your appetite." She motioned toward the plate, piled high, that Rae resumed devouring. "Can you feel your limits?"

Rae paused and closed her eyes. She reached inside the storm. The wind blew angrily around the three women, ruffling their clothes and whipping loose strands of hair. Rae was oblivious as she explored the storm inside.

When she opened her eyes, the wind left just as abruptly as it had come. "It's different from my fire. I don't feel the edges of my power, just the number of winds within the storm. I feel some sort of limit, but it's like threads, not the strands of sparks I'm used to." Nan and Luc shared a look before bursting into laughter.

"You Crafters are a strange bunch," Nan said. "I do not know what that distinction is, but if it feels different, it probably is. I'm perplexed about why your fire is gone, though." She sobered. "We need to be careful and make sure we're ready for the binding, should something change. I will consult the texts I have on Crafters and see if anything mentions having multiple Crafts." Nan patted Rae's arm and continued, "You look good child, but don't let your guard down, it could just be a matter of time before the Curse strikes again. You come and see me if anything changes."

"Of course," Rae replied, gritting her teeth to stop herself from arguing with the old woman.

The three continued chatting while Rae finished her breakfast. Before long, it was once again time to prepare to save their people. They could only hope this time wouldn't be as eventful as the last one.

Chapter Twenty-Five

Rae slipped into the Herbalists' medical tent as soon as Luc was satisfied the three acrobats knew what they were doing for tonight's show. It would be a little different, but they ran through the tricky bits a couple of times and felt confident they could pull it off.

Luc and Damien went to check on Abuela. She was trying to take part in the show despite the Healers' explicit instructions not to. They would have their hands full with the fiery, petite woman.

Rae took it upon herself to check on the last link in their chain. She nodded at the Healers as she passed by. She stopped when she could see Zeke's cot and found him talking to Freya.

"Are you sure I have to stay here another night? I feel fine. No, seriously! Hear me out!" Zeke grasped at her hands before she could walk away. Freya laughed and danced away from the bedridden acrobat.

"Oh, honey. Settle down and buy me dinner first." She winked and laughed as Zeke shook his head, still trying to plead his case. "It's not gonna happen, Zeke. You can holler 'til your throat gives out. The rule is twenty-four hours under observation with any head injury. The chief Healer does not take kindly to rule benders," she said as she took some last-minute notes about Zeke's symptoms.

Zeke noticed Rae standing outside the sheet separating his bed from the rest of the tent. "Rae! Come work your magic. Tell Freya she should risk bending the rules. I'm right as rain."

Rae stepped closer to Zeke's cot but shook her head. "I saw you fall Z. Listen to Freya." She looked at the Healer. "She knows what she's doing." Freya smiled at her before moving to check Zeke's vitals one last time.

"I knew there was a reason I liked Rae best." Freya winked and made her way to the exit of Zeke's section. She blew the two of them a kiss and disappeared.

Rae laughed at Zeke's sullen expression. "Oh, stop. You need the rest, Z."

"I feel fine, Rae." He bunched his blanket with both hands. "I feel so stupid and should have been more careful. I was so tired after our set, and I wasn't paying attention to my feet. I couldn't catch myself." Zeke hung his head.

"Z, you always tell me to stop being so hard on myself. Now it's my turn to say the same to you. Things happen." Rae squeezed her friend's shoulder.

"They didn't happen to the three of you," he countered, shaking off her arm. Zeke sighed. "Sorry for snapping, Sparks. I hate sitting in this med tent. You need to bust me out of here." He gripped her bare arm and recoiled. He shot her a look and then gripped her arm again.

"Rae, why are you so cold? Where's your fire?" he asked, flabbergasted.

"It's gone, Z," Rae said sadly.

"Gone?" Zeke sat up, alarmed by his trapeze partner's tone. "A Craft doesn't disappear."

Her eyes watered as she held his concerned gaze. "I don't know how else to describe it. I can't call a flame or even a spark, and my core is a raging storm." She showed him her hands, and a breeze blew across them. "All I can call is the wind."

Zeke licked his lips and swallowed. "You saved me, didn't you?" Rae looked at him with wide eyes. "The Healers keep saying my Craft saved me, that Duncan was distracted, so it had to be me. But all I remember is slipping and hitting my head, everything else is a blur. I would remember power being pulled from my core and into my veins, even if I did it subconsciously. There's no way I did it."

Rae hesitated before replying. "I think I saved you, too." She studied her hands. "I don't know how, but my wind saved you before I understood what happened to my Craft." The former fire Crafter crossed her arms as if she was trying to hold herself together. "Z, I know I should just be grateful I could save you, but there's a hole in my chest that aches. Nothing I've tried can fill it."

"It's okay to grieve losing part of your identity." He patted his cot, inviting her to sit next to him. She did so gingerly, careful not to jostle her friend. He took one of her hands in his and looked into eyes filled with misery. He continued, "Your fire made you who you are. It will always be a part of you, in here." He placed a hand on her heart. "We'll find your fire. It has to be somewhere inside you. We just need to find a way to access it." He took his hand off her chest and gave a sly smile. "At least now we can finally see if your temper was because of your fire or if your temper strengthened your fire."

Rae burst into a laugh and playfully hit Zeke's shoulder. "I've told you a million times, I don't have a temper," she huffed. Zeke lifted one eyebrow and gave her a look. She thought about the scene with George and relented. "Okay, so sometimes I can be a little hotheaded, but that doesn't mean I have a temper."

"Sure you don't," Zeke inflected.

Rae rolled her eyes. "You're the worst." She tilted her head back and closed her eyes. "Huntress, I've missed you. Promise me you'll never hurt yourself again," she said with a smile.

"Never getting hurt again. I swear upon my grave." Zeke kept a straight face, making his trapeze partner laugh. "Now fill me in on everything you promised me you would."

Rae sobered and tucked a strand of loose hair behind her ear. She laid down next to Zeke on his cot as he moved to give her room. This brought back memories of climbing into each other's cots whenever they had a nightmare. The familiar sense of safety comforted them both, and Rae told Zeke about the events of the other day. She started with the Crafter's curse and her conversations with Abuela and Duncan. She told him about trashing her tent, and the relief she felt in breaking things despite the terrible choice she faced. Rae finished with Tyee finding her, surprising her with his kindness, and vowing to be there when she went through the binding.

"Prick thought he could invite himself to something that hadn't been decided upon," Rae seethed, turning to look at Zeke.

Zeke rolled his eyes. "You're so thick, Sparks. The man wants to take you to his bed. He can't do that if you're dead." His eyes narrowed when he saw her move her head to hide her expression. "Continue," Zeke commanded, hoping he would find out why his friend was being so dodgy about the horseman.

Rae continued and told him about reaching the big top, the comfort he gave her without knowing anything, and the terror she felt when he fell. She described in more detail how she Crafted the wind that saved his life and went through the motions of wind Crafting despite never training with them.

"You called me Duncan," Rae said suddenly, remembering Zeke murmuring on the ground after the accident.

"I did?" Zeke shifted to look at her. "I was pretty out of it last night. Everything is pretty foggy from after I hit my head until I woke up this morning. Why would I call you Duncan?"

"The only thing I could come up with is maybe my wind Craft gave off a similar signature to his? It confirmed for me that my Craft was wind and not fire anymore."

"Hmm. I guess. What happened next?" Zeke prodded.

Rae told him about the agony of waiting for the show to end, checking in at the med tent, and how cringeworthy their friends were.

"Honestly, I love both of them, but they can be too much sometimes. And since when do they call each other their heartmates?" Rae vented. "Huntress, it's nauseating."

"So gross." Zeke nodded, before continuing, "I'm happy for them, though. It couldn't have happened to two more deserving people."

Rae sighed. "You're right. I shouldn't be so hard on them."

"Ha! Jealous much?" Zeke nudged Rae with his shoulder. "So did you go to the bonfire to find Tyee and avoid cleaning your tent? Or did you give in and put it to rights?"

Rae let out a burst of nervous laughter. "Neither," she spit out, before rolling onto her side, away from her friend.

"What? Hey, come back here. What happened?" Zeke sat up so he could get a better look at Rae's expression.

"I went back to my tent and found Tyee cleaning it for me," Rae replied.

Zeke knitted his eyebrows together and touched her shoulder, wordlessly asking her to turn over. "Why?"

Rae sighed and shifted on the cot. She murmured something too low for Zeke to make out.

"Say that again? I couldn't hear you," he complained.

"I think he cares about me," she repeated. Zeke motioned for her to continue. "I attacked him because I thought he was an intruder. When he explained he was trying to help me out, I couldn't process everything quickly enough. I kissed him." Rae threw up her hands before bringing them down and rubbing her face, slicking her hair back. Her hands cupped her face while her eyes went wide along with her smile, showing almost all her teeth. She gave Zeke a conspiratorial glance and continued, "Then I convinced him to stay the night."

Zeke gasped in shock. "You slept with Tyee?!"

"Shhh!" Rae motioned with her hands. "Not so loud, Z! This curtain isn't exactly soundproof."

"You slept with Tyee?!" Zeke whispered this time. Rae nodded, giggling. "You saucy minx! I told you it was going to happen," he said while Rae rolled her eyes. "Was it the best sex you've ever had?" Zeke gave a wicked grin.

Rae just shoved the acrobat and laughed. "You'll never know." Rae gave him a wink and laughed.

"Are you going to do it again?" Zeke waggled his eyebrows.

Rae bit her lip. "I don't know. We said no strings." She propped herself up on one elbow and shrugged her shoulders. "But I wouldn't say no," she ended with a dangerous glint to her smile. With those words, she moved to get up. Zeke clutched at her arms, trying to get her to stay. She was able to disentangle herself and stood out of arm's reach from the cot.

Zeke hung his head in defeat. "No. You can't leave," he pleaded. Rae felt a flash of guilt as her best friend looked at her with panic. She knew Zeke hated the med tent and the isolation it brought. When they were younger, he had to stay in the med tent for weeks because of a broken leg and refusing to take the Healers' tonics. He had panic attacks for years afterward whenever he entered the med tent.

The isolation brought back the fear of abandonment Zeke developed in his early childhood. His father left when his eyes changed and it was clear his mother wasn't willing to turn in their only son. He took Zeke's sisters and moved a couple of towns over, never to return or ask after his wife and young son again. When the Uprising took place, Zeke's mother fled without him, fearing she would be executed for treason and hiding one of the Magicae. She couldn't bring herself to kill her son, so she left without a trace.

Zeke was an orphan until the Circus came to town that summer.

In those early days, a couple of Shifters manned the gates and made note of any Magicae in the crowd. Once one was identified, they were tailed by a crew member and eventually brought to the back. Some Shifters could still sense the difference between Magicae and Mortals, making them ideal for the task.

Zeke was brought to the back, trembling, fearing for his life when he saw Rae playing with a flame in her hand, young and reckless with her Craft. She giggled when she saw Zeke studying her and waved him over. They were rarely seen apart from that moment onward.

Rae's heart squeezed as she stared into Zeke's eyes. She hugged him fiercely, whispering, "I'll be back in the morning, Z. Get some rest."

Zeke relaxed into Rae's tight embrace and responded, "Promise?"

"Of course." She ruffled his hair and chucked his chin before walking to where the curtain hung, pulling it back slightly. She brought two fingers to her brow and left her friend with a salute, ignoring Zeke's sigh as he considered everything she'd confided.

Duncan sat inside the empty big top, crouching with his elbows on his knees. He traced a pattern in the dirt as he gazed between his boots. He felt someone enter the tent and closed his eyes. Duncan sighed when the presence plopped down in a seat next to him. Silence stretched between Duncan and his new companion.

Finally, a throat cleared, begging the Ringmaster to acknowledge its bearer.

Duncan spoke, "What can I do for you, Chiara?" He looked up and confirmed it was the woman who promised she would find him again. Chiara placed a hand on his arm.

"You owe me a conversation." She looked at him through hooded lashes.

"Chiara—, you know now is not the time."

"Why not?" she challenged. When Duncan didn't respond, she tried again. "Talking may help you decide what needs to be done next."

Duncan sighed again. "Nothing is going to prepare us for what's coming." He shifted in his seat. "I talked with Nan... she wants us to go into the Forest."

Chiara inhaled sharply and withdrew her hand. "Certainly you aren't entertaining that thought."

"I have to. It's the only path I can see that doesn't end in bloodshed. Going south means long days on the road, avoiding towns, and risking lives. Our ranks are the fullest they've ever been and include young children not used to such travel. Speed will be limited. Chiara, we'll be sitting ducks out there."

"But the Forest, Duncan. The dangers... They're not just ghost stories. People die there."

"They disappear, Chiara. Nobody knows if they're dead or if they found what they went looking for." Duncan dusted off his trousers before leaning forward.

"Most people don't go to the Forest looking *for* something, they go there running *from* something." She rubbed the back of her neck. "The very trees clutch at you and little sunlight reaches past the canopy. Not to mention it's so thick in there you can barely move. How will we get the wagons through?" Chiara wrung her hands and brought them to her chest.

"Nan says there's a path only Herbalists can find. We'll be able to take the smaller wagons through. Chiara, please. I need your support in this." He grabbed both of her hands in his. "You asked me what you could do to help, and this is it. Your voice will help convince the others."

Chiara stared at the man that led them through everything. Duncan had been the first to mobilize and save their people. He was the one that pushed them to do more after they made it to Heimat, to actively seek their people instead of hoping they found their way to safety.

Chiara bit her lip. She knew the history of their caravan, she knew every face in the crowd, and she also knew they trusted her. She was the Head Herbalist on the Council and the most talented Healer in the caravan. Her tinctures and creams were unmatched, frequently saving parents from a fussy babe, children from their recklessness, and the elders from the onslaught of old age. She spent time with all their people, not just the Herbalists. Her word would go far to convince their people.

She needed to decide if she believed in Duncan enough to do what he asked of her. She searched his face and found desperation tinged with guilt. Chiara hesitated.

"I know this is a lot. But there is no second plan. We need tonight and tomorrow to go swiftly and smoothly, and then we need to flee. If our people don't come, I don't know what happens to them." He tucked a strand behind her ear and cupped her cheek. "I need you," he sighed, looking into her green eyes. "Think about it, Healer. If you have another way, I'm all ears." He took one of her hands, kissed it, and stood.

With one last look, Duncan left the big top. Chiara stayed seated and watched the Ringmaster leave the tent to make last-minute preparations for the second night of shows. She furrowed her brows and sighed. She had a lot to think about for the next couple of days.

Chiara got up and ambled back to the medical tent, to see what tinctures were low and whether new ones needed to be created.

Chapter Twenty-Six

George stood next to the ticket booth, shifting his weight from one foot to the other. He watched the crew of the Circus with interest as they hurried back and forth between the buildings and tents within the circus yard. Most ran supplies to various places, while others made last-minute fixes to drooping fabric or scuffed buildings, and others picked up loose trash and debris. They worked fiendishly, hurling insults and trying to one-up each other as they sped around the yard.

George was in awe of the way this nomadic city worked like a well-oiled machine. There was no denying its members believed in their mission and took pride in bringing it to light. He always thought Heimat was the pinnacle of a supportive community, but the Circus raised the bar to another level.

His musings were interrupted when a burly woman made her way toward him. He watched her face transform as she moved through the crowd. She smiled and waved at some, threw a teasing insult to a few teenagers, and ruffled the hair of one young boy around the age of ten. Her path was a beeline straight for him, making George settle onto his feet, preparing for whatever the woman had to say.

"Hail, good sir! You have a moment to spare?" she asked, moving to stand next to the Heimat man.

"Aye. And you are?" George held his hand out to the woman. She shook it with clearly restrained strength and beamed.

"Jess. I'm the Head Forger and resident Strong woman. And you're our contact for Heimat, correct?" she asked.

"Yes, ma'am." George dropped his hand and looked at the woman in front of him. She held herself with the confidence of someone in charge, despite the dirt covering her face and hands. He appreciated her blunt way of speaking, as he'd never enjoyed playing games when it came to conversation. George could slip through a crowd unnoticed but struggled to navigate conversations that went in circles.

"Great. We need to refill some of our supplies before heading out tomorrow night. If I get you a list, can you find someone to fulfill it?" Jess asked. She crossed her arms in a challenge when she caught him looking her over. "Or should I do it myself?"

George's mouth went dry. "It'll be done," he grumbled. "My apologies. I can't help but admire this community and its people. I meant no disrespect."

Jess nodded. "Accepted. I wouldn't look at any of the young lasses like that though, as most will knock your teeth out and the others would come for you in the night." She showed her teeth when she smiled. "It takes a while to be accepted as one of the players; a little longer when you go after one of their favorites." Jess shot him a pointed look.

George stuck his hands in his pockets. "I've never been known to bite my tongue and can't stand people that yell to get their way. I wasn't going to just roll over for the girl."

"Aye. But not even helping to clean up? Wasting resources we don't have?" she replied.

George ducked his head. "I could've handled it better, I guess." He looked Jess straight in the eyes. "Don't get me wrong, I stand by what I said, but I see your point that my delivery could've been better. That woman—"

"Stop right there. You shouldn't talk about someone when you don't know their story." Jess dusted off her costume and turned to take her leave. "I'll send a runner with my list before the show opening."

George gave a wave as Jess rushed off. He took his hands out of his pockets and ran them over his short-cropped hair. It looked like he might have to make an apology to the vexing Crafter.

He straightened his stance and kept his vigil by the ticketing booth. He had a job to do; finding his place in this new community could wait.

The sun started sinking on the western skyline while the Circus made last-minute adjustments. They had fewer recruits coming than last night, but a Shifter babe and his mother would be hard to hide. Everyone needed to be ready to hurry. Word had gone around that some soldiers and Vincenzio's higher-ups would be in attendance as well. The performers needed to impress their enemy and keep their Gifts and accumulation of people hidden.

Duncan's face was haggard as he grabbed a bowl of stew and some bread from the concession stand. He waved his thanks and leaned against the side of the building, shoveling food into his mouth. He skipped lunch earlier and knew he needed the sustenance.

He felt a presence to his left, deeper in the shadows.

"You can show your face, my dear," he said into the dark.

Rae stepped out and gave a soft smile. "I never could sneak up on you, huh?"

Duncan laughed. "Never. What's troubling you, my dear? Or did I take the wind from your sails?" he asked with a wry smile.

A flush crept up Rae's neck. "I tried to find you after breakfast, but Luc insisted we needed more practice since Zeke is out. It all happened so fast and I don't know how or why."

Duncan nodded, concern in his eyes. "The bad luck just keeps coming. First Abuela, now Zeke. How is he doing?"

"Upset that he's stuck in the med tent, but physically, he seems fine." Rae bit her lip. "Duncan, the wind moved through me of its own accord. Zeke could've died."

Duncan pulled her into a one-armed hug. "But he didn't. As terrifying as it was, hold on to that." He released the young woman. "I heard about what happened at breakfast after I left." He furrowed his eyebrows. "Your fire is truly gone?"

"It's like it disappeared without a trace. I can't explain it." She blew some hair out of her face to distract herself from the dark thoughts threatening to take over. She searched his face, taking the bread he offered. "Have you ever met a Crafter with two Crafts?"

Duncan took a couple more bites of stew before answering. "Just because I haven't seen it doesn't mean it can't happen. Abuela and I talked for great length about this. We think your fire is locked deep inside. You felt yourself losing control of it and buried it deep within." He finished the last few bites of his food and set his bowl down. "You need to find the key to whatever room you locked it away in."

Rae shook her head. "Why would I be able to Craft the wind then? Isn't Crafting in the blood? Isn't it something you're born with?"

"I don't know, my dear." Duncan stared at his hands. "A lot of what we knew about our Gifts was lost in the Uprising. The books from the State Library were burned by Myra years ago. A lot of the elder Magicae perished in the destruction that followed. We are at a disadvantage when it comes to the history of our people." He sighed. "Have you been training in your new Craft?"

Rae nodded and dropped into a crouch. She held one arm out and the other above her head, her feet staggered. She closed her eyes and breathed deeply. Rae focused on pulling a couple of winds from the storm inside and letting them slide through her hands.

She opened her eyes and smiled. She thrust the arm above her head out in front of her and brought her extended arm back. Her right foot swept to the side as her arms followed. Her movements were fluid and practiced. She went through the first several positions every Crafter learned at a young age.

Training started with learning the positions and the breathing that accompanied it. Rae's breathing matched her movements, breathing in, breathing out, thrusting her arms, and shuffling her feet. Occasionally, she crouched low and swept one leg out.

Once a young Crafter mastered the positions and the breathing, they could add Crafting to the mix. They would start by calling a flame or a pebble or such and gradually work towards more.

The thought process was once the body learned its movements, the Craft could become an extension of it, controlled by the movements and breathing of the positions. The basics were the same for each Craft but then became more specific as the student added more of their Craft to the positions.

Rae finished, breathing hard, and held a low crouch, a mirror of her starting position. Duncan beamed as he gave her a round of applause. For only having control of the wind for such a short time, Rae already demonstrated the promise of mastery. It was inspiring. She started, coming back to herself, and shot him a look.

"That was wonderful. You look like a full-fledged air Crafter. I can tell you've been practicing."

"I always run through my positions first thing in the morning. The first couple of times were hard, trying to get ahold of the wind, but I feel more confident with it now." Rae moved to stand next to Duncan and leaned against the wall with him.

"Once we get out of Heimat, we will start experimenting. Abuela is still looking in her books for something, but you and I both know Crafting is as much about feeling as it is about knowing. Keep looking, my dear, your fire's in there somewhere." Duncan squeezed her shoulder before grabbing his bowl from where it lay on the ground and striding towards the big top.

Time for the show to begin again.

For the wheel to turn and lives to change.

The gates opened, and the flood began.

George watched for purple bands. The crowds ebbed and flowed like the tide. People took the bandannas hesitantly, unsure of what they were for until ticket takers explained they were a way to bring the Circus home with them. They wanted the cloth to remind everyone of the memories made and entice them to come back. The people were relieved it was only a marketing tactic but disappointed the colors didn't grant certain extras to those lucky enough to get the right color.

George knew people craved eliteness more than anything. Despite the community he grew up in, he knew men and women both craved recognition.

Recognition came with power and power was the root of most evil in Kamore.

George knew that was why his home was in disarray. Power threatened his neighbors, his family, and the city he loved. Watching those bigots overtake his home had been the hardest thing George had ever done. Many days, Rich was the only one stopping him from doing something he would regret.

He couldn't decide whether this type of waiting was better or worse.

His heart clenched every time he thought past the next few days. He didn't know how he was going to leave his family, for Goddess knew how long. George's responsibility hung like chains, the weight crushing his soul; leaving felt unbearable, but he knew staying would be even worse.

A flash of purple caught his eye. He stuck his hands in his pockets and sucked in a fistful of air. He whistled an old Wharf tune and waited. George cracked a smile when he heard another whistle sing the chorus. *Good ole Eddy. Knew he'd figure it out.* George walked away from the ticket booth, whistling occasionally and listening for the responding tune.

He ended up on the opposite side of the concession stand before he stopped. He waited in the shadows until he heard footsteps. George whistled once more and came face-to-face with the Wharfman.

"Bollocks. Why'd'ya have to walk so far?" Eddy said, panting, leaning on his knees.

"We needed a safe place to talk," George replied.

"Aye, but I'm sure there are closer places than this." Eddy straightened and thumped George's arm. "This is to get me back for throwin' that knife at ya. Touché, my friend!" the man wheezed.

"Jeezez, Eddy. You need to stop smoking before every step leaves you winded," George scolded. "You got numbers for me?"

"Aye." Eddy held up a finger before coughing. He cleared his throat and continued, "Mikel's got ten kiddos and two adults, and Tamara's got fifteen and five." He turned his head and coughed a few more times. Eddy ran his sleeve roughly across his face and blinked hard. "Artist's Row has the highest numbers, a'course, cuz of the clientele it attracts. They should have just enough supplies and know to stagger. I think we're all ready."

George clasped the other man's forearm. "Goddess bless you, Eddy. That's all I needed." He squeezed the other man's arm but didn't let go. "I have one more favor to ask of you, old friend." His free hand pulled a slip of paper from his pocket. "The Circus needs more supplies. I was asked to see if I could procure it for them. Take a look and let me know if you think it's doable." He let go of the Wharfman and handed him the paper.

Eddy scanned the list of supplies and sucked on his teeth. "This is a lot of stuff, lad. It'll take me a day or two to get all this. You might be gone before it's ready." He glanced at his friend. "I'll gather what I can and send it tomorrow."

"That's all I can ask. Thanks, Eddy. I knew we could count on ya." George rubbed the back of his neck, contemplating what he'd tell Jess. "What did your people on the docks say to the backup plan?"

Eddy grinned wickedly. "They said they'll be ready tonight. They're all praying something goes wrong, so they have an excuse to stick it to our fabulous mayor." He shrugged his shoulders. "I told them they were fools, but they did little to heed my warnings. Headstrong lads and lasses that they are."

George chuckled. "We've all been there. Their passions will be rewarded one way or another. I'm sure they'll find a way to strike at the Mayor, no matter what happens."

"Aye, you might be right. Anyway, I have a brood I should check in on. Take care of yourself. I'll drop off supplies tomorrow around midday." Eddy saluted his friend before walking towards a group with purple bandannas proudly on display.

George watched quietly before making his way to the side tent, where Jess and Duke performed for the crowds. He would tell Jess the news and see what she had to say. He had a feeling she wouldn't be pleased by the lukewarm answer, but the time crunch made all things more difficult.

Tyee and his horsemen were performing in the big top. They were doing the same performance as in Windemere but added a big twist to the end. Normally, Tyee improvised the last trick, but tonight it was pre-planned. Instead of ending with individual tricks, they were going to switch horses. This meant they needed to know who would end up where, and which horses would tolerate each other long enough for the switch.

They practiced it during rehearsal, and it was a disaster. The horses kept fidgeting and hated losing their rider only to gain another. They almost gave up when one of his brothers suggested they tweak how they mounted and dismounted. After doing so, they practiced again, and it worked seamlessly.

Tyee was sweating as all five of them moved their horses into a tight circle in the center of the ring. They gave a nod and urged their steeds into a slow lope, keeping their circle tight and in sync.

They let out a yell and dropped onto the ground outside the circle of horses. They hung onto their saddles and ran alongside their steeds for a couple of oscillations. Then, releasing their mount, they slowed their speed, touching the stirrups of each horse as it passed.

With another yell, they gripped the saddle of the horse they were at and swung into a crouch, back leg stretched out behind them. They rode for several circles before dropping to the ground again.

They slowed until they were in line with the next horse and swung into the saddle. Their legs went over the horses' necks, so they faced backward. One last time, they swung down to the ground and ran until their original horse ran next to them. They kept speed with their horse before swinging into the saddle and breaking the small circle.

They ended in a line in the middle and bowed to both sides of the big top while the crowd went wild. Tyee's chest moved up and down rapidly, breathing hard with the exertion of trying to keep up with Koko for so long. He patted the stallion's neck, wet with sweat. He whispered in the horse's ear and leaned forward to scratch his ears. They exited the center ring in a group as the big cats made their way into the spotlight.

Tyee turned Koko towards the side ring and yelled to his brothers by choice that he would meet up with them later. Koko walked towards the side where Rae, Luc, and Damien watched the show.

Rae noticed him coming and made excuses to Luc and Damien. They shared a look before turning back to the performance.

He held his hand down and she climbed up behind him in her feathered leggings and tight, fringed top that stopped before her navel. Her eagle mask tickled the back of his neck as she looped her arms around his middle. They left the big top altogether and made it to the back of the carnival tent, out of sight from patrons and players alike.

She nuzzled his back before slipping down off of the muscular horse. Tyee swung his leg over and slipped down the side of his faithful companion. He found himself pressed against one of the poles supporting the carnival tent as Rae stepped closer to him.

He met her lips and deepened the kiss, slipping the mask off her face and dropping it to the ground. His hands roamed up and down her sides, sending shivers across her bare skin. She nipped his bottom lip and slipped her hands into his hair. She drove a moan from Tyee's lips as her hands traced his collarbone, sending shivers across his skin while a breeze ruffled their hair.

He gripped her waist and spun them both around so her back was now against the support pole. He kissed her more fervently, the need to be closer driving him to press her harder against the pole.

Rae moved a hand to his chest and pressed gently, the wind blowing in his face. Tyee pulled back unwillingly, chest heaving, recovering from the kiss filled with longing.

"Slow down there, Drifter." She graced his lips with one more touch of hers, taking in the smell of leather and horseflesh, and pulled back again. Her voice rasped, saying, "We still have a job to do." His eyes wandered to her lips as she bit her bottom one. "I have something I want to try. But it might be dangerous."

"Anything." He whispered against her lips, trailing kisses down the side of her neck, hands on her hips pulling her towards him.

Rae pulled back more forcefully, a gust blowing hard into his face. "Tyee, I'm serious."

He looked into eyes hardened into steel and tried to slow his racing heart. He nodded at her. "Shoot, Birdie. What do you need from me?"

She gave him a wary look. "I want to try pulling your life energy and seeing if it calls my fire." Her eyes widened, not believing she spoke those words aloud.

"Of course." Tyee pulled up his sleeve and presented her with his bare forearm, eyes still dark with desire.

"Tyee, think before you offer me your arm. I could hurt you. There's no telling this will work, but if it does, it could start an inferno."

"I'm not scared of getting burned," Tyee smirked as he rolled up his other sleeve. "Do it. Let's see what happens."

Rae searched his face and only found hard resolve. She furrowed her brows and gripped his arms. Her palms tingled with the contact as she closed her eyes. She focused on the energy inside him and opened her inner eye. She smiled when she saw the maroon energy within and gasped when she noticed it was glowing faintly from within.

Strange. His energy didn't do that before. Must be the change in my Craft... Rae mused while she focused on pulling the energy from his forearms to her palms. The energy felt like ice instead of fire this time but still echoed with that unnatural power. It entered her veins slowly while she took the time to look at the core, where her magic resided. She gasped and almost let go.

Tyee looked at the acrobat with concerned eyes. Giving life energy was risky, but he trusted her. He gritted his teeth and hissed as nails dug into his arms. He felt his knees growing weak but refused to stop her. *Just a minute longer. Then I either pass out or she lets go. Maybe both.* Tyee felt sweat trickle down his neck while he focused on staying conscious.

Rae let out a cry and dropped to the ground. Tyee knelt beside her when he felt her grip loosen from his arms. He moved her to her side as her eyelids fluttered rapidly. Her whole body shook a couple of times before going still.

The horseman went cold, watching the woman closely. He felt her neck and let out a sigh of relief when he felt a pulse.

"Thank the Huntress," he whispered while shaking the woman's shoulder. "Rae, wake up. Come on, Birdie, don't do this to me." Tyee looked about wildly, cursing their desire for privacy. He was about to yell for help when Rae stirred, ever so slightly.

"Rae, can you hear me? Come on, wake up, you reckless, reckless woman." Tyee hissed through the ache that started in his lower arms. They would ache for the next few hours along with some dizziness if memory served.

Rae's eyelids opened suddenly as she tried to sit up. Her hand went to her brow and she let out a groan. "Augh, maybe that wasn't the best plan." She closed her eyes again and lay there for a couple more seconds. "Your energy changed," she said with a cough.

She opened her eyes and propped herself up on her elbows. Tyee helped her sit up and sat next to her, their shoulders touching. Rae coughed again before leaning into Tyee's warmth. Her lips pulled up into a tired smile.

"It's in there."

Tyee turned to look at the woman next to him. "Your fire?"

"Yea. It's in the eye of the storm." Her brows pinched together. "It's curious though. I could've sworn droplets and pebbles were swirling with the flames in the center of the storm." She paused, and continued, "Do you think I can control all four Crafts?" Her voice ended in just a whisper.

Tyee was stunned but recovered quickly. "I wouldn't put it past you, but how do you get at the other three if the storm rages so fiercely around them?"

Rae started to respond but saw the lights flashing, signaling the end of inter-mission. "Shit. I gotta go." Both stood up and swung onto the horse that still stood next to them.

Tyee dropped her off at the secret entrance to the side tent.

"Continue this later?" he asked.

"Of course," she smiled and ran into the ring, where her friends already swung from the trapeze.

The sun was well past the horizon while the Circus began its second act. The streets of Heimat were empty, save for the occasional group of young people sauntering towards the Wharf and the trouble that followed. They were the only ones bold enough to openly deny the curfew order, only modified to allow people to attend the Circus. These young people tread on thin ice, banking on only needing to run faster than the soldiers plaguing their city.

A distressed call pierced the night.

"Momma!" cried a young girl around five. "Where are we going?"

"Hush Gemma, we're almost there."

The mother had the young girl's arm in hand, tugging her along the darkened streets. "We need to be quiet or the bad people might find us."

Gemma hated being quiet and didn't understand why they had to leave their warm bed in the first place. She always curled up with her Momma when Daddy was gone. It was their tradition and Gemma couldn't believe her Momma was changing it. The only thing keeping her quiet was the threat of the bad people.

All of Gemma's childish memories were colored with making sure the bad people didn't find her. Her Momma always said never to talk to strangers and never touch the plants. If she touched the plants and someone saw, the bad people would take her away from Momma and Daddy. They were always watching and her Momma even pointed them out several times. She said Daddy didn't believe in them, so it had to be a secret between her and Gemma.

Even now, the little girl scanned the streets, looking for those that were always watching.

"Momma! You're hurting my arm!" wailed the copper-haired, freckle-faced little girl.

Her mother had pulled her sharply into a doorway. She looked both ways down the alley, turned towards her daughter, and got down on one knee. She let go of Gemma's arm and brushed some stray hairs out of her face.

"My little wildflower. My sweet, strong, brave wildflower. Your world will never be the same. Promise me you will do exactly as I say, no matter what." She paused, waiting for a response.

Gemma looked deeply into her mother's bright, teary eyes and nodded her head. She could sense the seriousness of the moment and what her mother needed, so she nodded her head harder.

"That's my girl." Her mother quietly exclaimed as she stood up and took Gemma in her arms. "I love you so much," she said with a kiss.

Gemma giggled as she hugged her mom and whispered, "I love you more."

With Gemma still in her arms, Mirabella Vincenzio knocked on the bakery door in front of them.

Inside the bakery, Rich furrowed his brows. Tommy and Eddy wouldn't report back until tomorrow morning when suspicion couldn't be placed on the baker himself. He looked out the window discreetly and saw the woman and child. The woman looked haggard like only those harboring a secret could.

He quickly closed the curtain and opened the door.

"Come now, hurry young misses before someone sees." The old man closed the door as soon as the pair made their way into the warmth of his home. He studied them after clicking the many locks on his door back into place. The mother was young and looked oddly familiar. The daughter was restless and her stomach grumbled as she took in the smells of fresh bread.

The young woman scanned the inside of the bakery warily. She pursed her lips but hesitated. Rich gave her an encouraging nod as she pulled her little girl close.

"I need you to help my daughter," the woman whispered.

"And how would I be able to do that?" Rich asked, taking care not to give anything away. He couldn't shake the feeling he knew this woman, and it made him uneasy not being able to place her as a friend or foe.

"You need to get her out of this place." The young woman played with her daughter's curls. Gemma looked up at her momma with a concerned look. Before she could say anything, her mother's hand dropped to her shoulder in warning. Gemma stayed quiet.

"Why do you think I'm the type of person who could do such a thing?" Rich moved to a box to pull out a muffin for the daughter. Waiting for the mother to nod her permission, Rich handed it to the young girl. Gemma squealed in glee and took a bite of the treat. The baker chuckled, waiting for the mother to reply.

"I've heard whispers, and she's, well, let her show you." Mirabella crouched next to her daughter and took the half-eaten muffin gently from the girl's hands.

"Hush child. You can have this back in a minute," she stated when the girl fussed. Gemma looked at her mother through watery eyes. "I need you to show this nice man what you can do with the plants."

Gemma looked at Rich suspiciously before turning back to her mother. She whispered something into her ear.

Mirabella murmured, "I know it's hard, wildflower, but you need to learn you can trust some people. Just be careful who you place that trust in. Come here, love." Mirabella took her daughter's hand and led her to the vine that grew on the doorframe. "Show him. It'll be alright, the bad men can't see."

Rich watched in earnest as the little girl placed one hand out and closed her eyes. As she concentrated, the plant grew longer and formed new buds. Right before Rich's eyes, the plant flowered and burst into bloom. The little girl opened her eyes and smiled. She gently touched the flower and looked at her mother for approval.

"Very good, wildflower, very good." She pulled Gemma close one more time and looked to the baker. "Gemma is an Herbalist, a Grower specifically. I can't hide her Gifts anymore, there are too many plants in town." Concern clouded her eyes. "My husband can't know. He'd send her to the capital for Goddess knows what horrors. I need her to be safe." She ducked her head and recognition flashed in Rich's eyes.

This was Vincenzio's wife. The woman who appeared on his arm at all government functions. The woman he only saw from a distance always deferred to her husband. She must have been desperate to have come to him.

"Were you followed?" Rich peeked out the window, looking for soldiers, expecting some sort of trap.

Mirabella gripped his arm. "I was careful. No one knows your secret. I just need you to swear to me she will be safe." She searched his face with frantic eyes.

"I swear it. I will get her to where she needs to be, and she'll be safe."

"Thank you." Mirabella's eyes swam with tears as she embraced the man she just met. She knelt beside her daughter and held her tight. "Be a good girl, wildflower. Listen to what this kind man says. Be strong."

"Momma?" Gemma asked, confused. "I'll stay with you."

"No, no, wildflower. You need to go with this man. He will keep you safe from the bad men." Mirabella kissed her forehead. "I can't protect you anymore."

Gemma started crying and clutched at her mother. She stomped her feet and wailed while Mirabella ran her hands through her daughter's curls. She kissed her again and waited for the tears to end. When they did, she hugged her daughter tight and slipped Rich an envelope.

"This is for Duncan. Tell him I'm sorry." She cupped her daughter's cheek one last time and slipped out the door she came by.

Gemma cried silently as she tried to process the loss she suffered.

Rich knelt next to the little girl. "How about we get some rest? You've had a long day. I'll get the cot set up for you." He picked up the bag Gemma's mother left on the ground. He pulled out a stuffed dog. "Who do we have here?" He smiled when the little girl clutched the dog to her chest. "Well, he seems important. You hold on to him while I get your bed ready."

Gemma took Rich's hand and climbed the stairs to the living area above the bakery. She yawned while he set up a cot for her and soon fell into a fitful sleep, with nightmares of bad men and chasing after a mother that wasn't there anymore.

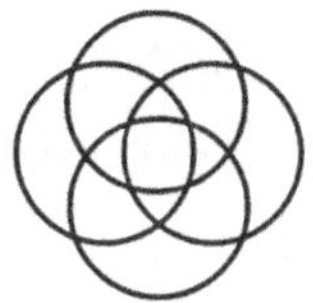

Chapter Twenty-Seven

T he second act went smoothly. Rae's lateness went unnoticed by most of the crowd, but Zeke's absence did not. Many people came up to the acrobats after the show and asked about the young man. They smiled and gave him the reassurance he just needed a little rest.

Rae was uncharacteristically quiet during the rest of the show.

She was trying to reach into the unrelenting storm at her core. She couldn't even get a glimpse of the Crafts held hostage inside the eye of the storm.

Her frustration made her ornery. Damien and Luc knew to let her be when she was in a mood like this. They let her stew in peace, not confronting her until they said goodbye to the worried patrons.

"You good, Rae?" Damien asked.

Rae stared blankly ahead, not acknowledging her friend.

Damien waved his hand in front of her face and tried again, "Rae-Rae! You in there, you vexing woman?"

Luc watched with concern. She knew her friend was going through a lot with losing her fire. The woman had worked tirelessly to master her Craft. She knew Rae was reeling from having it disappear in an instant. Her Abuela was looking for the answers to Rae's predicament, but a twinge in her heart insisted the answers Rae wanted wouldn't be found in books.

Luc placed a hand on Rae's arm, finally breaking the Crafter from her reverie. "What happened before intermission, Hermana?" she whispered.

Rae sighed, "I took more of Tyee's life energy." Luc and Damien exchanged a glance. "In doing so, I could see inside the storm taking over my core, where I pull my Craft from." Rae's eyes were filled with resolve as she clenched her fists. "I saw it. I saw my fire in the eye of the storm. But that wasn't all." She paused, wondering if it would be wise to say more. Knowing she had already said too much, she continued, "I saw water and earth in the eye of the storm, too." She looked at her friends with pleading eyes.

Luc gave voice to what Rae didn't say. "So you're saying you think you could have access to all four Crafts if only the storm subsides?"

Rae nodded profusely. "Exactly. If only I could figure out how to pull them out individually."

"Do you think they were always there? Like the inferno that used to be there masked the other three?" asked Damien.

"Oh! I bet you're right, Dame. But the question remains: how does she access them?" Luc mused.

"I'm going to ask Tyee for his energy again. If I can get a glimpse into the storm, I think I could call my fire out. I just need one more chance to see it."

Damien and Luc exchanged another look. "Rae-Rae, is that wise? You don't wanna take too much from the lad. And a gorgeous gal like you? He'll say yes every time," Damien stated.

Rae furrowed her brow. "Tyee wouldn't do that."

"You took him to your bed, gorgeous. He will do whatever you want for another chance to worship you in bed. Don't fool yourself."

Rae chewed on her lip. She sighed, "Then how do I get past the storm raging inside?"

"Would Zeke be able to help? Or Duncan? Could they give you advice on calming the storm? Or using all the wind inside?" Luc asked with a hand on her chin.

Rae kissed her friend's cheek. "You brilliant woman! I gotta run. See you two later!" Rae left in a hurry, without a backward glance.

Damien chuckled. "She may have lost her Craft, but her fire still burns bright as hell."

"Poor Tyee," Luc sighed. "I hope he knows what he's in for."

"Oh, amor. You know he doesn't. Nobody realizes how far in they are until it's too late." Damien ran a finger along her jawline. Luc leaned into the touch, feeling the shivers he caused as he touched her caramel-colored skin.

She closed her eyes and sighed lightly as Damien's fingers brushed the back of her neck. He gripped her gently and pulled her closer until their foreheads touched. They stood like that for a few minutes, relishing the closeness.

Luc opened her eyes and found Damien smiling gently at her. She tilted her chin up and captured his lips with hers. They shared a sweet kiss, unhurried and chaste. They pulled apart, but Damien threw his arm over Luc's shoulder and tucked her into his side.

He looked down at her. "Should we go check on Abuela?"

Luc beamed. "Great idea!" She looped her arm around his waist and they made their way to the old woman's wagon. She was doing better, but still needed a lot of rest. Frequent visitors helped her pass the time between meals.

Rae slipped into the med tent but kept her head down. She avoided Freya and her friends, rushing into Zeke's section of the tent. She pulled the cloth shut quickly behind her. Rae held her finger to her lips when Zeke shot her a questioning look. Rae stood by the entrance to his room and listened to the noise of the Healers walking around, checking in on patients, and triaging new ones. Several passed by Zeke's section but didn't stop. Rae waited a moment more before walking to her friend's cot.

Rae grabbed Zeke's hand and knelt close to where his head lay. "I have a proposition for you," she whispered.

"Buy me dinner first," Zeke grinned wickedly. Rae rolled her eyes.

"I'm serious, Z. I'll sneak you out of here, but I need your help." Rae watched Zeke's face carefully.

"Anything, Sparks. Just get me out of here," Zeke pleaded.

"Shhh!" Rae scolded. She whispered furiously, "Be quiet or else we'll be caught before we even get started."

Zeke smirked but it quickly turned into a smile. "I knew you'd come back for me even when you insisted you wouldn't. I'm too irresistible."

Rae snorted before shooting her friend a look. "Shut *up,* Zeke!" Rae couldn't hide her smile as she looked him over, still not moving from his cot. "Are you well enough to leave?"

"They gave me an immobilizer. Freya warned the chief Healer I was trying to get her to let me leave," Zeke shrugged. "It only targeted my legs though, so I can still feed myself and whatnot."

Rae let out a low growl and looked towards the entrance to Zeke's section. She dove under the cot as someone pushed the curtain aside. Rae held her breath as footsteps sounded in the small space. She heard Freya's voice move to Zeke's cot.

"How's our resident daredevil doing tonight?" Rae heard Freya up by Zeke's head, probably checking vitals.

Zeke's voice betrayed nothing as he said, "Just trudging along. Being a model patient and all."

Freya laughed. "Only because of the immobilizer we gave you."

"Yea, when does that wear off again? I think the chief Healer said something when he gave it to me."

"You cheeky bastard. You're going to have to wake up earlier than that to trick me into giving up information." She fussed with Zeke's pillow before smoothing out his blanket. Rae clamped her mouth shut, holding in a gasp when Freya leaned down to fix a corner.

Zeke drew Freya's attention before she could notice the Crafter under his bed. "Can't blame me for trying," he said, as Freya straightened to look him in the eye. "When am I free to leave again? In a couple of hours?"

"You'll be free to go after breakfast and a final examination tomorrow morning." Freya chuckled while grabbing his dishes from dinner. She gave him a look and dimmed the lantern by his bed. "Get some rest." Freya breezed out of the room as quickly as she'd come.

Rae waited for another beat before crawling out from under the cot. "Alright Zeke, we gotta move fast. We have a bit of time, but let's not waste it. I'm going to get you out of your cot and then—"

"Turn the pillows," Zeke finished for her with a grin. "Help me swing my legs around and then I'll wrap my arms around your neck. You can lift me down and rearrange the pillows."

Rae nodded and lifted the blanket before gently gripping Zeke's legs and pulling them to her side of the cot, opposite the curtain, shielding them from view. "Does that hurt?" she whispered.

Zeke shook his head. "It's the strangest sensation. I can see you pulling them, but I can't feel anything on my legs. They're just numb."

"Weird. Okay, put your hands around my neck and hold on." Rae waited until Zeke set his grip and wrapped her arm around his waist. She eased him off the cot and dragged him towards the wall of the tent. She crouched down, arranging his legs so they lay in front of him, and let him release his grip on her neck.

After he was settled, Rae returned to the cot and arranged pillows under the blanket to make it look like the acrobat was still in bed.

She felt a wave of nostalgia, remembering all the times she did this as a kid, sneaking out to join Zeke in his tent and chase the nightmares away. Or slipping out to meet her friends and practice the more dangerous tricks they were forbidden to try within eyesight of their teachers. They would meet outside the camp and run trick after trick, becoming more confident and daring as the days went on. Rae shook the bittersweet memories from her head and finished her work.

Once she was satisfied, she dimmed the lantern a little more to discourage Healers from interrupting a sleeping patient and returned to where Zeke sat.

"Any day now," Zeke whispered, tapping two fingers on his immobilized legs.

Rae rolled her eyes again and moved to crouch next to her friend. She signaled for him to be quiet as she felt along the bottom of the canvas separating the med tent from the outside alley. Her hands searched for a tie or give in the material.

She reached a pole next to them and found what she was looking for. Rae undid the bottom two ties before hastening to the next pole and doing the same. Undoing the ties gave enough slack for the two acrobats to wiggle under the fabric without ripping it.

Rae paused and listened to the world beyond the tent. She could hear a few voices but didn't recognize any of them. *Must be new recruits.* She chewed on her lip, debating whether it was worth the risk that they might say something. She glanced at Zeke before laying prostrate and pulling the side of the tent up, ever so slightly. Zeke's section of the med tent ran along the side wall, better than the front wall, but not as convenient as the back wall. The voices she heard came from the path to the right that led to the entrance of the med tent. She took another minute to scan the dark side of the tent, before dropping the canvas and rising to her elbows.

"I think we can make it. We just have to figure out how I'm going to carry you once we get out there." Rae searched Zeke's room, looking for anything useful.

Zeke thought for a second. "I got it. Have you used your wind Craft to carry anything before?"

"Z, I've had this for like a day. I haven't experimented much apart from my morning basics," Rae answered, still looking for something helpful. She frowned. "I guess you could say I lifted you when I stopped you from falling." Zeke nodded and glanced towards the trunk at the foot of his cot.

"Go into that trunk, and there should be a few extra blankets. Grab the thinnest one you can find. You're going to drag me under the canvas, place me on the blanket, and help me lift the blanket using my Craft." Zeke saw Rae's uncertainty and continued, "Trust me, Sparks. It'll work. I'll just need some of your energy to make it as far as the thicket. Assuming that's where we're going?"

"Aye, that's my plan. Hold on a minute," Rae held her hand up and listened. "We should go now." She moved to the trunk, opened it slowly, and grabbed the first blanket she could find.

Rae crawled out from under the canvas and spread the blanket out in the shadows of the alley. She pulled the canvas up and found Zeke laying on his back, waiting to be dragged out. Rae did so as quietly as she could, gritting her teeth as she pulled hard. Her breathing ragged, she positioned him on the blanket and waited for him to direct her on what to do next.

Voices sounded on the main path as Healers changed their shifts.

Rae and Zeke stayed as still as statues, praying the shadows would be enough to cloak them from prying eyes.

The crowd in front of the med tent dispersed.

The two Crafters held their breath when a distant figure looked straight at them. A voice hailed the figure before it could take a step toward them, and they sighed in relief.

Zeke held out his hand and whispered, "Just channel your Craft into me. I'll do the rest."

Rae gripped her friend's hand and looked inward. The storm inside was a tempest. Rae clenched her jaw and teased out a single thread of wind. She willed it to move through her veins, down to their joined hands, and into her closest friend. Zeke nodded as he felt the incoming power fill his veins. He closed his eyes and moved his free hand in a circle. The blanket he sat on rose and hovered a couple of inches off the ground while Zeke held his hand flat, palm facing up. He moved his hand forward and the blanket beneath him moved in the direction his fingers pointed.

Rae stood up and took off at a brisk walk to keep pace with the clever Crafter still clutching her hand. They kept to the shadows and continued quietly making their way out of the player's yard and into the forest butting up to the edge of the yard. Both Crafters concentrated on keeping their power flowing, so Zeke stayed aloft. The air was tense as they crossed the open space before the tree line.

Neither noticed the figure stalking their steps since they left the side of the med tent.

Rae gave a small whoop in celebration once they passed into the trees, but quickly grasped at the storm inside when Zeke started to sink.

The sudden rush of wind leaving her core allowed Rae to get a glimpse of the three other Crafts hidden within. Concentrating with all her might, Rae started trying to push the storm out of her core and into her link with Zeke.

She heard a cry in the distance but kept concentrating on the storm. Its lines grew thinner and thinner as she pushed more and more.

Rae heard a snap and lightning flashed within, momentarily blinding her.

When her inner eye cleared, the storm was back, weaker than before but still strong enough to mask her other Crafts.

She let out a frustrated cry before noticing her surroundings. Rae felt empty air where there was once warmth from Zeke's hand in hers. She looked down and saw Zeke sprawled across the now stationary blanket, knocked out cold.

A trickle of blood seeped from a gash on his forehead.

"Z," Rae whispered, her hand covering her mouth. She blinked rapidly and knelt by her friend. She could feel her heart beating in her throat as she placed a shaky hand on Zeke's neck. Rae sighed when she found a pulse, but her own kept racing as she wheeled about, looking for something she could use to help him.

A twig snapped.

Rae straightened and stepped towards the sound, putting herself between Zeke and the unknown intruder. Rae's chest heaved, eyes scanning the dark woods frantically. She grasped at the storm inside, but could barely call a breeze to her fingertips. She reached down and grabbed the twin daggers from her boots.

Leaves rustled.

"Show yourself!" Rae roared, desperately clutching inside for the fire she knew was there and holding her daggers high in a defensive position. Her arms trembled as she fought to keep her arms up despite her exhaustion. Rae knew she needed to protect her friend at all costs. Her selfishness put them in this predicament in the first place. She tried to swallow the knot in her throat, thinking about what she might have cost her friend.

The bushes rattled.

Rae steeled herself for what was to come. The forest was rumored to be filled with monsters, human and animal alike. She took a step forward, ready to take the offensive.

A figure stepped out of the undergrowth, and Rae attacked. The intruder held up his arm and yelled, "Rae, stop!"

Rae swung her leg, but the intruder hopped over it, anticipating the move. She growled and tried another attack when a cry came again.

"BIRDIE! YOU'RE GONNA HURT ME!"

Rae paused, breathing hard. Keeping her daggers drawn, she cocked her head. "Tyee?"

The figure nodded as he held up a lantern, illuminating his face.

Rae finally lowered her weapons and turned back to Zeke's still form. "I hurt him. Stupid, selfish, idiot."

Tyee approached slowly and moved the lantern to light up Zeke's form. "What happened?" he asked gently.

"I pushed too much of my Craft into him. I was trying to see if I could push enough out to get to my fire." She hung her head. "I was selfish." She ran her hands over Zeke's body, taking comfort in the shallow breaths he took. She used her sleeve to dab the blood from his forehead. Tears welled in her eyes. "He's never going to forgive me. I took him from the med tent and experimented without his permission. This is all my fault." She wiped angrily at her face. "I need to fix it," she said with a growl.

"Let me help." Tyee bent down and lifted the acrobat, careful not to jostle his head too much. He lifted him over his shoulder as gently as he could and strode out of the woods.

"Tyee! Wait!" Rae yelled and ran after him.

Tyee turned toward her and lifted an eyebrow. He waited for her to continue.

"We need a plan," Rae said.

Tyee scoffed. "What do you mean, we need a plan? We bring him to the med tent and tell them what happened. They set him to rights. Simple. Effective. What else is there?"

"I don't know if the Herbalists will be able to help."

"Rae, he's bleeding. They'll at least be able to help with that and monitor his vitals."

"We leave tomorrow, though. They'll be moving any patients into wagons. We're better off bringing him to Abuela's wagon." Rae straightened her spine and crossed her arms. They stood at a standstill, neither willing to break eye contact.

Tyee felt Zeke stir on his shoulder.

The horseman's eyes went wide when Zeke let out a groan. He quickly set the young man down on the ground while Rae rushed over.

"Z? Can you hear me?"

Zeke mumbled under his breath. Rae looked to Tyee, but he shook his head. She turned back to her friend and wiped his hair from his eyes.

"Say that again, Z."

Zeke's voice rasped while he tried to open his eyes. "Bloody hell, my head hurts." He placed a hand on his still-sticky forehead. "Ugh, must have hit it pretty hard, eh?" he asked when he felt the blood still seeping from his wound.

Tyee left the pair and disappeared into the forest.

"Rae, what happened? All I remember is feeling too much power coming through the bond, but I couldn't let go. You couldn't hear me and the next thing I knew, my world went black. Did you lose control?" Zeke's eyelids fluttered before finally opening. Rae knelt by his side and put an arm under his shoulders. She helped him lean forward and put the blanket behind his head, balled up to provide support.

Rae felt Zeke's eyes on her face, but she stared at her hands. She balled them into fists and took a deep breath. She forced herself to look Zeke in the eyes and said, "I didn't lose control. I was trying to see into the storm and kept pushing my Craft through our bond. I saw my flames and didn't think." She swallowed, still holding Zeke's gaze. "I'm so sorry."

Zeke broke eye contact with his partner, but not before she saw the hurt flood his eyes. "You could have just asked," he murmured, falling silent at the thought of his body being gambled with, like all those Magicae in the capital.

"I know, Z, I feel awful. I'm so sorry." Rae reached for Zeke's hand, but he shook her off. Silent tears leaked from Rae's unnaturally hazel eyes.

They sat in silence until leaves rustled from the treeline. They looked up to see Tyee coming out of the woods, plants in his hands.

He shot a puzzled look between the two acrobats, feeling the tension in the air. They both watched him approach but said nothing. Tyee knelt by Zeke's side, opposite Rae, and grabbed a knife from his waist. He placed a handkerchief on the ground and started shredding the stems of the plants he carried. Once satisfied the pieces were small enough, Tyee grabbed the waterskin at his hip and gathered the pieces in his hand. He carefully funneled the broken bits of bark and stems into his waterskin and shook it vigorously.

"Drink this. It'll help with the headache." Tyee held the waterskin to Zeke. Rae helped him sit up, but Zeke hesitated before taking the skin and pressing it to his lips. He drank deeply, surprised at his thirst, and tasted bitterness mixed with splinters as the concoction passed his lips.

"This tastes awful," Zeke spluttered, wiping his mouth. He held it out for Tyee to take back, but the horseman motioned for Zeke to keep drinking.

"You have to drink it all for it to be effective." Tyee caught Rae's eyes, and she mouthed her thanks. He nodded and addressed the acrobat. "Willow is a natural pain reliever. It's better as a tea, but beggars can't be choosers. You need the water, so best to drink it all."

Tyee looked to Rae before continuing, "We should get you to the med tent, Zeke. They'll be able to help you more than we can."

"I'm not going back there." Zeke shot an accusatory glance at Rae. "I just need some rest. You can't take me back there." He clutched at Rae's tunic, eyes filled with determination at not losing his freedom.

"We won't take you back there. We'll figure this out." Tyee's eyes snapped to Rae's, blazing.

"Fools." Tyee shook his head and stood up. He took one last look at the pair and marched towards the player's yard across the field.

Rae gently lowered Zeke back to the blanket and took off after the stubborn horseman.

"Tyee!" Tyee ignored her. She tried again, "Wait! Tyee, stop!"

Rae grunted when she ran into Tyee's front as he wheeled around.

"Why should I?" he spat. "If you and Zeke want to risk his health, that's none of my business. I've tried to be here for you and you throw it in my face. I'm done."

Rae took a step back, chest heaving, and fists clenched. They stood glaring at one another before Tyee turned around and walked away. Rae watched him go for a moment before turning back to where Zeke lay on the ground.

She helped her friend stand on shaky legs and pulled his arm over her shoulders, holding onto his wrist. Her other arm gripped his waist, and they started the long journey back to the player's yard.

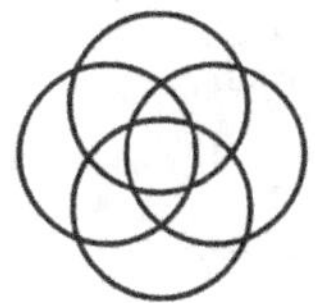

Chapter Twenty-Eight

The morning on the third day of Circus shows dawned swiftly. Performers and crew woke with purpose, needing to pack tents, close up the permanent structures, and prepare for the last show. Everyone needed to work together, including the new recruits from the past couple of days.

An air of anxiety crept over the players as tensions regarding the Circus's next steps mounted. Friends snapped at each other, parents yelled at their children, and the packing grew frantic.

Heads turned when the bell for the show circle tolled.

Performers and crew members stopped what they were doing and streamed into the big top.

Duncan stood in the middle of the ring, hat, and cane in his hands. He watched his people fill the seats of the tent. Mothers held their babes close, the old were escorted by younger family, and friends found each other in the crowd. Some people took their seats right away, while others stayed standing, waiting to hear what their Ringmaster had to say.

Duncan watched the crowds. He saw the unease, the despair, the nerves, and everything in between. He nodded when people raised a hand in greeting and smiled when he saw eyes filled with fear. The Ringmaster noted Zeke hobbling in with an arm over Rae's shoulder and Nan arriving with Javie behind her, ready to support her should she grow weary. He saw Jess and Kaiser and Gar and so many more. Damien and Luc arrived, sitting next to Rae and Zeke, checking in on their friend. Tyee slipped in and stood on his own in the shadows.

Duncan watched everything, looking for one figure in particular.

Chiara arrived and locked eyes with the Ringmaster.

He raised one eyebrow, and she nodded. The tension left his shoulders as a smile lit his face. She made her way through the crowd and sat next to her son.

Duncan breathed deeply before raising his hand to his lips. "Please take your seats, my friends." He waited for the crowd to quiet, then continued, "We need to talk about what happens next." He put his old top hat on his head and switched his cane to his right hand.

"A lot of you have expressed your concerns about the people we are leaving behind." His eyes found the young recruit that stopped him at breakfast. "The truth is, our caravan is not ready for a fight. We leave Heimat tonight, but only for a spell. I have consulted with the Council, and tonight, we travel into the Great Northern Forest."

Gasps sounded across the stands. Whispers broke out as people questioned the wisdom of their leaders.

"I know this is scary. But like our ancestors before us, we are stronger together. Our Gifts and talents will guide and protect us. I intend to find a safe place to settle and then the actual work will begin. Some of you heard Abuela, but in case you didn't, everyone will need to make a choice. War is coming. We will leave some behind to care for the young and the old, but the rest of us will return to reclaim Heimat.

"The Resistance will begin in force. We will take back what was ours and put Myra in her place."

The crowd was silent, stunned by the man in the middle of the ring. Myra's name was associated with death, destruction, and terror and her reputation for power and cruelty proceeded her.

Defeating her seemed impossible.

Rae started clapping. Her fellow acrobats did the same as Jess yelled in triumph. Slowly, the audience's energy built to a crescendo. Friends and family looked at each other, starting to believe in the possibility of exacting revenge for the horrors they faced after the Uprising.

The crowd became a roar.

Duncan watched in silence. He knew his people were caught up in the rush of being part of something. Revenge and retribution could make anyone salivate with anticipation. Duncan knew that doubt would follow the frenzy.

His eyes drifted until they met Chiara's blazing ones. He knew she disapproved of his methods, but she couldn't argue that they didn't work.

He grew up to become an advisor to the president, and manipulation was something he exuded with every breath. He couldn't help saying the words he knew would yield results.

He had more in common with Myra than he'd like to admit.

Duncan didn't break eye contact with the Healer as he shrugged his shoulders and his eyes turned apologetic. He hated disappointing Chiara, but he did what was best for their people, no matter how much it ate away at him. The roaring died down as Duncan and Chiara held each other's gazes.

Silence permeated the big top as the crowd waited for their Ringmaster to continue.

Duncan broke the staring match he was in and looked at the crowds of people.

"If you want to say something, now is the time. The Council and I started talking about new strategies to combat our circumstances after Tiva. We started running through backup plans should our safe places fall." He straightened his coat, needing to get his emotions in check.

"We never thought we would need them so soon.

"Now is the time for suggestions before it is too late to change course." Duncan turned in a slow circle, looking at the crowd, beseeching them to say something, good or bad, and break the silence.

One of the kitchen crew stood up. Duncan nodded to them, holding a hand up to amplify the man's voice.

"The Forest is a bad spot. We can't send our children and elderly there. They won't stand a chance against the monsters inside." He sat down after saying his piece.

"The Forest will provide protection from Myra's forces. It is the last place her hand doesn't reach. Aye, there are stories claiming monsters and criminals roam the trees, but stories have been twisted before. Settling in the Forest will give us food, water, and safety. We will need time to prepare for war; the Forest will give us that and more."

A woman stood up. She spoke once Duncan gave her a nod, her voice projected by the wind so all could hear. "I understand that argument, but what if we get there and the monsters are real? What if we go and only meet heartbreak? What's the backup plan?"

Duncan scanned the crowd, feeling anxiety creeping in on many people. "We leave. We move east to the northern part of the Ridgeback Mountains. The land is less fertile and more open to the elements, but it's our best bet at finding a place remote enough from the capital to be safe."

The woman nodded, satisfied with his response, and sat back down.

A couple more stood and voiced their concerns about going into the Forest. Duncan reiterated that the benefits outweighed the risks and the plan should the Forest prove too dangerous. The dialogue was reaching a standstill, with people on both sides refusing to listen to one another.

Chiara stood up.

Duncan met her gaze, and she nodded, eyebrow raised. Duncan held his hand aloft and her voice filled the big top.

"Many of you are scared and I would be lying if I said I wasn't. I grew up hearing stories of the shadows lurking amid the trees in the Great Northern Forest. My mom told me it claimed my father and her father before him. Her voice and hands shook whenever she spoke of this place. She feared it with every fiber of her being. When Duncan told me this was the plan, I protested. I told him I would not and could not support such foolishness." Her eyes met his again before she turned to the people behind her and continued, "He pleaded with me to reconsider. Duncan is a great man. He gave us a home when we had none. He risked his life to save our people from ruin. That we've survived is in a large part because of him.

"He's asking us to trust him once again. It's a lot, but it's all he asks. There's a path the Herbalists can find. It will lead us to where we need to be. Take heart, my friends. We need to follow in our ancestors' footsteps. They too doubted their leaders, but those that remained steadfast were the first settlers of Kamore. We need to be strong and we need to try. We all want better for our children."

Chiara paused and looked down at Damien sitting next to her. He nodded at his mother, proud of her for speaking to their people despite her misgivings. She gripped his shoulder and didn't let go. "We need to keep our wits about us and find the best place for them to be safe. Our strength will falter if we fracture now.

"Have courage, my friends. The long night is ending. Now is the time to let our light shine the brightest."

With a flourish, Chiara sat down. Silence filled the tent. Duncan waited a moment to let her words sink in.

"My friends, we have one more night. We need to get the last of the children out, then pack and leave. Think about what has been said here. I need every one of you to turn the tide against Myra, but I refuse to force you to do something against your wishes. We all have a choice. Take today, and make yours."

With those last words, Duncan left the big top.

He went to the edge of the trees and prayed to the Huntress his words would be enough. The members of the Circus spoke in hushed tones as they left the tent. They had a lot to consider as the sun climbed higher in the sky. Preparations for the last show began slowly, as families discussed what they would do when the last curtain closed on the life they once knew.

Rich had spent the night tossing and turning. He woke before dawn, contemplating what to do. The little girl deserved safety, like any of the children they rescued. But her absence would alert the mayor more surely than anything else.

Rich and his associates would be left to deal with the consequences of Vincenzio searching the town for his little girl.

He checked in on her, finding her asleep with a frown on her face. His expression turned somber as he shut the simple wooden door. The girl was going through a terrible trauma, while Rich only thought of the consequences her presence would bring to his door.

He sighed and shook his head.

He went down the stairs to the main part of the bakery and started his tasks for the day.

Rich's father started the bakery when he was just a boy. He had many fond memories of learning to stoke the ovens and knead the bread just right. His father was a simple man but loved his son something fierce. He always spent the morning telling Rich stories of the old days while checking the rise of doughs made the night before. He taught Rich how to shape dough into different forms and what temperatures to set the ovens to for different loaves of bread.

After they got the bread in the oven, they could move on to making treats that parents would buy for their kids and the lunch items they served their patrons around midday. After the lunch rush, they closed up shop to get prepped for the next day. Dough needed to be made so it could rise by the morning, inventory of ingredients needed to be taken, orders needed to be put in for supplies, and the bakery needed to be cleansed before they could call it a day.

It was hard work, but being with his father was all that mattered.

A small smile graced Rich's lips as he thought of those happy times, always accompanied by the yeasty smell of bread in the ovens. He reminisced while stoking the embers from the night before. Soon, a fire blazed as Rich added more fuel to the oven. He left it to burn while he tended to the bowls filled with dough, kept under flour cloths on the counter across from the oven. They had risen to almost twice their size thanks to the warmth emitted by the coals left in the oven. It was an old secret passed down from his father.

Rich wiped the wooden counter before covering it in flour. He gently tipped one bowl onto the dusty surface and kneaded it gently to knock the air out.

He portioned the dough into thirds and rounded them into balls before setting them aside. The baker did this with the other bowls, working himself into a rhythm. He rubbed the sweat from his brow and finished the last batch of dough.

He turned and checked the oven, and once satisfied with the flame, he took his wooden paddle and placed the balls of dough inside. He whistled while he worked, hands covered in flour and head filled with a list of tasks ready to be tackled.

He turned around and almost ran into the little girl that was supposed to be asleep upstairs.

"Heavens, you scared me, lass." He raised his hand to his chest in surprise. He looked the little girl over carefully, looking for signs she was upset. Her hair was a tangled mess, her face splotchy with dried tears, and she clutched her stuffed dog with both hands. Her eyes shone with unshed tears and she wiped at her nose with her sleeve. Rich pulled an old chair over and motioned for her to stand on it to get a better look at the counter he was working on. "Climb on up here and you can help me with the sweet treats."

The little girl climbed onto the chair, still clutching her stuffed dog tight to her chest. Rich had a wave of déjà vu as he remembered his daughter and granddaughters standing on that very chair. He wiped the extra flour from the counter and brought out ingredients and bowls to make the turnovers his bakery was known for. The girl watched with wide eyes as the splotches slowly faded from her face and she set the stuffed dog at her feet.

He wiped her hands clean with a soapy rag and placed a bowl in front of her, taking the other one for himself, the ingredients between them. Rich moved slowly, explaining each step in the process so Gemma could mimic his movements. He praised her good work and laughed with her if she spilled.

They worked together for over an hour, creating batters for cookies, tarts, and cakes. Rich pulled the bread from the oven, the yeasty smell taking over the small space they worked in. Before long, Rich's daughter showed up to help. She smiled when she saw her dad interacting with the little girl.

"Well, this is a familiar sight," she said, closing the door quietly. They would welcome their first customers in a little over an hour.

Rich looked up in surprise. "Melody! Come meet our newest helper!" He waited for his daughter to hang her coat and make her way to stand on the opposite side of the counter. "This is Gemma."

Melody smiled. "Hi, Gemma. Very nice to meet you." She crouched so she was at eye level with the young girl.

Gemma hid her face and clutched her stuffed dog. She slid down from the chair and went to gaze at the oven instead of meeting Melody's kind face. The little girl was still wary of strangers.

Melody was unfazed by the little girl's shyness. She had two little ones of her own that did the same thing around strangers. Her heart squeezed, guessing this little girl had lost her mother in some shape or form.

She turned a questioning look to her father as she straightened.

Rich responded in a whisper after scanning the room. "This is Vincenzio's daughter." Melody's eyes widened. "Her mother brought her here last night, said she's an Herbalist and needs to be taken before her father finds out."

"Poor dear." Melody shot a look at the little girl mesmerized by the flame in the oven. "Last night? Seems a little abrupt, doesn't it?"

"It is what is, Mel. I'm sure she had her reasons."

"What did she expect when she married that monster?" Melody spat.

"Melody. We don't know her circumstances. She might not have had a choice. Whether that was real or imagined matters little. Be kind."

The woman hung her head. "You're right, Da. I shouldn't say such things. I just hate seeing so many families being ripped apart. The girls are noticing the absences." She lifted her gaze to her father. "The adults might not, but the kids do. They keep asking me if it's because they have Gifts. I explained as best I could, but they see in black and white. They can't begin to understand why the children they grew up with, are friends with, and love have to hide who they are. I did my best, but I don't know if it's enough."

Rich smiled at his daughter. "The joys of parenting." He reached over and patted her cheek. "Chin up, lass. You're doing a great job. Those girls love everyone something fierce, just like their Momma. They will spread a lot of good in their lives."

Melody sighed. "I worry that love is going to get them in trouble or hurt someday."

"It might. But it's better than having a heart of stone. The next few years are going to test everyone's resolve. Once the dust settles, we will need those hearts to rebuild."

Their conversation was interrupted by the sound of footsteps coming up the back stairs. They looked to the cellar door and heard the distinct three-rap knock of the city leaders.

Rich opened the door and Tommy came in with a huge grin plastered on his face. "Melody!" He cried, launching towards the baker's daughter and one of his closest friends. He lifted her and spun her around before shaking Rich's hand. Melody laughed and shook her head as he said, "Everything went according to plan. They have an impressive setup over there. I knew they had their act together, but damn, they have it down to a science." He stopped when he noticed the little girl next to Rich. He shot a glance between Rich and Melody. "Who do we have here?"

After a moment's hesitation, Melody spoke up, "She's a new recruit."

Tommy's gaze snapped to Melody's, brows furrowed. "Why isn't she with her family? Do the other three know?"

Melody shook her head and looked at Rich. The old man sighed, "She is Vincenzio's daughter. She's an Herbalist and her father doesn't know. Her mother brought her here last night. She wanted to get her daughter to safety."

Tommy's jaw went slack. "You can't... He's going to... Rich, this is danger-ous," he spluttered, trying to find the words to explain the thoughts swirling inside.

The older man ran a hand through his hair. "Aye, it is. Look at her, though. We can't pin the sins of the father on his daughter. She deserves our help, as much as any other child."

Tommy breathed deeply and rolled his shoulders back. He looked at the little girl, still holding tight to her stuffed dog, quiet with two new strangers in the room.

"Do you want me to take her to Tamara or Mikel?" Tommy asked, thinking about his children.

"Just let Tamara know she should pick her up on her way. I don't want to risk her being seen in the daylight. There will be enough distractions with everyone crowding for the last night." Rich looked at Gemma and patted her head. He said to the girl, "I need you to go back upstairs, lass. We'll be having customers come in soon and we need to keep you hidden. Take this loaf upstairs and give it to the nice lady up there. She'll cook you a proper breakfast." His eyes crinkled as Gemma nodded profusely. She grabbed the loaf he offered and took the steps two at a time.

"How's Ma doing?" Melody asked with a frown.

"She has good days and bad days. Just like the rest of us." Rich offered a tight smile. He turned to Tommy. "Anything else to report?"

"No, Sir. It was all quiet when I left this morning. I'll find Tamara before I head back and give her the news. I have to drop off these extras, so the last of our people can take them to the Circus." With a salute, Tommy went back through the door he came from, heading towards Artist's Row and the glass studio where the Forger could be found.

Rich and Melody exchanged a glance before returning to making the bakery presentable for their customers. They cleaned the counter and filled bins with bread, fruit tarts, and turnovers as quickly as they left the oven and cooled on the counter in front of them. They worked in unison, exchanging gossip and stories. Customers slowly filed in and bought their bread for the day, some getting treats for the yawning children they dragged behind them.

Warmth spread inside Rich's chest as he interacted with his customers and observed the way Melody did the same. His daughter greeted everyone with a confidence he didn't find until he came into his old age. Melody made everyone laugh and slipped a treat into the bags of those with young children. His daughter made the work easy despite the creak and ache in his bones. His eyes twinkled as the day went on and customers continued to file through.

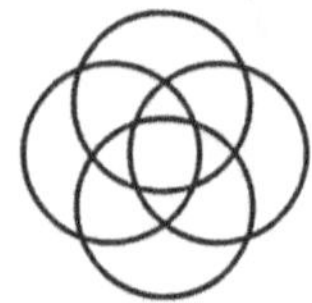

Chapter Twenty-Nine

An air of melancholy surrounded the Circus. Emotions and tempers ran high as performers and crew struggled to complete their work while the choice loomed over them.

The crew was as varied as the performers; there were cooks, blacksmiths, stable hands, farmers, carpenters, seamstresses, washers, and so many more. Losing one individual would mean a hit to the collective knowledge base of the Circus itself.

Most felt there wasn't much of a choice.

Leaving the only family many of them had ever known felt like a betrayal. Some raged internally at the prospect of a choice that wasn't a choice. Would anyone leave knowing it meant risking everything and abandoning the people that cared for, helped, and laughed with them? Resentment rolled off some individuals in waves, while others only felt a renewed sense of dedication to the mission. They were ready to fight back against their oppressors and finally claim a place in the society that shunned them. These were the people sick of responding to the problem instead of trying to fix it.

Change was coming whether they were ready or not.

They worked in tense silence, recognizing the divide between them. They had never spent such little time in Heimat before, so packing was proving more difficult than they thought. The grounds where they set up had permanent buildings for the ticket booth, concession stand, and livestock pen. That left the carnival tent, med tent, big top, and the tents in the player's yard to be packed.

Many of the crew had little to do besides wait for the run-throughs to end so they could finish packing the players' tents. The supply and livestock wagons were ready, and the carnival tent would be packed after intermission, leaving only the big top to physically dismantle after the show.

This meant most of the crew were left with time to consider what would happen next, and thus, were the first to notice the smoke coming from the other side of the river.

A lot of people watched the smoke closely, praying it didn't mean what they thought it did. Their stomachs filled with dread as chilling memories came to the surface.

Midge stood straight as a board, hand clutching her chest. Memories of fire and screaming and death filled her head. Her eyes scanned the city frantically, praying to the Goddess she wouldn't see the destruction spreading.

She held her breath when a second plume of smoke joined the first.

Not Heimat. She motioned for a runner to come close.

"I need you to run as fast as you can and find Duncan. Tell him he needs to come and see this. Go!" She pushed the girl towards the big top, never taking her eyes off the city that was once a safe haven.

Rae stood next to Damien and Luc, waiting for Kaiser to finish his run-through with the big cats. She nodded when her friends looked at her, but her eyes kept straying to where Zeke sat in the stands.

Sleep had finally taken them when they crashed onto her cot. Zeke refused to see a Healer or go to Nan's wagon, but Rae had snuck some tonic into his breakfast. The immobilizer finally wore off after Duncan's speech, but her friend was still out of it. He sat dozing, trying to fight the effects of Chiara's tonic. He wouldn't be performing with them tonight, but Rae hoped he was back to his normal self by the time they left Heimat.

Tyee didn't even look at her after his run-through. The horseman was avoiding her after the disastrous incident last night. She would not apologize for standing by her friend, but he deserved an explanation. Rae knew Tyee was trying to help, but she didn't know how to explain Zeke's aversion to the med tent.

What were you expecting? You've slept with him and made out a couple of times, not exactly trust-building exercises. Physical intimacy and emotional intimacy are two different beasts. You've got a ways to go before you've conquered either.

Rae bit her lip as she thought to herself. She knew things with Tyee were complicated, and she was lying to herself if she thought the only thing they had was physical.

She pushed those thoughts and the tingling they brought to her toes to the side. She needed some room in her head to analyze what was going on with her Craft. A breeze played with her hair as she looked inside. The storm still swirled with no way to see past the clouds and winds. Rae sighed in frustration and kicked the dirt with her boot. She shook her head when Damien and Luc shot her questioning looks.

She walked to the side ring, still attempting to look past the storm inside. She slumped to the ground and played with the ties on her boots. Rae let her mind wander while her fingers tied and untied knots with the strings of her boots.

Her hands stilled as an idea took shape in her head.

Rae focused on the storm inside but didn't open her inner eye. She knew what she would see and the frustration it would bring.

Keeping herself in the dark, she reached into her core and felt the wind inside. The breeze followed her from the main ring and blew harder as she pulled and prodded at the quivering ball of energy inside. Slowly, she coaxed the storm to unwind and pulled the winds until they formed three strands.

Then she started to braid.

She hummed while she worked, twisting the winds around one another to form a plait.

Rae kept her inner mind shut to what was happening in her core, not wanting to mess this up. Hope was lodged in her throat as warmth gathered where the storm once raged. The breezes around her quieted until the air went still. She took the braided winds and used her arms to spin them into a ball to the side of her center. The clouds found their way to the new epicenter of the swirling winds and a smaller storm took root.

Tears fell from her eyes as a single spark grew into an inferno. Her core was molten once more as she felt the magma enter her veins. Rae gritted her teeth and pushed back, using her sense of touch to guide her. She needed to get her flames under control, or else she would end up in need of a binding after all. Her flames didn't want to cooperate, but she pulled them until they resembled glowing wicked-hot cords. Humming the same tune her parents once sang to her at bedtime, she braided her flames. The inferno fed itself into her plait and she placed it next to where the storm sat.

Rae barely had time to register her accomplishment when she felt water rising rapidly around her. She spluttered as waves buffeted her and knocked her off her feet.

Her inner mind spun.

Rae squeezed her eyes shut, sending a silent prayer to the Huntress, hoping she could stop herself from opening her inner eye.

Her breathing came in rasps as cool water spread through her veins. Rae let the waves crash over her and felt herself sink to the bottom of the ocean taking residence in her core. She felt panic creeping in but kept herself calm using the memory of a lullaby. She hummed the tune to herself and took a wide stance. Rae moved her arms in rhythm with the currents and slowly coaxed them into three large strands. She proceeded to pull them into a braid.

She felt the power of the water in every drop. She shivered as the currents fell into order and gathered at her feet. Rae felt the waves becoming less powerful and soon the ocean was only waist deep. Her plait of currents held the mighty roar of millions of droplets of water at bay.

She gripped one end of her plait and tried walking towards where her flames danced, contained by the cords she wrought, but the water at her feet pulled her back. She bit her lip and took halting steps, putting all her strength into moving against the water at her waist, keeping a firm grip on the currents she had ordered. Rae made slow progress until the pool around her sat next to the small inferno.

Rae stepped out of the water and felt its power leave her veins. She stumbled to her knees but still refused to open her mind's eye. She let her hands dig into the dirt around her and felt the ground she knelt on shake.

The ground continued vibrating while she heard the sound of earth groaning. She stood to her feet and hit her elbow on a newly formed rock face. She gulped, realizing the earthquake inside was causing mountains to form within her core. Rae struggled to keep her footing, so she dropped to a knee and let out a cry.

Her body felt heavy as dirt and bits of rock entered her veins. She felt impenetrable, her skin becoming armor. She almost looked to see before squeezing her mind's eye even tighter. Rae contented herself with running a hand over her face and torso.

Her body was unyielding beneath her fingers, it was rendered unrecognizable. She let out another cry as the ground shook harder.

Clenching her jaw, Rae tried to pull the dirt and rocks into a rope. Everything kept slipping through her fingers as she tried to create a plait like the others. She growled in frustration and hit her hand against the dirt. A spire of earth shot from the ground where her hand hit. Rae sat still and noticed the rumble and shaking of the ground ease for a few moments. She hit the ground again, and the same thing happened. A spire shot up, and the shaking eased. She traveled around in a circle until hundreds of spires pushed into the air and the ground only groaned. The rocks and dirt in her veins subsided, leaving her skin as vulnerable as before.

Rae brought herself back to the present and knelt as her heart beat rapidly, and her breathing slowed. She wiped sweaty palms on her breeches and cradled her head in her hands. Tears flowed freely as she felt the power inside, ordered by the constructs she placed on it.

"RAE! GET UP!"

Hands pulled at her, forcing her to her feet and dragging her towards the entrance of the big top. She blinked, trying to process what was happening. She realized Luc and Damien had grabbed her arms and forced her to run with them. Rae closed her eyes when she was blinded by the sun outside the big top.

The acrid smell of smoke assaulted her nostrils, and fear gagged her. She pulled at the hands dragging her and her friends stopped.

She stared with wide eyes at the Circus in chaos. Individuals ran wildly, shouting and panicking, while three dark plumes of smoke rose from the town across the river. Luc and Damien tugged her towards the tents and wagons that were being packed haphazardly and as fast as possible.

Rae dug her feet in.

"What's happening?" she asked, trembling at the answer.

"Heimat is burning. Rae, we need to go. Duncan ordered us to march. We have to leave now." Luc gave Rae's arm another tug.

Rae shook her head and clenched her jaw. "What about the kids? What about the people we were supposed to collect tonight?" Her voice cracked as tears streamed down Luc's face and Damien's eyes clouded over. She pulled out of her friends' grips and angled towards the bridge. "I can't do this. I'm going to find them."

"Rae! Don't be stupid. Come with us." Luc clutched at her tunic.

Rae grabbed her hands gently. "Luc! Stop. There's no time. Go with Damien and get out of here. I'll try to find the kids and get them out. If I don't make it, just go. There's no time to argue, Hermana. Abuela and Javie need you." She kissed Luc on the cheek and placed her hands in Damien's. His eyes pleaded with hers to stay, but she shook her head and raised her fist.

He matched her movements and gave a heavy sigh. Rae watched them head to the wagons before turning back to the bridge.

Her feet pounded the ground in rhythm with the pounding of her heart.

She dodged other performers and crew as they wheeled about, gathering others and things, before heading to the wagons and tents. Some yelled she was going the wrong way, while others simply shouldered past her. Rae made it to the bridge in time to see George racing into the city, minutes ahead of her.

A tug on her tunic stopped her in her tracks.

She wheeled around to see Zeke standing behind her. "Zeke, go to the wagons." She tried using his arm to turn him around but stopped when he resisted. "I'm serious Zeke, find Luc and Damien. I need to go help George find our people."

The cry of a falcon pierced their ears. Both looked up to see Bane soaring after the town leader. They exchanged a look and Zeke spoke before Rae could cut him off.

"I'm coming with you. No time to argue. I'll keep up." Rae pursed her lips as Zeke bounded ahead of her and crossed the bridge, a slight limp the only indication of his previous afflictions. Once they were across, an explosion sounded and they were thrown to the ground. Both acrobats' ears rang as splintered wood rained down on them.

They brushed themselves off and shared a look. The bridge was decimated, and so were its twins, one upriver and one downriver. George must have set the fuses before making his way back to the city. It was one of their fail-safes to make sure the Circus could get away should danger appear.

Rae gulped, realizing it would be a long time before she saw her friends and family again. She walled those thoughts away and pulled her daggers from her boots, throwing Zeke a feral grin.

Nobody was going to stop her from finding those kids.

The sound of marching soldiers announced their fate before the screams could. The bakery had been empty for a couple of hours, which was odd, but Rich chalked it up to excitement for the Circus. The silence should've been their clue. No one in town noted the absence of the soldiers, but that spoke louder than any warning could have.

The search for Gemma Vincenzio had begun.

Rich sent Melody to fetch the little girl. He would have to get her to a safe house until the raids quieted. He knew across the city, the last three leaders would do the same. The safe houses would have to do until they could find a better way to get them out of danger. He hoped Duncan would keep his wits and get the Circus out of there. If they didn't make it, the Magicae didn't stand a chance of mounting any kind of resistance.

Melody thundered down the stairs with Gemma in tow, backpack snug against her back and hood hiding her curls.

"I'm taking her to Tamara."

"Don't be silly, Melody. I'll take her. I won't let you risk yourself like this." Rich protested.

"It'll be less suspicious if a mother and daughter are fleeing the streets compared to a grandfather." Melody laid a gentle arm on her father's forearm. "Da, you're too prominent. You'll be stopped. They won't trust you. Please, let me do this." She gazed into her father's bright eyes, filled with doubt. "I can do this. I'll take care of her." She gave her father a fierce hug and patted his cheek. "Take care of Ma. I'll be back soon."

She gathered the little girl in her arms and exited through the cellar.

Moments after the door shut behind them, soldiers banged on the baker's door.

Before Rich could open it, three big brutes shouldered their way in and started searching for something. They didn't say a word, just upended tables and bins, reaping destruction in their wake. One held him at sword point while the other two went to search the rest of the house. He heard his wife scream as he tried to reason with the soldier in front of him.

"What is this about, sir? Heimat has been a gracious host to all of you. Why the violence?" he asked.

The soldier grunted in response, refusing to move his sword.

Rich tried again, "Are you looking for something? Maybe I can help?"

The soldier gave Rich a once-over before spitting on the ground next to his feet. Rich tried to hide his wince but wasn't quick enough. The soldier sneered at his discomfort.

"Scared of a little spittle?" He let out a grating laugh and slapped his knee. "You're too stupid to know anything, old man."

Rich gritted his teeth. "Try me."

The soldier laughed long and hard. "We search for the rats hiding in our fair city. General Vincenzio has let them fester for too long. The purge begins today." He continued laughing as his comrades came back down the stairs.

"She's not up there. Let's keep going." The lead soldier said.

The three left as swiftly as they came. Rich rushed upstairs to his wife. They held each other and cried as their city burned. They prayed incessantly for their daughter and that she returned home safe and sound.

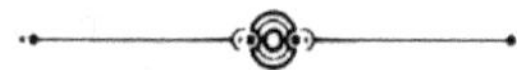

George ran with a single-minded determination. The bridges slowed him down but were effective. The soldiers wouldn't catch the Circus anytime soon. He needed to find the children and get them to safety. He sped through the Upper Districts and headed straight for the Barracks.

Reg would have his group spread between two safe houses. He slowed as he reached the first one. Keeping to the shadows, he avoided groups of soldiers and panicked townspeople alike. He went to the cellar and gave the signature three-rap knock.

He heard a latch unlock and quickly slipped inside. He was engulfed by wiry arms with no intention of letting him go.

"Reg, you're squeezing too tight," George managed. He swatted at his friend. "Let go, you bastard."

"I could'n help it, Georgie. I'm so happy, I could kiss ya!" Reg beamed, forgetting the others in the room with him.

George pushed his friend away, trying to count the few figures in the dark. "None of that. How many are here?"

"All of them."

George stared at his best friend. "What do you mean, all of them?" he repeated, trying to blink away his disbelief.

A pained look crossed Reg's face. "The other house was raided. They're gone." He hung his head.

George put a hand on his friend's shoulder. "Are you sure?"

Reg nodded. "I saw 'em with me own eyes, and I woulda' tried to get 'em back, but these kiddies needed me. I could'n leave 'em."

George's grip tightened, recognizing his friend's grief. "Only thing we can do is keep moving forward. Now I have an idea, but it might not work."

"Anything to get us outta this mess, Georgie."

George motioned the kids and adults in the cellar forward and told them his plan. Some raised their eyebrows, some cowered in fear, but most put their trust in the town leader and nodded along. Once everyone knew the plan, George listened to the world outside the cellar door.

As a hush descended, he saluted Reg and slid into the chaos outside.

Rae pulled Zeke around a corner as a group of soldiers entered a house to their right.

"Be careful," she hissed.

"Trying," came his reply.

Rae gave Zeke a once over, noting his slight limp and the way he winced every few seconds. "You're still not feeling okay."

Zeke shot her an incredulous look. He waved one arm at the streets crawling with military personnel. "They don't care, Rae. It doesn't matter. We need to figure out a plan."

Rae searched his face. "I care, Z. I worry about you." She touched his cheek but pulled back when he winced. She sighed. "I don't know how to do this. We need to find those kids, but I have no idea where to st—"

The cry of a falcon interrupted Rae's train of thought. She looked up to the familiar sight of Bane in falcon form. He chattered at the two of them before taking off down the alley to their left. Rae looked at Zeke, who shrugged. She turned back and heard another cry, followed by more chattering.

The pair made their way down the alley and found Bane perched on the streetlight outside a charming townhome, with white trim and cheery colors. He chattered at them when they hesitated.

He went around the back of the house with the two acrobats in tow. The back door was knocked in and the sounds of fighting boomed inside. Rae held tight to her daggers and took light steps toward the door. She stood in the entryway and peeked inside.

Seeing nothing, she signaled for Zeke to follow.

In the hallway, a soldier moaned on the ground, blood pooling beneath him. They kept walking until they made it to the living room. More carnage accompanied the smell of blood and gore. Several soldiers, a civilian, and a child lay dead.

The acrobats held their breaths and kept walking. The sounds of fighting were distinctly coming from upstairs. Rae and Zeke made their way up, keeping their wits about them. They were met with the sight of one man standing in front of a door, facing off against two soldiers. Three other bodies lay motionless on the ground at their feet.

Rae reached deep inside and froze.

The four elements sat in glorious splendor within her core. They pulsed with their elemental power, waiting for Rae to call on them. She hesitated about how to take a little power without unwinding and losing control again. She pulled a couple of strands of wind loose and called them to her hands.

The winds looped across her wrists before knocking the two soldiers against the wall as she thrust her hands forward and to the left. The force cracked their skulls and left them still on the ground. Zeke went to the man guarding the door with hands raised.

"We're here to help. Are you one of the contacts for tonight?"

The man coughed. When he pulled his hand away from his mouth, it was bloody. "Mikel. I'd shake your hand, but I don't think you want this on you." He coughed again and sank to the floor. His hand strayed to a bloom of crimson on his side.

Rae knelt next to him and attempted to get a closer look at the wound. He swatted her hand away. "Let it be. Nine kiddos behind that door need your help. Find Tamara. She has a glass shop along the riverbank to the east. Follow the bank and you'll find her." He broke into a coughing fit, spewing blood. "Quick, before more come. Save them. Please." His voice was a rasp as he devolved into shakes. Rae and Zeke exchanged glances before opening the door behind him. They both touched the man's shoulder as they moved past him into the room.

Rae's heart squeezed at seeing the children behind the door. They were crying, distraught, and filled with fear.

She went to the youngest, no more than four, and picked him up. "Shh. Dry your tears, little one. We'll get through this." She rocked the little boy slightly and turned to the other children. They were aged from the four-year-old to newly minted teenagers. Pain filled Rae's face. They were so young. She quickly wiped the pain from her expression and gave a tight smile to the children gathered before her.

"Listen closely, friends. Things are bad out there. There's a lot of fighting and blood and death. No, no, no, now is not the time to cry. I need you to promise me you will save your tears for tonight. I need all of you to be strong for the next few hours. That is the only way we will get through this." Rae looked into teary eyes and let determination blaze in her own as the children nodded and wiped their faces. She set the young one down. "Good. Yep, we can do this. We just need to work together." Her gaze went to the older children. "We need to find Tamara. She has a glass shop on the riverbank. Does anybody know where that is?"

All the children shook their heads sadly.

Rae glanced at Zeke. "Okay, no worries. We'll figure it out. Now, when we get outside, there are two rules. Ready for them?" She paused and waited for their nods. Once she had them, she continued, "One, nobody gets left behind. Keep your eyes out for danger and look after one another. Two, stick to the shadows. We are going to stick out like sore thumbs, so the darkness is our best friend. Got it? Any questions?"

The children shook their heads and got ready to leave the room Mikel had made his last stand in front of. Rae warned them of what they would find and encouraged them to avert their eyes and hurry past the awful scene. Lethargy would be their enemy if they let it grab hold.

They exited the house without complications and met up with Bane, keeping watch from the fence. He started chattering when he saw Rae and Zeke but stopped when he saw all the children. Rae held her arm out, inviting him to use her as his perch.

Bane glided effortlessly to the outstretched arm.

"You found them, Bane. We got to them just in time. We're supposed to take them to a glass blower's shop along the riverbank. Tamara is her name. Be our eyes?" she asked the stoic Shifter.

A cry was Bane's only acknowledgment as he took to the wing and steered toward the river.

Rae and Zeke picked up the two youngest ones and led the other children quickly and quietly through the streets still crawling with soldiers.

Melody pulled her hood tighter over her head and shifted the little girl in her arms. They kept to the shadows, but her heart raced every time glass shattered and fire roared. The laughing of the soldiers grated against her and the constant beat of marching feet frayed every nerve. The glass blower's place wasn't far, but it took some creative planning to get there unseen.

The girl in her arms was so quiet, she had to check frequently that she was still breathing. She pulled the girl's hood down firmly, taking care to brush the copper curls from her eyes and tuck them into the hood itself.

Those curls would give her away before anything else.

They looked around one last corner and Melody spied the shop she was after. Melody scanned the scene before her and stepped towards the shop.

Suddenly, a soldier appeared on the cross street and leered at her. She walked briskly and rapped three times on the door to the glass shop. She set Gemma down and edged the young girl behind her. The soldier slinked toward her but got distracted by a young boy running past him.

The door opened, and Melody pushed the little girl into the opening before following her.

Melody's stomach dropped when she felt someone grip her by the hair and pull her out of the doorway, onto the street.

She screamed as she was thrown onto the pavement and her world went dark.

Blood pooled underneath the young mother as the city of Heimat continued to burn.

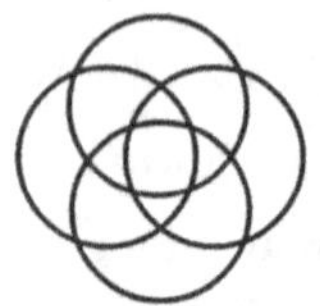

Chapter Thirty

George raced through the streets, short sword in hand. He struck down soldiers when he couldn't avoid it but kept hidden as much as he could. He got to the safe house in the Upper Districts and his stomach tied itself into knots when he saw the back door swinging on its hinges.

He held his breath when he entered, fearing the worst. Flies were already buzzing around the carcasses. George gagged when he reached the living room, only pausing to say a prayer for the father and son dead on the floor.

He heard a groan from the second level and thundered up the stairs.

"Mikel." George rushed to the man's side and gripped his arm.

The dying man let out another groan. George fumbled for something to stop the bleeding when he felt a hand on his. He looked into Mikel's tired eyes and saw pain.

"Ta-Ta-mar..." Coughs racked Mikel's body as he tried to communicate. "Ki-ki-s..."

George puzzled over the broken speech before it clicked. "The kids. They went to Tamara's?"

Mikel gave a nod before his head lolled to the side and his whole body went still.

George used his thumbs to close the man's eyes and sent up another prayer for the dead.

He left the house of death and made his way to Tamara's.

Bane found the glass blower's shop long before Rae, Zeke, and the kids even got close. He scouted the area and convinced some of the other nearby birds to distract the soldiers he did see. He flew back to the pair and their charges to be their eyes in the sky.

They made it to the shop with little hassle. Rae and Zeke got in one scuffle and took down two guards each. Rae tried not to dwell on whether they were dead or simply knocked out. They got to the shop and went to the back entrance. Rae let out a couple of breathy laughs of relief when they saw the door remained strong and intact. Anything was better than an open door and death within.

They knocked several times, waiting for an answer that never came.

Zeke scanned their vulnerable position and said, "We need to keep moving, Rae. We're begging someone to find us being out in the open like this."

"I know." Rae held her hands to her head, struggling to think with the screams of innocents and the banging of doors filling her head. They needed to find somewhere safe. She bit her lip and looked at the kids. They could risk the river, but she wasn't confident enough in her water Craft to trust the lives of others with it. Most of the kids probably couldn't even swim.

Too late, the sound of footsteps sounded, barreling toward them. Zeke and Rae hurried the kids to stand behind planters and bushes lining the backside of the house. They whirled around, weapons ready, and faced three guards.

Rae spread her legs into a wide stance and took a deep breath to ground herself. She reached within and pulled some strands from her plait of wind. Before she withdrew, her flames thrummed within their confines.

Curiously, she pulled a couple of strands, delighted by the comfort of holding her fire close.

Coming back to the present, she stood with fire in one fist, engulfing the dagger she held, and the wind coating the other. Breathing hard, she concentrated and thrust the wind forward, knocking the soldiers down. While they were on the ground, she advanced on them, the flames dancing to engulf both daggers in her hands.

The soldiers tried to scramble away, but one couldn't find his footing. Rae leaped and plunged the flaming dagger into his pant leg. Rae miscalculated her thrust and felt the soft give of flesh as her dagger plunged into his leg.

The man screamed in agony as the flames scorched the wound, cauterizing and burning the flesh around it.

Rae removed her dagger quickly, the blood draining from her face while the soldier struggled to his feet, clutching his wound and patting at the flames.

Rae panicked and reached for the water she felt inside. Grasping too many strands at once, water gushed like a geyser from her palms, buffeting the man until he collapsed meters away. Smoke billowed from where fire once raged. Drenched in sweat, Rae put her hands on her knees and took giant gulps of air, trying to slow the thundering pace of her heart.

Zeke passed a glance to where the children hid, frowning with worry. He knew the toll trauma could take on a young one. He floundered between going to them and helping his friend. Zeke looked at Rae, bitterness tinging his vision. Rae's betrayal of trust and using him to her own ends still weighed on his mind.

"We need to get out of here." Zeke moved to get the kids when a sound piqued his interest. He stood still and sent the wind to bring back the sounds he could barely hear.

Sure enough, they were light footsteps headed in their direction.

Rae swallowed and finally gained control of herself. She was still white as a sheet and drenched in sweat, but at least she wasn't heaving.

Zeke held up a finger and pointed to where the footsteps sounded from. They both took up defensive positions, Rae lighting her daggers again. The flames were less bright, but still made an impressive sight. They heard the footsteps just before the figure rounded the corner to their position.

Bane let out a familiar cry, distracting the two below. In that instant, George rounded the corner and put his hands up.

Zeke and Rae turned back to the figure, hackles raised, only relaxing once they realized who it was. George stepped over the soldier with the charred leg, knocked unconscious by the ordeal.

"Are the kids with you?" George asked, trying to find the telltale signs of adolescents around him. A tremor in the bushes gave them up, and he rushed to it. He pulled the youngest boy from his hiding spot and held him close. "Thank the Goddess. Come on kiddos, let's go inside." He held his hand out to the other kids crouching in the bush.

"It's locked. Nobody's there. We need to keep moving." Rae glared at the easy way George took charge of the children.

He smirked and walked to the door, the young boy still in his arms. George shifted his load so he could free one of his hands. He used it to rap three times on the back door. Rae glanced at Zeke but was met with a shrug.

They waited for another couple of moments.

Before Rae could reiterate her sentiment, they heard locks turning and the door opening slowly.

A woman with ebony skin and bright white tattoos beckoned them inside. Her tattoos covered every inch of her skin, shining eerily in the dark interior of the glass shop. She twirled a fire poker in one hand, the tip red hot and fresh from the fire. She wasn't taking any chances.

"Hey, Tam. Got room for a dozen more?" George gave a lopsided grin, still holding the trembling four-year-old.

The fire poker fell to the floor as the woman threw both arms around the town leader. "Thank the Goddess. Yes. Get in here, all of you." She reached down and grabbed the poker before anyone could step on it. She hurried the troupe inside, nodding to Zeke and Rae and their choice of weapons. The woman checked both sides of the alley behind her house before shutting the door behind them, barring the locks once more.

"How many you got here, Tam?" George asked, setting the young boy down to join the other children.

"About twenty." Tamara raised an eyebrow when George leveled his gaze at her. "What? The glass shop has plenty of hiding places and enough hazards to discourage even the keenest of guards." She lifted her chin, daring George to contradict her.

He held up his hands in deference. "Today, your arrogance is only an asset." Tamara chuckled lightly and turned to the two Crafters.

"Name's Tamara. Call me Tam." She held out her hand to them. They sheathed their weapons and shook the woman's hand with a grin.

"I'm Rae and this is Zeke. We're better known by our stage names though, Golden Eagle and Silver Falcon." Children gasped as they stuck their faces out from their hiding places, ears perked by the sound of the performers they idolized. "We have one more, Bane, waiting outside."

Tamara frowned. "Well, we should get him in here." She stepped to the door when Zeke held an arm out to stop her.

"No. He's a Shifter in his falcon form. He's keeping watch and will be our eyes as we move through the streets," Zeke explained.

"Ah. A powerful friend indeed." She turned to George. "What's the plan? We heard the bridges blow." She gave a pointed look towards the lanky man.

George turned sheepish. "It had to be done. If they went after the Circus, everything would be for naught."

Tamara nodded and ran a hand through her short, wiry strands that fanned out to create a halo around her head. She walked to a bench that had a map of the city laid flat. Black marks covered the parchment, indicating danger or dead ends. Her fingers tapped lightly on the marks where the bridges once stood.

"They're tearing the city apart looking for the mayor's daughter and any Magicae they can get their hands on." She motioned someone from the shadows. A woman stepped forward, face dirty and hair a mess. She held a little girl in her arms. "Unfortunately, we have both." All three's eyes widened, connecting the dots. "Our brave Melody got her here safely. She didn't make it, but the girl did." Tears pricked the glass Forger's eyes.

George's face fell, and he clenched his jaw. He wiped angrily at his eyes. "Melody's gone?" Tamara could only nod in answer. They embraced, sharing their grief as the young woman took the little girl back into the shadows.

George pulled back and said quietly, "Mikel is gone too." Tamara's eyes clouded with pain, but she nodded.

"I figured the worst when he didn't arrive with you." Her eyes gained a far-off look. "So much death, so much pain." The group sat in silence for several moments, giving their respects to the ones they lost. Rae broke the silence and cleared her throat.

"I know grieving is a necessity. I've been there. But we need to come up with a plan to get everyone out of here. The soldiers will pull this city apart before they stop looking." She gazed at the map, hands tracing paths and alleys winding through the sections of the city. Her finger stopped by the Wharf and she frowned. "I think I heard Duncan talking about a boat. Is it ready to sail?"

George composed himself before looking at the Crafter. "That's why I came here. I met with Reg and we decided the boat would be the best way to escape. We need to get everyone there before they close the docks for good. Eddy said they were already prepped last night."

He squinted at the map, running different routes in his head. He tapped several places and rubbed his chin. "The alleys along the riverbank would be best." He paused, hearing glass shatter and screams nearby. The four exchanged looks and refocused on searching the map. George traced hidden alleys before snapping his fingers. "We sneak along the bank, cut in by the old inn, and run like hell until we reach the Wharf."

The other three studied the map carefully before nodding. It was the most direct route with the least vulnerable positions. They nodded and moved to fill in the children and other adults, using their talents to inform how they would distribute the children between them.

Reg signaled to his party to wait. They followed the plan George gave them exactly and were almost at the docks. They had to leave the safety of the alley, cross the street, and make it to the third dock on the left.

Reg looked both ways and keeping his eyes peeled, he scanned once more before signaling the first group to make their way across. He had two other adults and eight children in his group. They split into groups with one adult and two or three kids each. This made them less noticeable and faster moving than a large group.

The first group made it across the street and kept running to the docks, out of sight from the street. Reg held his arm out when the next group threatened to go. He shook his head as several soldiers thundered past. He watched them closely, breathing in relief when they turned right towards the Fringe instead of heading to the docks.

After a couple of moments of silence, he signaled the next group to go. They disappeared into the maze of containers and extra piles of wood as another group of soldiers appeared.

Reg looked at the two kids in his care and gave them an encouraging nod. The brothers kept their heads held high, but couldn't hide the tremor in their legs. Reg returned to his vigil, waiting for another group of invaders to transverse the road in front of him.

He bared his teeth in the shadows, hidden from sight, the raw feelings of grief pulsing within. Losing six of the people he was charged with protecting weighed heavy on Reg's heart. He pushed the grief aside as their opportunity beckoned.

They sprinted, Reg holding each boy by the hand, dragging them faster than their little legs could handle. Reg didn't take a breath until they were lost from sight on the docks. The three slinked forward carefully, making their way to the ship that would take them to safety.

The two boys rushed forward when they made it to the dock, bounding up the gangplank to reach their friends. Reg strode behind them, glancing behind, keeping an eye out for suspicious activity. He boarded the ship with one last backward glance and a smile for the ship's crew.

"Ready to give 'em hell?" Cheers rose as they waited for the last of their people.

George, Tamara, and the two acrobats led a group of almost thirty Magicae through the streets of Heimat. Bane flew above them, scouting the way, and giving a cry should they need to pause.

The alleys along the bank were mostly deserted, making it easy for the sizeable group to make good headway towards the docks. George led the group with Rae beside him, twin blades alight with flame. Tamara and Zeke took up the rear with the five other adults interspersed among the children. They came to the spot where they could be seen and gathered as a group.

George whispered words of encouragement, making it clear the adults and children should keep moving at all times, no matter what happened. Their only job was to get to the third ship on the left as quickly as possible. Tamara, Zeke, Rae, and himself were the only ones that would stay and fight, should it come to that.

The four fighters knew their group would draw attention. It was just a matter of time. They needed to prolong the inevitable as long as possible.

They waited in the shadows of the last alleyway, waiting for a large group of soldiers to pass. The roar of fire, fighting, and screaming rang in their ears, throwing the children off balance. Many had tears streaming down their face and snot dripping from their noses, fear being the only thing keeping them quiet.

George signaled for the group to go and everyone took off at a sprint, with the youngest children carried in the arms of the adult Magicae. They made it to the outer edge of the Wharf before the first soldiers descended upon them.

Rae and George engaged, waving at the group to keep going. Rae swung her daggers, catching one soldier's sword between them. She whipped her arms and sent the weapon flying. The soldier charged straight into Rae's daggers, his clothes catching fire as she slashed his arms and torso. She thrust the wind forward and knocked him against the stones. She looked in time to see George get past the soldier's guard and slide his sword into the man's side. He pulled it free, wiped the blood on his breeches, and kept running.

Rae took off, catching up to George as he took the lead of their group again.

A lone soldier barreled toward them.

Rae sent a jet of flame from her dagger, knocking him over, and lighting his clothes on fire. George nodded as they kept running.

A falcon's cry caught Rae's ears as the docks came into view.

She turned and gasped.

Vincenzio himself led a squadron of soldiers down the road behind them.

She grabbed George's arm and turned him around. His expression turned grim and he yelled at their group to run harder. They watched their people stream past them and joined Tamara and Zeke at the back.

Rae's mind spun as she scanned their surroundings for something to help them. She bit her lip, deep in thought.

"We need to slow them down!" Zeke yelled above the sound of soldiers marching.

"No shit!" Tamara fired back, chewing on the inside of her cheek.

George said nothing as he repositioned his grip on the sword in his hands. He took a wide stance and stared down the man destroying his city. "Tam, go. Tell them to take the ship and leave. We'll slow them down for as long as possible."

"I'm not leaving you, George. You can't ask me to do that," Tamara countered.

George wrenched his gaze from the oncoming soldiers and pleaded with the glass Forger. "Reg is already up there. He won't let them leave until it's too late. You need to make sure they leave."

"George... I can't," Tamara protested. George gripped her arm and tried to turn her around. They squabbled some more, the squadron looming ever closer.

Rae tore her gaze from the oncoming soldiers and looked at her friend. "Do you trust me?" she whispered.

Zeke looked at her abruptly. "Of course, Sparks," he said, pushing the bitterness away given their situation.

"Good." She gave a sad smile and turned to the other two. "I need both of you to go." Their heads turned to the young woman. "Now. I'm going to do something, just get those kids out of here. Don't wait." She pushed both of them toward the ship. "Please, it doesn't make sense for us all to die. They'll need both of you. Go," her last word was a command. Tamara gripped her forearm once before following George to the ship, against their better judgment.

Bane was doing his best to dive-bomb the soldiers and blind the ones he could. Rae let out a cry and held her arm up, calling Bane to her. He did so, chattering to communicate his displeasure.

"Bane, Zeke, I need your life energy. I'm going to use the earth beneath us to create a barrier, but I need more strength. Can you help?" Zeke nodded, but Bane hopped to the ground.

He Shifted into his human form for the first time since arriving in Heimat. He took the shirt Zeke offered and wrapped it around his waist. Bane opened his mouth, but only a garbled sound came out. He coughed a couple of times before trying again.

"Ugh. I always forget how troublesome vocal cords can be." Bane's voice lost its hoarseness as he continued, "I'm in."

The two men placed hands on Rae's bare shoulders and channeled some of their life energy into her. She took it in, surprised by the pure power emitted from Bane's Gift in liquid form. Shifters were considered the most powerful Magicae for a reason.

She closed her eyes and channeled the energy to her core. She opened her mind's eye and felt the power thrumming in the spires of earth jutting from within. Rae stroked one gently and called it forth into the world around her.

The men behind her gasped as the ground in front of them shot into the air. Rae heard their shock as if they were at a distance. It was the only confirmation she had that what she was doing was working. She continued, moving more quickly. Soon, a legion of spires jutted across the road. Rae continued until she felt Zeke squeeze her shoulder.

"That's enough Rae, come on, let's get on board that ship." Zeke shook her until her eyes lost their clouded look and she was back in the present. She nodded and took a step forward, but fell to the ground, crying out in pain. Bane leaned down and threw her over his shoulder. He raised his eyebrow when Zeke shot him a look.

"We both know you're still not at one hundred percent. Move." Bane took off before Zeke could respond. They heard soldiers pounding against the spires of dirt and rock, trying to knock enough down to get through. Zeke and Bane didn't spare a glance backwards, eyes focused on the ship pulling away from the docks.

They saw Tamara waving her arms and yelling at the crew, stalling them from leaving port. Bane and Zeke made it to the end of the dock, feet from the ship.

A boom sounded at the first dock. It exploded in a mass of splinters and metal. Bane and Zeke shared a look. Their time was limited.

A rope ladder was lowered from the gunwale.

"Go. I'll use my wind to help."

"No, we go together." Bane stared at him in defiance. The next dock blew apart, the heat and splinters reaching the place they stood. Their dock was next.

"Fine, take my hand." Zeke felt Bane lend him some life energy.

They sprinted, Bane still carrying Rae on one shoulder, and jumped just as their feet left the dock. A gust of wind propelled them into the side of the ship. The impact jarred their clasped hands apart, and they scrambled for purchase on the rope ladder. Bane gripped it with both hands once Rae was steady, Zeke holding onto one of his legs. They shielded their faces as the ship pulled away as fast as she could.

Stray metal and pieces of wood rained on the three Circus members as the dock blew up before the ship was out of range. Strong arms pulled the ladder up and took Rae from Bane's shoulder. Bane and Zeke fell onto the wooden deck of the ship and lay there panting.

A young woman dressed in black breeches, black boots, and a loose white top helped them to their feet. She wore a maroon bandanna in her hair and a gold earring on her right lobe. She gave them a wicked grin.

"Welcome aboard the *Vengeance*."

Tyee sat atop Koko, brooding over the events of the day.

The Circus had scrambled to pack the chuckwagons before taking off. They needed to get to the forest before the soldiers organized enough to take boats across the river.

The sun was setting as they reached the tree line of the Great Northern Forest. He glanced back and could still see the town of Heimat, smoking in the distance. He rubbed Koko's neck, offering comfort to his friend and seeking it for himself. The horse bobbed his head and nickered his contentment.

The Forest would be full of dangers, but thoughts of a blond acrobat with eyes of liquid gold were all that clouded Tyee's mind.

He prayed to the Huntress he would see her again.

And with that, Tyee guided Koko into the trees behind the last of the wagons.

GET THE FIRST CHAPTER OF SPARK OF RE-SISTANCE, BOOK TWO IN THE CHRONICLES OF KAMORE SERIES

Couldn't get enough of the world of Kamore?

Join my email list to get the first chapter of book two, featuring a look into the Capital and Myra's response to the events in Flicker of Defiance.

I believe in building relationships with my readers and send out occasional newsletters with updates on my writing, extra insight into the world of Kamore, and a behind-the-scenes look at the life of an indie author.

You can get this first chapter, for free, by signing up at https://authorcalewis.com/myra-chapter/.

*Free Chapter
Link*

Cast of Characters

<u>The Circus</u>

- Bane- Shifter, Raptor forms, son of Gar, Star of the Raptor Show

- Betsy- Mortal, Head Cook

- Carlos- Herbalist, Head of Medical Tent

- Chiara- Herbalist, Healer, serves on the Governing Council as Head Herbalist, mother to Damien

- Conrad- Shifter, Tiger form, serves on the Governing Council as an Elder, Big Cat Performer

- Damien- Mortal, Acrobat, Son to Chiara, White Raven

- Duke- Mortal, Strongman

- Duncan- Crafter, Wind, serves on the Governing Council as Head Crafter, Ringmaster

- Eva- Forger, Wood, Elephant Performer

- Freya- Herbalist, Healer

- Gar- Mortal, serves on the Governing Council as an Elder, Head of the Raptor Show

- Izzy- Crafter, Unknown, Young girl that loves Nan's storytelling, Daughter to Marv

- Javie- Herbalist, Grower, Brother to Luc, Grandson to Nan

- Jess- Forger, Iron Material, Strongwoman

- Juno- Shifter, Elephant form, serves on the Governing Council as Head Shifter, Elephant Performer

- Kaiser- Mortal, Son to Nymeria, Big Cat Performer

- Kim- Mortal, Young girl

- Luc- Mortal, Acrobat, serves on the Governing Council as Head Mortal, Black Swan

- Mac- Mortal, Head Cook

- Marv- Mortal, Ticket taker

- Midge- Forger, Cloth Material, serves on the Governing Council as an Elder

- Nan - Herbalist, Healer, "Abuela," serves on the Governing Council as an Elder, Fortune Teller

- Nymeria- Shifter, Lioness Form, Mother to Kaiser, Big Cat Performer

- Rae Freeman- Crafter, Fire, Acrobat, Daughter to Naomi and Andre, Lighting Crew, Golden Eagle

- Tyee- Mortal, Horseman

- Wren- Crafter, Unknown, New Recruit from Windemere

- Zalia- Crafter, Fire, Lighting Crew

- Zeke- Crafter, Wind, Silver Falcon

Townspeople of Heimat
- Eddy- Mortal, Wharfman

- George- Mortal, Liason to the Circus, Brother to Tommy, Best Friend to Reg

- Johanna- Forger, Animal Hide Material, Resides in the Fringe

- Luna- Mortal, Mother to a Shifter Baby

- Melody- Mortal, Baker, Daughter to Rich

- Mikel- Mortal, Resides in the Upper Districts

- Reg- Mortal, Resides in the Barracks, Best Friend to George

- Rich- Mortal, Liason to the Circus, Baker, Father to Melody

- Sara- Mortal, Wife to Tommy

- Simone- Mortal, Resides in the Lower Districts

- Tamara- Forger, Glass Material, Resides in Artist's Row

- Tommy- Mortal, Resides in the Norther River District, Brother to George, Husband to Sara

Myra and Her Supporters
- Gemma- Herbalist, Grower, Daughter to Mirabella and Darren Vincenzio

- Mirabella- Mortal, Wife to Vincenzio, Mother to Gemma

- Myra- Mortal, Tyrant of Kamore

- Darren Vincenzio- Mortal, Myra's right-hand man, Husband to Mirabella, Father to Gemma

Deceased

- Andre Freeman- Mortal, Former President of Kamore, Father to Rae

- Helene- Herbalist, Healer, Best Friend to Naomi

- Jason- Herbalist, Healer

- Jose- Forger, Metal Material

- Naomi Freeman- Mortal, Former First Lady of Kamore, Mother to Rae, Best Friend to Helene

- Naveen- Mortal, Sous Chef

- Rocky- Mortal, Carnival Tent Worker

Acknowledgments

Writing a book is an enormous endeavor, and I am blessed to have so many people to thank.

First and foremost, a huge thank you to Joseph for always supporting my dreams. I promise I'll make it up to you one day. And to Ruby, Walter, and Lena for being the best writing companions day in and day out.

To the best Beta readers around, Amy and Kate, you helped to make this story what it is today. I am completely indebted to both of you.

To Rachel for creating an extraordinary cover that is significantly better than everything I tried to create.

To all the friends and family that have encouraged me along the way. Your excitement and constant wondering about when the book would be ready filled my heart more than you know. Special shout outs to Mom, Dad, Adam, Sophia, Cody, Emma, Deb, Greg, Val, the Cabin Crew, my aunts, the Kickball Team, Laura, Craig, Abby, Tyler, and Sydney for never failing to ask about how everything was going.

To the indie authors that came before me, providing so much information on the best ways to self publish a book. You provide more inspiration than you know for a new author like myself.

And finally, to all the readers that gave this book a chance. It's an honor to have somebody choose my book amongst all the options out there. Thank you for taking a gamble on the stories inside my head.

About the Author

C A Lewis grew up reading stories filled with dragons, swords, and adventure. Her books transport readers to other worlds where magic and fantasy reign. Her debut series, The Chronicles of Kamore, highlight themes of found friendship, defying the odds, and perseverance despite what life throws at you. She is based in the Twin Cities of Minnesota with her husband, Labrador Retriever, and two cats.

https://authorcalewis.com/

https://www.facebook.com/authorcalewis

https://www.instagram.com/author_c_a_lewis/

Sign up for my newsletter at: https://authorcalewis.com/landing-page/

Newsletter
Link

www.ingramcontent.com/pod-product-compliance
Lightning Source LLC
Chambersburg PA
CBHW070613300726

48975CB00006B/1805